Nov 13

# NEW BERN

## 1710 IN THE CAROLINAS

a novel by:

### Jimmy C. Waters

His voice thundered as he shouted from his pulpit, "The New Bern Colony, conceived wholly in greed, and founded in so much blood, will most assuredly be cursed by our benevolent Deity, damned for all eternity by Almighty God!"

*Rev. Josiah Ipock, Itinerant Minister,*
*New Bern Settlement, 1711.*

"Saints or sinners, Suh', makes no damn difference! We facin' pirate cannon, and all of us gonna' die in this hea' ditch!"

*Dunker Tim, Slave of William Brice,*
*serving with Martin Bender, in the New Bern*
*Militia along the Cape Fear River, 1718*

Currahee Books™

# Dedication

This historic fiction novel is dedicated to those marvelous peoples, mostly German and Swiss, who created our city of New Bern, the first true city anywhere in the North Carolina Colony. This story is, in reality, the story of the settlement of the entire North Carolina Colony, and is thus a story for every Carolinian, in some sense for every American. This is who we all are. The men and women of early New Bern, both free and enslaved, showed a faith and gritty determination that allowed them to survive more challenges than any peoples in any other colony in the new world. As we celebrate the first three hundred years of New Bern and our state, we shall look forward to the next! In that moment, however, let us all pause each in our own way, to honor, to remember, and perhaps to give thanks to these, our ancestors.

## Acknowledgements:

A special word of thanks to Ms. Stephanie Gullion, Ms. Norma Snyder, Mr. Tanner Ruhlen and Mr. Jim Henderson for help in reviewing this book prior to publication. Thanks also to Mr. Tucker Ruhlen who contributed the initial artwork for the several battles. Also, Mr. John Garcia did an splendid job on the cover and book design. It is always a pleasure to work with him and his wife, Renee at The Freelance Design Group! Thanks to all of these folks!

This and other works are available from the Publisher:

## Currahee Books™

766 Collins Road, Toccoa, Georgia 30577
**www.curraheebooks.com**

Cover & Design by Freelancedesign.com • Asheville, NC • 828.645.9336

# Prologue: Men at War
## *Hill 861, Khe Sanh, South Vietnam, February 1968*

Jesse, a short squat eighteen-year-old boy was, in spite of his age, a veteran. Much like his ancestors his abbreviated torso was tight and well defined. His chest and shoulders were not large by the standards of the Marines in his company but he was well toned and quite strong, having survived Marine training at Paris Island only eleven months before. Now, after five months in country, he knew when to shoot and when not to, when to duck and when to run, and when to fight like hell. He was by this time, a well oiled fighting machine—a trained professional killer in the service of the United States Government, just like the recruiting posters said. In short, he was a Marine.

This evening he wore his boots, trousers, flak jacket, and helmet—nobody in the company had worn more for the last three weeks. He held his rifle tightly, but unconsciously. In truth he felt like he'd been born with it, like it was merely another appendage, a part of his body, but that was the illusion that the Corps liked to create in every Marine.

THIS IS MY RIFLE! (Shouted while holding up rifle in right hand)
THIS IS MY GUN! (Grabbing male private parts in left hand)
THIS IS FOR KILLING! (Holding up rifle again)
THIS IS FOR FUN! (Grabbing male private parts)

I know that seems a bit out of context here, but that's what Jesse was trained to feel, and the Marines out there will understand.

Jesse was lying face down in the sandy, yet semi-dark, earth just behind the upper lip of the defensive berm, hoping that he did not die in the approaching dusk. He wasn't particularly excited about dying at eighteen, but try as he might, he really didn't see any other realistic hope for his small band of Marines in the farthest observation post from the headquarters (HQ). His unit was five hundred meters outside the perimeter of Khe Sanh, South Vietnam.

Jesse's OP—observation post—was the first line of the defensive position. Any Marine knows that the very purpose of any OP was to die loudly and gloriously. Sometimes the Marines in the company called these positions the OD post, which stood for "Observe while Dying"! If they made enough ruckus in the OP on Hill 861 during the initial skirmish, they would at least warn the men in the main defensive perimeter to the rear, that the enemy was coming. These men in the OP were the first to receive enemy fire, and the first to die.

And die they did in this mud at Khe Sanh, at a rate of five to twenty men per day. In this battle, the enemy, the North Vietnamese Army (NVA), was committed. Lying before this far-flung, ill conceived OP was a hardened, angry enemy—a veteran force of fighters who withstood unspeakable hardships, like having no shoes for weeks at a time during the cold months, or eating only small portions of rice with a ration of water each day. This hardened enemy met any test in order to defend their native soil, while at the same time, exhibiting an amazing willingness to die. Yeah, this enemy force was hard, battle-tested, committed. This was the worst type of enemy to face.

As Jesse lay there the enemy artillery (arty) was firing on the next position over on the left flank. Those guys were catching hell—getting murdered in their holes. Next, the arty would move onto his position and after softening the line for a while, the enemy would move forward for today's massive charge. When the arty moved down the line in his direction, he intended to slither back into his bunker—it had a pretty good reinforced cover—and hope for the best. He didn't want to die in a hole, but in there he was sure the end would be swift. In his hole, he wouldn't even know it when he died, and it may even be preferable to the gnawing fear and uncertainty he was now used to experiencing, or the shooting battle that was sure to follow the arty barrage. The NVA were at least consistent. They'd begin their barrage around dinnertime, and attack at dusk, preferring night battle for their massed charges into the American laid killing zones. They'd done the same thing for the last three days.

Amid these thoughts, Jesse noticed an ant crawl over the top of the berm and begin to make his way down the near side. He laughed to himself and said, "Just like the damned dark dirt of Carolina. You never escaped the ants there either! At least this one is heading into the hole for safety!" Admittedly strange things go through your head in battle, and Jesse didn't realize he'd spoken out loud, as he waited for his opportunity for fiery, explosive death there on Hill 861.

"Don't you be bad-mouthin' Carolina! My people come from there!" Jesus spoke up from the opposite side of the hole.

"Bullshit, Jesus," Jesse said. "You're from Tennessee, 'least that's what you said!"

The two Marines in this particular hole had the same last name, but couldn't have been more different. Jesse, at five feet ten inches, was built like a fireplug—short, bandy legs that held amazing strength and arms that looked downright fragile, but still enabled him to get through some of the roughest physical training ever devised by man. He survived, and even thrived in the Marines, because of his will to succeed.

Jesus, on the other hand, looked like a mountain; his sheer strength seemed to be that of five normal men, and that alone carried him through. He stood six feet four inches, with massive forearms that acquitted him well in high school football only two years before, not to mention hand to hand combat during Marine training. His face was flattened, and his dark skinned forehead seemed somehow too big to be human, giving him the appearance of a bloated, beefy demon with a rifle—at least he hoped that's what the NVA thought. Why these two guys, who looked so incredibly different, should ever become such friends was beyond anyone's comprehension, but friends they were. That's why they shared the same hole in this god-forsaken OP, on this god-forsaken hill in the middle of nowhere.

Maybe it was the thing with the commanding officer only three months before, when Jesus had just arrived. While standing at attention in ranks that day, the CO had shouted for "Bender!" Jesse answered of course, but then so did Jesus! That was weird!

Jesus had just arrived in country, and had only that day been assigned to the company. Julian Christopher Bender was a brand new Marine, and didn't realize there was another Bender already in the company. When he heard his name, he responded, "Yes Sir!" with the gusto that only a new Marine can muster.

The Master Sergeant, always the bastard henchman of the CO, thought he had a new idiot in the company, so he immediately charged in Julian's direction and shouted, "Did you think somebody called your name, Numb-nuts? What the hell is your name anyway? You do know your own damn name don't ya?"

Jesus responded in confusion, "Yes Sir! Bender Sir! Uh, Yes, Sir!"

"Yes Sir? Do you see a sir before you Numb-nuts? I'm Master Sergeant Thompson, Numb-nuts! Master Sergeant Thompson, not Sir! You got that?"

"Yes Sir, uh." Julian damn near died when he realized he'd said it again. "Yes, Master Sergeant Thompson!"

"Are you dumb or just plain stupid, Numb-nuts? Did your Mama have white babies too?" (Julian Bender was black, very very black, as in BLACK, the dark color of rich ebony).

Jesus just answered again, "No Sir! Uh, No Master Sergeant Thompson!"

By then Master Sergeant Thompson had caught on that two Marines named Bender—one white and one black—now served in the company.

"Your name is Bender? That right Numb-nuts?" he shouted.

"Yes, Master Sergeant!" Julian had gotten the hang of it now.

"Well that will never do." Master Sergeant Thompson shouted. "We already got one damn Bender here and that's one too many! We don't, by God, need another!" The Master Sergeant continued. "What is your full name, Marine?"

"Private First Class Julian Christopher Bender, Master Sergeant Thompson.

United States Marine Corps!"

"Well this won't do," the Master Sergeant shouted again. "This won't do at all! I don't want confusion in my company. I don't want confusion in my beloved Marine Corps! Private First Class Bender. Is your name really Julian Christopher?"

"Yes Sir! Uh, Yes Master Sergeant!"

"Well Julian Christopher, that sounds like JC to me. You want to be JC? Maybe you want to be Jesus! Do you want to be Jesus, Private First Class Bender?"

"Yes Sir! Uh, No Sir. Uh, No Master Sergeant." Julian was really confused, and he wondered, like every Marine has at one time or another, why all Master Sergeants seemed to shout all the time.

Of course, by that point it was absolutely inevitable. Private First Class J. C. Bender became Jesus from that moment on—he was called Jesus by every single Marine in the company!

Within the next month, Jesse and Jesus had gotten to know each other, since they both shared the name Bender. They endured the jokes about whose Dad had visited whose Mom, from blacks and whites alike in the company.

Then, several months later, the company had been tapped to defend the ever-shrinking death trap that was to be known as Khe Sanh, Vietnam, which is where Jesse and Jesus were sharing their hole. The 26th Marine Division had encamped in that rotten coastal defense position two weeks ago along with elements of the 9th Marines, thinking they would face only a few starving Viet Cong. The brass knew this position would really piss off the Viet Cong, but the Marines just thought of themselves as bait in a very large trap. Their location was intended to draw out the enemy for the big naval guns and air power to destroy. At first, they had planned on staying only a couple of weeks, so their food and ammo was limited.

Instead, the NVA had, much to the chagrin of the Marine commanders, moved in considerable strength onto the field and encamped on the overlooking hills. From those hills, these pesky little men could lob their artillery fire onto the entire American position whenever they damn well pleased. Including both the HQ area and the airfield, which was the one lifeline the Marines had, once they lost their fortified positions on the roads. To make matters worse, heavy weather settled in, and at least for a time, the US had nothing to throw back at the offending NVA positions only a few miles to the west. They had no advantage in air cover, with the clouds this thick and the enemy so near, and the big naval guns were silent, again, because the NVA was so close to the American positions.

Yeah, Jesse fully expected to die here, as so many were already doing. At that very moment he was wishing that he was back at home in New Bern, NC. He wanted nothing more than to drive around the Charburger again. It was a cheap hamburger place out on the south edge of town, just beside Highway 17. He'd be drinking beer with the guys from his high school football team, and playing with the girls who were also driving around the Charburger. That was where they all hung out.

Jesus spoke up from the other side of the hole. "Hey, Jesse. You still enjoying the scenery or are you gonna get your sorry white ass back into this hole?"

Jesse heard the voice of his friend, but he didn't even look back. "Bite me, Jesus. I just want to see them if they come over the rise early. I'll come back before the arty gets to us."

Jesus laughed. "See um, you dumb ass! How could you miss'em? We've got concertina up every fifty meters, and claymores in between. Those gooks'll make noise for sure. Most'll be meat before they get here."

Concertina wire was a barbed wire with sharp razor edges, similar to that used at the top of prison fences. It was up all along the perimeter, some two hundred meters away. Jesus thought it should at least slow the NVA down.

"Sure, Jesus. Tell that to Freeman," Jesse said, as a joke. As soon as he said it, he wished he hadn't.

Freeman was a big black grunt from West Orange, New Jersey, a real bad-assed dude from a rough city and one hell of a mean Marine. He seemed to never forgive Jesse for his southern background. In fact, Freeman had given Jesse all grades of hell from their first days together in the 26th eight months ago, but it had always been in good humor—well almost always. Jesse would ask to borrow something, maybe a pair of socks. Freeman would toss them over and then holler, in his approximation of southern lingo, "Yes' suh! Massa. Got 'em right heaaa!"

To Jesse, the joke was getting old, but months and months of eating the same battlefield dirt bonded men together in ways that no civilian could ever understand. Jesse really didn't mind the ribbin' too bad, and everyone knew when the shit hit the fan, Freeman was a man you wanted beside you. He was a fighting demon! Everyone knew, he was one hell of a Marine!

Funny thing, Freeman picked on everybody in the company but Jesus—once he learned Jesus was from Tennessee, he stopped. "Damn! A big bad-assed black man in Tennessee! That's deep south, man! Sheee-it! You mutha's have had it as bad as we did in Jersey! And now, with Jesse here, you got to live with your ol' massa all over again! Sheee-it!" Therein lay the summation of discriminatory racial practices in the Americas, as seen from the prospective of the black community of West Orange, NJ in 1968.

Freeman was the first in the company, after the Master Sergeant, to use the nickname Jesus, but soon the entire company picked it up. They all liked having Jesus in the company, sort of like God in our bunker, or God on our side, in some weird way.

Most of Freeman's face had been blown off by a mortar round just before yesterday's evening attack. He never knew what hit him—one moment here, the next gone. He'd died instantly since most of his upper brain was gone. Some of it was on his chest and back and some was just lying in his hole, and head wounds really bleed a lot. The mortar round left his body face down in his hole, and the blood just seemed to drain out of him, while his heart beat a final few times. The rest of his body had been picked up last night, after the fighting stopped.

Most of Freeman was now in a black body bag, Code Number 26D-621-A: Khe Sanh. He was in a warehouse with a hundred and sixty-nine other dead Marines, awaiting shipment home. The cargo planes, the only means of re-supply for this base, were getting knocked out of the air right over the runway fairly frequently, and nobody wanted to put bodies on them just yet. So the dead were stacked in a warehouse freezer, next to the hamburgers that the company would eat the next day for lunch. Die out here; they put you in a freezer.

Of course, some of Freeman's skull and brains were still in the drying mud of the next fighting hole, fifteen yards to the left. Yeah, Jesse should have kept his damn mouth shut about Freeman.

### The Artillery

Artillery—arty—can be your best friend or it can ruin your whole day. That night Jesse saw both. The first explosion on their position shook the ground so fiercely that Jesse felt it in his bones. He didn't even realize that the pressure wave lifted him fifteen feet into the air. He was thrown up and over the face of the berm toward his enemy, falling some eighteen feet, barely clearing the coil of concertina wire at the rim of his own hole. He had a deep cut on his shoulder and another on his lower back that he didn't even feel. The pain would come later if he lived that long, and his left eardrum was blown by the pressure wave. He did feel the eardrum blow. It felt like his head was cracked wide open, and at the time, he was sure he had a severe head wound. He thought in that split second, "I'll die the same way Freeman did, with a hole in my head, and my brains in this damn dark dirt!"

His left hand went to touch the side of his skull, and the blood from his ear convinced him he was mortally wounded. To make matters worse, he'd landed on his back, thus exposing his chest, belly, and balls to anything the NVA wanted to toss his way.

He remembered thinking, "Sheee-it! This is just no place to be." In reality he'd shouted those words to himself, but with the sound of more artillery fire demanding everyone's immediate attention, he didn't realize he'd been shouting. Of course no one else heard. His next thought was something like "I'm toast!

They'll ship me home in pieces if I don't get the hell out of here."

He looked quickly over his left shoulder towards the top of the berm, noting the concertina wire still formed a solid piece, and thus presented a four foot barrier to his return. Jesus stuck his head up at the top of the hole for a moment, and then disappeared again. He was seven feet away, but it might as well have been fifty miles. There was nothing at all that he could do for Jesse.

The arty explosions were moving further back behind the defensive line now. As that danger moved away from him, he realized he was "hidden" from jagged metal that each round sent his way—protected by the back side of the berm, but he was facing the enemy and exposed in that direction! Still some sharp eyed gook with an AK was bound to see this prostrate Marine lying out here big as you please on the wrong side of the berm pretty soon. He'd be dead in a heartbeat. He had to find cover fast and getting back on the defensive side of the berm did not seem to be an option. Like the veteran Marine that he was, he did the most illogical thing in the world. He rolled over, grabbed his rifle, crouched low, and ran like hell charging toward his unseen enemy!

Seemingly stupid that, but in reality it was the only logical choice. If he could make it just a few yards forward and into one of the holes left by yesterday's artillery, he'd at least be hidden in a hole again and might even live through this. Of course he'd be way out on his own when the inevitable charge came from the pissed off NVA. It was so slim a chance at life that it wasn't really worth considering, but he decided that after he'd begun his run, and he couldn't stop now. So he continued forward some twenty yards, and flung himself into the first hole he saw, a hole seven feet wide and four deep with steep sides front and back. He still had his rifle—a minor miracle that—as well as some ammo. He figured he'd die fighting, just like Marines are supposed to. He'd be covered in blood and that damn dark dirt. Again he thought, "This shit looks just like the sandy, dark dirt of a Carolina tobacco field! What a place to die!"

As Jesse checked his load, he heard nothing. Still he felt every explosion of the arty in the marrow of his bones and in a few seconds the pressure in his ear stopped throbbing. Then he felt—rather than heard—something that terrified him! Something landed right in the hole to his left and he thought he was a goner! An unexploded mortar round must have found his hole. He stupidly looked over to see his certain death.

There grinning from ear to ear was Jesus, big, ugly, and black as night! All six foot four of him, sitting there, and he was shouting something to Jesse, obviously very proud of himself. He looked like some massive high school kid who'd just won the hundred-yard dash. In a way, maybe he had.

"You got to be the dumbest, damn Marine on this whole damned planet!" Jesse shouted, "You'll never get back to the world if you do this kind of dumb shee-it. What the hell are you doing out here?"

"Screw you very much!" Jesus answered. "I couldn't let you have all the fun. Besides, the arty got most of the defensive line. They didn't even have time to call HQ. NVA inside the southwestern perimeter, bigger than shee-it! Marines on that end, in a world of hurt, screaming like a beat bitch!"

Jesus took a ragged breath, and then continued. "Saw you fly over the berm. Knew you was too damn dumb to find your way home, so I thought I'd come too! Saved my ass, too! I got out of the hole just before it blew."

Jesse thought a moment, and then replied. "This is bad news, man! You mean that HQ knows we're getting pounded, but can't raise us on radio. The OP is toast, and the next defensive line is gone? Am I hearing this?"

Jesse paused for a moment, as both Marines thought about their unfortunate position. Jesse then continued, "They could waltz in here with a small company and get all the way to the HQ, hell maybe even the airfield, with no resistance."

Jesus, ever the practical one, merely said, "Life just sucks, don't it? Think Charlie got all that figured out yet?"

"Hell no! They had, they'd be here by now. Big time screwin' for us!" Jesse checked his jacket, finding what he wanted pinned to his breast. "I got two grenades. You got any? We're for sure gonna need 'um."

Both men looked up briefly, as the arty barrage swung further behind them. At least that was one advantage of hunkering down in this most unlikely position—no artillery falling here. Then, Jesus adopted his joking voice, a somber voice that he imagined sounded like God—it was a play on his nickname in the company, and he "quoted" something that never appeared in any Bible. "And behold, a light shown from the wilderness, and Jesus, the Son of God, brought forth the instruments of death!" As Jesus spoke he opened a knapsack filled with ammo and grenades. He also had two claymores and wire. Then he dropped the joking religious tone, and got down to business. "I figure we'll plant these claymores. Gooks come, they're toast!"

Jesse grinned at his friend's antics, and then continued the thought. "Put them about twenty, twenty five yards out, angled at 90 degrees to get overlapping coverage. Anything in that area, definitely be toast when we trip 'em off." Then Jesse looked up at his friend. "Good thinking Jesus. I'm surprised you had time to pack before you came to visit."

"Hell Jesse, when I saw your scrawny white ass go over the berm, I grabbed what I could and ran. Damn lucky too—like I said, just in time." With that, both looked back at the now destroyed hole that had been the OP.

Then to business. The two opened the sack and took out the claymores. Each of these explosive mines would fire a lethal array of projectiles in an 85 degree arc for almost a 180 degrees of coverage aimed away from the newly adopted fighting position, with an overlapping arc of fire directly in front of their hole outward for fifty meters. When all else failed, when their ammo was nearly out, when they couldn't contain the onslaught of NVA charging at them across the distant concertina wire, they'd throw the switch and pop off the claymores. Had to be careful in their placement though, the NVA had gotten smarter lately; at times they snuck in and actually moved the claymores around to fire directly back at the Marine positions. Even with that danger, there was the possibility that these two beauties would help them live a few minutes longer—though neither had any real hope of survival.

Such was the plan for two Marines who were shit out of luck, and stuck five hundred meters outside of the second defensive perimeter line, in a filthy place called Khe Sanh, a place nobody wanted to be. These two had NVA regulars before them and deadly artillery behind. Hell, even if they did try a retreat after the arty stopped, their own guys would cut them down before they could ID themselves. That was exactly when the NVA usually came to visit.

In the distance, they could hear the screaming of other Marines who were still under fire from the artillery barrage. These were the lucky ones—wounded but not dead. Most of them would see the world again, while neither Jesse nor Jesus thought that they would. In a few minutes, the NVA would attack in force all along the perimeter. To add to their danger, the mortars from their own company would be zeroed in on the very place that these two proposed to defend. After all, there were supposed to be no dumb-ass Marines out this far. As Jesse thought it through, he was sure he'd been right in his earlier assessment. He said "We be screwed, man!"

The two men checked and reloaded their weapons. Then each headed over the lip of their hole to plant the claymores. A trip wire would have been nice, but it was quicker to just run a hard-wire and pop off those bad boys manually, so that is what they did. Each Marine returned in less than a minute, laid on his back in the hole, and breathed several curses under his breath. Neither thought he would live through the night.

## *A Moonscape of Death*

When the artillery began to let up—with the last few rounds cooking off somewhere near the distant airfield, both Marines had the same thought, "Oh shit, they'll be coming now." Yet the attack this night was not as immediate as it had been in the previous few days. There seemed to be a hole in time, a sudden quiet after the final explosions. Jesse thought to himself, "When did it get dark?" A pitch black had settled over Hill 861 on the Khe Sanh perimeter. Jesse could barely see Jesus, his skin was so black, but then most of that was the damned black dirt.

Each man lay face out, in the prescribed 45-degree angle to each other, their backs to each other some four feet apart in the hole. Each waited, in the intense heavy quiet after the artillery stopped. After perhaps a minute of exquisite silence, a magnesium flare was fired from the defensive perimeter behind them, lighting the darkness and floating quietly, almost contentedly to earth on its small parachute.

"See anything Jesus? Where are the lil' Gooks?"

"Don't know Jesse. I'm sure they'll be here in a while."

The flare continued its slow drop to the earth, and another joined it in the night sky—again turning night into a surreal moonscape of charred, turned earth and concertina wire. The razor sharpness of the wire reflected the descending lights of the flares, appearing as a hundred thousand small mirrors reflecting the shining light back into their eyes. Shadows moved, grew larger, or shrunk as the various flares climbed into the heavens or descended and burned out—each light changing all the unnatural shapes in this eerie battlefield of death. Some scattered rifle fire was heard from the left flank, towards that end of the defensive perimeter, adding to the sensation of unearthly terrain. The picture before them could have been the backside of Mars.

Jesse said, "I hope the left flank got their OP in before the fun started over there. Sounds like it started on their end."

"Nah. I don't hear no AKs. It ain't started yet. That's some bare ass baby shootin' his wad at a shadow! Dumb shit bare ass, wastin' his load like that." Inexperienced recruits, newly arrived from the world, were typically clean shaven, with nice haircuts, and smelled like soap—the veterans called them "bare asses," or "bare ass babies." Usually the newly arrived babies were unsure when to shoot, so they shot at everything or nothing depending on the circumstances.

"He'll know soon enough," Jesse said. "He'll need that ammo before this night is out." Again the two men waited, while another couple of flares were fired along the line.

"Do you think we need a plan?" Jesus asked, after a few more moments—moments that seemed like hours. "After we fire off the claymores, do we drag ass back to the line or what?"

Jesse thought about it for a minute. "I don't know. We'll have to see who's engaged where, see who's taking fire. We can't go back if it means crawlin' towards our lines right beside the NVA. We get mixed up in that advance and our own guys'll frag us quicker than ape shit."

Jesus contemplated. "Yeah. I don't want to go in under a flare either—they'll shoot our ass for sure." He was quiet for a moment, then said, "We are big time screwed, ain't we Jesse."

Jesse said, "You're a dumb shithead, Marine, Jesus! I told you that five minutes ago." Jesse tried to sound brave joking with his friend, but merely came off as a tense fear.

Jesus, like Jesse, contemplated his imminent death, then said, "Seems like a couple of hours already. Sure it was only five minutes?"

"Four, maybe five minutes. Don't time fly when you're having fun," Jesse said.

Several more minutes passed, very slowly. The men waited as the fireworks show of flares continued to transform the battlefield. Life was on temporary suspension in this surreal world.

"Jesus, what did you mean about Carolina?" Jesse asked.

"Huh?"

"What did you mean about Carolina? About you being from Carolina—you always said Tennessee before," Jesse repeated.

"Oh. My family came from there. You white motha's owned my people; don't you know your history, white boy? Some town called New Bern, according to my Ma, but we was shipped outa there way back, couple hundred years ago! Massa moved to Leesville, Tennessee. My people were born slaves way back, and we was owned by a man named Burdine Bender; whole bunch of Burdines in our family but the first came from New Bern in the Carolinas, 'least that's what my Daddy always said. Your people were ass-kicking mean, and they owned us for damn sure! My Granddad and my Dad remember all the stories."

Jesse grinned. "Hell, my people owned your people! Weird that you think of that now!"

"Only every damn day, Jesse," Jesus responded. "Every damn day! Brothers think about that shee-it all the time!" Here Jesus paused just a moment, to let Jesse stew on that one. Then he continued. "But you know, we might also be kin! You ever think of that?"

Jesse said, "Yeah, I'm sure my great-granddad needed some dark nookie, one night! Head out to the slave yard, right? The history books didn't talk about it, but in high school I had a great teacher for Carolina history. Master and the slave girls! Still, most folks don't much talk about it. Hell my Granny Mildred would kill me just for sayin' that!"

In the momentary lull, during a desperate battle, men can and often will, talk about anything!

Jesus thought that over for a minute, while his eyes scanned the horizon for the enemy. He said, "Yeah, my Grandma still tells stories about her ancestors, brave men, been free men for some time before the Civil War, but 'fore that, slaves sure enough! Last little while, my folks was fighting to keep the family all together in Tennessee and hoping the North would win, and sure enough, here come 'de Jubilee! Heard about that shit all my life! You should hear my Dad!"

At that point, Jesus mimicked what was obviously supposed to be his Dad's tone of voice. "Your family has done much for you Julian. When you return you shall repay that debt. You will go to college with the money from the GI Bill, and me and your Ma will pay for the rest. You will get an education, and you should never forget how your family, slave and free men for hundreds of years, have struggled just to make that possible!"

"Guess so, cousin." Jesse said, and grinned again. "We'll make sure you get your education, if I can get your sorry black ass out of this! In fact, we'll look all that shit up too. Find out if my people owned your people, about being cousins, we'll check out all 'o that. Hell, my Granny would probably know all about it! But for now, how 'bout getting your dumb Marine ass back into the game. Get on your side of this hole, keep your head down, and your eyes open."

They waited what seemed to both like another few hours—in reality it was only three minutes or so, then Jesse said, "You know we really should look up that shit about your ancestors. My folks settled in New Bern real early, and my Granny is real big on family history. Yeah, Granny Mildred could really tell you some stories, but she always says there are some things no one in the family should ever talk about! We should look into that. Hell, we may be cousins! Wouldn't that be a bitch! In New Bern, it would really piss off all the right people!"

Jesus smiled to himself. He'd never heard a white want any kinship with a Negro before, but strange things happened in this battlefield moonscape. "Yeah, Jesse. Your white ass sure 'nuff looks like my damn cousin! We'll look that up for sure, if we get our ass out 'a this fix and back to the world."

Jesse smiled at his friend. "Sure, Jesus. We'll figure it out one day, we sure as hell will!"

Neither thought at that moment that anything would ever come of this conversation, but in many ways, this talk both began and defined their friendship for over four decades. Weird things really do happen to men, bonded together, in the midst of battle, and at those times, the last thing they notice about each other is their skin color!

### They're Coming

One or two more minutes passed then, each one slower still. A couple more flares lit the night sky, and all that desolate world changed shapes again. This time Jesse saw movement in front of his hole, about a hundred meters out.

"See 'um, Jesus? I got a shit load out here in front coming over the wire. Maybe twenty or thirty Gooks."

Jesus said, "They must not be in the dead zone yet. They'd be tripping the claymores between the wires by now."

"Yeah," Jesse said. "If anybody's alive in the defensive perimeter to trip 'um." Just then a massive explosion rocked the earth, followed immediately by two more. As another magnesium flare lit the sky, the defensive perimeter guys fired more claymores. Then all the claymores between the outlying wires were cooking off right under the advancing line of the NVA.

"That'll shut you up, won't it?" Jesus said. More flares were fired and all was still for the moment, as the last flare burned down towards the ground.

As those shadows grew in number they began to move again, and Jesse realized that the number of approaching human forms had increased. Worse, there was a large gap in the concertina wire—but then he also noticed some of the NVA lying on the ground.

Jesus said, "Guess those claymores got a few of 'um."

"Guess so, and we still got our two right out in front. Should slow 'um down some," Jesse said, and then he thought of another problem. "Jesus, if we let them know we're out here alone we'll get all their attention. Let's hold fire until our mortars start, and then we'll open up. We'll be lost in the shuffle then, maybe."

"Sounds good, Jesse. Just keep your sorry white ass in this hole will ya? I don't want to follow you around no more tonight."

"Sounds like a plan, Jesus." Jesse though for a moment. "You know, I think we're really in a world of hurt this time."

Jesus considered for a moment, and then answered. "Yeah Jesse, but there's nowhere to go man. We can't get back in now in the middle o' this! We try, we're toast!"

"You're right. Guess this just has me worried a bit," Jesse said. "By the way, Jesus, I'm glad you came over the berm. It would be mighty damn lonely out here right now without you."

Jesus chuckled, "Yeah, well, no real choice man. And screw you very much too."

When the next flare fired some thirty seconds later, the enemy seemed to have moved drastically closer, and Jesse thought he'd have to shoot in the next few seconds or be spotted—either would be certain death for the two Marines. Just as Jesse prepared to pull his trigger, the Marine mortars opened up with two ranging shots. The NVA knew that this meant certain death if they didn't move fast, since those mortars were sure to have the range now, so they jumped up in mass, and charged straight towards Jesse and Jesus, just like the previous three nights. Jesse thought he saw over a hundred NVA charging directly towards his position, but he silently thanked God for the mortars. They'd taken out plenty already, and he still had two claymores in front of his hole.

The next mortar shots landed a hundred and fifty meters in front of their position, but were even then too far out to reach the small yellow men crouching low and running in their direction. The mortar teams quickly corrected and fired a concentrated barrage directly into the charging line. More flares lit up the sky, and within two seconds of each other Jesus and Jesse began firing, their noise now lost in the growing battle.

The Marine rifle in 1968 was the venerable M-16, a light weapon that was capable of single shot fire, sustained automatic fire, or three round burst fire. A single shot was deadly, but sustained automatic would cut a man in half. The weapon was effective out to five hundred meters and deadly at two hundred. These NVA were only a hundred meters away. Like almost all Marines of the day, both of these men chose burst fire, since three rounds were more likely to hit something than one, but didn't clean out your ammo as fast as the full automatic fire. Also, burst fire was less likely to garner attention to their position than two automatic weapons on full "rock and roll"—their term for automatic fire.

With their first burst both Marines cut men down, men who were only eighty or ninety meters out to their front. Then they picked other targets and fired. The NVA regulars were by now charging directly at them in a massive human wave, and each time a gap appeared in that line, each time someone was taken down by claymores, mortars, or rifle fire, someone else seemed to fill the gap. The enemy line rushed on into a hellish death, shown in the low black-and-white light of the flares from the defensive perimeter, flares that calmly rode their tiny parachutes down from on high above the battlefield, like little angels passively observing this deathly horror.

Jesse was surprised that the NVA didn't seem to know that two Marines were firing on the line from this terribly exposed position, but he was counting himself as incredibly lucky. He turned his head towards Jesus and shouted, "In just a few, we'll fire the Claymores."

Just as he turned back, a round caught him in the left shoulder tearing a gaping hole just under his collarbone. Jesse felt like he'd been kicked by a horse, and he wondered if he really was going to die that night. He spun with the impact and was tossed back about three feet onto his stomach. Only then did Jesus note that something was wrong.

As Jesse fell into the hole, Jesus shouted, "Wait hell! Gem'me that switcher!" He grabbed the switcher between them and fired off the two claymores. Each sprayed on array of pellets into thirty-five NVA soldiers who had the misfortune of charging into their deadly kill zone. One NVA was too close to Jesse's claymore and caught the full charge. He was blown in half by the blast, absorbing much of the force into his abdomen before his body came apart.

Before that guy's torso landed askew on its own legs, Jesus had grabbed his rifle again, switched it to full auto, and laid out lead all around the front of the hole. The noise of his M-16 was murderous, but the claymores, AKs, and mortars were all firing at once, and Jesus couldn't even hear himself shouting, "Screw you, you little piece of shit" over and over again as he auto-fired his full magazine.

Jesse meanwhile, was rolling over onto his back, as a jumble of thoughts flew through his mind. The sharp pain in his shoulder let him know he'd been hit bad, but he had the distinct impression that he wasn't dead yet, and he wondered how long it would take to bleed out in the hole. Still, he had the presence of mind to realize that Jesus was on full auto and would quickly empty his magazine. When that mag went down, and Jesus was changin' it, the NVA were sure to charge the hole. Jesse crawled to the opposite perimeter of the hole and lifted his M-16 with his right hand. He opened on burst fire just as Jesus ran empty—just in time to waste three NVA coming in from that side. They each died within fifteen meters of the hole.

As Jesse looked for another target, Jesus changed his mag—accomplishing that task in four seconds flat. He then peeped back over the rim. At that moment, he took a minor wound in the face. Shrapnel cut him below his left eye, leaving a gash down to his chin exposing part of his jaw and several of his back teeth. It bled like hell but was not serious. That last sentence sounds crazy, but again, the Marines out there will understand.

The last of the flares were dying but two more were climbing into the sky, and that mixture of light sources painted the battlefield into a horrid field of death with bodies, and parts of bodies, scattered haphazardly across the earth like rocks in a streambed. Jesse noted the wound on his friend's face, with only passing interest. Jesus was still fighting and that was what counted—Jesus was one hell of a Marine.

For ten more minutes, each man fired as rapidly as he could. It seemed to them like hours had passed in that ten minutes and Jesus had switched back to burst fire to save ammo. They changed mags when needed, and checked to make certain not to change them at the same time.

Jesus was scared shitless, and that made him more deadly. He selected his targets and killed in rage, angry at the killing but joyous at the deaths. He shouted curses as he fired, and he hated his enemy at that moment.

Jesse was the opposite, a man who killed quickly but with no passion, displaying almost a casual lack of interest as if he were delivering mail rather than supersonic death from the hot barrel of a deadly assault weapon on burst fire. Neither man thought of anything else. They were lost in the killing. A target presented itself—a target went down. Neither man thought of his own life, the life of his enemy, or his own future any longer. There was not any time for that. At precisely that moment, each was a pure killer. Each man in his own way was merely an instrument of destruction, cruelly efficient, hardened, and each was certain he would die that night; it seemed inevitable.

Then all of a sudden it slacked off for a few minutes, and at some point, perhaps twenty minutes into the fight, neither Jesse nor Jesus could find a target. Each stopped firing, and automatically checked his load. Flares continued to light the sky, but the mortar rounds were slacking off too. Jesse had slid around to the back of the hole by then, and was actually firing at the backs of NVA who had already passed their position. The enemy seemed, for some unexplained reason, to be unaware they were there. Neither Jesse nor Jesus realized then, that they had killed almost an entire company scattered all around their hole, and had thus created a gap in the NVA advancing line. As for the NVA, they never seemed to notice the high rate of fire from their rear.

When the firing in their immediate area stopped, Jesus spoke. "Jesse, what the hell is happenin' man?"

"Don't shout Jesus. I still don't think they know we're here."

"You gotta be shittin' me! How can they miss these damn dead dummies all around us?" With that Jesus nodded his chin, pointing out the corpses near their position. Jesse saw the cheek skin on Jesus' face hanging down and flappin' whenever Jesus moved.

"Don't know man," Jesse said. "But they still ain't payin' us any attention, and I want to keep it that way."

Again, the moonscape seemed to quiet down for a time. Now the flares were the only explosions that were heard. Still, men were screaming, seemingly all around the two Marines who were still stuck way out in the middle of this hell.

"Jesse, are they still out there?" Jesus whispered.

"What did you say, Jesus? I can't hear from that ear."

At that comment, Jesus looked around at Jesse, and noted the blood streaming from his ear. For a moment, Jesus thought that was his friend's only wound; then he saw the blood on Jesse's shoulder and back too. Jesse then turned his head to get his good ear close to Jesus.

"Oh man," Jesus said. "You look like shee-it. How you feeling?"

"Been better, I guess," Jesse said. "Shoulder hurts like hell. Besides, you ain't no spring rose either, you son-of-a-bitch! Your Mama won't even kiss your ugly face now, unless she wants to suck on your damn back teeth! Didn't I tell you not to come out here and get all banged up?"

"And didn't I tell you, had no choice man?"

Jesse looked out of the hole for a second, then said, "Guess I'm glad you came all the same. One M-16 wouldn't have stopped those dudes. I'd been real dead; a big-time goner, just like Freeman."

"Got that right, man. Guess we did each other a favor. Takes two to really rock and roll!"

The two were quiet for a few seconds, the firing was dying out around the entire perimeter, like it sometimes did when men on both sides of the battle line asked themselves, quite seriously, the inevitable battlefield question: "What the hell am I doin' here?"

Meanwhile, the flares kept lighting up the sky, every minute turned into an hour, and the ever-changing scene, changed yet again.

## *A Quiet Enemy*

Sometimes death on a battlefield was actually quiet, sometimes loud and violent. In Khe Sanh, South Vietnam, you could never tell. The quiet at that moment on the field was thick and rich. You could almost breathe in the quiet, and the flares continued to paint the horrid moonscape in slowly moving shadows, a breathing, surreal scene of death.

"Think they still out there?" Jesus asked after a few ragged breaths. By this point both men were exhausted. "Maybe they slithered on back up to their hill top for the night."

"Not a prayer! I think they just laid down where they were. They're still all around us," Jesse whispered. "And keep your damn voice down. I'm only deaf in one ear, and those bastards can still hear just fine!"

Again, the two Marines waited. One minute, two, three minutes passed, how could time pass any slower?

Then, a shrill whistle like sound, and it started again. As one flare lowered in the sky, the shadows all seemed to move at once. When the next flare climbed up enough to light the night, over two hundred NVA were running towards these two Marines. Some were even past them, once again, out to their left flank. Mortars started again, and this time they were landing right beside the hole. It made sense when Jesse thought about it. They were right in the middle of the NVA at that point. Explosions, screams, rifle and mortar fire, all combined to make the world one big explosion. The very air seemed to be deadly. Jesse felt the earth move under him from the various blasts and he sensed all kinds of lead flying past his head.

Suddenly, Jesus was firing again on burst fire, and he shouted, "Jesse, I need you bad!"

Jesse stopped his firing at the NVA running thirty meters out to the left flank, but as he turned away he saw a mortar round land right in that spot. The sound was felt more than heard, since he was already deaf in that ear. Still he did see a number of NVA lifted off the ground and thrown a number of feet into the air, limbs all spread out. A satisfying sight, that.

But not the sight that greeted him when he turned—a group of NVA, a whole platoon maybe, were chargin' at the hole, directly at him and Jesus. They were only twenty meters away now, and this batch was really pissed.

Jesus was changing magazines and shouting, "Oh, shit. Oh, shit. Oh, shit." He was quite repetitive when he got either angry or really scared. At that moment, he was both.

Jesse switched to full auto and stood up. He began popping off, firing right over Jesus' head. He'd be plenty empty real fast, but he had to stop the NVA out there, and not in his hole. As he opened up, several of them took cover, and others seemed to crumple into the dirt. Jesse guessed that he got some of them, but they were falling down way too damn close. One caught several of Jesse's rounds in his chest, but kept staggering forward as he died. He actually fell forward onto the rim of Jesse's hole only six or seven feet away, and that was just too damn close! Just at that moment, out of the corner of his eye, Jesse saw Jesus stand up and run.

Jesse remembered thinking, "Where the hell is he going?" just before he saw Jesus jump down, taking a position in the next artillery hole about twenty five feet to the right front. That way, they could at least set up some type of crossfire angle on the NVA, and they needed to do something real fast. These NVA were really just too damn close to screw around with now. Jesse's auto fire kept the NVA down just long enough for Jesus to get into the hole, where he rolled just like they taught Marines to do. He came up firing on burst fire again, just as Jesse's mag ran dry.

The two couldn't coordinate changing their magazines out now, and Jesse was out, but he knew that Jesus had changed mags while running. A good Marine always did. Jesse popped out his mag, and grabbed another from the bag by his feet—only a few magazines left, he noticed. Then he thought, "Oh shit. We'll probably be dead before we use 'um up anyway." In five seconds he was firing again.

Just as Jesse shot, Jesus stopped. Jesse saw his friend look at him briefly and then the ground all around Jesus flew up into his face, and the next hole was lost in a cloud of dust. Three mortar rounds had landed within seconds of each other, right between him and Jesus, and those rounds had probably killed his friend. Jesse knew he had no options left, so he switched to full auto and fired at anything that moved. Two more flares rose and he changed mags again. Now he could hear Jesus firing once more. "At least he's still alive," Jesse thought, then he noticed that Jesus was on single shot fire. He was running out of ammo too.

Then Jesse heard a high pitched squeal in his right ear—he was sure for just an instant that he was hearing the one artillery round that was coming straight for his hole. He knew for sure that he would die in a horrible flash, but strangely enough, his final thought was, "I'm sorry, Jesus, but I guess I'll be leavin' you alone now."

No explosion, no fire. The squeal continued. It wasn't artillery. It was something else. Another whistle, maybe? What the hell was that?

He saw the shadows move again, some of them were NVA getting up to run, but none of the moving shadows were close to him now. In fact, yeah, many were moving away. They seemed to—what the hell?

Yeah, they were moving back towards the cuts in the concertina wire. They were retreating on that signal. Some NVA blows a whistle, and they run away? Jesse decided he really had to get himself a whistle. He'd for sure get one, if he lived through this. The mortars from the defensive line kept pounding for another few seconds or so, but the NVA were definitely moving back. Jesse surprised himself when he thought, "I may have made it. I may live through this!" As soon as that thought struck, he turned to find his friend.

And there he was, big, black, beautiful, and filthy, looking mean as hell, sitting right next to Jesse, right on the edge of the hole. Jesus had that big damn dumb grin on his bleeding face and a couple of back teeth were still showing above a section of his lower jaw.

Jesus had already managed to crawl back over to Jesse's spot. All Jesse could think to say was, "You big dumb damn nigger. You really piss me off coming in here all the time, uninvited. You've done it twice tonight!"

Jesus grinned though his half-face. "Don't call me nigger, you damned lil' redneck cracker. Only brothers get away with that!"

Jesse just grinned again at his friend, and then turned back toward the enemy.

It was really happening. Out in that flare lit moonscape that the NVA were retreating. By then the field all around the hole was littered with over a hundred dead or dying men, all NVA, more than a full company as it turned out. A few were still alive, and several cried out in their foreign tongue for help or for a merciful death. Perhaps they shouted out to their friends to come and get them. One NVA was breathing his last some twenty feet away, and the two Marines heard his gurgled breath as he died, drowning in his own blood.

"Better him than us!" said Jesus.

"Yeah," said Jesse.

The two Marines stayed low for a couple minutes more. Some of the enemy was still out there, and a few were bound to have loaded rifles. The Marines looked over the scene. Only then did they smile at each other as they realized they were still alive, and were likely to stay that way for another day.

"Jesse, are we gonna make it?" Jesus asked, not quite believing it himself.

"Shit, Jesus. How in hell should I know?" Jesse said. "I'm just glad they're runnin' the other way, man. I'm for sure getting me a whistle!"

"You got that right, white man."

"OK. You can stop that shit right now, Jesus," Jesse said as he laughed. "Right this minute. I'm damned filthy and at least as black as you are right now—what with this mud and black sandy dirt and all. Besides Freeman ain't here man, and the cracker jokes grow old."

"Hey, don't get so pissed, white boy. You'll bleed to death!" Jesus said. "In fact, why don't you let me take a look at that shoulder for you? It looks bad."

Jesse said, "You should see your damn face, you think I look bad. You know, I do think they're through for tonight."

Jesus looked out again across the field of the dead. "Yeah, but I'll bet that their arty starts up in ten minutes or so when they're sure their guys are back in. In fact, we don't need to be out here then, my man."

"Got that right," Jesse said. "Lets start singing the God Damn Marine Hymn and hustle on back to see what's left of the defensive perimeter. Maybe our guys won't shoot us if we're singing about the good ol' U S of A!" Jesse looked around behind him, surveying the scene of carnage. "There sure ain't no reason to be out here no more. Ain't nothing left of the OP."

"Semper fi, you son of a bitch! Sounds like a plan, to me!" Jesus said. "But I thought, massa would want to sing Dixie or some shit like that!"

"Gimme a break Jesus, will ya?" Jesse said, but he couldn't help giggling a bit as he thought about it. "But wouldn't that freak 'um out. It would 'a really pissed off Freeman too! You know it? Us singin' Dixie like that!"

Jesus, always a hellion, mumbled, "Hell, I guess they couldn't frag nobody that was dumb enough to be out here singing Dixie, could they?" Jesus thought it over again, for about two seconds flat! Then he grinned, leaving one flap of his left cheek dangling the wrong way, down towards his shoulder. He looked gross, but he was excited—he would live through this night!

"Let's do it!" he shouted! "Let's stand up bigger'n hell and piss off Freeman! We'll march right back to HQ singing Dixie louder than shee-it!"

And that is just what they did.

The news back in the world about Khe Sanh was huge. It was the largest battle fought in South Vietnam up to that date, and folks watched most of it on TV. Vietnam was the first war brought to your very own living room by Col. Sanders Fried Chicken, Kellogg, and the other fine sponsors of the morning news. It was the first televised war in history and the first war where televised battle scenes were even possible. Everybody knew about Khe Sanh.

For Marines, that battle will always command respect. The grit, determination, and bravery shown by the 26th Marines in that battle are unsurpassed in military history. Today, the seventy-seven days of the siege of Khe Sanh are revered as one of the proudest examples of courage in a long history of selfless sacrifice, one of the finest of many fine Marine traditions. This battle is only one of the several reasons that, for every Marine, the very word "Marine" is always capitalized. Marines out there will understand that too.

While the battle itself has been somewhat overshadowed by the Tet Offensive, which took place roughly during the same time period in 1968, the name Khe Sanh still brings great pride, and usually a moment of silent reflection among the men who fought inside that tough perimeter. A lot of good Marines died there. In the end two hundred and five men left that field in body bags. In the hearts of their fellow Marines, they are merely on permanent patrol. They will always be remembered and revered for their stand on that muddy, black-dirt, ground. Their sacrifice allowed many others, like Jesse and Jesus, to come home.

Many other remarkable things happened on Hill 861, as well as the entire Khe Sanh perimeter, not the least of which is that these two Marines—these Bender boys—became best friends for life. Fighting a hopeless battle and surviving against all the odds sometimes has that effect.

Within two months, the 26th Marines got a Presidential Unit Citation awarded by President Johnson on the White House grounds, for their actions at Khe Sanh. All who were ambulatory attended, including the Bender boys, one black and one white. They were fast friends by then, but they had to search a bit to find a bar in Washington at that time that would even let a black man and a white man share a beer together when they came to town for the White House ceremony. Apparently, they could die together in Khe Sanh but they couldn't drink together in DC. After what they had been through, that didn't seem too important at all.

It has often been said that it is impossible to find an atheist in a foxhole. Men need God with them when they face the possibility of instantaneous death, and thus, God manages to show up all the time in war. In a similar way, it is all but impossible to find a racist in a foxhole too, just another offshoot of that same principle. Skin color doesn't matter when a man is fighting beside you and saving your life.

When men share their labor, their dirt, their blood, their horror, their food, farts, ammo, and most of all their fear, they soon begin to ignore each other's complexion. Jesus and Jesse were Marines who had lived together in a hole in the ground at Khe Sanh. No one else was there in that hole—no one else would ever be bonded to these men as they were to each other, and skin color had nothing to do with that at all. Jesus could have been an albino as far as Jesse was concerned, and it wouldn't have made any difference. In Jesus' view, Jesse was just a kid that always needed help! When one bartender gave the Bender boys a weird look before serving them in upstate Virginia in 1968, they just looked in each other's eyes, and chose to ignore it. Life was too short and way too sweet to worry about such minor crap. These guys were alive and back in the world, and they were friends for life, much more than that really. Again, the Marines out there will get that one, too.

A variety of other medals were passed out that day at the White House, as Marines who fought all along this tough battle line were recognized. Jesus and Jesse received no individual recognition. No one had seen their battle, and none knew of it until after the fact. Still, these Marines are, today, immortalized in the folklore of that Marine unit, and such a Marine legend is probably the highest praise any Marine can earn from his fellow Marines. They had upheld the highest traditions of bravery and sacrifice, a long proud tradition of one of the premier battle forces ever known to man. These men were, after all, United States Marines.

With all the metals awarded and all the speeches finished, the unit stood down for the first time in over a year, and these two Marines went home. Khe Sanh became history. Still for the men who were actually there, the living hell of Khe Sanh is forever entombed in their minds and in their nightly dreams. For these men, the battle is best remembered by the defiant fighting spirit of two loud, proud, bloody, severely-wounded warriors, one black and one white. One was wounded in the shoulder and was so filthy he seemed dead, as if he shouldn't be walking at all. The other, black as night, was so massive that he seemed a giant from hell itself. He was calmly walking along with half his teeth exposed from a bloody wound in the left cheek, and his jaw seemed to hang down to his shoulder. These two, arm in arm and supporting each other, occasioned an array of comments when they wandered back into the HQ around midnight.

Their story quickly spread, and a timeless legend was created. The legend of the Bender boys is remembered in Marine folklore to this day. Five hundred meters out in front of the Khe Sanh perimeter on Hill 861, these two Marines wiped out an entire company of NVA regulars in a moonscape of shadowy death. Then, arm in arm, looking like death itself, they marched back to HQ at midnight, while singing "Dixie" just as loud as you please!

One can never predict how men will respond to battle, or how they might respond when it is over. Some want to get back to the real world, as if a battlefield is not real enough, and just begin their life again. They never want to see their fellow Marines, preferring to move on with life, and leave the horror as well as most of the memories behind if they can. Others need their fellow fighters in some way, and live the rest of their lives feeling as if no one could ever understand unless they themselves had been there. Many men came home scarred for life, with the horror they had known manifested in their lives in terrible ways, drunkenness or drugs, post-traumatic stress, or suicide.

The Bender boys felt none of that. They had gone through their hell together, and that made it more bearable somehow. They had survived because of each other, and they knew it.

They were like most of the Marines who came home. One went to New Bern and became a history teacher, while one went to Tennessee and did indeed finish his college education, just like his Daddy said he would.

Jesus would carry for life a terrible scar on his left cheek, and with his size and that scar together, he was always fearsome. He joined the marchers in the Civil Rights movement throughout the South from 1970 onward, demanding full participatory rights in the nation he had fought and bled for. For he, more so than most, had earned those rights.

By now you've probably figured out that I was one of this strange pair. Jesus and I kept in touch through Christmas cards and a phone call or two. When we traveled near each other, we would visit over supper. We never talked about the battle itself. Strangely enough, we did talk about looking into our family history, but we never really got around to it somehow, until much later.

In fact, most of that work would really wait until my Grandmother, Mildred Carmichael Bender, died. She passed away at the very young age of 99, in 2005, and what a remarkable life she had! She had lived through both World Wars, and the Great Depression. She remembered Pearl Harbor like it was yesterday, not to mention FDR's death, the Cuban Missile Crisis, the Kennedy assassination, Nixon's resignation, and 9/11. She had sent one son to fight in World War II, and a grandson—me—to fight in South Vietnam. She had more great-grandchildren, nieces and nephews, than either of us could count!

When she was born, the whole world was pulled by horses or oxen. Cars had been invented by 1906, but nobody in Pollocksville, NC had one! Still, she lived to see men walk on the moon. Her life was longer than the entire history of the Soviet Union, and she cried both when the Berlin Wall was built, and when it came down in 1989. What a life she had!

Not only was she the family historian, saving all kinds of letters, documents, and diaries from forever ago, she had lived history—she was history. I was crushed when she died.

My Dad had already passed away when Granny died, so I had the task of clearing up her things. Any furniture the grandkids or great-grandkids didn't want, I gave away, but when I realized that she'd collected so many family papers, my curiosity got the best of me. I am a history teacher after all, and I love history with a passion. My Granny, as I said, lived it!

My Dad had always told me that Granny saved everything, and it seemed she knew everything about everyone in the family. What she'd saved over the years was remarkable. It included old family papers, deeds, letters, old diaries, store or farm invoices, tax records, and other papers of the family going back for generations. Though she had married into the family, it was like those letters from her husband's family were her treasures. They went back, I initially thought, four or five generations. I knew I'd love going through it all, and when I took seven boxes of the stuff from her hall closet, I moved it right into my office at home. I figured I'd spend several happy afternoons looking through all of that old junk.

I was dead wrong!

It took three years!

Even with the help of many in the family, it was tough and slow going. Many relatives played a role, and when I found stuff that I thought different ones would be interested in, I shared it with them. Most often, they got interested too, and began to dig for more of the family history, and that made the task take even longer. Turns out the Benders have quite a history.

Then I opened one old box and found some things that were apparently much older than the other material. These papers were barely legible, and were written in the time when the letter "f" was used instead of the letter "s". Some were from eight generations ago! In fact, several of those papers, and one diary, dated from the founding of the colony of North Carolina! That, however, was not to be my biggest surprise.

Among the oldest of those documents I found something that absolutely floored me, a name in a diary that sent my mind reeling. I knew my buddy Jesus would die to learn of this. Yeah, I should admit up front, that he will always be Jesus to me, Dr. Julian C. Bender, cardiologist of Nashville, Tennessee.

One of Granny's papers, listed a land title for a Martin Bender, and a subsequent will probated in 1750, identified that same land as going to his two children, Daniel and John. What really shocked me was subsequent correspondence between these two! Several old, barely legible letters were there, written by these brothers as well a large collection of documents written by their father, Martin Bender, that dated from the early to mid 1700s. I also found that my ancestor, John Bender, had kept a diary of those distant times, even as he saved his own father's papers! As it turns out, Daniel Bender had moved to Leesville, Tennessee, along with his half-brother named Burdine Bender. Does that ring any bells?

I remembered Jesus' conversation about his Dad's weird name, Burdine, and that the name had come from a white "massa'" in Leesville, Tennessee which was only about twenty-five miles from Nashville. I gave him a call immediately, and told him what I'd found and I must admit that I was dying to know (and here comes my weird sense of humor!), what would Jesus do?

Jesus got even more excited than I was and was visiting with me in less than a week. Together over that long weekend, we really began to dig. We now know that we really were distant cousins after all, but that was only part of what Granny Bender was hiding. She knew a lot more than she'd ever talked about and she kept most of it hidden for decades, for a whole host of reasons.

Today, we don't think of the settlement of New Bern, the first true city anywhere in the North Carolina Colony, as the settlement of a rugged "frontier" but we certainly should! Those Germans and Swiss who came to this beautiful land nestled between two of the most picturesque rivers in the world, including Jesus' and my ancestors, were truly courageous! Here they faced a barely settled, rough wilderness and suffered unspeakable hardships. Hundreds died. Disease, war, slavery, piracy, rebellion, Indian massacres, all were endured right here in our fair city, and these placid streets, lined now with high end boutiques, antique shops, and eateries, hold more stories than could ever be told. More blood was spilled here than we, today, can possibly imagine, and it does not speak well of us that we should remain so ignorant of this rich history. I was as guilty as anyone, and as a teacher of history and one who is truly passionate about this subject, I should have known better. Until Jesus and I began to explore my Grandmother's papers, I was wholly uninformed, and it is clear to me now that I had ignored this rich, human, tapestry of local history for much too long!

This is the story, as best it can be told. What Jesus and I could not document, we created based on our study of the history of those times, or other written histories from the period. Thus, even those less well documented parts of this story are more than educated guesses—they are, at a minimum, based on history or the general logic of the situation, as well as on the belief systems and/or the technology available in those times. For example, we surmised how it must have felt for a young boy, our ancestor Martin, to land in a new world, or how the local Indian tribe might have felt about the new white settlers. We studied hard to enable us to consider what those black slaves must have experienced in the early days of this colony. Within two generations, this family had not only helped settle a new colony, but had also helped create a new nation. At a minimum this is a story about creating a new world in New Bern and the Carolinas, a term used at that time for both North and South Carolina.

This is a story of and for all Carolinians, if not, indeed, for all Americans. This is the story of America in some fundamental sense. This is who we are.

In another sense, Jesus and I sought to explore critically important racial relationships in this history. Jesus insisted on it, perhaps because we trusted each other so completely or perhaps because we had shared so much in that hell of South Vietnam. He felt we could and should explore that tough topic. In this work, we wanted to discuss the dynamics of black/white relations in our common history. Nothing has been as convoluted as racial relations in America, and because our personal history exemplified that, we both hoped that this story can shed some light on that tough issue. Of course, these are lofty goals, but my friend and compatriot, Jesus, always aimed high. I love him deeply, and no man has ever earned my respect and love more. I could say much more, but well, there it is.

As for the rest, I'll have to let the story speak for itself.

Jesse Bender
New Bern, North Carolina,
December 2008

# Chapter 1
# A New City in a New World
## *A Ship of Death*

The boy was terrified as he watched his father, Henrig Bender heave the few remaining contents of his stomach over the side of the rickety, leaking, forty-foot schooner, named strangely enough, *Desire*. The small shallow-draft ship wallowed in the stormy five-foot seas of Pamlico Sound, and every soul aboard, like the boy, was terrified, except the Captain. Storm clouds merged with the rough inland sound, and rain pelted the boy and his father alike as they sat on the top deck along with the Captain and crew. Still, with his illness, the father had to be here exposed to the storm, since he was throwing up minute by minute.

The boy had hoped that the ship, if one could call it that, would not roll quite as much once the mouth of the Neuse River was sighted, but the *Desire*, only a river craft really, still seemed to sag slowly, wallowing some sixty degrees off center, one side to the other, with each monstrous wave. Just when he thought it couldn't dip any further, it would go down another ten degrees or so, such that the masts seemed pointed directly at the distant shore, fifteen miles away. Then, slowly, as if by the afterthought of a forgetful God, the masts would begin a slow steady climb to the upright, remaining there only a few seconds before dipping in the opposite direction to point eventually toward the other distant shore. The boy, Martin, had felt that sixty-degree roll of this small vessel for three of the last five days.

Martin had found something to occupy himself as boys often do, while his father continued to cough and heave. Martin sat low by the gunwales on the top deck upwind of his father, about ten feet away, and watched a solitary spider ignore the storm and weave his web in the shadowy corner where the deck met an upright holding the pulley assembly attached to one of the sheets carrying the mainsail. Once in a while a sailor would run by, responding to a shouted order, grab the line attached to the pulley, tighten it or loosen it, making adjustments to the sails above but as Martin watched, the spider calmly continued building his home in the dark place just under the wooden joint. Martin thought, "It is good to have a home," and with that thought, he looked back at his Dad, and noticed again how weak the man seemed amid his coughing, as if he were coughing his very life away. Martin knew that others had died on this voyage—he'd watched many die.

Since leaving Europe, over half of the 695 migratory souls, those would-be settlers heading into a wilderness to build a new colony, had died. Well over three hundred had been lost without even seeing their new home! Martin feared his father would soon follow, as he asked himself, for the hundredth time, "Where then will be my home?" The spider of course, ignored his audience as well as the growing storm and billowing seas. It calmly, determinedly, weaved its web, creating its home seemingly from its own body.

At that moment, Martin recalled a Bible passage—for the Bible had been drilled into him by both his mother and his father for his entire life and various memories of passages would sometimes come to him, seemingly of their own accord. They often brought him a renewed strength, random though they might seem.

*"The foxes have holes, and the birds of the air have nests; but the Son of Man hath no where to lay his head."*

As strange as it seems, from that brief memory of a Bible passage, Martin drew a measure of strength.

Martin's mother had said goodbye to her husband and son on the docks in the distant Virginia Colony, in order to continue her travels to the new colony of New Bern in the remote Carolina woodland. She was staunch Anabaptist in her religious beliefs, today we would call her Mennonite, as were most of the others traveling on this voyage. Because neither the Swiss nor the German authorities wanted such religious deviates in their country, a businessman, Christopher de Graffenreid, offered them the chance to immigrate to the New World. De Graffenreid knew the potential riches that could be gleaned from a successful colony, and he had put together a group of investors specifically to secure land for this venture. The poor German Palatines, many of them Anabaptists had been persecuted and rejected in their homeland, and they now provided him with the settlers his colony needed. The wilderness between the Virginia and South Carolina settlements provided him the territory.

In this cold March of 1710, Martin's mother was traveling with ninety-two families, over 287 settlers, heading overland from Virginia to the bluff that joined the headwaters of the Neuse River and the Trent. In fact, the overland settlers should have arrived by now. At the union of those two rivers, these Germans would make their new home. From that union of rivers, the bluff, only ten or so feet above the waterline, takes its name, Union Point. Here the dark, deep, acidic waters of the Trent River meet, but seemingly refuse to join with, the shallower, brown, silt-laden waters of the Neuse. As the rivers' courses merge, each seems unwilling to mix its waters with the other, and one can often see a line stretching far out into the river southeast from Union Point, where the colors of the rivers are still unmixed. Then, finally, the Trent River gives up its name and identity to join the much larger Neuse, but it doesn't wish to give up its character or its dark, rich, color too quickly. These rivers are both stubborn, like many of the souls who would dare to settle along them.

Unlike her husband Henrig, Martin's mother had been healthy when this group of storm-tossed settlers landed in the Virginia Colony, in the cold winter of 1710, after a desperate sea voyage of thirteen weeks. She and the other healthy ones had been welcomed warmly by the authorities there. Women were in demand in every colony, as their survival rate on any rugged frontier was much lower than that of men. However, given the persistent cough Henrig had when the ships arrived in Virginia, and the high death count on the trans-ocean voyage itself, he had been rejected, and was not allowed to land in the Virginia Colony. The colonists there feared any disease born by the newly arriving immigrants from Europe. Henrig, and many others, some with only a cough or hint of illness, had been forced to remain on board the ocean-going ships in the harbor of the Virginia Colony, until they either got well or died. After almost three weeks, with no real improvement in his cough, the authorities there had placed Henrig Bender and seventeen other desperately ill German immigrants, aboard the *Desire*, a small, rickety, coastal craft for a five-day sea journey from Virginia to the newly formed Carolina Colony. This group, like many to come to these shores, had been rejected yet again in their first try to get into the new world. Martin's mother had wanted to take her son with her, since he showed no sign of illness, but the Captain of the *Desire* asked that he remain to tend his father.

At that moment as Martin watched the spider complete his home, the task of tending his father seemed somewhat temporary. Everyone on board expected Henrig to die within the hour. Martin would then have to watch as the Captain, along with his three man crew, calmly tossed the body of his father over the side, as they had done with seven other bodies on this cursed death ship. In fact, the persistent cough and heaving were sure signs that the end was near for Henrig, and Martin, while telling himself that he would soon watch his father die, was also praying that God might spare the man, at least until the *Desire* reached the shore in the new city of New Bern. There Martin hoped to rejoin with his mother. So much of every man's life is made of such mundane hopes and prayers.

Perhaps a more benevolent God would have granted the prayer of a fifteen-year-old boy on that day. Martin had turned fifteen years old the previous April, and who would wish that such a boy should be forced to face life in a turbulent frontier colony without his Father? Still, in this instance, God was not kind to Martin and within an hour he heard his father's final heave, followed by broken, shallow breathing, then none at all.

The Captain had been watching for this, and walked to the dead man on the deck, even as the ship continued to roll alarmingly from side to side in the stiff wind. "Come on boy," the Captain said to Martin, "We'll say only a short prayer in this storm, and then we'll have to be done with your father. Can't take long, as we'd best land by nightfall. This storm is still rising."

Martin noted that the spider had finished his work and was now resting in the center of the web. He stood and looked at his father on the deck, as the Captain casually glanced at Martin, hoping that the boy would be alright. Having another desperate scene, with yet another family member about the death of a loved one was to be avoided if at all possible. Apparently satisfied that Martin wouldn't cause a scene, the Captain ordered one of his men from the stern of the ship to come help with the disposal work. After a brief prayer for the soul of the deceased, the Captain asked Martin if he wished to say anything, but Martin could think of nothing to say. He did not cry, but he did quietly wonder once again, "Where will be my home now?"

Thus, even at the moment that Martin Bender came to the new world, he had to assist the Captain and one crewmember, as they picked up his father's body and tossed it over the side, into shallow waters of the broad Neuse River. The body would wash into the coastal marshes within forty-eight hours, where it would feed the various creatures of the inland sounds along the Carolina coast.

The rolling waves never abated, but the rain did pause from time to time. A few hours later, just at dusk, the schooner reached the mud flats at the shores of New Bern, and began to anchor beside two other, smaller ships. On shore, Martin could see only a few tents and some makeshift cattle pens that indicated the tentative existence of a new colony. Of course, no dock was in place as yet, so as the crew made the schooner fast with anchors, they lowered the dinghy into the Trent River. The Captain, had himself, rowed ashore along with four of his healthy passengers, Martin among them. Martin began to suspect that the Captain wanted shed of the now-fatherless boy as soon as possible.

### *The Arrival*

Along the wooded banks of the Trent River, they were greeted by the governor of the new colony, Robert Cary, and many others who were expecting family members on this ship. Cary was slight of build, but even with a soft voice he could be dominating in character. He had served as governor since 1708 and was aligned with a group of Quakers who, strangely enough, tended to dominate politics in this colony at that time. He owned a plantation along the Pamlico River near Bath, the only other town in the North Carolina Colony.

Bath, formed as the very first town in the North Carolina Colony in 1705, was destined to forever remain a relatively small village. In 1710 it consisted of only eight cabins and a tavern. Still, with Cary's plantation and several others nearby, it served as the capital for those early years, though the real political power in the colony rested with several plantation owners along the Albemarle Sound near Virginia. From his plantation in Bath, Cary managed his own affairs and governed this growing colony of North Carolina. When Martin Bender arrived in the new settlement of New Bern, Cary happened to be on his way to the South Carolina Colony in his small sloop. He had merely stopped by the new settlement for a few days to help establish the new town of New Bern.

The rain faded into a light mist, and even before tossing a line to those on shore, the Captain cried out in German, for he knew that most of the settlers in this new colony spoke only that language. "Eight dead, and two still likely within the next fortnight!" He then shouted the names of the deceased and those still ill. Most were women or children, and with each name someone on shore gasped, or burst into tears for a family member they would never see again. This Captain clearly was a no-nonsense man, who obviously believed in getting this cruel news out first and fast. Many men of the sea in those days, tempered by the vagrancy of years on the angry oceans of the world, shared that trait.

Martin understood the terrible finality of that roster of the dead. He had seen them die on both the ocean crossing and on the brief voyage down from Virginia. Still, ever hopeful, he looked for his mother amid the throng of people on shore, and while he didn't see her immediately, what he did see frightened him even more.

Rough men led lines of three, four, or more savages held in chains. Two groups of these wretched savages, chained together, passed nearby while Martin stood there. The Indians held their heads down and averted their eyes from any white man. Martin later learned that to stare directly at a man was to show disrespect in their culture. The savages wore only rags around their midsection and were largely exposed to the cold. Some of their bodies were painted, and others were tattooed. Martin knew these Indians were now slaves, soon to be sold to the first ship heading for South Carolina or Virginia. He'd seen the same type of scene in Virginia.

One group of slaves attracted Martin's attention. It was a line of four slaves, chained together by collars around their necks, with their hands bound together at the wrists. They were led by a man who appeared to be a slave himself. He was a large black man, with a full beard of unruly hair, whose head was deformed through either battle or intentional torture. He was a barrel-chested mountain of a man and his black skin was exposed to the freezing rain from the waist up, which he didn't seem to notice. He wore a whip around his neck and one mighty shoulder, and was missing his right ear altogether, with his head presenting only a scarred hole where the ear should have been. Martin, of course, noticed that gross deformity, but he did not stare. He did hear one of the sailors address this large man as "Black Jambo," with a rough sailor's voice that cut through the evening noise.

"Black Jambo! Are those savages bound for Virginia?"

"That's right! Mr. Foscue sent me along with four of 'um for passage in the hold. Can you take um?" Black Jambo replied, looking not at the sailor, but at the Captain.

The Captain looked toward his small sloop and nodded. "We'll load out in the morning. Bring um' back then."

Black Jambo merely nodded and jerked the chain to get the slaves moving on along the shoreline, but what then captured Martin's attention, was the slave at the very end of that string. She was a young savage, with shoulder length hair, and was dressed in deerskins from the waist down. Her skin was olive toned and her young breasts, firm and fully exposed, were wet in the evening rain. Martin stared at that girl for only a moment before telling himself that his staring was sinful, and that he should look away. Just as he was about to turn his head, however, she turned toward him, and seemed to stare directly into his eyes. That captured him, gripped him, and held him in check for a time, as he stared back into the girl's face. She was quite pretty, and could not have been older than twelve. Her face was rounded and well formed, except for the mud and what appeared to be dried blood on her lower lip. Martin wondered what had caused that injury.

Then he realized that she was not looking at him, so much as looking through him, to the boats along the shore. He realized that for her, those boats were terror itself. The boats meant she was being shipped away from her family and her home. The singular thought hit Martin like a blow from a hammer. He was looking at the most terrified face he had ever seen. Then she quickly looked away, averting her eyes from any of the white men along the shore, lest she show them disrespect.

Even in the earliest days of the New Bern town, there were men who sought to make money from the sale of slaves. While only a few black slaves were in evidence on the shore that day, Black Jambo among them, slaves were present in New Bern from the earliest days of the settlement. Black Jambo, like most of the other Blacks, had been purchased in Virginia and either belonged to the few local plantations or had come down to the new settlement with the several other farmers in the area. In contrast, Indian slaves were seen in this new settlement in abundance. Most of the slaves in New Bern during the earliest period were Tuscarora Indians.

Several whites were leading other groups of Indian slaves. These rough, uncouth, frontiersmen leading these slaves were not Germans. These rough men had been in other parts of the Carolina or Virginia colonies for some time— some had been born in Virginia—and they were accustomed to the demands of frontier life. Most of these frontiersmen wore breeches of cloth, but these were covered with skins, dried and sown into cloaks or loose shirts. They spoke a language that Martin did not understand, but did recognize as English. These earlier settlers, perhaps from Bath or some of the established plantations along the Chowan or Pamlico Rivers to the north, considered this new town as merely another opportunity to ply their gristly trade in human flesh. Whenever they could, they captured the local Indians, the Tuscarora, with the intention of selling them into slavery.

While later generations of slavers would have to purchase black slaves in Africa and transport them halfway around the globe, in the earliest days in North Carolina, slavers merely rounded up the Tuscarora when they were hunting alone or in small groups. Sometimes they took women or children from their villages. They then beat them into submission and chained them, soon to sell them to the next ship passing by. Of course the profit was enormous, since no trans-oceanic transportation was involved, but fate would soon show that the price for such cruelty to this warlike tribe would be high indeed! A bloody war would soon result from this barbarism toward the Tuscarora, and whites throughout the Carolinas would pay a stiff price.

However, that was unknown on the day Martin arrived, and the frontiersmen transported their Tuscarora slaves without a thought as to the consequences, which is why several groups were at the shore that day. These sought passage for themselves and their cargo on the *Desire* or one of the other ships when they sailed.

Martin however, being ever observant, noticed something else in that first look at New Bern. Strangely, these rough frontiersmen mixed comfortably it would seem, with persons obviously of a more genteel nature. These were the German Anabaptist settlers who had come to the new town at the behest of de Graffenreid. Martin immediately felt he would be most comfortable among these persons, for they were speaking German, which was his only language at that point, and they dressed in more refined clothes than the frontiersmen. He recognized some from the earlier ocean crossing. This group seemed downright cultured compared to the others. Yes, he and his mother would fit in among these genteel souls, and for a moment his heart knew peace.

Then he again looked in the crowd for his mother, hoping to find some loving face to run to. While he was still terrified, he was also glad to soon have solid land under him again after a fourteen-week voyage. As the small boat hit the shore, he jumped out and looked through the crowd repeatedly, hoping to see her, but for some reason she was not there. After debarking, the Captain ordered his small boat to fetch the remaining passengers, as all around Martin, the newly landed refugees were greeted by family. The Captain shouted for someone to "Come and take this boy off my hands!" However, Martin and the Captain both noticed rather quickly, the downcast look of the other settlers, as they began to disperse.

Finally, a smallish man with balding hair and a slight limp, strode toward the Captain and Martin. The Captain recognized the governor of the Carolina Colony and said, "Oh. Hello Gov'nor Cary. It is good to see you here sir, and glad I am to be ashore, also. For I fear a worsening of this storm tonight."

Some have found it interesting that Governor Cary met the German settlers when they first reached the conflux of the Neuse and Trent Rivers, but that must be seen as simple expediency. None of the other leaders were available. De Graffenreid himself had chosen to travel with his Swiss immigrants, rather than the Germans, and that party would not arrive in New Bern until September of 1710. De Graffenreid did have his son travel with the German Palatines, but he never became the leader one might have hoped.

John Lawson was the only other local leader, but he was engaged in Virginia when the new settlers arrived. For many reasons, Lawson must be considered the first true North Carolinian. He was an educated man, if a bit hot tempered, but with his background as a surveyor, he was commissioned in 1700 by the Lords Proprietors in London to undertake an expedition deep into the hinterlands of the Carolina wilderness. He was the first white man to do so. At that point, Charleston, on the coast of South Carolina, had long been settled but few understood what the interior of either North or South Carolina might hold. Lawson undertook his famed "Thousand mile trek" in 1701 through the interior of both states, leaving Charleston, moving deep into the foothills of that state, traveling up through what would become the Waxhaws area near present day Charlotte, North Carolina. Thence he visited the Haw River Indians near the future site of Burlington, and later the Tuscarora, who dominated the interior of the coastal plains from upstate South Carolina all the way up to the western shore of the Chesapeake Bay. Lawson then traveled outward toward the coast, heading at first to the English settlements in the Albemarle Sound region, but then turning a bit south to emerge at the joining of the Trent River and the Neuse, which he labeled "News River" in his travel log. A later misspelling of that early label for the river, resulted in the name Neuse.

At that joining of the rivers, Lawson discovered several other early settlers, including some French settlers, along the Trent River, and an Englishman, William Brice, who was carving out a plantation on the south bank of the Trent River by 1706. Lawson lived there for a year or so, refining his log, along a creek that bears his name to this day. He then set sail for London to publish his book on that expedition. That text is available today as one of the primary, authoritative sources on the savages of the interior of the Carolinas. By 1708, this man knew more about North Carolina than anyone, and had even surveyed the New Bern site for de Graffenreid himself, in 1709. Still, like de Graffenreid, he was unavailable when the Germans arrived in New Bern, so it fell to Governor

Cary to greet these Germans in March of 1710.

Speaking in English, Governor Cary replied to the Captain, "Welcome Captain. We are glad to see that you made the journey quickly, and arrived before this storm grew worse. I too fear a gale this night, and I've decided to stay here until the storm passes." The man then turned away from the Captain and looked directly at Martin. He switched to German. "You are Martin Bender, son of Henrig Bender, yes?"

Martin merely nodded, as an all-consuming fear seized his heart and seemed to freeze his entire body. He held his breath and felt that he knew what was coming. Unfortunately he was right.

"Your mother is dead," said Governor Cary with no further preamble. "She was attacked last week, by several Coree Indians and was killed."

Death came in many ways in the early years of the Carolina Colony, and Indian attack was one of the most feared. The Coree Indians were one of the smaller tribes along the upper coast of North Carolina, but like their allies the Tuscarora, they were warlike and did not respond well to the enslavement of their kinsmen. They killed the new colonists wherever and whenever they could. Of course, because of the location of their towns, they were much more of a problem for the settlers in Bath than in New Bern, since they too lived along the Pamlico River to the north.

The governor continued, "She gathered water for us near my home in Bath on her journey here, when the savages struck. They attempted to capture her and carry her off, but she and one of the other women fought them. She was killed by a blow to the head, and left on the ground, so she was not captured like the other woman. That would surely be a fate worse than death." Here the governor paused a bit to glance at the boy, and then he continued, "When our men heard their screams, they quickly drove away the savages, so at least her body was not mutilated. She is buried in the churchyard in Bath. I am sorry."

The governor paused again to assess the effect of this news on the adolescent before him. Seeing no imminent emotional breakdown, he decided to push onward and address the obvious question. "You will stay with me this evening at the Brice Plantation across the river, and we will then seek an apprenticeship for you. I'm sure many will need able young men, with all the work to do here." With that, he gestured to the few hovels made of wood bark on supporting posts, and the beginnings of the log structures that held some cattle and hogs behind him. That is all that then existed of the town of New Bern.

Again, Martin did not cry. In fact, he seemed to show little overt reaction to this horrid news. Overt displays of emotion were not in the nature of this young man, as we shall see, but he did feel a searing pain in his heart for his mother and father, both gone before reaching their new home. He wondered, yet again, what this meant for his future, and strangely enough, he thought again of that spider on the ship—at least it had a home on this rainy winter night.

However, immediately after that thought, Martin realized that the governor had spoken of him as a "young man" and not as a boy. That surprised him a bit when he thought about it, and at that realization, he made certain that he stood a bit straighter, and that his voice was low when he spoke. He used of course, the guttural German tongue that would remain as one of the main languages in this new city for a few more years.

"Thank you, sir. I will work hard in whatever task you may have. I can hunt, if provided with a musket. I am a good shot." He then paused, but realizing that the governor was still evaluating him, he quickly continued, "I am also good with livestock, hogs, sheep, or cattle, and I can milk."

The governor seemed pleased with that response, knowing that several families would like to have the services of this young man. Strong backs were always in demand in every new city, and this fifteen year old seemed to possess a fine character, which would become more apparent as he matured. Of course, the governor also knew that whatever family did acquire this young man as an apprentice, also received a measure of wealth in the form of management responsibilities for his money, not to mention this boy's land and livestock.

Unknown to Martin, all of the funds of each settler family had been deposited with de Graffenreid prior to the voyage, so Henrig Bender had left what few funds he had in safekeeping with the authorities, and Martin was now entitled to those funds. Moreover, every settler family was to receive land, livestock, and tools to begin a farm. Each family had been promised two hundred and fifty wooded acres of land on the Neuse River or the Trent, along with two cows, two calves, five sows with pigs, two sheep, two lambs, seed for planting, and tools for felling trees. These would now pass to Martin, since only he remained of his family. Without even knowing it, Martin was now as well off as almost any of the other settlers, and of course, the governor realized this. In fact, he had even considered taking this boy on himself, since any master of this apprentice would control those lands, livestock and whatever meager funds there might be.

Standing nearby, however, was a large, rather squat, barrel-armed man named Johannes Simmons, who was busily hugging his petite wife, Margaret, with great vigor. Johannes had parted with Margaret in Virginia for the same reason that Martin's mother had left him and his father. While Johannes had never been ill on the ocean crossing, Margaret had suffered greatly, and at their parting in the Virginia Colony, her husband thought that he might not see his wife again in this life. On the more recent voyage down the coast, Margaret had coughed as much as Martin's father, and for a time both the Captain and Martin thought she might die also. Martin had helped to tend to her as he had his father on that voyage. However, in defiance of expectations, she had recovered completely from her illness over the last two days.

Margaret was hugging her husband, but was also watching the scene just behind the governor. She saw the trepidation in the young man's face, as he clearly wondered about his fate. However, during the stormy voyage down from Virginia, Margaret had come to appreciate his help and also to respect this young man's character, noting how closely he tended to both her and to his dying father, even on the most terrifying days of that sea voyage. While she was unaware of Martin's wealth—she would have been quite surprised by it in fact—she felt that she saw into his soul, and of course she recognized the obvious question as to where this young man would live. Her heart ached for his loss, and she knew he felt great apprehension.

In that very moment, God convicted her heart, letting her see clearly her immediate course of action! Without even consulting her husband, she stepped toward the governor saying, "Governor Cary. I have seen the character of this young man on the recent voyage, and our family would be honored if he would come to live with us."

She paused and noticed that the governor seemed surprised by her forwardness, and her husband was now standing beside her with a look that could only be characterized as complete astonishment! Still, never being one to defer to men simply because of her sex, Margaret ignored their obvious surprise and continued. "He can apprentice with my husband and learn to be a cooper. Many barrels will surely be needed as we begin to ship our produce to Virginia."

As Johannes Simmons continued to look on in surprise—for what man would take on that additional challenge during the uncertainty of colonial settlement on a rough frontier—Margaret made her final point. "We will certainly love him as one of our own, and we'll take good care of him until he grows. I shall direct him myself and see that he learns his letters, his numbers, and his Bible."

That statement alone settled the matter. Clearly this woman believed she was doing God's bidding, and no one would dare raise even the slightest argument after that point had been made! For throughout the centuries, men on every continent of the globe, men of letters, and men of great wisdom have all learned that no force in the known Universe will stand when confronted by the simple assurance of a Mennonite Frauline who is certain she is doing God's will!

Of the men assembled in the drizzling rain on the shore of the river, Johannes recovered most quickly from his surprise. Sensing the inevitable, he proposed to do what virtually every one of those doggedly religious Anabaptists in this new colony would have done at that precipitous moment—he said simply, "We shall pray."

Without even thinking about it, all standing within earshot of that voice bowed their head, as if commanded by some unseen force. The governor, the Captain, Martin Bender, his adoptive parents Johannes and Margaret, and several of the smelly, rough, frontiersmen, all bowed. Even Black Jambo paused and bowed his head as Johannes raised his voice to God. In the rainy drizzle at dusk, on the shore of a new settlement that would one day become a great city, Johannes Simmons began his simple prayer in German.

*"Father, we thank you for bringing our family together again. We ask your blessing on this boy who comes to live with our family, as well as your blessing on the souls of this boy's father and mother."* At that moment, Johannes realized that he didn't even know the names of the boy's parents, so he could not mention them by name. Pausing undaunted for just a moment, Johannes quickly determined to continue anyway. *"God, we recognize that they stand with you even now, with their lives completed and fulfilled in your presence. Grant them peace in the knowledge that we shall keep this young man, guarding him from the works of the Evil One. He will work hard, and he will learn his letters, his numbers, and his Bible. Thank you for this addition to our family and let us discipline this young man, rightly and correctly, in your ways, Amen."*

Thus, it was done. Martin Bender now had a new family and a new home, in a new world.

## *The Simmons Family Hovel*

That very night, Martin moved into his new home, along what would become South Front Street, though the "home" certainly left much to be desired, and the street as such, did not yet exist. Johannes, like the others in the overland group, had been in New Bern only twelve days, and was sleeping with his other two children in what was essentially a pen for livestock. The "home" was merely a small hovel of several branches and wood bark, tossed diagonally against a low log livestock pen. These family hovels were nestled along the outside of the fence, and on the inside of that large, single fence, was where the cattle and sheep slept. Hogs were, of course, tied outside, as they made too much mud. Thus, would this family and many others, live for the next few months as they felled trees, using the first timber for fencing the livestock. This group had essentially been a "cattle drive" when coming down from the Virginia Colony, leading over a hundred head of cattle, sheep and pigs through the wilderness with them and the housing needs of the livestock, on which their lives would depend, came first. Only after a stout livestock pen was constructed to corral the animals, did families begin to build their rude log cabins and individual livestock pens.

These log huts and livestock pens would characterize this early town for the first fifty years or so. Hogs, during that time, would run free in the streets since they could not be penned anyway. They would always root out under any fence the townspeople could build. Only a few citizens in those early days had horses, and these were tied to the side of the family hovels, as they were much cleaner than the other animals.

There was one exception to this general building priority, of course. The very day the overland group arrived and the first log was felled to build the new town, that log was placed as the foundation log for the community church along what would become Middle Street. In those early days, God came first in this new town, and this amazing group of religious zealots would not think of using all of their labors selfishly for their own survival, until their God had been honored with a new church home.

During the first weeks, each day at approximately 3:30 in the afternoon, all males stopped working on the livestock pen or their own cabins and moved toward the center of the small town to work, for the last two hours of the day, on the church. It would be the first large building completed in this new town, and would be finished in an astonishing forty-five days.

There had been a previous edict from the governing authorities in Bath that all citizens would pay a tax to support the Church of England—the Anglican Church. In fact, that had become the official religion for the whole of the North Carolina Colony, though de Graffenreid had promised religious tolerance, as long as his settlers paid the tax. Still, in only a year, this church tax edict would lead to rebellion in the Carolinas, but that was unknown on the day Martin arrived in New Bern. With Governor Cary's sympathies lying firmly with the Quakers, that edict was soon merely ignored in most of the farms along the Pamlico River, as it would be in the new city of New Bern. Thus, it bothered these immigrants not one whit that the church *building* was to be Anglican. God was God, and God needed a home in this new town. Therefore, their job was to build Him one.

Moreover, these devout Germans, men and women alike, worshiped in a ruggedly independent frame of mind, another characteristic that would dominate this new town for hundreds of years. These Germans had left Europe when they were totally impoverished, in order to seek a place to worship their God in their own manner. With Governor Cary and his Quaker Party generally demonstrating a live and let live policy on spiritual matters, these new settlers saw no problem in this confused state of religion, at least for the time being. They built an Anglican Church and paid taxes to support it as required, and then they worshiped as they damn well pleased, or more accurately, as they felt God led them to worship.

After the prayer, Martin and his new family said goodbye to the governor and walked along the low fence, past areas designated for other families. They soon came to a low hovel with two young girls inside who were playing with wooden "dolls." In reality, these were merely sticks with rough faces carved on one end of them, but with the amazing imagination of children, these became the equivalent of the finest toys in the world!

One girl, Christina, was only four, and smiled sweetly as her parents returned with this young man. She was of pleasant disposition and would eventually marry well, becoming the wife of a farmer named Earl Claude Banks, who settled along the Trent River some miles below New Bern. She would birth nine children, leading to the foundation of that wonderful extended Banks family in lower Craven County—a family that would lead the community as farmers, plantation owners, and eventually as political leaders for well over 200 years.

However, that was well in the future and unknown on this particular night in 1710. In fact, other than a brief nod in her direction, Martin did not look at Christina at all. Rather his attention was completely captivated by her older sister Katheryn. At 13 years, she was only fourteen months shy of Martin's own age, but Katheryn had just begun to reach puberty. Still, for some young girls, their beauty is obvious prior to becoming women. Katheryn looked somewhat like her mother, and had almost reached her mother's height. She had flowing bright yellow hair and laughing blue eyes, as did many in this colony of German settlers, but Katheryn seemed to offer so much more. A quick, demanding intelligence seemed to lurk there in the lightness of her face, and while she was of sweet disposition and did laugh often, one could never mistake her for one of those mindless pretty girls with nothing to offer but a pretty face and a giggle. She had something of a serious side, and would often pause to carefully consider her words prior to speaking, certainly a trait not characteristic of most girls that age.

Given her gentle, ever-ready laughter, her serious yet playful nature, and easy smile, she would captivate men, old and young alike, throughout her life. As she developed, she would grow to have her mother's strength and assurance, but she would temper that with kindness, more so than either of her parents. Katheryn, even at the age of thirteen, was sure to become an impressive young woman, and all believed she would become a woman of substance in this growing town. In truth, she was a gem that any man would be lucky to capture, when she came of age, and everyone in New Bern seemed to recognize that fact, in spite of her youth.

As Martin was introduced, he was invited to sit on a large log that served as the only bench in the middle of the hovel and just then, the one remaining family member took it upon himself to make his presence known. A large, incredibly hairy, dark brown dog marched directly toward Martin and sniffed Martin's crotch twice. Johannes apparently knew what was coming, so he said firmly, "Max, Don't!"

Max, of course, ignored his master completely, as dogs frequently do. He had already determined that smell or no smell, Martin was ripe as a make-do love interest, so he hurled his massive forepaws into Martin's lap and immediately began to hump his left leg. Martin was shocked and didn't know what to do, and this behavior caused immediate shouts from Margaret and Johannes both. Their daughters laughed outright as Johannes rushed to kick Max in the side, and thus disentangle Martin's leg from the overly passionate cur. Once disengaged, Martin was quite embarrassed and the girls continued to laugh loudly, despite his obvious discomfort. Margaret then offered Martin some tea and the situation began to relax into normalcy, as Max drifted back to the opening in the hovel where he lay down as if nothing had happened. Such was Martin's welcome into his new home.

Normally, Katheryn would have then invited Martin to join in their play. However, on this day, she seemingly sensed that something was different about this young man coming into the hovel with her father and mother. After her mother explained that Martin would be living with them as an apprentice to her father, she decided to coyly keep a distance from Martin. In that sense, one might say that Katheryn chose that very day to become a woman. For at that moment, she was carefully selecting what parts of herself to share with a man, and which parts to jealously guard and hold in reserve, as do women of substance in all cultures. This trait has driven men around the world to total distraction for eons and women in all cultures seem to understand that implicitly. While Katheryn was always civil—indeed she was quite nice—to Martin, she was never openly joking with him during that first year, as she was the others in her family. Perhaps she sensed even at that young age, what the future might hold.

Overtime, Martin noted this reserve and assumed, rather stupidly, that this meant that Katheryn didn't particularly care for him, or resented him in some way. He thought she might realize that he was eating precious food out of the mouths of her family, and often wondered if that was the seed of Katheryn's distain for him. He determined, for that reason, to work extra hard to help meet his obligation to this family for his keep, and that habit of working hard would characterize him throughout his life. Of course, such thoughts had nothing to do with Katheryn's behavior towards him, and her behavior remained pretty much the same, even when his value to this family later became apparent. Clearly, Martin was much less sophisticated in his judgments and assessments of the inner dynamics of relationships than Katheryn, and that fact would plague him—as it turns out—for the rest of his life.

Still, all of these things were unknown to him on that first night. He was thankful merely to have a roof—any type of roof—over his head. When Johannes indicated he should sleep at the far end of the hovel, well away from the two girls,

Martin didn't realize that even then both Johannes and Margaret were aware of the way Katheryn was acting differently toward the new boy in the house. They had each, without speaking to the other, determined to watch this friendship carefully, lest some intervention become necessary to separate these two. Such is the way of parents, particularly parents of daughters, the world over.

Just before bedding down, Johannes took out the most precious possession of his family, the family Bible. He then read a few verses in German to his family. He selected some verses from Matthew that he thought appropriate.

*"And into whatsoever city or town ye shall enter, enquire who in it is worthy, and there abide. And when ye come into a house salute it. And if the house be worthy, let your peace come upon it."*

Johannes then ended the Bible time with one simple statement; "May all who dwell here, find this home worthy in God's sight, that there be peace in this house." With no further comment, Johannes then offered an evening prayer. Martin would soon learn Bible readings and prayer were to become a daily occurrence in his new home. After lying down, Martin also offered a silent prayer for his father and mother and asked God for strength, once again. He then fell asleep almost instantly.

## *The Early Days in New Bern*

The next day, Johannes took Martin with him to begin his work on the new town. On this day, the two would help the other settlers clear the first two streets of trees, thus creating logs for individual homes as well as the church, and any other necessary livestock pens. Governor Cary had dictated that all men of working age would work for two weeks on clearing streets, the livestock pen, and the church, and only then begin construction of their log cabins. Of course, the city of New Bern that we know today was in the distant future on the day when Martin Bender began felling trees to help form the several planned streets. With the overland group only recently on the scene, the central community livestock pen, and of course the church, had demanded most of the construction efforts during the first weeks. That pen lay about two hundred yards from Union Point, somewhat towards the east along the Trent River, on ground that would one-day hold the seat of government for the entire colony. Today, that patch of higher ground is known as Tryon Palace, but in those settlement days, the higher land was considered good for the communal livestock pen. It was high and dry, some five feet above the river level and was downwind of the proposed settlement—carefully placed there for obvious reasons.

The town itself existed only in the minds of the new citizens. The plan developed by de Graffenreid and his surveyor, John Lawson, involved two major avenues laid out to resemble a large cross. De Graffenreid himself described the town plan.

*"I accordingly ordered the streets to be very broad and the houses well separated one from the other. I marked three acres of land for each family, for house, barn, garden, orchard, hemp field, poultry yard and other purposes. I divided the village like a cross and in the middle I intended the church. One of the principal streets extended from the bank of the Neuse straight on into the forest and the other principle street crossed it, running from the Trent River clear to the Neuse River. After that we planted stakes to mark the houses and to make the first two principal streets along and on the banks of the two rivers, mine being situated at the point."*

The upright of the cross, running east to west and thus parallel to the Trent River, came to be known as Broad Street, while the crossbeam running north to south and thus parallel to the Neuse, was named Hancock. This original plan for the framing of the city is observable even today, though the streets are now interlaced with other streets in the downtown area. In those early days, those crossing streets did not exist. Of course, the unplanned avenues that seem always to run parallel to any waterway quickly became busy thoroughfares, and these came to be called South Front Street along the Trent River, and East Front Street along the Neuse. The strangest feature of this newly planned town, however, sat just a bit further to the west where a ghost town of sorts appeared, with the houses constructed from the bark of trees!

While New Bern was the first large white settlement in this immediate area, it was not the first town here. The Tuscarora had lived at this river junction for years. They called their community "Cartouca," a Tuscarora term meaning, "Where the fish are taken from the river." While this particular town was deserted, several of their dwellings were still visible in 1710 just west of the new grid of streets.

This tribe lived, as did many woodland Indians of the period, in wooden covered longhouses, some of which were thirty feet long. Constructed of saplings, covered with tree bark, these homes were quite comfortable and very durable, and tended to house extended families or entire clans. Some longhouses could sleep as many as sixty people. The Tuscarora had lived at the conflux of these two rivers for centuries where they enjoyed hunting, fishing, and some cultivation of grains, as they carved a comfortable living from the land. This woodland tribe was not known to corral livestock in 1710, rather taking their meat from the bounty of the woodlands in the area. Of course, this made the hunting grounds around the area precious to the Tuscarora and they resented the constant felling of trees as the whites cleared field after field along the rivers and streams.

Previously, de Graffenreid, with John Lawson acting as his agent, had purchased this land from the local headman for the Tuscarora, and the Indians had moved from their village along these two rivers. But those decaying structures could still be seen when Martin arrived along the banks of Trent River. At that point in 1710, no Tuscarora were living inside the city of New Bern, but some small villages were within twenty miles of the new town, just to the west up the Neuse River, and other Tuscarora lived along the Pamlico River some thirty miles to the north. Each day, members of that tribe came to trade and often brought meat, deer or bear, they had taken from the forest, which they traded for iron pots, cloth, beads, knives, or anything else that took their fancy. Mirrors, in particular, were highly prized by this tribe, but they were very scarce in the new city.

When Martin saw several longhouses, as he walked along with Johannes, he paused a bit. Johannes interpreted that pause as fear. He knew the boy had lost his mother to an attack by the savages, and while the boy did not witness that attack, such an event would certainly cause terrible emotional scars. He thought to himself, "Thank God, the savages didn't make off with his mother while she was alive, or mutilate her body!" At that thought, he looked at Martin again who was standing and still looking at the several longhouses in the distance.

Johannes quickly sought to offer some comfort. "Do not be concerned Martin. Those savages moved out several months ago, and we won't be seeing them again, now that there are more of us here in the town."

At that, both Martin and Johannes began their walk to join the work crews, many of whom were even then picking up their axes to begin cutting trees and clearing the newly planned streets. Logs, at that point, were still headed to the church grounds.

It might help us understand Martin's reactions to the new town a bit better, if we consider what Martin didn't see in those first days of New Bern. At this point, there were no real roads at all anywhere in this area of the North Carolina Colony. While an Indian trail, redone as a cart path did wind its way northward to Bath, it could not be called a "road" by any stretch of the imagination. In fact, the overland group of de Graffenreid settlers, while following that trail, had, at some points, stopped in their travels to fell trees that would have blocked passage of the two wheel carts that held their tools. Of course, in 1710, no road at all went to the south of the settlement, and any travel to South Carolina involved an ocean voyage.

Further, in addition to the absence of roads, even the most basic industry of the day was nowhere to be found. There was no water powered saw mill to make lumber—trees were felled and used as logs for the early construction projects. There was no grist mill for grinding corn; there was no blacksmith, no tannery, no cobbler to make shoes, no baker, no silversmith, no cloth to be purchased, and no work sheds in which anyone could complete any of these most basic tasks for settlement. While the settlers themselves had been hand-picked to include men skilled in these tasks—Johannes Simmons was a skilled, master cooper for example—all of their tools had been unceremoniously stored in a separate hovel along the side of the livestock pen, and were, as yet, unpacked! The first demands in this new town, next to constructing a church, were associated with survival, and not civilization.

However, these Germans were not the first white faces in the area. The upper and central parts of the North Carolina Colony along the Albemarle Sound had been settled to some degree by traders coming down from Virginia. Also, by 1710 there were several growing plantations in the immediate area of the new city. Further, there had even been an earlier settlement of French Huguenots in this vicinity in the 1690s. Those robust Frenchmen had streamed down from Virginia around 1694, with some settling around the Pamlico River near the site of Bath, while others came further south and settled along the Trent River where, in the distant future, the town of Trenton would flourish. That settlement had died out completely by 1710, leaving only a few historic documents, and John Lawson's journal as proof of its existence. This came to be known among historians as the "Second Lost Colony of the Carolinas," though few citizens today even know of this interesting people or of their history. Still, it is strange to consider that New Bern, a settlement that in one generation would be entirely English in character, was originally formed by settlers who spoke either German or French, and probably spoke no English at all.

Meanwhile, to feed the new colonists in New Bern, some of the earlier frontiersmen were selected and paid to hunt deer or bear for the stew pots. A couple of locals who had wandered down from Virginia, One-Eye Benny Sutton and Able Ward, always seemed to be able to bring in some bear or deer. Another earlier settler, Jim Grimsley, was locally known as Gator Jim because he was reputed to capture alligators, skin them, and sell both the meat and the dried skin. He lived with a Tuscarora woman, if the rumors were true, out in the swamps near Catfish Lake, some ten miles south of New Bern. He came to town once a week or so, and brought in meat of one kind or another to trade for his few necessities—salt, and maybe a bit of rum.

On occasion, when Johannes did not need Martin in the shop, Martin joined that group of experienced hunters, One-Eye, Able, and even Gator Jim on occasion, and he learned much from each hunt with them. He hunted on Saturdays, and even on some weekdays from time to time, and he brought much meat back to the Simmons family. The Tuscarora also brought in some meat, as mentioned previously. Other settlers fished in the rivers to feed the group, and the townspeople, of course, ate much of the supplies they had brought with them from Virginia. The several plantations in the area grew some extra food, and two fairly large plantations had only recently been carved from the wilderness; each did manage to produce some grain or corn for the settlers.

James Edward Foscue had built a rather large house on the western bank of the Trent River about eight miles below the proposed site of New Bern. Foscue Plantation held twelve slaves; Black Jambo included, and supplied many needs of the growing town. Today the Foscue Plantation house—the second grand house built on that plantation—stands in mute testimony to the fortitude of those early settlers along the lower Trent River.

William Brice, an Englishman, owned a plantation across the Trent River several miles up from the new town along the eastern bank of Brice's Creek. Fortunately for these new German settlers, he grew an excellent and large crop of corn, which helped feed these people during that first winter, until they could get their own crops in the ground. His main export of course, was tobacco, which had caught on in Europe quite nicely, and pitch—a tar like substance gathered from pine trees, and used to caulk the hulls of the wooden ships of the day.

However, even with these local plantations providing what they could, securing the needed supplies of food for the new settlers would prove all but impossible. Several ships came to the settlement each month, bringing various food items and the more rare items needed in a new settlement—items such as spinning wheels, pins, gunpowder and lead for molding shot. Still, food was the basic concern. While much livestock had been trailed down with the overland group from Virginia, the new colonists didn't want to merely kill off that livestock for food. That livestock was to be their breeding population and was intended to generate more livestock for the new settlers. Finally, much of the stores that were supposed to arrive with the colonists had been used previously on the trek down from Virginia. Thus, even in the earliest days of New Bern, food was quite scarce.

Within this new settlement, a town that existed only in the minds of the settlers, the need to secure food and build a home dominated the next months of Martin's life. Each day he and Johannes would fell trees along with the other men, and when the final livestock pens were completed and the church built, the families began to build their own rude, dirt-floor cabins. In Johannes' case, he and Martin built a log cabin approximately twenty feet long, with a fireplace in one end, and a half wall that bisected the interior. They also built a loft amid the rafters where the daughters could sleep. Martin, of course, stayed downstairs near the fire with his overly passionate companion, Max, while Johannes and Margaret slept behind the half wall, thus giving some measure of privacy to the married couple.

Margaret and her daughters planted some corn, beans, potatoes, and a strange plant never seen before by Europeans—squash—which they acquired from the local savages. The women in the town tended the small gardens that soon sprang up beside every log cabin. They gathered eggs from the chickens, newly acquired from the Brice Plantation, and when ships arrived in the river, they hurried down to the shore to see what new items might be bought or traded for. While funds were scarce, these settlers did, occasionally, purchase some of the metal items they could not yet fashion for themselves—a sewing needle, a metal ax, or perhaps a large cooking pot for the hearth. Max, the family mutt, kept a staunch lookout over the family cabin, and entertained himself by occasionally chasing the chickens around in the yard.

On Saturdays, all of the men were allowed to hunt for their families, and both Johannes and Martin could shoot. Unfortunately, only one musket was available, and it seemed that the two had to range further and further from the settlement to find rabbit, deer, or on occasion, bear, for curing. When such wild meats did become available, Margaret and her daughters worked wonders, with some water, a few vegetables, and a bit of salt, to create hearty stews that would sustain and enrich life for all in the cabin.

Of course, these Germans did not know the skills of the frontier—tanning of hides and drying meat. Thankfully, the slaves, on both the Foscue and the Brice Plantations along the Trent River, did. Most of those earlier slaves and frontiersmen had been in the Carolina Colony a while and Germans, if anything, are fast learners. Within only a few short months, many of these rugged settlers would be as seasoned by life in this rough frontier town as any men on Earth, Johannes and Martin among them.

Initially, only twenty families lived in New Bern with the rest of the Germans, taking two-hundred and fifty acre farms along the Neuse, or settling to the south of New Bern along the Trent River and its tributary, Mill Creek. De Graffenreid, ordered that a saw mill and grist mill be constructed along Mill Creek in the lower part of Craven County some fifteen miles below New Bern. Also, the Germans living in that area constructed a two story "blockhouse" type of log fort on the bank of the Trent River, just across the River from the mouth of Mill Creek. That blockhouse and several rifle pits—redoubts, in the military terminology of that day—were intended to protect the settlers in that area from the savages. The blockhouse is clearly depicted on de Graffenreid's early map of the New Bern area, which has survived in the historic record, and many living today, remember the interesting "holes" in the ground behind the sand beach, where children from the Mill Creek area swam for almost three hundred years. Those holes were the remains of the rifle pits dug in 1710, just after de Graffenreid arrived in New Bern.

Johannes Simmons and all of the other citizens in the town were selected for this new settlement because of particular skills. Johannes was a cooper—a barrel maker, and all of the produce, along with the export crops of the colony, would require barrels for shipping. Within three weeks of landing, the tools for the various craftsmen were unpacked and delivered to various work sheds in the town, with the explicit instructions from de Graffenreid to "Make money!"

De Graffenreid and his investors did not choose to settle this land for altruistic motives! Indeed, they demanded and expected that this colony would soon support itself and make a profit in exports for the investors. De Graffenreid knew that both the Virginia and South Carolina Colonies were now exporting large quantities of tobacco to Europe, along with pitch, wool, rice, and some fruit, and he saw no reason that his new town in the North Carolina Colony could not do the same. Other products included indigo, (a crop used to make a deep blue dye for cloth, which was in high demand in London), and animal hides. Some of these, such as tobacco and hides, were shipped in large oblong barrels called "hogsheads" whereas other products—tar, pitch, and indigo—required standard barrels in various sizes. Johannes would make the hogsheads and barrels along with various others in the cooper's shed, including several black slaves leased from the Foscue or Brice Plantations. The slaves would fell the trees and deliver the wood to Johannes' cooper shed.

Thus, Martin's first year in the colony was spent either building fences, log cabins, felling trees for barrels, hunting on Saturdays and sometimes on weekdays, or shaping the wood into barrel staves. Martin was big for his age, with broad shoulders, and his hands were often bloody with splinters. Sometimes he felt that if he had to shape another piece of wood he would simply lie down and die. Still, all men must bear burdens, and Martin was a deeply religious boy—in reality, a man in the making—who knew that he was indeed fortunate to have been bound over as apprentice to such a fine couple as Johannes and Margaret. He worked hard for them and was ever thankful in his daily prayers, for such good fortune. If he missed his mother and father, he realized his good luck to be living with this particular family. For he had seen other newly orphaned youngsters, bound over to very cruel men who seemed to view those apprentices as merely slaves to be worked to death.

Sundays were set apart in this religious community. On Sunday morning, nowhere could be heard the bite of an ax into a tree trunk. No distant gunfire was heard, since all were expected in Church, and no one would be hunting on this morn, at least none of the Germans. On these days, all put on their best clothes, and the entire German population would gather in the church for prayers. Many Bible passages would be read and a message would be delivered by one of the lay leaders of the congregation—for no ordained minister had yet ventured into the new settlement. Still, hymns would be sung, and prayers lifted to God. An offering was taken and, after a careful accounting, some funds were turned over to the authorities for use by the Anglican Church in other parts of the colony. However, much of these funds were used by the local congregation to support the poor—a designation that included almost everyone at that point.

Each evening after the evening meal, the family would read a Bible passage and hold an evening devotional, attended by the ever caring Max, who liked nothing more than to lay by the fireplace when all members of his family were within sight. Johannes liked to discuss the Bible passages a bit and would often lead with statements on the importance of a personal relationship with God. For the Anabaptists were the radicals in the reformation and staunchly advocated for a direct, personal, immediate relationship with God that was not dependent upon a priest or reverend as a liaison. Johannes mused on every man's intimacy with the Divine.

In contrast, Margaret most often contributed thoughts on how God might be reflected in nature—within a beautiful sunset across the Trent River, or in the myriad colors of the leaves along Broad Street. Once in late November of 1710, after a snow of some depth, all of the trees bent with the weight of ice and with the ground covered in a snowy white, she commented, "God has surely made an ice palace for all of us to enjoy!" Of course, she made that remark nestled comfortably on a bench with Max at her feet and a large fire in the fireplace, warming the entire cabin. Martin, who had been out hunting all day, saw the snow quite differently. While cold and inconvenient, it was the best way in the world to track a deer!

During these evening Bible readings, each of the daughters and Martin would be expected to read a bit, and thus their reading skills increased over time, until it seemed quite natural to read long passages of scripture. Unlike some of the other families, Johannes and Margaret chose to teach their daughters to read right along with their instruction to Martin, so Bible reading was a daily occurrence, even among the women. Of course, the Bible was the textbook, since it was the only book in the cabin. They read of kings and conquering armies in the Old Testament. They studied a jealous, punitive God and his swift retribution for any offense. However, Martin, Christina, and Katheryn all quickly detected the more forgiving God pictured in the later books of the Bible, a loving, caring God represented by Jesus that could forgive all sins, and was ever present in the lives of his people. Both Christina and Katheryn seemed much more comfortable with this milder, more loving image of God, but Martin preferred the more understandable, if more firm, divinity of the Old Testament.

Unlike the girls, Martin was becoming exposed to a wider world, including both the growing town and the harsh world of the frontier. He felt in some sense that the wilderness surrounding New Bern was best represented by the older representation of the Divine, rather than the latter, and he related more to the unforgiving, harsh nature of God pictured in those ancient books of the Old Testament. For Martin, any mistake or failure to take great care while he hunted alone in the forest miles from New Bern would surely result in swift and cruel punishment. Once or twice he had hunted on property that Johannes had assured him was his own section of land—a two hundred and fifty acre patch of wilderness along Mill Creek and a small depression called Baleakack Branch some twelve miles south of New Bern. That woods was truly the back end of nowhere, and out there God and the elements, were both very unforgiving!

Martin knew of other boys his own age and even full grown men who went hunting for the family stew pot and disappeared forever. In one instance, a young man named Kenneth Traynor was absent for two whole weeks, and only then came stumbling back into New Bern from the wilderness to the west, half starved, and stripped naked, telling tales of being captured by savages and tortured. His tales were extreme and he would have been considered crazy, save the evidence of torture all over his skin. The Tuscarora were adept at embedding one-inch twigs under the skin and then setting them afire for their amusement. John Lawson had described exactly this form of torture in his journal, noting that several of the Native American tribes employed this gristly cruelty. When he did finally return, Traynor had very little skin left on his entire body! He was a walking mass of wounds and blisters who nevertheless managed to survive his injuries. He lived out his life in New Bern and even hunted a bit from time to time, but he never again hunted alone in the distant woods.

On every trek Martin made into the wilderness surrounding New Bern, each time he went beyond the settlement and into the endless woods beyond, he learned to practice patience and stealth. He studied the ways of the deer and other animals prior to killing them and he learned the ways of the wilderness trails. After only a few months, he could move through the forest without any sound whatsoever, since his life depended on that very skill. He could track game and hunt with skills learned from Gator Jim, or Able Ward. He rarely missed a shot. He mastered these skills not only to approach his prey, but also to avoid trouble with the Tuscarora hunting parties that shared his wilderness. Death in that harsh world could come unexpectedly, at any time, capture by the Tuscarora, by snakebite, or merely being eaten alive by the bear, wolves, or panther that roamed the area. Surely God punished those who were weak, or unskillful, and the harsh vengeful God of the Old Testament fit that profile.

In understanding how these Germans confronted their rough world, a world of disease, cruelty, and the possibility of instant death, it is important to understand their spiritual dimension. For these Anabaptists, God was a daily, ever present reality, much more so than today. These men and women left Europe because they could not practice their religion as they saw fit—Mennonites and

Anabaptists were considered the extreme among the religious radicals, even during the reformation—a period of known radicalism. They were persecuted by both the Catholic Church and the more reformed Lutherans and Calvinists alike! They came to these shores because the enduring message of this new world was a message of religious freedom. Here these marvelous people sought only to live, to work hard, to worship their God, and most of all, to be left alone! This independent spirit would characterize this colony and indeed the new nation that arose from it for the next three hundred years.

Of course, Martin did not think in that fashion—for who among us truly considers his place in history during his lifetime? Rather, Martin merely lived his days, chopping wood and shaping barrels, praying, hunting, butchering his prey, and predictably enough, clandestinely observing his "sister" Katheryn, a young woman who seemed more compelling to him with each passing month.

Katheryn seemed merely to tolerate his presence, though she did often joke with her sister or the other family members. Still, Martin thought of her quite often. Moreover, her body seemed to be changing right before Martin's eyes. He would notice how one moment she would be playing with the dolls she and her sister had so often enjoyed, and the next she and her mother Margaret would be discussing how corn should be planted or cloth sown—discussing womanly things. She seemed to change daily, and he felt he was watching her grow into a woman.

Once, during a reading of the Bible in the evening, Kathryn was jokingly commenting on how King David had run naked in celebratory dance, as a way of worship. Then Kathryn, with an amused look, asked her father if he ever wished to celebrate their new life in such a worshipful fashion, dancing naked in the streets of New Bern! Johannes, conservative and paternal, looked at his daughter sternly, and was about to admonish her for mocking God, but was interrupted by the immediate, robust laughter of his wife Margaret, who then shouted, "I'm sure Father will certainly not dance naked here or anywhere else!"

Johannes lost it immediately, and had to drop any pretense of discipline. He laughed along with Christina, Katheryn, and Margaret. Max even lifted his head a bit, and apparently wondered what was so funny, but detecting nothing out of the ordinary, he calmly laid back down beside the fire.

While theirs was a sternly religious home, the beliefs of the Simmons family were not harsh or oppressive. Their religion was serious, but it was not a weight around their necks, as it can be for some. Rather, their spirituality was a scaffold supporting their life and they had that most marvelous ability to laugh occasionally at their own beliefs, as well as at themselves. Even Martin was seen to smile a bit, as the rest of the family seemed to feed off of each other in their joy at the mental image of their father, Johannes, running naked out on Broad

Street! By then, Margaret was holding her hand to her mouth, she was laughing so hard, and Christina was bent over, leaning on Katheryn in her joy. And that is when the most unexpected happened.

Katheryn, sitting on the rude-made bench beside Martin, looked at his hesitant smile, and joyfully placed her hand on his arm, saying, "It's alright Martin. We can all laugh at the thought of Father naked in the street. Surely none of us will ever see it!" With that, the laughter of everyone became even louder, as Martin joined in the joy. Still, for Martin, that single touch, along with that joke directed his way, was electric. He fell in love in an instant, though he could not voice that thought for years. Moreover, at that moment he realized for the first time that Katheryn did not hate him, but rather, was choosing to be reserved around him. He became, in an instant, much more confident around her, and much more comfortable also. His world changed in that moment and he would remember that single instant for the rest of his life.

As it turns out, Martin would share his feelings about that moment many years later with his son John, a story about the moment when he fell in love with John's mother. Fathers through the ages have coached their sons in matters dealing with women and such sessions inevitably end with honest men ultimately admitting to little or no understanding of women at all! Martin was no exception to that general rule, but his remembrances did find their way into his son, John's diary.

{Author's Note: That is how the story got passed down through the folklore of the family, with John Bender's diary and many papers written by Martin Bender himself ultimately ending up in the hands of Mildred Bender over two hundred and fifty years later. That diary Jesus and I found among the papers in the old box in the closet of Mildred Bender, just after she died.}

Life continued for many months in this way. Johannes and Martin built barrels by the scores, but soon they were paid almost as well for the crude furniture they fashioned for various family cabins—benches, tables, cupboards, and stools. While the women tended the garden, gathered eggs, milked their cow, collected wild blackberries, figs, and other fruits in season, Johannes and Martin worked on these various wood projects. Max lay around and guarded the yard, or chased the chickens, depending upon his mood on any given day.

A planting season came and went in 1710, and in the first year the harvest was good. Of course, that harvest was merely food for the next year—it would be some time before this settlement would not only be able to feed itself, but also invest time on cash crops such as indigo or tobacco. Like all coastal settlements, disease was always a danger in the summer, and yellow fever, that scourge of early settlements throughout the colonies, did take many lives in New Bern in 1710, but during that first year, it did not touch the Simmons family.

The new city seemed to be moving forward. The Germans were all learning English, though Johannes was struggling more than most in that endeavor. Many settlers, like Martin, were becoming adept at living on the frontier. Within the first year, men were gathering pitch and tar, and that proved to be the only cash export for the settlement during the early years. Life was indeed pleasant for a time, and could have continued that way, but the fates were not to be so kind.

## *Rebellion in the Carolinas*

Like every gathering of people, the colonists in the Carolinas needed a government, and like many new settlements, they could not seem to agree on one. In this colony, there had been a long-standing dispute between the earlier Quaker settlers around Bath and the Anglicans situated along the Albemarle Sound and up in Virginia. The disagreements were mainly religious in nature. From the 1670s onward, a number of Virginians had settled just south of the Virginia border in the northeast section of the Carolina Colony, and those areas like the Virginia Colony itself were Anglican. The area around Bath was settled somewhat later, and when a Quaker missionary came to call at Bath in the 1690s, many of those settlers converted to that strange and peaceful religion. By 1700 Quakerism was the dominate religion of the entire colony, other than the Albemarle. Of course, this truly angered the Anglicans that dominated the Albemarle and both the Virginia and South Carolina Colonies. At various points, one group accused the other of overt discrimination in the governance of the newly settled colony in North Carolina.

By 1710, Governor Cary, who had initially sympathized with the Anglicans, had switched his allegiance and was now strongly supportive of the Quaker Party. Cary no doubt recognized that the area around Bath included a large number of Quakers, so perhaps he was merely playing politics with his newfound enthusiasm for that party. While paying lip service to the Anglican authorities in neighboring colonies, he and his official Quaker Party pretty much ignored their dictates. Still, neither Virginia nor South Carolina, being Anglican in their beliefs, was disposed to send much help to "those damned Quakers" along the Pamlico and Neuse Rivers. Those distant settlements would have to grow their own food or starve. Starve they did, and starvation will inevitably lead to brutality. In many cases, it leads to war.

One stark, harrowing fact, known to historians worldwide, is that any population on Earth is exactly three meals away from a revolution. That is how long a father can watch his wife and children go without food. Any father on Earth will then begin to steal, and thus starvation often leads to the breakdown of authority, and frequently to total barbarity. Such starvation and the resulting barbarity arrived in 1711, almost crushing the new settlement of New Bern.

In January of that year, a newly appointed governor arrived for the North Carolina Colony, Governor Edward Hyde, who was known to be staunchly Anglican. Thus, he was in immediate conflict with Governor Cary, as well as all of the officials that Cary had appointed, since all of them, to a man, were supportive of the Quaker party. This situation was deemed intolerable by Governor Cary and his followers, most of whom held plantations in Bath, or along the Pamlico River some miles north of New Bern.

Governor Cary met this challenge from Hyde simply and directly. He merely refused to step aside to let Hyde assume the governmental duties! Of course, within only a fortnight this conflict was the talk of the town in both New Bern and Bath, and anyone who mattered, began to take sides in this conflict. This conflict thus set the stage for the very first true rebellion among white men anywhere on the North American continent.

Martin had listened to discussions of these political problems for a number of months while holding his own council when other citizens in the shop wanted to discuss the pending conflict. He listened carefully when community members argued about the imminent troubles, and indeed the differences between Governor Cary, and the would-be Governor Hyde, were the talk of the town. Even the girls at home, Christina and Katheryn, heard of the troubles and began to ask their father about the potential conflict.

One day in the early spring of 1711, William Brice, the owner of the large plantation across the river, came into the cooper's shed in which Johannes and Martin were carving barrel staves. He arrived riding a beautiful black stallion that was known to be one of the fastest horses in the area, and he was accompanied by his slave, a large black man named Gideon, who rode behind him on a mule. Brice dismounted and calmly tossed his reins to Gideon who caught them in midair, seemingly without even looking. Brice then strode into the shed and spoke. "I say, Sir. Are you the proprietor of this business?"

Both Johannes and Martin had by then, learned English well enough to be understood, and if the syntax was a bit obscure, the meaning was usually clear. Johannes calmly replied, "I am. Welcome Sir, for you coming to my shed! How I help you?"

"Thank you for your kindness," Brice answered. "I'm very pleased that a cooper is now working in these parts. My fields across the river grow some of the sweetest corn in the world, but my slaves cannot seem to get the knack of making barrels, and I can't ship it anywhere! Now that you are here my good man, I shall need quite a few barrels for the coming harvest in three months. I am hoping that you can supply them."

Johannes was excited about this possible order for his wares. William Brice was one of the earliest settlers in this area, having begun his plantation on the southern bank of the Trent River several years before the settlement of New Bern. He was rumored to have eighteen black slaves now working on his plantation, making him a wealthy man indeed. Further, he was known to produce much corn and high quality tobacco for export. This could turn into a substantial order for Johannes' business.

Johannes replied. "Sir, happy be I and mine to supply you. I make barrels, finely of all in this colony! How many you may need?"

Brice smiled at the convoluted English of this German cooper, but without a pause, he mentioned an exorbitant number, just to see how this new settler might respond. "I'll need fifty barrels over time." Seeing no response in Johannes' face, and judging that to be a good sign of stability, he then temporized a bit. "Let's start with twenty barrels and then see how the harvest looks after the corn is up. I'll have tobacco to ship also, but I'm putting in more corn this year, since there are many more mouths now to feed here along my river." Brice always spoke of the Trent as "My River", and even today the largest single tributary of that river bears his name.

Brice looked at the cooper once again to be sure he had been understood. He believed that he had been. Everyone was well aware that within only six months, they would all be facing another cold, long winter and food would have to be on hand to help the colony survive. Most of it would be stored in the barrels made by Johannes and Martin.

Johannes replied, "Certainly, very yes. Twenty barrels in autumn. Can do we will! Before corn is corn in harvest!" Johannes had meant to say, "Before the corn was ripe for harvest." Brice smiled again at the fumbled attempt at English. Still, all three realized that such a large order would demand that Johannes hire more help for felling trees and carving, but that was certainly possible. In fact, Brice would ultimately lease out one or two of his slaves to assist, since they could finally learn the art of barrel making from a master cooper, making them more useful to Brice, not to mention more valuable. Skilled slaves had almost twice the value as healthy field hands, and Brice never missed an opportunity to get various skills taught to his slaves.

Brice continued, "Yes, I think things should go rather well with our crops as well as our new colony this year, unless that rogue Hyde begins to kick up his heels again. I don't understand why Governor Cary doesn't merely toss the bugger in shackles and send him upriver for the Tuscarora to play with, uh?"

Martin cringed at that thought. Surely no white Christian would send any other white man to that fate! However, he was surprised to hear Johannes question Brice.

"I'm sure governor send not man Tuscarora! Not Hyde." Johannes had meant that even Governor Cary could not be so callus, but he wasn't sure he'd made himself clear.

Thus, Martin stepped into the conversation, since his English was more refined. "But Mr. Brice, how do you see this conflict progressing? Johannes and I fear that the authorities in Bath may offend those in the Albemarle or in Virginia and we are sorely dependent upon their assistance in these troubled times. How can they continue to support us with food shipments unless we acknowledge the rightful governor?"

Brice was pleased with the improved English and looked over at Martin. This boy was well spoken, and seemed large for his age. Brice paused, considering his answer. He was not only a successful plantation owner and farmer, he was also a man of letters, and a thoughtful man, and in politics he carefully considered his positions. "I too fear offending the Virginians and without the coastal freighters that deliver food, cloth, and slaves to our docks each week, our new settlement would not survive. Still, the authorities in Bath are solidly behind Governor Cary, and I don't see how they can toss him out merely at the whim of Hyde, the Anglicans in the Albemarle, or the Virginia governor."

Therein lay the problem. The North Carolina Colony was surviving during that first year almost totally at the behest of the earlier settlements in the Albemarle Sound region of the North Carolina Colony, as well as the Virginia authorities. To understand this, we have to look at the geography of the coast that so determined the location of the settlement, and thus the politics of those early years. Because of an accident of geography, North Carolina was the bastard child among the colonies—having been settled much later than all of the other colonies save Georgia, which wasn't settled until 1733. Strangely enough, coastal geography accounted for the tardiness of settlement.

While South Carolina and Virginia both had fine deep water ports—Charleston and Jamestown—the North Carolina coast, in between the two, was cursed by a series of long, narrow barrier islands, not to mention thousands of square miles of inland sounds and swamps. These geographic features effectively prohibited early settlement in North Carolina for scores of years. Moreover, the sounds all along the North Carolina coast averaged only four feet deep—much too shallow for the deep draft ships of the 1600s and early 1700s, and that meant that the North Carolina Colony was settled much later than either Virginia or South Carolina. By 1620, both Charleston in South Carolina, and Jamestown in Virginia, were settled English villages. Whereas the first incorporated town in North Carolina—Bath—would not be organized until almost a hundred years later in 1705—all because of that cursed set of barrier islands and those shallow sounds!

Since North Carolina was such a new colony, it played second fiddle to South

Carolina and Virginia, and would continue to do so for almost two hundred years! It is no real surprise that Virginia tried to dominate North Carolina in the early decades of the 1700s, since many, if not all, of the early settlers in Bath and along the Albemarle Sound were transplanted Virginians anyway. Settlement in the Albemarle area of North Carolina had come not via great transoceanic voyages of settlers seeking new frontiers, but by men and women coming overland, almost due south from Virginia, into the swamps and forests and continuing until they hit higher, dry land. Even de Graffenreid's German settlers had landed in Virginia and come to the Neuse and Trent Rivers from that distant Virginia colony. For that reason, many Virginia authorities considered the settlements in North Carolina to be merely extensions of Virginia—there was even some move to merge the colonies at one point.

From such accidents of geography are politics sometimes made, and the colony along the Neuse and Trent Rivers would be subject to this curse of shallow sounds and inland waters for the next few centuries. In 1711, the fact is that the North Carolina settlements were much less important than Virginia or South Carolina, and to be blunt, few in distant England even knew or cared what happened in North Carolina.

Thus, when they sent a new governor, Governor Hyde, to the colony at the behest of the Anglican sympathizers in Albemarle and Virginia, they neglected to perfect the paperwork mandated by such a transition of power. Therefore, when Hyde arrived in Bath, he had nothing official to present to Governor Cary or to the other authorities that clearly named him as the new governor! This oversight led to war and it is a strange historical fact that the first rebellion anywhere on the North American Continent would take place, essentially, as a result of a typo in the paperwork.

Of course, William Brice, Johannes Simmons, and Martin Bender each understood all of this during their discussion that day in the cooper's shed, as Johannes' business was then called, in the new settlement of New Bern. What Brice didn't know was where these particular settlers stood on the controversy. Who supported Cary and who supported Hyde?

Never one to either temporize or mince words merely to further his business, Johannes addressed this issue directly. "I don't know much of this matter, but I know Governor Cary helped me."

Brice smiled knowingly, glad to hear of the cooper's support for Governor Cary. He quickly agreed. "I could tell at the outset that you were a stable man and a good judge of the situation! I am for Governor Cary also, for he is one of us, and if need be, I will stand beside him when the time comes." At that the men shook hands, and Brice turned to his slave, Gideon, and reached for the reins of his horse. Gideon had anticipated his master's desires, as required by his position, and was already holding out the reins toward Brice. After Brice mounted, he turned again to Johannes in the work shed. "Twenty barrels within three months it is! And now I know I can depend on you should Governor Cary need our support!" With that, both he and Gideon rode off, the stallion prancing through the streets of the growing town, the mule plodding along behind.

Martin however, was curious as to what the conversation might mean, so as he and Johannes returned to their carving, he switched back to German and asked, "Do you think, sir that real troubles might arise between the governor and Hyde?"

Johannes temporized a bit, but then responded, "No, I don't think it will come to that." Johannes spoke clearly and correctly in German, and his English did improve over time, though he was always more likely to misspeak in English when he was excited or under stress. He laid down a finished stave and picked up another of the wooden boards from which the next would be shaped, then continued, "I think that politicians love to talk loudly, but when real disagreements come, they let others do their work. We'll hear about arguments, and challenges for duels, but I don't think either has the stomach for real conflict."

Within a month, Johannes would learn how wrong he'd been. When the conflict began, hundreds of men would be armed, and both Johannes and Martin would find themselves in the thick of the battle, though not on the side they anticipated.

### Gathering Clouds of War

Governor Cary resolutely refused to relinquish power and merely continued to govern from his plantation in Bath. With no official capital yet established for the North Carolina Colony, one location was as good as another and only Bath and New Bern had yet been established as official cities in the entire colony. Cary continued to make various appointments and write edicts that continued to hold the force of law, while seemingly ignoring Hyde's appointment entirely.

Edward Hyde, however, was even more direct. Knowing that the real power over the colony lay in Virginia, he proceeded to Williamsburg, just up from the Jamestown settlement, and returned with word from the Virginia governor that he would soon receive a "personal bodyguard" of British troops, since he was now the governor of the North Carolina Colony. Bypassing Bath altogether in his return trek, he arrived in New Bern, and using the Virginia letter of support as his "authority clearly granted by Governor Spotswood in Virginia", he began to call up the militia to assume his place in government.

One problem became quickly evident; there was no militia to call up! None had yet been organized in the New Bern area since the town was only one year old. None had, to date, been needed. Undaunted, Hyde looked over the new town for a few days, and determined that William Brice was both well educated and the most senior plantation owner in the area. Brice was immediately appointed Captain in command of the New Bern Militia and was ordered to call forth a militia that did not, as yet exist.

Now Brice had previously been loyal to Cary, but he saw various advantages to this appointment, not the least of which was a Captaincy that gave him some degree of recognition and authority in the new city. Perhaps he truly believed that British troops would be arriving soon to support Hyde, and of course no one wanted to stand against the King's troops! While his motives are unclear, it is known that in the spring of 1711, he switched his allegiance to support Hyde.

Thus, in May of that year, the call to arms went to all able bodied men in the city of New Bern and the surrounding farms. All men were ordered to report for duty with the New Bern Militia. Over 90 men responded, including both Johannes Simmons and Martin Bender, though some were rejected for various reasons. Martin, now seventeen, would have been considered too young had he been living with his own family, and perhaps Johannes could have protected him from this call up, but neither was aware of that fact. Also, Martin was becoming a fairly big young man and he often hunted in the wilderness alone on the lower Trent River many miles from New Bern. He knew woodland skills, and many knew that Martin was a very good shot with a musket, so he answered the call, even when others his age didn't.

The men were told to bring their muskets or a shotgun along with provisions for ten days, and a blanket. The New Bern Militia met at noon on a Monday, in a rude tavern owned by Toby Mallard, that had recently been established just to the north of the New Bern settlement beside the ferry landing on the Neuse River. In colonial America, taverns seemed to spring up in almost every colonial town and along every early wagon trail, since they served as a combination, eatery, hotel, meeting place, entertainment center, and courthouse all rolled into one. Mallard's Tavern, on that particular day, served as a meeting hall for the very first meeting of the New Bern Militia.

When a number of men had gathered, Hyde began to speak. "Men of the Carolinas. You all know that I hold the charter from the Lords to rightfully govern the North Carolina Colony and that the governor of Virginia is sending a contingent of His Majesty's troops to support me in that government. You all know that the former governor, that rogue Cary and his cronies in Bath, refuse to step aside. You all know that his band of damned Quakers has governed to their own advantage, and left out good Anglicans like those here."

On that point, of course, Governor Hyde was utterly wrong. While Brice and a few of the earlier settlers in the area were Anglican, most of those present were the stalwart Germans, practicing Mennonites, who really wanted nothing to do with this conflict. Hyde, on that day, either didn't realize that fact, or chose to ignore it completely.

Hyde continued, "With the aid of Governor Spotswood of Virginia, I will raise the militia and remove Cary from his position, to be bound to London in chains to account for his actions. We will join with another militia force from the Albemarle and the Virginia Colony, and confront Cary and his followers in Bath. You men will accompany me to that meeting, and in the confrontation to follow. I do not anticipate any real conflict, once that bastard Cary sees our resolve. The matter should take no more than five or ten days and you men may return home thereafter. We will leave for Bath immediately."

William Brice, much more so than Hyde, knew the measure of the men in that makeshift militia. While resolute and confirmed Christians, these Germans were not particularly supportive of either Hyde or Cary, and most of them knew Cary better. Brice sensed that he should do a bit more to rally support for Governor Hyde, and with that on his mind, he rode or walked along with various groups in the New Bern Militia during those first days of travel, to do what every effective commander does—talk openly and directly with the men he proposed to lead into combat.

Thus Brice found himself walking beside Johannes, Martin, and several others at one point on that first afternoon, while hiking up the North Trail to Bath. He spoke up. "I say, men. I share Governor Hyde's thoughts about this matter. He has been appointed governor clearly at this point, and perhaps we can get a better shake from him than from Cary and his lot up in Bath. We are now much larger than Bath, and perhaps we can persuade Hyde to govern the colony from New Bern. At any rate, Hyde is our new governor, duly appointed for us, and I think we have to support him, though I don't really think that any fighting will come in the matter."

That assurance was not good enough, or perhaps not clear enough, for Johannes. As Martin and the others listened, he questioned Brice. "But Captain. All we like Cary. He treated us fairly to all. Do we know Hyde? Do we know what does he for us?"

Brice held his thoughts for a moment carefully considering the question, and then he responded. "Johannes, you have asked a critical question. While I'm not sure what Governor Hyde proposes to do, I do believe he is the legitimate governor of our colony, and I am a British subject. As such, being a loyal subject of the Crown, I can only support the governor appointed by those in London!"

Martin Bender reflected on the matter. While he was German, the authorities in Germany clearly didn't want him or his family. Indeed, they wanted no one with their beliefs anywhere in their country. By coming to this British colony, had he and Johannes and all the rest not submitted to British authority? Did they not owe rightful allegiance to those governors appointed by the British? However, and perhaps more to the point, was such a responsibility worth fighting and maybe dying for?

Of course, that begged the question as to who was the correctly appointed Governor, Cary or Hyde. Cary did tend to side with the group that had come to be known as the Quaker Party, and that did not suggest that his group would be as liberal in their governance as the Anglicans, led by Hyde. Moreover, the Anabaptists group, to which both Johannes and Martin belonged, depended totally on that religious tolerance. While Cary had helped greatly when Martin was uncertain of his future, by helping him to get settled with Johannes Simmons and his family, the Anglicans promised more tolerance of this group of Germans and their rather unorthodox beliefs. Clearly, Martin's thoughts on the matter were unsettled, as were those of many in that makeshift militia. There was a great deal of uncertainty on this march up to Bath and, of course, Captain Brice knew that and was trying desperately to calm the fears.

All of these questions rambled through Martin's mind as he walked along with the others for three days, up the North Trail. Still, with nothing further said at that moment, Brice's comments seemed to settle the matter, at least for a time, and the men proceeded on towards the showdown in Bath. Brice moved down the long line of men to talk with others, repeating essentially the same message.

Martin had noticed one other thing on this march that caused him additional concern. He was absolutely sure that this New Bern Militia was totally, and woefully unprepared! Of course, he had shot pheasants and rabbits in Germany, and since he arrived in New Bern he'd learned many more woodland skills. He'd killed deer and bear within the last year, and he felt he knew his way around the forest and had developed some skills as a marksmen. Even at the age of seventeen, he was quickly becoming a frontiersman. However, he knew that some of his compatriots had never held a musket before at all! Indeed, he was very much aware that this was the first time that the New Bern Militia had been called to service. This group was totally unprepared for going into battle and had never even trained together. As Martin considered that matter, he realized that most of these men were shopkeepers, sailors, pitch harvesters, farmers, rope makers, cattlemen, sheepherders, blacksmiths, or others specifically selected for their settlement skills and not their military prowess. Should this force confront a trained, armed, and well-prepared militia, Martin feared not only for his safety, but for all of the men in this ragtag army.

There was, however, one small group of men walking with the militia, but not a part of it, that seemed to walk with confidence—the slaves that accompanied their masters to the conflict. In those times, many gentlemen, Hyde, Brice, and four others in the party, carried their personal manservant wherever they went, and in this instance, Brice had brought along two servants. Thus, history records that at least six slaves traveled with this group, and interestingly, those slaves could shoot muskets quite well. Further, being personal servants, they had much more prestige than the typical field hand slave. Several of these personal servants, Gideon among them, even considered themselves superior to most of the Germans in the party. In the later years of institutional slavery, such attitudes became more rare and it would be illegal to arm slaves, but in the early decades of the 1700s, not only were some slaves armed on occasion, they were required to hunt for much of their own food.

Martin Bender had learned much of his newly acquired hunting skills from the slaves of Captain Brice, who were known to be some of the better bear hunters in New Bern. Martin took some comfort from the fact that, at a minimum, those six black men could shoot if needs be and he noted on the march that each carried their weapons comfortably, as if they were used to them and knew what was to come.

That night the men camped in a wooded forest, next to a small plot of land owned by a family named Thigpen. The army had managed to bring enough bacon and beans to eat without having to impose too much on the family, but should they have needed it, they would have merely confiscated anything needed from that farm. Such were the powers of the militia in every colony since the presumption was the militia was there to protect the colonists. On this evening, however, the only imposition requested was use of the bedroom loft in the cabin for Governor Hyde's and Captain Brice's sleeping quarters. Here the leaders of the militia could sleep, while the other officers had their tents for cover. The other men, of course, rested with their single blankets on the cold ground outside, or in the small barn with the several cattle Thigpen owned.

Several large fires were built and the men huddled around them for warmth. Martin listened that evening to the conversation, mostly in German, at the campfires near where he and Johannes planned to sleep. He realized that many men shared his thoughts and concerns, and those with the most fear sought to reassure themselves that no battle would be necessary, that merely a show of force would convince Cary and his supporters to surrender.

Johannes had observed Martin's mannerisms during the day and knew that his young protégée was gravely concerned. Late in the evening, he sat beside Martin, slightly away from the others, and spoke; "We seem to be going into a battle with little preparation and less reason to fight."

Martin replied, with a point he'd recently heard voiced by others around the fire. "Yes, many here do not know how to hunt, or shoot, much less how to fight. Still, Captain Brice is a commander of some experience and has lived on this frontier for some time now. He's captured Tuscarora slaves and even tamed black slaves. He will know what to do."

Johannes considered this for a moment, and liked the way this young man, even when frightened, sought out a positive point to make. That suggested a courage, or at the very least a determination, not to succumb to fear. Johannes then shared his thoughts, "Perhaps he will. If a battle should begin, stay next to me if you can, and we will watch out for each other. Perhaps it will not come down to fighting."

At that moment, Martin knew he had found a family that truly valued him. This man, Johannes Simmons, had taken Martin into his family when Martin had no home at all, and with those kind and reassuring words on the eve of battle, Johannes had truly become his father. Martin almost wept at that moment, feeling a profound love and gratitude for Johannes, even in the midst of his fear. It is often the case that men going into battle or during a battle develop a profound love and respect for their fellow warriors. These two untested men had, without realizing it, discovered the one fundamental truth that helps men survive the hell of war. The only thing a man in battle can depend on is the man fighting beside him, and if one is very lucky, that man will be worthy of such a profound trust.

Without even voicing the thought, each man knew what he needed to do at that moment, and again with no word between them, they bowed their heads. Johannes, as the senior man led the prayer for them both, speaking softly, in German.

*"Father, tonight we prepare ourselves for war. As we sit tonight below the splendor of your heavens, we see the many wonders of your creation. We thank thee for thy gifts to us this day and for all of these great treasures. Tonight we sleep away from our family as we travel to a battle. We ask thee for courage to see thy will, and the strength to accomplish thy desires. Make our hands thine that we may fight for thee. Make our minds thine that we understand thy will. If we have to fight tomorrow, be with us at every step. Make our arms strong and our aim sure, for thy glory. Protect us from harm while we do thy will, and make us mighty in strength for thee. Grant us peace in the evening of tomorrow to return to our lives in our new city of New Bern. Amen."*

Martin knew it was time to sleep and he could think of nothing else to say, but it was one of those moments when something needed to be said between men going to war. Each man contemplated his life and his situation at that point. The senior man, Johannes, was a thirty-five year old cooper, who had some experience with a musket, and no experience at all in war.

The junior man, Martin Bender, was only seventeen on that march, but was quickly becoming one of the better hunters and frontiersmen in the new city of New Bern. Strangely enough, he was surer of himself and his skills with a weapon, than he was of many of the others, but he was terribly unsure as to the outcome of this battle, as well as the military skills of he himself and his colleagues. Still, with Johannes beside him, he would fight as well as he could.

With that thought, Martin finally came up with the right thing to say. "I will stay beside you, Father." It was the first time Martin had used that term for Johannes, and both were acutely aware of that fact. Martin continued, "We will fight together, and if need be, we will die, but with God's blessing, whatever comes, we will do it together."

At that, both men paused a moment and Johannes almost allowed himself to cry, but neither of these Germans was emotionally constructed in that fashion. Johannes merely coughed to clear the slight catch in his throat, or perhaps in his heart, saying only, "God's will be done, with us my son. Goodnight Martin."

"Goodnight, Father," Martin said the term again. They then went to sleep beside the fire.

### An Ugly Proposition

On that very same night, as Martin and Johannes prepared for bed, Governor Cary was busy seeking one of the ugliest political alliances ever proposed anywhere in the Carolinas. He was sitting in the longhouse of King Hancock of Catechna Town, an important Tuscarora village near where the city of Grifton, North Carolina would one day grow. King Hancock was the leader of the southern band of the Tuscarora. Cary had come to this village with his interpreter, an honor guard of six troops, and a guide to seek an ugly, possibly bloody alliance.

The odors of the longhouse—odors the Tuscarora were quite used to—disturbed the sensibilities of Governor Cary considerably, since they were almost overpowering. The drying scalps of several Catawba warriors hung from the ridgepole in the chief's longhouse, and Cary noticed those immediately upon entering. The white settlers in the Carolinas had already learned that the Tuscarora had fought with the Catawba since time before memory, over hunting grounds far out to the west. On this night, the aroma of those nearly rancid, human trophies mixed with the smell of dung—for the Tuscarora were used to sharing their longhouses with much of their livestock, and several goats were tied in the other end of the longhouse.

In spite of the overpowering smells, Governor Cary was not to be distracted. He sat in that longhouse with a mission in mind and through an interpreter, he presented his case, rather succinctly. He laid his gift of two iron axes and two muskets before King Hancock, since presentation of gifts from petitioners was the custom when one was beginning negotiations with the Tuscarora. "Tell King

Hancock that the followers of Hyde capture the Tuscarora and sell them into slavery in Virginia and in the south islands. I hope he will attack and destroy those who would capture his women and children."

As the translator translated this message for King Hancock, the King paid no attention whatsoever. Unknown to Cary or any other white man at that time, King Hancock could speak and understand English quite well. In fact he also knew and spoke French, some of the Cherokee dialects, and of course, his own language. It is a little recognized fact of history that white negotiators in colonial America often dealt with Native Americans who were quite often, bi-lingual or multi-lingual.

King Hancock knew French since the very first settlement anywhere in his territory had been that long forgotten settlement along the upper Trent River of a group of French Huguenots, in the 1690s. King Hancock had also been discretely learning English for years. He found it to his advantage to know things that one's enemies may not be aware of, so he pretended to listen to the translator, a half-breed Tuscarora, named Two-Nose, quite seriously.

Two-Nose was so named by the Tuscarora because he lived quite well in both the white world and the Tuscarora world. The name was intended as a mild insult and a play on the odor of the whites, but Two-Nose didn't seem to mind. During the translation, King Hancock was carefully considering Cary's proposal, and wondering as to Cary's real motives.

By the time the translation was over, King Hancock had decided to play with this upstart Cary, a would-be governor, now displaced. King Hancock put a scowl on his face as he pretended anger at all whites. "All whites steal the children of the Tuscarora. Why should we only attack some of them?" Of course, no Tuscarora Chief would admit that any white could or did capture fully grown warriors, so the pretense had to be maintained that only women and children were taken as slaves. Cary had been briefed on this belief, and had formulated his proposal to be respectful of that position.

Cary responded, again through the interpreter. "That is not so. Only the followers of Hyde and the Church of England capture slaves! Quakers do not do so!" While Cary was technically correct in that Quakers had almost always stood against slavery, he was also lying, since many in the Quaker Party, including he himself were not Quakers, and thus many in that party owned slaves and worked them on their plantations. However, to be strictly fair, in that particular year Cary had only black slaves on his plantation, and did not, at that time, own any Native Americans as slaves.

That subtly aside, Cary continued. "The followers of Hyde will steal many more Tuscarora in the coming months as the sun grows in the sky before the harvest season, and we should fight them together. I would like to fight beside the great King Hancock!"

King Hancock was called by that English name, since so many Tuscarora names were essentially unpronounceable in English. His name, in his language, meant "Wise killer of bears," because he had killed a bear early in life. The English in Bath had named him King Hancock after the first white trader to meet with him, Jacob Hancock. At first, he'd been called merely Jacob Hancock's King, but then the name "King Hancock" took root. The Tuscarora leader of the northern Tuscarora villages was called Tom Blount, for essentially the same reason. A white trader named Blount, had been the first to meet with him.

King Hancock was considering his options. As an important Tuscarora village headman, his word would carry influence throughout most of the southern towns of the Tuscarora. He would not be able to influence the upper towns of the Tuscarora in the Albemarle Sound region, who followed Tom Blount, but he could and did command between five hundred and a thousand warriors from the lower villages at that point. He had known that whites were capturing any Tuscarora they could subdue in the wilderness, including some warriors, and he had even lost one of his own sons just three months previously. That son, like the others, had "gone missing." Of course, in the wilderness one never knew if a bear, wolf, or panther had taken a hunter, of if the hunter had been captured as a slave. Still, Hancock had reason to resent the whites, and more than enough reason to go to war with them—the prospect of revenge felt good, and the Tuscarora could take many slaves themselves among the whites, just as they had captured many Catawba slaves for decades.

King Hancock was interested to see what might be involved in this proposition for his tribe, so he asked, rather bluntly. "Our forests hold many bear and deer, and our women find many berries. Our water from the Great River (the Tuscarora name for the Neuse River) is sweet. Why should my people make war?"

Cary was prepared for the question. "Your people will capture many guns, axes, blankets, and much livestock from the farms of those who make slaves of your people."

King Hancock considered this response, and knew it to be true. There could be much plunder in striking the outlying farms and perhaps even the towns of the smelly-pale men. To the Tuscarora, white men had a distinct, somewhat unpleasant odor, stemming from the fact that many in frontier colonies bathed only once a week or so, whereas the Tuscarora "went to water" each morning for a ritual cleansing. Thus, human body odor marked whites as smelly from the perspective of the Tuscarora. It also marked them as non-Tuscarora, and of course, their pale color had to become a factor in the tribe's name for this unusual race. To the Tuscarora, all whites were smelly-pale men or merely smelly-pales.

King Hancock knew that the smelly-pale before him was considered a leader, but he did not understand why. This Governor Cary was clearly not a warrior. This was a bald, fat man who walked with a limp, and no matter how foolish the smelly-pales might be, why would any race follow a man like this? King Hancock had already determined what this man wanted and why he wanted it. For many Tuscarora were interacting with smelly-pales daily, trading deer hides for blankets, or knives, and those warriors had heard of the political struggle between the two smelly-pales who wanted to be governor.

It is interesting to note that in this discussion, like many others in the years to come, the white leaders had completely underestimated their Native American counterparts. Cary was a former governor who spoke two languages, and had received the benefits of a college education at Cambridge. He was a successful plantation owner, and his entire background and training demanded that he view King Hancock, as a savage and as a much less capable man.

In contrast, King Hancock was a powerful man, standing nearly six feet high, in an age where the average white man stood only five feet, four inches tall. Further, King Hancock had thrived throughout a lifetime of warrior competition and training in a warrior oriented society, and he had risen to lead via that rough and deadly competition. King Hancock spoke four languages—two more than Cary. He was tested in battle many times over, whereas Cary had never led in a conflict before. Moreover, King Hancock's followers had absolute confidence in his judgment and fighting ability. Cary would have been shocked to learn that King Hancock felt nothing but contempt for the balding, limping smelly-pale before him, a pitiful man who could never be considered a warrior.

In the broader sweep of history, we may well ponder who was the lesser man? Suffice it to say that in this negotiation, as in many such negotiations in the centuries to come, white men dealt with Native American rulers who were much more experienced and learned men, and in many ways more accomplished men than the white leaders themselves, yet these Native American leaders were consistently underestimated by the whites who dealt with them.

At this point, Cary mistook the silence of King Hancock for interest, so he pressed on with his proposal. "My men will tell you which farms and cabins to attack. You should kill everyone. You may have all the livestock and anything you find in the cabin. For each scalp you bring to us, we will pay you with a musket, and much powder and shot."

And therein lay the ugly proposal, starkly stated. Cary was offering a bribe of battle spoils, if King Hancock would release his warriors to slaughter other white settlers in the Carolina territory! History later records quite a few instances of whites using various Native American tribes to fight against their enemies, and thousands died at the hands of Native Americans who were thus, serving as surrogate fighters in white conflicts. Those deaths were terribly cruel, and in many cases pointless; for what women and children, carefully tending their farms in outlying areas, could influence the governmental squabbles between Cary and Hyde?

Yes, this tactic of using Indians to fight white battles continued throughout the next two centuries, but this may have been the first recorded instance of this on the North American Continent, and certainly was the first instance in the Carolinas. It was an ugly proposal indeed!

Had King Hancock agreed to that proposition, history would have been considerably different and much more negative for the Carolina colonists. However, King Hancock and his tribal elders were so repulsed by Cary in general that they turned his proposition down flat. His younger warriors, of course, wanted to fight with Cary, and said so in the council meeting, but young men often wish to fight—such is the nature of things—as it is the nature of older, wiser men to exercise caution. In this instance, caution won the day. Cary and his entourage left the longhouse that evening, quite disappointed in their lack of ability to win the Southern Band of the Tuscarora as allies, but they were still confident of their ultimate victory.

In that confidence Cary was dead wrong. For it is a historical certainty that men who underestimate a potential ally are also likely to underestimate their enemies, and Cary was a man who was destined to do both.

### Two Militias Join Forces

Two days later, Martin and Johannes were marching along with their comrades in the brisk spring air. As the militia approached Bath, a rider approached and spoke with Governor Hyde, seemingly conferring information or secrets. Governor Hyde then turned in his saddle to address Captain Brice and the several other leaders at the front of the column. Johannes and Martin were near enough to hear the discussion.

Hyde said, "It seems the rebel Cary has flown the coop! He is not at his plantation, but has moved up river. This man believes he is at the plantation home of one of his henchmen, a Robert Daniels, so we will move in that direction. The column from Albemarle is to join us down the road a bit." Hyde then kicked his horse and began the move toward the fight, while Brice, the other officers, and the men followed along behind. Sure enough, within a mile, the militia from New Bern began to pass men standing alongside the trail, and rumor quickly spread down the marching line that, "This is the militia from Albemarle. They are filthy!"

And they were! What a sight, what an image those rugged frontiersmen made! Unlike the Germans who were dressed in cloth garments, and seemed in that context to be so very unsure of themselves when out in the wilderness, the new arrivals all seemed to be predators of the forest and they dressed in the skins of their prey. Moreover, they seemed to be cocksure of themselves, and forthright, these wilderness bred frontiersmen, men long of the colonies in the northern area of North Carolina and lower Virginia. Unlike the majority of the New Bern Militia, most of these men had been born in the colonies, and the way they held their muskets suggested a comfort with their weapons that made the heart of Martin rejoice. "Look how they stand, Johannes," he exclaimed. "They hold their rifles as if they were born to them. They know this wilderness!"

Perhaps that phrase best summed up these ungainly frontier fighters. They were almost to a man native Virginians, born into the wilderness having never laid eyes on Europe, and they had survived and thrived on a rough rugged frontier. Many had fought with Indians in various battles previously, and all had used a musket since they were four or five years old. These men sported breeches made of tough deer hide, and leggings of bearskin or beaver. That was the type of clothing that allowed a man to survive in the wilderness, and men accustomed to the great wilderness of these woodlands would depend upon such clothing for the next two hundred years. Almost without exception, they were unlettered, uncouth, and smelly, and while that caused some negative comment among a few of the Germans, it was apparent to all that these rough men were exactly the men one wanted to have at one's side in a tough fight on this frontier. These men had clearly fought before, and they knew how to win.

Without saying a word, and with no order given, these rugged Virginians and men from the Albemarle joined on at the end of the marching men from New Bern, and in less than fifteen minutes Hyde's force had grown from seventy-five untried men to a fighting force numbering just over a hundred and fifty. At times, one experienced fighting man can turn a group of two or three novices into a capable fighting force, many times stronger than would be expected by merely the numbers. This is exactly what happened over the next days. As those days passed, many of the Germans began to adopt not only the swagger, but also the uncouth language of these rough men of the Albemarle and of Virginia. More importantly, they watched how they cared for their muskets, and they undertook target practice together, alongside these Virginians. Thus did a formidable fighting force emerge from these two very different groups of men.

Within two more days, Hyde's militia approached Cary's. On May 29, 1711, these combined militia groups with Hyde and Captain Brice in the lead, made a final turn in the trail. The column had veered off the main road to Bath several miles before and now they were headed a bit more to the south, towards the cleared fields of Robert Daniels. As they topped a rise in the ground, several fields came into view, and a few black slaves were working there. Captain Brice spoke to one of them. "I say, you there." Here he pointed to one of the larger black men who held a hoe standing in the middle of a patch of corn. "I say, is this the home of Robert Daniels?"

The slave well trained by his master, cast his eyes downward as was proper, and answered in the low mumble so characteristic of slaves. "Yes 'um. It is, Suh!"

Brice continued, "Is your master yonder at the big house?"

Here the slave temporized a bit, and then mumbled, "Not sure, Suh! I don't get up to the big house much."

Brice and Hyde had paid little attention to that answer. They knew that slaves lied to whites with every breath, and they had both noticed something odd. They were looking over the big house in the distance, and the barns and slave cabins beyond and they quickly noticed that absolutely nothing and no one seemed to be moving. Nothing was happening around either the house or the large barn immediately behind it. Moreover, near the several slave cabins, they noted a lack of any movement at all, and at that realization, warning bells began to sound in their minds. This plantation was much too quiet! Not a slave, nor any slave children, not a chicken, nor a hog, or anything else was visible at all. Even the few cattle near the large barn seemed subdued.

At first it seemed the plantation house was empty. However, as the militia approached the two story home, curtains were pulled back from the eight front windows, and muskets were seen. These deadly barrels seemed to spring, two at a time from each window sill, and when the front door to the upstairs porch was cracked several more showed up there. But the real harbinger of death rested in the open lower door of the barn—there the barrel of a single smooth bore cannon was visible. In light of these preparations for battle, the men topping the hill became suddenly aware that they were in for a tough fight. For hundreds of years, men have faced artillery in battle, but throughout all history not a single man has ever been happy about it.

At that moment, however, Hyde and his approaching militia were wholly unaware of the real threat. They knew from spies that reported to Governor Hyde that Cary had only forty-five or so armed men with him, and while the smooth-bore cannon was a surprise, they felt they could neutralize that single cannon in the barn by merely avoiding its firing arc. However, unknown to Hyde, Cary had hidden four other artillery pieces, carefully sequestered in various buildings around the open ground approaching the plantation house, and while one cannon can cause one problems, five field pieces can ruin your whole day.

It was into this deadly maelstrom that Johannes, Martin, and one hundred and forty nine other militiamen under Governor Hyde, rode. They would need to charge the plantation house and grounds, across about half a mile of open ground, under fire at every step. The plantation buildings were set up in a semi-circle fashion, with the plantation house in the middle and several barns, a spring house, and a meat house forming the wings of the group of buildings. Overall, the scene looked very tranquil until one contemplated the muskets and the cannon in evidence. Cary and his men had concealed the additional artillery pieces in most of the other buildings, each loaded and deadly, creating a terrible crossfire into which the New Bern Militia would charge, and no one in that force saw that danger.

Eyeing the one cannon in evidence and understanding how such a weapon could cut down a line of charging men, Martin spoke in a whisper to Johannes. "Captain Brice won't send us across that field. He's too smart. He'd be wastin' half his militia, if he did."

However, before Martin finished speaking, he heard the shouted command, "Form battle lines!" That shout made his blood run cold.

While the New Bern Militia had never trained together, Captain Brice and their officers had at least explained a battle line formation to them, and clearly the Virginia frontiersmen knew the formation. In the set piece battles of those days, men often had to shift from a marching formation involving long lines with two men walking side by side, to a formation more conducive to fighting. Men would shift from marching in that familiar two by two formation, with two men turning into a line moving to the right, and the next two turning left. Thus a line of men would be formed, and at a shouted command those lines of men would turn 90° to face the enemy as one armed battle line. From that formation every man in line had a clear shot toward the enemy and could charge, or retreat as necessary. Thus did Martin and Johannes remain side by side in the battle line.

After their turn, while he marched just behind Martin, one of the frontiersmen, Cooper John Mosely, spat on his thumb and put the precious moisture carefully on the end sight of his rifle. "Well, I recon' Hyde wants those rebels out of that house. Cary is about to find out Hyde means business." Cooper John finished his clean up of his rifle sights, and scratched his right calf, while verbally offering up the lament of every fighting man for the last five thousand years. "Damn bugs!" He swatted his leg, and scratched again. "Chiggers. How in hell can they get on me every month of every damn year?" In addition to picking up the language of the rough Virginians, Johannes and Martin had listened to Cooper John and his companions from Virginia and the Albemarle and had acquired a few choice curses!

Captain Carmichael, one of the Albemarle leaders, was riding beside his men in the changing formation and heard that irrelevant discussion of lice. He decided he needed to stop that talk before it degenerated further. "Alright, men. Keep it down for now. We'll get the order to move forward, and I want to see the battle line moving forward together. Hold fire until it can do some good. Don't shoot before you see anything to shoot at!"

Captain Carmichael had directed that last comment toward a 14-year-old lad near Martin who was named Tooty Cash. His nickname, Tooty, was memorable, and Martin couldn't even remember his real first name. Cash had claimed to be 17 just last week when the militia was called up, but it was clear that he was much younger than Martin. He wasn't even shavin' yet. At that precise moment, Tooty looked like he was about ready to pee on himself and he probably would before he got across that field—if he got across that field at all. Martin was frightened, as were many men on that field, but Tooty was truly and absolutely terrified.

As Martin contemplated the fear he saw around him, his own fear set in. It is a fear that only battle tested men can know. That fear is palpable, heavy; it is a physical thing at times like those. Martin thought to himself, fear can get into your guts and make the most experienced soldier cry like a newborn babe. In the last few miles of the march, on that cool spring morning, Martin had heard some of the frontiersmen from Virginia speak of this fear. Many of those men were only one or two years older than Martin, but they were frontiersmen and were many years wiser. They had fought Indians and trained for months with either the Virginia Militia or the militia of the Albemarle.

In contrast, Martin knew that he, Johannes and most of the men from New Bern were not yet tested. Even their leaders had only limited experience fighting Indians and had certainly never faced a force armed with cannon before. Again, this caused Martin a moment of pause, as it would any man.

In an instant, Martin heard the cannon fire with a thunder louder than he could imagine, and a cannon ball careened towards his group of militia. Seemingly without effort, that solid shot decapitated a man only five men down the line from Martin, and his brains sprayed far enough to reach Martin's own face and arms. Thus, Martin was covered in blood from the first seconds of the battle.

Many men would have panicked at that moment. Even men hardened by previous battles can lose control of themselves when the brains and guts of their comrades are sprayed on their own faces and bodies, but for some reason, Martin did not. He wiped some loose particles of meat from his face, and looked back toward the battle, much to the bewildered astonishment of those beside him.

Captain Brice took position just behind the battle line, and dismounted. He stood for a moment and withdrew his single shot pistol. With his saber in his other hand he yelled, "Hold ranks! Battle line, hold position!"

He glanced toward the decapitated body and in only a second or so, though it certainly had to have been longer, the word came to advance. Martin checked his powder in the flash pan and, along with the rest of the men in the battle line, he began to move forward.

As the men in the barn reloaded the first cannon, doors flew open on the pack house, the spring house and several other buildings, each revealing a loaded cannon aimed at the New Bern Militia. Seeing the devastation about to envelop his men, Brice did the only thing he could do. At the top of his voice he shouted, "Charge!"

By ordering a charge toward the guns, he hoped that many of the men could get below the arch of the cannon fire quickly, and changing positions is almost always a wise course of action in battle. As the militia groups from New Bern and the Albemarle charged across the field, Martin could feel the battle in his very bones. They ran into the open field toward the plantation house that bristled with rifle muskets, and the now-obvious cannon. At some point, Martin noticed a door swing open on the distant barn, and still another cannon appeared. All of a sudden, almost unexpectedly, all of the big enemy guns went off and Martin saw at least two other cannons firing. In that instant when the reality of this battle hit him, he believed he was a dead man, but like so many men throughout history Martin and the others in the charging battle line seemed to turn into automatons—racing toward the battle, shouting, running, charging, firing, reloading, all without thinking.

Those who do not know battle can only imagine the horror of an artillery barrage, but when one is under fire, it is quite personal, terrifying, and deadly. It is like an infinitely loud thunder that rolls through the air, louder than anyone could ever imagine, louder than anyone could possibly believe. The noise of the big guns consumed Martin, and the horrid sound sucked the breath out of him. He felt the vibrations of the cannon in his heart, his lungs, his balls, and his ribcage. He and the others began to run, and he realized then that he was screaming at the top of his lungs, just to see if he was still alive, and able to scream, or able to hear himself scream. His musket fired seemingly by itself, and then he was reloading while he was running toward the cannons to get below their angle of fire. The line of rifles from his battle line sounded like massive, sweet and noisy friends, sounding in his body, and then the enemy guns answered. The noise was only a small part of the sensation because he soon felt the ground around him shake, as he flew through the air. He tasted dirt in his mouth, then blood, all the while he hoped that it wasn't his own, but he knew that it might be. He found himself laying face down in the dirt, when he was supposed to be running, and he saw Johannes run past. So he got up with dirt on his lips and cheeks, and guns firing all around him, and he ran some more and screamed some more, and then jumped into another depression in the ground.

Martin did not know how many times he reloaded his weapon in that shallow depression in the ground, and he did not realize that he had bit his own lips all the way through, several times. He was merely trying to survive. He did note that Johannes was lying at his side, and like Martin, he still loaded his musket and fired. Martin's mind registered that it was his own blood he tasted. It tasted the same as if he'd lost a tooth, and then he realized that he had lost a tooth. A musket ball had sideswiped him, taking only his front two bottom teeth.

Then, Martin was up and running again, because he'd heard Captain Brice shout, "Move forward," and because everyone else was or because he'd be scared to be the only one not running forward. Men dodged from one cannon hole to another in the field, or tried to hide in shallow cornrows, as they loaded their muskets to fire. Some of the Germans remained standing as they'd been ordered to do, but no shouted orders could make the Albemarle Militiamen stand and fight when every ounce of their being demanded that they find cover, any type of cover, from which to shoot. Those rugged frontiersmen knew "Indian fighting" which involved seeking concealment in battle, and they ignored the proper European field formations. The Germans soon adapted the same idea; seek cover, and then shoot. They quickly decided that this idea would help them live a bit longer.

But staying stationary for too long in any battle is a mistake, so Martin and the others were soon up and running again. Another cannon shot whizzed past, then another, until the ground shook all around. Then somebody's head popped open like a ripe melon, dropped on the ground right next to Martin, the brains and the blood covering his face again. Another man was hit by the solid cannon shot and his chest disappeared while he was still screaming. It's hard to look at the expression of disbelief on a man's face when his body has been blown apart, and he breaths his last, but Martin and Johannes saw that gristly event several times that day during the ninety minute battle. Those dead men didn't even realize they were dying, at least for a brief moment, and they always looked surprised somehow.

Once, about sixty minutes into the fight, Martin saw a cannon ball take a man's leg off in the next company over, and the man kept screaming and running on his good leg, one step, then a hop of sorts, then another hop, until he fell over. Then he looked down and realized why he'd fallen. He looked directly at the stump below his knee, and then, for no reason other than random chance, he looked directly into Martin's face. He bled to death in just a minute or so, with only one leg left.

Just then, Martin looked to his left and saw one of the most horrible sights on any battlefield; a musket ball striking an already dead body. The body was really only a torso; the head and one arm had already been blown away by the cannon, but the musket ball hit the body nonetheless. That time the shot brought movement and the torso seemed to jump a little with the impact. The stomach and the guts were ripped open uselessly. The sight of a lead musket-ball tearing into flesh was bad enough, but tearing dead, gray, yielding flesh was unimaginably horrid. Martin knew he never wanted to see it again, so he just keep screaming and running, running into the cannon fire toward the barn and the buildings.

Then he felt himself lifted up, and he tasted the dirt again. The very dirt that was clinging to him seemed to reach out for his heart and soul. He felt that sick, despised feeling every soldier knows—the sense that death can't be worse than this. He felt his stomach turn and he lost his breakfast in that dirt, then, he heard the shouted command of Captain Carmichael. "Let's move on up, you bastards! We're dead if we stay here!" He was up and running again, with Johannes by his side, still firing.

Then the real hell began. While the enemy cannon had been loaded with solid shot initially, soon enough the enemy guns opened up with the newly developed explosive shot. At that point in history, when walls need to be breached, or buildings destroyed, or enemy guns silenced, the loaders behind the cannon loaded solid shot, and that was what most of the early fire had been in this battle. That shot could take out fifteen men in a battle line if it hit the line at the correct angle, and it certainly killed anyone it hit directly.

However, when explosive shells were used, they destroyed anything within a certain radius, and thus decimated whole sections of the battle line without mercy. This weapon sent men and body parts flying through the air. When a line of men advanced on a fortified position, at this period in history, and explosive shot was available, it was loaded forthwith. With one blast, hundreds of men could be wiped out. Explosive shot was not terribly effective in the early 1700s against fortifications or earthworks—it did not have the explosive power of later, similar explosion shot—but it was an excellent antipersonnel weapon. In 1711, explosive shot was exclusively a man-killer.

Martin was loading his musket, while lying in yet another depression in the ground, and perhaps by that stroke of luck, he had time to notice that all five of the enemy cannon seemed to be loading at the same time. In an instant he understood what was about to happen, a massed cannon shot from all five enemy guns, though of course, he didn't then realize it was a preplanned firing of the explosive shot. Still, he saw the danger of five cannon firing at once, so he shouted at the top of his lungs, "New Bern Militia, DOWN!" Almost sixty members of the New Bern Militia heard that shout and thought it was an order, so they hit the dirt, finding what cover they could in the cornrows. Martin thus saved scores of lives with that single shout, just by keeping his head in battle, and thinking about what his enemy might be up to!

Five cannons each loaded with explosive shot thundered together toward Martin and the other men in the field. The effect was devastating.

Sometimes battles hinge on a single occurrence and that thundering, fateful shot, was such a time. The New Bern Militia took causalities of course, but the Albemarle Militia was decimated. They were on the other side of the advance and many had not heard Martin's warning shout. The five enemy guns all fired explosive shot and all struck home hitting the exact center of the militia formation out in the open. It left Hyde's combined militia immobile in the field. Forty-four men went down in that devastating blast and most were men of the Albemarle. Martin and Johannes were both quite lucky that they had jumped in a shallow ditch when that blast occurred. Martin, with blood on his face, had looked sideways from the ditch just in time to see many of the Albemarle men fall.

Tooty Cash died in the same blast. Martin watched him fall, only twenty feet away. Tooty had been at war for exactly seventy-five minutes, and because of his fear, he had loaded his musket repeatedly, but had neglected to fire it. He had never, not even once, shot his musket at the enemy. After the battle Cary's men would find a dead boy with a musket loaded with six different balls and six different loads of powder. Had it been fired, it would have blown Tooty's head apart.

By then the New Bern men were completely in it, and every man was running and screaming. These new colonists were running forward as one and firing their muskets at anything that moved. With no plan at all, other than to close with the enemy, getting close enough that Cary's men wouldn't fire their cannon again, these militiamen moved forward in the hope that they could overrun the enemy. They advanced in mass into more firepower than any of them had ever seen before. They were close enough now that they had some targets, so they fired at the men behind the windows in the plantation house or in the spring house. Everyone was firing, and soon almost all of the militia had found shelter behind tree stumps at the edge of the large field, or in a furrow of the freshly plowed earth. Men, who had never seen battle before, now tried to make themselves invisible in a four inch depression in the ground while they loaded and fired.

Martin had loaded and fired twice, while lying in a furrow that ran, unfortunately, directly toward the plantation house and for that reason, his particular ditch gave no cover from that direction. Only the dense smoke that characterized every battle in this period provided him any cover at all; for by this point in the battle, he could barely see a hundred feet in front of him, the smoke was so thick. Smokeless gunpowder was in the distant future, and men in the 1700s learned that the dense smoke of a battlefield, coupled with perfect

# Battle of Daniel's Plantation

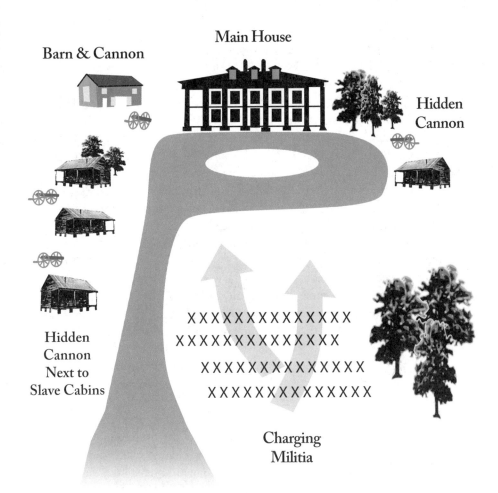

Barn & Cannon

Main House

Hidden Cannon

Hidden Cannon Next to Slave Cabins

X X X X X X X X X X X X X X
X X X X X X X X X X X X X
X X X X X X X X X X X X X
X X X X X X X X X X X X X

Charging Militia

stillness, could at times, be their only hiding place and thus their only hope of survival.

While Captain Brice was nowhere to be seen, Captain Carmichael still felt the burden of command. He didn't bring his militia unit to this field to lie in the dirt, and his only real chance to live through this was to keep moving and overrun the damn rebels in the buildings. After he loaded a fifth time, he shouted to his unit, "Let's move' um on out boys. We ain't doing much good here!" He was wounded within only a few seconds and both Johannes and Martin watched as he fell to the ground.

At just that moment, however, the enemy cannon stopped shooting, and Martin thought, "What is goin' on, now?" He reflected only a moment as he saw the brigade to his right use the pause in enemy cannon fire to advance a bit. When they moved, Martin realized in a flash what was about to happen, in spite of his total lack of experience in war. He shouted, "They're coming!"

He didn't realize he'd shouted it, since his eardrum had been damaged at that point, and almost every man on the battle line was partially deafened by the cannon. Still, Martin was certain that the only reason for the enemy to stop their cannon fire was to advance their own line. The enemy clearly believed they had wounded enough of the militia that they could charge and finish them off! Thus, with no authority at all, Martin knew what needed to be done. He shouted to Johannes and the men around him. "They are coming, so load now. Have your knives out and be ready to fight!"

Had one asked Martin at that moment, he would have sworn that he meant that suggestion only for Johannes, but in battle there is so much terror that every man on that field desperately sought out any strength, courage, or good advice that they could find. Martin's shouted command carried the weight of authority, and at the ripe age of seventeen, he alone was now effectively in command of the New Bern Militia, and every man within earshot knew it, even if Martin didn't!

He began to reload and made sure his hunting knife was still on his hip. Only a few of his men, those nearest, could hear him in the lull of the cannon fire, but they began to reload too, and others watching began to do the same.

Sure enough, Cary's men soon materialized out of the smoke and haze that hung low over the deadly ground. At first they looked like so many ghosts, only vaguely present in the drifting smoke. With little wind, the smoke tended to hang around longer than usual, and every man on that field by this point in the battle, hated the smell of the gunpowder. Still, here they came, at a trot, and as Martin and the other militia spotted targets, they began a withering musket fire that stopped Cary's men cold. One or two of Cary's followers made it as far as the militia battle line while the New Bern men were busy reloading. One even jumped into the same cornrow that Martin was in. As he brought his musket barrel toward Martin, however, a musket went off right by Martin's ear. Johannes had fired his weapon over Martin's shoulder, and both heard the sickening sound of the ball tearing flesh from the chest of the man ten feet away.

Martin, realizing what had happened, looked into the eyes of his enemy, which were even then fluttering in death. The man fell toward Martin, the killing wound, a second wound, having come from the knife stuck deep in his back by Gideon, Captain Brice's black slave, who had landed in the other end of the row. The dead man fell away, brushing Martin's arm, just as another musket nearby exploded. Martin looked into Gideon's face, as their eyes locked on each other for only a moment. Martin nodded his thanks. Then both began to reload their muskets, having never said a word.

Then, a shouted command, "Militia retreat to the wood line!" Col. Brice's voice cut through the sounds of the battle. The New Bern Militia men scrambled up and helping their wounded comrades began an organized retreat, having been stopped cold by a much smaller, but better armed and entrenched force. Martin, without realizing it, took up the call. "New Bern Militia, retreat to the wood line. Take your wounded with you!" He believed that he had merely repeated the command so others would hear, and he did not at that time realize that such was the prerogative only of officers on the battlefields of those days. Once again, for a third time in just under fifteen minutes, he had taken command of a battle line in the field without realizing it or intending to do so.

As Martin looked around, while escaping the hell of that cornfield he realized that the New Bern Militiamen weren't doing too badly. Some were left dead or dying in the field, but Martin could see that most seemed to be moving back toward the tree line, and mercifully, the enemy didn't seem to be firing much anymore. Martin passed a young black slave who was hobbling toward the tree line holding his hand over a wound in his upper thigh, so Martin grabbed his other arm, placed it around his own shoulder and helped the man to the woods. The enemy couldn't see the New Bern Militia at that point with their line of sight blocked by the dense smoke and within only a minute or two the firing stopped altogether.

"Thank ye, suh!" the slave said, as they hobbled together toward the trees.

Martin was not used to begin called Sir, so he merely said, "I'm Martin Bender."

"I'm Dunker Tim, and I'm sur' nuf' thankful for your help!" Just as they reached the tree line, Martin laid the slave beside a tree with several other wounded men, and went looking for Johannes.

"Thank ye a 'gin, Suh!" The slave shouted.

As they reassembled in their units and prepared to leave the battlefield, men all around began to look at Martin in a different way, including even Johannes.

Martin was known by every member of the New Bern Militia as a hunter, a good shot, and a frontiersman—still, something had changed on that field. While Martin had entered that battle as a rather large 17-year-old boy, he'd left that battlefield as an experienced field commander in the New Bern Militia, without really intending to! All present realized that he had that most elusive of command qualities, he could keep his reason when under fire, and every militiaman who fought near him that day had witnessed that interesting and rare phenomenon more than once. Even then, Martin Bender was a commander, because from the age of 17 on, he never once refused to make a tough decision, and that quality would make him a man of substance for his entire life.

Of course, nothing was said on that day, but all present knew that Martin was a leader, including surprisingly enough, Martin himself. Within only a year, his fellows would defer to his judgment when another battle came, and they would do so willingly, since they had seen the measure of this young man under fire. They would, and did entrust their lives into his care.

However, the unfortunate truth is that this battle accomplished absolutely nothing. While over sixty men died between the two sides, Cary still had his armed men at Daniel's Plantation, and more local supporters in the Bath area rallied to his side after that battle. Also, the New Bern and Albemarle Militias under Hyde had suffered the loss of thirty-two men and many more wounded. Out of one hundred and fifty eight militiamen, Hyde now commanded only sixty-two effectives as he marched back towards the city of Bath.

While the town itself was filled with Cary sympathizers, it was for lack of a real alternative, serving as the capital of the North Carolina Colony. Hyde did have some supporters in the area, so Hyde would remain in Bath with his militia for a fortnight, while the small army collectively licked its wounds.

### *A Pirate Comes Calling*

One interesting occurrence did take place during that four day respite in Bath, an occurrence that Martin would remember his entire life. One morning, just at dawn, a small mizzenmast ship hove to in the wake of the point on Old Town Creek, just beside the Bath docks, and a large brightly dressed man disembarked. He was extremely tall for that time, standing over six feet four inches, and carrying an amazing two hundred and forty pounds of solid frame, he was essentially a giant in that age. As two of his seamen rowed him ashore, his size became obvious, but even more striking was hair. He had a full head of shoulder length hair that was raisin black, and with that he sported a full growth beard of the same color.

In Bath he was known as Edward Teach and was considered a Captain of an armed merchant vessel. He had recently married a young woman of sixteen years, Mary Ormond, the daughter of a local farmer. No children ever came from the marriage, but in that town Mr. Teach was considered respectable, since he maintained a nice house, and supported his wife fairly well. He was also known to be an acquaintance of Governor Hyde himself. However, even then the world knew this massive character as Blackbeard—perhaps the most notorious pirate in the world during those years, a time that is now known as "the Golden Age of Piracy."

Historians can only speculate on how this brigand became a "respectable man of commerce" in this small backwater community of Bath, but respectable he was, at least in this one location. Teach paid his taxes respectfully to the governor's appointed minions at the customs house, and even attended the Anglican Church when he was in port along with his wife. It seems almost miraculous today, and we can only wonder how he did it. How did a man who was literally hunted by the British Navy—the most powerful armed force in the world at that time—not to mention the French Royal Fleet, the Netherlands, and every single Spanish galley throughout the seven seas—how did he live a simple quiet life here in Bath?

Part of the answer is simple—the same accursed sounds and shallow inland waters that kept this colony as a backwater for so many years, sheltered hundreds of pirates. Blackbeard's ships, and indeed most pirate vessels, were most often smaller coastal freighters with a draft of five to eight feet, so he could navigate the channels in these rivers and sounds all along the North Carolina coast. Also, Bath itself was small enough so that no one dared challenge Teach when he came to port. Those citizens figured that they had better leave this rude, cruel man to his own, and each time he visited, there were many who hoped that he would depart the waters soon, which he usually did.

However, one of the frequently overlooked aspects of his pirate career is his relationship with Governor Hyde, and later with Governor Eden. Blackbeard had met Hyde when he was visiting in Jamaica previously. It was rumored, even as early as 1711, that Hyde sheltered Teach's criminal activity, and for that service Hyde was reported to receive a cut of the spoils. In fact, many merchants noticed that Hyde seemed to never have his own cargoes confiscated by Blackbeard or other pirates, whereas most plantation owners, such as Captain Brice, suffered some losses each year to pirates in the sounds and coastal waters of the Carolina Colony.

As he landed on this morning, Teach immediately inquired as to the governor's health, and when he found that Hyde had survived the battle and was still the titular governor, he paid his respects to the governor himself. Martin and Johannes happened to hold guard duty that particular morning just outside the house in which Governor Hyde reposed, so they both got a good look at this gigantic man when he came to call. They of course knew the rumors about Teach, since they, like the citizens of Bath, lived in a seaport town and no rumor spreads in a seaport town like rumors of piracy. Still, the governor's secretary, Mr. Tobias Knight, greeted the brigand with a calm, welcoming smile and soon ushered Teach directly in to see Governor Hyde. Rumors of the time also suggested that Mr. Knight received a cut of the pirate booty, but nothing was ever proved.

Shortly thereafter, they were relieved of their guard duty and did not see when Teach departed, but they did note two days later when Blackbeard's ship raised anchor and departed for the open sea. Apparently, Mr. Teach had enjoyed his wife only briefly on this visit and the call of the seven seas was demanding. In only a few weeks, this interesting and rather unusual relationship between Governor Hyde and the most notorious pirate sailing the seven seas was to have an impact in the Cary rebellion, but that was not apparent during that particular visit.

### Governor Cary and The Carolina Navy!

In spite of the pitched battle at the Daniel's Plantation, the Cary Rebellion was far from over. Cary, emboldened by the failure of Hyde's forces to capture him, had gathered more men and numerous cannon in only a few weeks. He decided to bring the battle directly to Hyde himself.

Meanwhile, Hyde was still trying to determine which course of action he should take against Cary, knowing that many more men were joining Cary's cause daily. He began to be concerned that the area immediately surrounding Bath was too strongly sympathetic to Cary, and he worried about being caught in a trap. For a few more days, he considered his options. Within only a week, however, Hyde led his remaining militia force, now all experienced fighters, down the river a bit toward the coast, where he encamped at one of the several plantations of another of his subordinates, Col. Thomas Pollock. The early colonists in that area were much more aligned with the Anglicans in the Virginia colony, and being camped nearer to the large Pamlico Sound meant improved escape options should the need arise. At the Pollock Plantation on the lower Pamlico, Hyde considered himself relatively safe.

However, in just over three weeks after the first battle, Cary had learned of Hyde's whereabouts and armed a small ship with six cannon. Further, he armed two other, smaller fishing vessels with two cannons each, and thus he had something never before seen on the sounds of the Carolinas, a multi-ship brown water Carolina Navy! Of course, anyone might have predicted by the lack of trails and roads in the colony at that time that the next battle of Cary's Rebellion was to be a sea and land battle. However, Hyde stupidly neglected this important point, and thus failed to choose a safe encampment area. In fact, every single building on the Pollock Plantation house lay within firing range of the small cannon that Cary and his rebellious henchmen had mounted on his ragtag navy vessels. With those three small ships and around a hundred men, Cary proposed to attack Hyde and the remaining militiamen at the Pollock Plantation. He first declared himself the rightful governor of the colony, presumably for the sake of posterity, and then on June 30, 1711, he began his attack.

As in the previous battle, the firing raged around the plantation house itself, its outbuildings, and the fields between the big house and the river. However, in this instance, Martin Bender, Johannes Simmons, and all of the other New Bern Militia, still fighting for Hyde beside the frontiersmen from the Albemarle, were inside the buildings and not approaching across the fields. As the cannon from Cary's navy fired upon the buildings, Martin noticed that they tended to poke small holes in the wood siding, but unless the splinters from that strike hit someone in the face, little damage was done.

By this point, Johannes had been placed in charge of a squad of militiamen who were in charge of guarding the barn. While many of the New Bern militiamen knew of Martin's bravery in the previous battle, and clearly Martin exercised influence over many of the men, he was still considered too young for formal command, so almost as an afterthought, Johannes was assigned to command a squad, with Martin as second in command. Thus, they jointly commanded twelve members of the New Bern Militia. The Albemarle Militia were all more experienced and would not stand for the "damn German" or "the boy" to be in command, so they fought under separate leaders elsewhere that day. In contrast, the men from New Bern had seen what both Johannes and Martin had done in the previous battle, and in their minds either was now worthy of command. Johannes was the oldest member of that group, and was awarded that honor.

Hyde's militia did have two cannon mounted in earthworks in the front of the plantation house, and as the battle began, those cannon returned fire on the Carolina Navy and Cary's followers. With Cary's cannon fire hitting all of the plantation buildings, the twelve members of the New Bern Militia that were in the barn with Johannes and Martin were under fire, but were not able to return fire since the Carolina Navy was well out of musket range. However, Cary and his commanders had transported over a hundred men in the various crafts and with no return fire from the buildings, they began to land the men on the plantation grounds.

In the big house, Captain Brice and Governor Hyde temporized, and could not determine what course of action would be appropriate, since they only had approximately seventy-five men to oppose over a hundred. As the cannonade continued from both sides they had almost reached a decision to remain in the plantation and earthworks and let the attackers come to them.

Neither Johannes nor Martin realized that of course, nor had either ever learned how command structure in a militia unit was supposed to work. To Martin in particular, it seemed reasonable to move forward to within musket range of the Carolina Navy and fire on the men who were just beginning to disembark on the shore. Throughout history it has always been easier to stop an invasion force on the shore than to let them disembark unmolested and then begin the battle. Martin seemed to understand that fact intuitively, so he turned to Johannes and said, "I think we should move forward to that group of trees and fire on them. It will slow them down and we will be concealed in the trees, while they unload at the dock. They will be exposed."

Johannes didn't even respond directly to Martin. He merely turned towards the others in the barn and said, "Let's move out." With no hesitation at all, the twelve stalwart Germans grabbed their muskets and slipped out the side door of the barn.

In the plantation house, the commanders still temporized, unable to reach a firm decision. When they saw men streaming from the barn, they immediately got angry. With limited manpower they felt loosing twelve militia members was a poor waste of their resources. Nevertheless, the men left the barn heading for the trees, apparently with the youngster Martin Bender in the lead and his stepfather, Johannes Simmons, just behind.

"Damn this independent militia! Damned these Germans! They run like rabbits when the battle begins!" Captain Brice shouted. "This rabble cannot be considered a fighting force!"

Hyde replied, rather dryly, "One can never have confidence in untested men." He paused for a moment. "Can we send a runner to recall them? Do we have any others in that barn?"

Colonel Pollock, unlike both Hyde and Brice, had some degree of military training, having attended a military academy for part of his education. He also had considerable experience fighting Indians throughout the Carolinas and Virginia and knew the value of cover during a battle. Finally, unlike the other commanders, he knew a good idea when he saw one! "Perhaps we should let them be for a moment. I don't think they are escaping to the woods. I think they have the idea of striking at Cary!"

Brice couldn't believe it! "What?" he shouted. "Who gave that order? I'll throttle the bugger, damn his hide!"

Colonel Pollock merely smiled to himself, realizing at that instant that the untrained Germans in the barn had a better conception of what needed to be done than either Hyde or Brice. "They are attacking. They are heading to the tree line, just there. See?" Pollock said. "Let's support them with the cannon. They seem to be setting up a skirmish line in the trees to bring fire on Cary's men at the docks."

Sure enough, Martin, Johannes, and most of the others had reached the tree line, and as soon as they took up their protected positions behind a stand of large oaks, with no orders whatsoever, they began to fire on the few men in Cary's band that had reached the shore. Of course, firing on the enemy almost always means that one draws the enemies' fire, so Cary's men were soon beginning to fire on Johannes, Martin, and their group of men up in the trees.

Once that firing actually began, Colonel Pollock decided he had had enough of the temporizing of Captain Brice and Governor Hyde. The battle had begun, and such indecisiveness must come to an end, so he recommended another decisive action. "Perhaps we should support those men at the tree line further. If we send another unit into those trees on the opposite side of the lawn, we can catch Cary's troops in crossfire, and hold him up for some time."

Pollock waited only a moment to see if he heard any objections. Hearing none, he issued orders. "Captain Carmichael, form a squad of twelve men with all haste, and double time march into those trees where you will immediately bring fire on the disembarking troops."

Carmichael, still favoring a slight wound from the previous battle, responded immediately. "Yes, Sir." He then called the names of twelve men whom he knew to be good shots. He wanted men who had had men in their sights before, and without any consideration for political correctness, socioeconomic status, or early race relations, he managed to include five slaves among the twelve that he took into the tree line, including two men belonging to Captain Brice—Gideon and Dunker Tim. He knew these men could shoot and on this day that is what mattered. Carmichael at that moment cared not one whit about the fact that they were chattel.

Martin and his group were now drawing heavy fire from the troops on the lawn, but like many European armies, those troops under Cary preferred to fight in a standard battle line. Their commanders had received training to indicate that such was the correct battle field formation, and so they lined their men up in the battle line on the lawn just beside the dock, making themselves highly exposed targets for Martin and the other Germans in the trees. For the New Bern Militia, now somewhat experienced with their muskets, it seemed they could not miss! Cary's men were still disembarking, and while most of those Germans were engaged with Cary's battle line, Martin aimed at the men who were just climbing over the sides of the boats. When those men fell wounded into the water, or sometimes even into the boat itself, they created even more confusion for the enemy, slowing down the unloading process even more. Martin thought he was doing more for his side by continuing to shoot at those targets, and he was wise in that decision. One of his missed shots even hit the upright mast just behind the head of Governor Cary! It did no real damage, other than to terrify the former governor.

Within only a minute or so, Martin became aware that another group of militia was firing at Cary's ships from the opposite tree line across the lawn, creating even more hell for Cary's supporters. He recognized Captain Carmichael across the way and waved to him rather stupidly, it would seem, in the midst of the battle. Strangely enough, Carmichael waved back, and then went on with his business.

While Cary's men outnumbered those men beside Martin, the men who were still in the ships could not enter the battle without exposing themselves to fire. Still, the battle odds did seem to be swinging towards Cary's men, as he now had over fifty effectives unloaded and formed into two battle lines, one facing Martin and the other facing Carmichael and his men in the opposite woods.

At that moment the battle could have turned either way, but for two fortuitous events, both resulting from strange strokes of luck. Often history does change on such seemingly unrelated events, and this was to be one of those lucky days for Hyde and his outnumbered force. These two unexpected factors would make him the undisputed governor of the Carolina Colony, and thus change history forever.

First, a lucky shot from one of Hyde's cannon near the plantation house took out the main mast of Cary's largest ship. With that mast gone, the ship could still maneuver but would be very slow in the water, and relatively ineffective as a warship. However, that, coupled with the next, totally unexpected event, changed history.

At that exact moment, with cannon firing and muskets cracking all along the shore, a lonely pirate returned to port, his ship slipping peacefully by, across the mouth of the river, just at the edge of the bay some eleven miles away. Near the Pollock Plantation dock, on one of the ships of the Carolina Navy, Cary's subordinate caught sight of the mizzen-mast vessel sailing past, across the wide bay. Grabbing his looking glass and extending it with great precision, he inspected the vessel carefully, seeking certainty in his conclusions before he pointed out the ship to Cary. Within less than a minute, he was certain: the ship belonged to the notorious Blackbeard!

Of course, all of Cary's men knew of Blackbeard's support for Hyde and believed the rumors that Blackbeard paid Hyde for protection. While they were willing to fight the pitifully outnumbered militia at the Pollock Plantation, none of the Cary supporters wanted to engage an armed ship, commanded by the legendary pirate, fighting beside his notorious, well trained, and deadly cannon

# Battle of Pollock Plantation

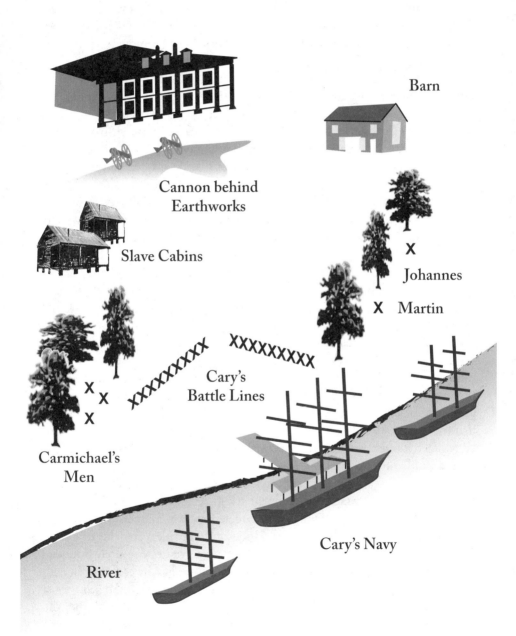

Barn

Cannon behind
Earthworks

Slave Cabins

X Johannes

X Martin

Cary's
Battle Lines

Carmichael's
Men

Cary's Navy

River

crews. While Cary's men were not afraid of a fight, they were not completely insane!

When the distant sail was pointed out to Cary, who was standing near the compass on the deck of the largest vessel, he took only a moment to realize the gravity of his situation. His mast was down. He could not maneuver his main fighting vessel, and his men onboard had never engaged in a sea battle before. His vessel held six cannon, whereas Blackbeard's ship was rumored to carry over twenty!

He clearly had no desire to fight Blackbeard, and he, like every man on that vessel, was certain that Blackbeard had appeared to support Hyde. Noting the devastation on shore, where his men were still receiving fire from two concealed positions, and looking again at the multitude of cannon ports on Blackbeard's ship in the distance, Cary ordered a general withdrawal.

History records that on that particular day, Blackbeard had no intention of fighting, and in fact most of his men were lying around the deck completely drunk. Not two hours previously, he'd ordered that rum be made available for most of the crew, since they were sailing upriver in what was essentially, for Blackbeard, protected waters. In that river, he knew he wouldn't have any opportunity for capturing prizes or any need for fighting. On that particular morning, he was merely a lonely sailor going home, and while he certainly heard the cannon across the river, he had neither the desire nor the intention of getting involved in that fight. Blackbeard, while manic, cruel, and some would say insane, was not an outright madman! He saw no gain in the political battles of that backwater colony, and he had already decided to merely sail on home to Bath to spend some time with his most recent wife (he was rumored to have twelve wives, in various ports, but no one ever counted, and certainly no one complained!). In this fashion, did the sweet, relatively innocent Mary Ormond play a minor role in history. Blackbeard chose to ignore the sounds of battle, though he did note that the several ships at the Pollock Plantation appeared to be hoisting sail and preparing to depart. Before they could make way, he sailed calmly on by, destined for Bath and home, where he docked three hours later.

Meanwhile, on shore, Johannes and his small contingent of men realized that Cary's followers were now heading back to their ships, and while they did not understand why, they found fewer targets for their muskets. One by one, they began to fall silent, as did the cannon on both sides. As Martin looked down the line of men beside him behind the trees, he saw one severely wounded with a gut shot. The others were reloading weapons, just in case, but he also noticed that each man save the wounded one was grinning as if he'd just won at a local turkey shoot! These men had fought together, and won, though they did not really understand why. Still they had fought and survived, and that is what mattered at that moment.

Martin clasped the man next to him in a bear hug, and as soon as the others saw that, a cheer went up, which was quickly joined by Carmichael's men across the lawn and the other men behind the earthworks at the plantation house. Martin and Johannes then lay their muskets against a tree and hugged each other, as Governor Hyde, Colonel Pollock, and Captain Brice calmly strolled across the front lawn, looking quite pristine, as if they were preparing to hunt pheasants or spend a day at the horse races. Captain Brice was the first to speak.

"I say, Sergeant Simmons. That was a bold maneuver leading your skirmish line into the trees to oppose the landing. Good decision, indeed!"

With that praise, Johannes began to temporize, not really knowing what to say, so he mumbled, "Martin's idea was it. It seemed right thing."

Brice had never seen any commander share credit for a good battle maneuver with a subordinate before, and while he knew that the boy was apprenticed to the barrel maker, he did not realize the extent of their relationship. Still, he felt a need to continue. "At any rate, jolly good show! It drove off those Cary bastards forthwith!"

Governor Hyde, looked on and said nothing, but his small smile was noticed by Colonel Pollock who was the only one on the field that day to correctly guess the reason for Cary's withdrawal. While everyone had seen the mast go down on the larger vessel of the Carolina Navy, only Pollock had taken note of the distant sail, and recognized that ship for what it was. It would be years before Thomas Pollock would disclose the presence of Blackbeard on the river that day, or the likely effect on Cary and his men. On that day, Pollock, like the rest of the men, was merely glad the fight was over, and that they had survived an attack by a larger force, armed to the teeth.

A few weeks later, Cary tried once more to raise a force to oppose Hyde, but when a contingent of His Majesty's Marines arrived from Virginia to show support for Governor Hyde, Cary's force dwindled to less than ten men. While battle with Hyde's militia was one thing, no one in all the Carolinas could be found who was willing to fire on the King's Men. Within a month, Cary was captured and shipped off to London in chains, just as Governor Hyde had promised. Cary's Rebellion had lasted less than two months, and Johannes and Martin had remained active in the New Bern Militia for that entire time.

As history goes, Cary's Rebellion was not much of a conflict, and most who live in that region of the Carolinas today do not even realize that such battles ever took place in those parts. In fact, a much larger and more devastating war was about to commence, but no one on the lawn of the Pollock Plantation knew of those future events on that day. Still, the repercussions of Cary's Rebellion were devastating, and soon became clear for every colonist in New Bern, Bath, and all of the Carolinas.

While the fighting had taken only two months, the plain fact is, there had been no effective government in the Carolina Colony for well over four years! Taxes had been collected in various locales, paid in grains or tobacco, but those stores were left to rot in the storehouses, since no one knew where to ship the grain or tobacco in order to pay the taxes. Further, when Hyde finally became the undisputed governor, all of the Cary appointees, every magistrate, every local judge, every local sheriff, immediately resigned in order to appear to be supporting Hyde, and not Cary's lost cause. Had he been smart, Hyde would have immediately re-appointed them and that is what most of those officials expected. However, Hyde had his point to prove, and stupidly refused to do so!

Any anarchist who has ever desired to have no government should consider the sad state of the North Carolina Colony in those years from 1708 through 1711. Literally nothing could get done; no new settlements recognized as townships, no new counties formed, even land deeds from that period became suspect, so no one could legally buy or sell land. Further, with the militia called out, the infant industries that had begun came to a screeching halt. Crops were left untended in the fields, and no one was cropping tobacco or harvesting pitch from the forests, since no one was available to do such harvesting.

Suffice it to say, the colony, including the only two towns that then existed in North Carolina, New Bern and Bath, were totally non-functional. In this dysfunctional political environment, all of the New Bern Militia followed the way of fighting men throughout history. After the battle ended, they left the plantation of Colonel Pollock and went home.

However, one more thing resulted from this battle. As they reflected and discussed the leadership skills of Colonel Pollock, Governor Hyde, Captain Brice, Captain Carmichael, and others, Colonel Thomas Pollock's leadership began to outshine all the rest. A mutual respect and admiration was formed and these men wished to honor their only truly effective senior officer in some way. While heading home, someone tossed out a possibility that was realized over a hundred years later.

A small village, just a couple of cabins really, had arisen eleven miles up the Trent River from New Bern. It was then called Trent Mill, for the grist mill built near the joining of Mill Creek and the Trent River at the direction of de Graffenreid. The grist mill serviced several German farms on the Trent River and up its tributary, Mill Creek. Someone suggested that they rename Trent Mill in honor of Colonel Thomas Pollock. It took over a hundred years for that to transpire, and during that time the village became known as Trent Bridge rather than Trent Mill. Still, in time the village did eventually assume a name that would honor Col. Thomas Pollock for all time. Today the beautiful, small village of Pollocksville still placidly sits along the lower Trent River, eleven miles south of New Bern. Ultimately, that village would be Martin Bender's home.

At that time, however, one got to Trent Mill using the only trail that then existed to the south, by crossing the Trent River at New Bern using a ferry, passing Brice's Plantation and then riding along a trail known as Island Creek for twelve miles. One then came to a smaller bridge and the newly built grist mill on Mill Creek. Crossing the small bridge where Mill Creek joined the Trent, one found oneself in Trent Mill. From there one could travel for many days and not see another white face until one arrived in the settlements in South Carolina. The large river port on the Cape Fear River, a port city known first as Brunswick, and later as Wilmington, would not exist for another twenty-five years.

## New Bern Men Come Home

After a five-day walk to the south from Pollock's Plantation the New Bern Militia arrived home. There was no victory march after Cary's Rebellion since Captain Brice had not returned with the men and he was the only local leader who would have ever considered organizing one. Rather, the men merely walked into town and disbursed to their homes, where they completely surprised most of their wives.

Johannes and Martin arrived at the cabin, which stood on the newly named South Front Street beside the cooper's shed, and a sorry looking pair they were! Grimy and smelly from hundreds of miles of foot travel, and Johannes was heavily bearded. They walked in at just after 1:30 in the afternoon on a Thursday. Margaret was not in the cabin, having gone to the mill on East Front Street to pick up a sack of meal. However, Katheryn was cooking at the fireplace in the cabin, and her reaction upon seeing Johannes and Martin shocked Johannes to his very core!

Upon seeing the two men just inside her cabin door, her first thought was that these filthy men were robbers, and she began to reach for the old shotgun kept by the fireplace, but her father's voice saying, "Hello Katheryn," arrested her completely. She paused for only a moment more and then she squealed with glee, shouting the phrases used by women worldwide, when their men return from a war. "You're home! Oh thank God! Thanks to the Lord Almighty, you're home safe and sound!" With that she flung herself across the small cabin and Johannes despaired momentarily of catching her when she jumped into his arms.

Then he received the shock of his life! She was not running to Johannes! She flung herself into a hug with Martin—that shocked both the young man and the father, and as Martin spun around bearing Katheryn's weight in his arms, Johannes was mortified! In that split second he understood, while he'd left a young girl here only two months previously, now a budding young woman had taken her place. And at that moment, that young woman was joyously, and with no apparent self-consciousness, hugging his apprentice!

Martin meanwhile, every bit as surprised as Johannes, merely hugged the girl saying, "There, there, we're fine Katheryn." He repeated himself twice. While this young man was extremely resourceful and a natural leader of men, Martin would always be rather dull when it came to dealing with women, and simply put, he could think of nothing else to say.

Before either he or Johannes explored this unexpected behavior further, Katheryn had disentangled herself from Martin and jumped into her father's arms as he had expected her to do previously. That of course, brought a smile to Johannes face, as it would any father, and that smile only increased as he saw Margaret rushing across the street and toward the cabin door.

Margaret did not see the men as yet, since the inside of the cabin was dark compared to the bright sunny day outside, but as Margaret crossed the small yard she screamed to Katheryn, "Have ye gone daft, girl? Why are ye screaming and shouting like a banshee?" But then she saw her husband, and in a flash she was screaming herself. Then she was in her husband's arms. No one ever answered her question.

Neither Martin nor Johannes returned to work that day, since they were both quite exhausted, and as soon as Margaret determined that state, she immediately ran both Christina and Katheryn outside with instructions to make not a sound as they worked in the garden—on pain of death should they disturb these men who needed a day's rest so badly.

Still, around the dinner table by the fireside that evening, Katheryn and Christina both asked their questions about the battles, and Bath, and what cannon sounded like, and what war was like, and how an armed ship looked, and what Blackbeard really looked like, and why the men smelled so badly when they arrived at home. Johannes and Margaret both noticed that Katheryn seemed particularly attentive whenever Martin spoke of his sense of the battles and when Martin described how he and Johannes and the others had chosen to head to the tree line on the Pollock plantation to oppose the landing of Governor Cary's henchmen. Katheryn lamented, "But you both could have been killed!" Then she looked unhappily at both Johannes and Martin, neither of whom knew what to say to that blatantly obvious assertion. For it is a certainty, proved repeatedly by history, that in any battle, men get killed.

Later that evening, still sitting by the large fireplace, the family again read the Bible. On this night, at the behest of Johannes, Katheryn read most of the text, and the sound of the Holy Scriptures soothed the rest of the family. Johannes suggested that most beautiful of passages that has always meant so much to men going to or returning home from battle.

*"Yea, though I walk through the valley of the shadow of death, I will fear no evil; for thou art with me; thy rod and thy staff, they comfort me."*

Johannes, as head of this Christian household, felt it his duty to instruct his family each time a Bible passage was read, though in truth, his wife Margaret was much better versed in the Bible. Still, Johannes wanted closure on this topic of battles, and he commented, "Men in battle have sought the comfort of those very words for thousands of years. Perhaps that should be our last word on this recent fight, and God willing, in the morning we can turn to our proper work again building this city. We can then leave the battles behind forever."

The family considered those words for a moment, sitting by the fire and all were glad that the recent troubles seemed to be over. Then, however, Martin spoke in disagreement with Johannes, which was indeed a rare occurrence in this household. "I think I'd like to read one more passage. It is a passage that has helped me many times in my life."

He then reached out for the Bible and Katheryn handed it to him, and smiled. That smile brightened his heart. He quickly turned to a passage even more beautiful and more treasured than the previous one, by men in a desperate fight. When he found the verses, he read calmly with the assurance of a young man who had been tested in battle and had passed the test.

*"In all of these things, we are more than conquerors, through him that loved us. For I am persuaded that neither death, nor life, nor angels, nor principalities, nor powers, nor things present, nor things to come, nor height, nor depth, nor any other creature in all creation, shall be able to separate us from the love of God, which is in Christ Jesus our Lord."*

Again, no one spoke for a moment or two. Then, Martin spoke up unexpectedly. "I think that in battle, men are in hell, but even in our hell, God is with us." That simple statement demonstrated a faith that would last Martin Bender a lifetime. He paused, for another moment, then using the honorific he had used the night before the fight he said, "I think Father is right. We should let our Lord's Holy Word be our final talk of war. In the morning we can turn to our work, again." Then he stood to prepare for bed and said, "I bid all of you a good night. Thank you all for your kindness to me. It will be good to sleep at our home again."

Everyone then said goodnight, but again Johannes noticed that Katheryn's "Goodnight, Martin," seemed to linger a bit in the air. He knew then with a certainty what he had suspected since her earlier greeting. Not only had Martin turned into a young man during the recent war; Katheryn had turned into a young woman. He was a bit surprised by that thought, as are parents the world over when their children grow up seemingly in an instant. Then he smiled a bit to himself, at the thought of those two perhaps together one day. He could imagine many other men in the new town that Katheryn might eventually marry. Surely many would seek her hand, and some had made known their intentions already to him, but as he reflected, he realized that he could find none any better that his apprentice, Martin Bender.

## *Life Begins Again*

The very next morning, Johannes and Martin were up bright and early, and together they returned to the cooper's shed and took inventory of the various supplies of wood and barrel hoops. After two months, they found very little to work with and no orders were waiting, so they determined that they should collect wood, as a first step and build the smaller, multi-purpose barrels that could be used for storage of almost anything. Surely these would sell in time, and their labors would bring them some cash. They returned to the cabin and found the axes they'd used to harvest the necessary wood for their building projects, and in the next weeks they felled trees, and shaped barrel staves and barrel hoops in the shed.

However, in the next few days they noted that not many customers were coming by to place orders. In fact, they'd not seen Captain Brice or Mr. Foscue or any of the several other large plantation owners at all since the recent troubles had ended. Upon reflection they realized that they had seen little evidence of any commerce at all in the small village of New Bern.

In spite of that fact, it was obvious that the little town was still growing. It now had two new streets running parallel to the Neuse River. De Graffenreid had imported a new group of settlers, Swiss immigrants, whom he settled on lots along the new streets. They were immediately put to work producing food in any and every way imaginable, such as harvesting fish from both the Trent and the Neuse Rivers or picking berries in the nearby woods. Those who knew how, hunted deer near the town, though with over two hundred white settlers now in the town (no one bothered to count the slaves, which were a growing population even in those early years), the hunters had to travel much further to find any sizable game.

One group of men, led by one of the frontiersmen from Virginia, had hunted for over a month by traveling up the Neuse, and then overland. They had reached low mountains far to the west of New Bern and came home with strange tales of many Indian tribes, and rivers almost as large as the Neuse, and deer and bear aplenty. Martin knew that one day, he too would hunt in those distant strange lands in the colony and see the mountains of the Carolinas, but that was to be in the distant future.

As Martin and Johannes became increasingly concerned with the apparent lack of business in the colony, they talked together about what they should do. Johannes suggested that they talk with Captain Brice about business and seek his advice, but he was nowhere to be found. Martin then made the suggestion concerning the tavern. "Johannes, in the recent troubles, the rough, experienced men from the Albemarle went to taverns in almost every settlement to talk matters over. Perhaps we should go to Mallard's Tavern this evening, and find out why there seems to be so little business."

This was a rather radical suggestion for these two men to consider. While they had earned the right to be respected as fighters, and indeed Martin's hunting and woodland frontier skills improved with each weekly hunt, neither man drank and certainly neither frequented taverns at all, viewing them as somewhat sinful. These men preferred instead, peaceful, Bible filled nights at home. Still something had to be done, and the tavern seemed to be the place to get some ideas, or at least find out what others were doing.

To understand the import of this decision by these overtly religious Germans, one needs to understand the meaning of the tavern in frontier America. Throughout the colonial period, from the 1600s until well into the 1890s, taverns were scattered along each frontier trail at a distance of around twenty miles or so, roughly the distance a wagon, a mule, or a man could travel in a single day. Certainly taverns provided a meal and a warm bed, but taverns were much more than merely a place to rest for the night. Taverns in those times served the functions not only of hotel and diner, but of a hospital, a news establishment, a coffee shop, a convention center, a post office, a business center, a theater, and on occasion, a courthouse, all rolled into one. Any man traveling in colonial North Carolina in those decades was dependent upon the taverns along his route, and the taverns existed in virtually every settlement of any size. While only two towns existed at that time—the state government was so dysfunctional no new towns were established during those troubled years—every little crossroads settlement on every trail held a tavern.

The tavern at New Bern had been built within a year of the first cabin, though it was not constructed by the Germans, but rather by a settler from Virginia named Toby Mallard who was often well into his cups. Toby was never suspected to be overly inclined toward religion, but he ran a small, clean establishment, and he was known to be generally honest. He did quite well in those early days. The rough trail that provided customers for Mallard's Tavern reached south from the Virginia settlements through Bath and down to the Neuse River where one boarded a ferry for the river crossing into New Bern. Mallard's Tavern was next to that ferry dock on East Front Street in New Bern, and was in that fashion, the first building one came to when entering New Bern from that direction.

That trail and the Neuse River Ferry provided a steady stream of traffic for the tavern. Later that trail would come to be known as the "King's Highway." Still later the name would change again to Route 17, the Ocean Highway, but in 1711 it was merely known as the North Trail, since it was the only trail to the settlements in the North. No real trail existed which headed to the settlements in South Carolina, and all interactions with those plantations near Charleston, were by sea.

Many of the wandering souls along the North Trail, as well as many locals, stumbled into Mallard's Tavern in the evening. The travelers brought the latest news from Bath or Virginia. These travelers wanted nothing more than a dram of rum and a good, cheap meal. Some slept for a ha'penny by the large fire near the hearth on the floor of the tavern, but the more sophisticated or wealthier, paid a shilling or two for the privilege of sleeping on a real bed with several strangers in one of the upstairs rooms. In tavern bedrooms of those days, bed space was sold by the head and one never knew when a stranger might join one on the same mattress. Three or four men, who were total strangers to each other, often slept together in a double bed, though most taverns did make some effort to keep the men in one room and the women in another, unless of course, one wished to pay a bit extra for that privilege! Every tavern worthy of the name either included, or had immediate access to, a whorehouse, and Mallard's was certainly no exception.

In the new settlement of New Bern, on any evening of the week if you wanted excitement, a quick drink or just good conversation, Mallard's Tavern was the place to be. Only on court days up in Bath, in particular on "hangin' days," was any other tavern in the Carolinas livelier! At Mallard's, cock fights were held in the stable every weekend and the occasional bear baiting—pitting someone's hunting dogs against a raging bear, if one could be found—was sure to draw bettors from all across the area. Of course, few of the community leaders, and fewer still of the overly religious Germans, would grace such dubious festivities as those, but if one wanted a sense of what was happening in the community in the 1700s, one went to the tavern.

Further, in the 1700s and 1800s, all classes of folks came to the tavern. Local farmers like the Banks family, plantation owners like Captain Brice, or local businessmen just like Johannes Simmons, all would show up most evenings at the local tavern for a dram. Slaves hovered around the tavern, having accompanied their masters, and even these individuals gathered what news they could to share with other slaves, when the opportunity presented itself. If they had a coin or deerskin to spend, slaves became customers, who were allowed to sit in the back by their own tables as they enjoyed their rum. All of these, along with the rough river-men, frontier hunters, sailors from the docks, wagon drivers from the North

Trail, or the "soiled ladies" of the day (Mallard's prostitutes), showed up in the tavern, where the men would compare notes on the crops and the weather, gossip a bit, and listen to the day's news. Sometimes they would compare notes on world news, if anyone was lucky enough to have received a newspaper from any of the other colonies like Virginia, South Carolina, or Maryland. On occasion, they received news of the world elsewhere, from a seagoing sailor or ship's captain.

Thus, like the necessary houses (that is, the out-houses) of those times, the taverns welcomed all. These rough taverns were the great equalizers of the day. No matter how few teeth a man had, how bad he smelled, or how sour his breath, every man who could pay his tab was equally welcome at Mallard's Tavern and every other tavern in this frontier colony. While it is relatively easy today to jest at the pretenses of civilization manifested in these rough frontier taverns, we should humbly remind ourselves of a fact long noted by historians: In the humble taverns of that era began the great American dream of equality! For every free man had his place, every free man was received, and indeed every free man was respected as a man, at the frontier tavern. From that dream of classless equality, a great nation would later emerge.

## *An Evening in Mallard's Tavern*

One evening in early August of 1711, Johannes and Martin wandered into Mallard's Tavern and while each was not disposed to drink, their courage and their fighting skills were widely known by this point and widely respected. Thus, even though this was the first time at Mallard's Tavern for them both, they were greeted warmly by several other customers. Toby Mallard had heard of Martin and Johannes leadership in the fight at Pollock's Plantation, so he welcomed them loudly so his other customers could hear. "Glad I am to have men of such courage in my humble tavern!" He shouted loudly enough to be heard over a rather loud argument at the other end of the room. As yet, Mallard's didn't have a "bar" to speak of, so men sat around the fire, or huddled around the few tables. "Come here Johannes, and bring young Martin with ye. At this table, the first dram for our local heroes is free, if you agree to tell us all the story of how ye charged the tree line and drove off Cary and his bastards!"

Clearly, someone had embellished the story a bit, but both Martin and Johannes were happy to be welcomed, and they quickly headed over towards Toby's table. There they sat, and sipped a dram of rum, as they told their tale.

The business deal that would shake the foundations of the North Carolina Colony to the core took place at Mallard's Tavern, on that very evening, and the deal transpired because of a simple event that did not take place. On that particular evening, Archie Carmichael showed no promise, whatsoever, of getting drunk enough to fall into the fire.

Archie, short for Archibald, was a distant kinsman of Captain Carmichael from the Albemarle, but no one could ever determine how. He'd recently fought, like Martin and Johannes, with the New Bern Militia, but on this evening, like most, he leaned precipitously on the stacked rock wall next to the hearth at Mallard's Tavern. He was perched on a recently carved three legged stool with only the two back legs actually making contact with the rough wooden floor. As he slept off his drink, he snored loudly enough to be heard clear down to the flatboat docks on the river just over thirty yards away. There were several flatboats in from the Albemarle Sound, and one small sloop from Jamaica. There were usually at least a few river-men or sailors—a tough lot those guys—drinking their cares away on any particular evening in Mallard's Tavern, and they all watched old Archie snore, and looked forward to his anticipated fall. Some thought that Archie would fall into the fire sooner this evening since he'd begun drinking earlier than usual, but others thought he'd fall the other way, and thus upset the spittoon two feet away in that direction.

Archie himself had had a goodly portion of the homemade liquor made by Mallard. It was a famous corn whisky distilled right up-river at the Mallard farm. Archie never failed to sleep for several hours each evening after partaking of such fine local whisky as that. Every once in a while he'd entertain the entire tavern by falling into the fireplace, whereby he'd come alive again, and cuss as only a Carmichael could.

Now the Banks brothers, who had settled down river from New Bern, made their own brand of sour mash whisky. The liquor that sprang from the branches of that proud family tree would, by the turn of the century, make "Carolina Stump-Slung Whiskey" known far and wide in colonial times. Everyone knew that any of the Banks brothers cooked up a mean brew, but while their whisky was powerful, it was a bit too strong for Archie's taste. When Archie had a little coin in his pocket or a chicken, pig, or deerskin to trade, he drank the upscale whisky made by Mallard himself. So on this particular night, he treated himself to the finer brew, prior to getting drunk enough to fall asleep leaning against the wall by the fireplace on the south end of Mallard's Tavern.

Archie frequented the tavern for his evening drinks almost every night, and having a reputation for not holdin' his liquor well, his evenings were always entertaining to the local crowd. At various times, many of the local folks in these parts were known to take bets on when Archie would tumble over—the river-men bet on Archie every night, but then again, they'd bet on anything. Side bets were placed on whether he'd fall toward the front door or the other way, thus landing on the hearth or maybe even in the fire itself. Bets were often placed on the time of the fall, as well as the direction, and Archie catchin' fire, if he happened to fall that way, was an extra bonus.

Captain Brice once won an entire bottle of imported French wine from Toby Mallard himself, the owner/proprietor of this fine establishment, on just such a bet. On that memorable evening, Archie had leaned a bit before he woke up and thus he rolled squarely into the fire in the big floor level hearth, and caught his deerskin breeches on fire. He rolled on the floor until the fire was put out, with the entire tavern crowd laughing at him all the while, and with nothing but his breeches and pride damaged, he joined the laughter while his pants were still smoking. Still, later on, whenever he told that story, he cussed loud and long about that fall!

Now this particular Carmichael was like most of that scattered, "poor white trash" family from down in the South Carolina Colony, in that Archie could barely name his Mammy and his Pappy, and he wasn't real sure about the latter. He had no clue who his Granddaddy was, though he sometimes wondered. He'd been told by his Mammy that their great Granddaddy had fought the French in one of the innumerable wars of the 1600s, but he didn't know whether to believe that or not. He'd left South Carolina only a year ago, after noticing that his Pappy wasn't called Carmichael at all, but sure enough someone aware of his dubious family lineage had spilled the beans on his kin even way up here in this new town! Still, Archie had learned in his twenty-eight years, not to ask too many questions about the family lineage.

Archie was like many of the Scots in the colonies in that he was happy to hunt a bit, raise a decent crop of corn, beans, and maybe a bit of tobacco for sale down river. He was a poor man, owning no slaves, and only a few acres of tillable land, with a rough cabin on it along the Neuse River just outside of New Bern. Still, he had come to New Bern with his bride in tow. Further, he had a cow for milk, several goats, a hard working mule, and a few skinny pigs that he'd cut up when his missus needed bacon. He enjoyed his woman once or twice a week and she worked harder than the mule did! He hunted and tended his crops and looked forward to having a bit of corn whisky each evening at Mallard's Tavern. He neither wanted, nor expected, much more out of life, and he'd learned that most wonderful of lessons, that to be completely happy, one need only choose to want what one already has!

Top that healthy attitude off with a fine sense of humor, and he really didn't mind the bettin' on his anticipated evening tumble. Hell, he'd even placed a bet or two on himself! Such was the evening's entertainment in Mallard's Tavern in the early days of colonial New Bern.

There were several folks at the tables across from the hearth who lost interest in Archie when he snored loudly again, though that particular snore was only slightly less loud than the former effort. However, Archie had snored from a relatively stable position and showed no promise of an interesting tumble into the fire on this night, at least not yet. Talk at Mallard's Tavern soon turned to other things.

Able Ward, well into his cups, took another swig from his glass of rum as he turned away from Archie. He then slurped loudly, mostly to announce that he had something to say. "If you ask me, there's money to be made in slaves. Capture Tuscarora, or Coree, or Catawba and sell 'um in Virginia, I say. We'd do well to ship the lot of 'um out!"

At that point he burped rather loudly, possibly to emphasize his point. "There's gold to be made in those slaves, savages the lot of 'um! But gold to be made as sure as my pecker's a foot long! All we got to do is catch um!"

His friend, One-Eye Benny Sutton, was drinking with him in the tavern. One-Eye was a river-man who had lost his eye to the back swing of a large branch while hunting one day. He liked to claim, however, it was because he could see better with one eye than most men could with two! "Hush your fuss, you old coot. You ain't figured out how to catch 'um without gettin' your damn throat slit and neither have I! And if your pecker's a foot long, I'll be a caged whore waiting on a weekend." One-Eye had heard much the same idea from Able for damn near a week now, and he really didn't know what had set off Able's most recent get-rich-quick scheme. Still he couldn't miss an opportunity to poke some fun at his drunken friend.

Distracted from thoughts of slaves and gold, Able simply had to respond to the slight to his manhood. "Damn too is a foot long!"

At that point, One-Eye gave up entirely, not wishing to discuss the private parts of his friend further. Thus, he now tried the tactic of agreeing with him. "Yeah, I recon' so," he said. One-Eye had learned that this approach was the quickest way to get Able to shut up.

These rough gents would have never guessed it but their conversation was being listened to quite intensely by several other folks at Mallard's Tavern at that moment. Toby Mallard, the proprietor, was serving drinks to a table full of local farmers at the far end of the room, but he'd previously been talking to Captain Brice, a plantation owner that Toby knew always needed more slaves. Both Brice and Mallard were well known in these parts; each was well respected as a shrewd businessman.

When they heard the idea about rounding up the Tuscarora and selling them in Virginia, they both realized that the idea would provide them the cash to purchase black slaves in that colony to work in the new town of New Bern. They both realized that they could not capture the local Indians and work them on plantations in town. The desire to escape would lead to losses, runaways, or worse. However, catching the endless supply of Indians and selling them in another colony was possible. Indeed, it was already being done to some extent here as well as in both Virginia and South Carolina. One fact, little recognized by folks today, is that slavery did not begin with importation of black slaves. It began with enslavement of Native Americans, and in the North Carolina Colony that meant enslavement of the proud Tuscarora.

As Toby approached the table where Brice had been drinking alone, he voiced his thoughts. "Able may have an idea there, Captain Brice. I know you could use many more slaves, if the price was right, and I fancy I know a couple of rough son o'bitches, what could capture a wildcat if'n they tried!" With that, Toby Mallard looked over at Able Ward and One-Eye Benny. Toby was known for his colorful language, but not only was Captain Brice smiling, he was also listening to Toby. Meanwhile, Able spit his chew of tobacco in the general direction of the fire, missing Archie Carmichael by a full foot, and almost hitting the top of the spittoon.

Toby continued talking since Captain Brice seemed interested. "We'd want to get a few, say ten or twelve Tuscarora, but if we could store them at your plantation for just a couple o' days that should be enough time. Course, we'd want to send them on along right smart quick, and not store 'um here!" Again, Toby noted that Brice had not responded, but was still paying attention. "I don't think capture would be a problem, but we'd want 'um shipped out double quick, least wise their cousins might get ornery!"

Brice sipped his dram and looked thoughtfully at Mallard. Of course, true gentlemen never participated in the slave trade, but strangely enough in that century such refined objections to slavery related to the actual breeding, acquisition, shipment, or trading in human cargo and not to owning slaves themselves. Still, Brice was always willing to listen to a business proposition, and this one sounded as if it might have some merit. After a few more moments, Brice responded. "I say, Mallard. You do realize that we'd have no income from this venture until the stock is sold in Virginia. Also, as businessmen, we'd need to split the initial costs of capture, storage and shipping."

Seeing no objection from Mallard to that prospect, Brice continued. "You know old man, I do have a small sloop that can get the cargo into Virginia for sale rather quickly. I think that, if you can provide the cargo, I can certainly get it there and get a good price."

Toby nodded and grinned showing his remaining five teeth proudly. Brice paused for another moment, and then continued, "I think this might just work to our advantage. Yes indeed, I think, by God, we should try it!"

Thus, the broad outlines of the horrid deal were struck—a deal to capture the local Tuscarora and sell them as slaves in Virginia. This deal was one of the ugliest episodes in Carolina history. Slavery in any form is an anathema to the modern mind, but in this period, it was casually viewed as merely business, as shown by that unholy deal in Mallard's Tavern that night. Today, we cannot imagine viewing another human being in that fashion, literally believing that a human being has no soul, and thus is merely chattel. It is hard to even conceive of what slavery meant at that time, because the very mindset is so alien to our sensibilities today. It is far easier for the modern mind to vilify and dehumanize an enemy in battle in order to prepare oneself for killing. That is how human beings became "Japs" in World War II, "Gooks" in South Vietnam, or "Ragheads" in the more recent desert wars. But even in the depths of that dehumanization we still believed those human beings had a soul. Slavery, today, is a totally alien thing, but cruelty often breeds cruelty, and slavery bred, perhaps, the worst cruelty of all.

None are wholly innocent. Most Native American tribes kept slaves themselves—the Tuscarora included. Further, many free Blacks in the South owned slaves—either black or Tuscarora. However, in those manifestations of slavery, the slaves were most frequently of the same race as the slave owners, and no real racial prejudice undergirded the slavery. In the case of the Native Americans, slaves were most often captives from inner-tribal wars. Eventually many of those slaves became fully participating members of the new tribe. Those slaves were treated much better than in the later instances of inter-racial slavery.

Still, the enslavement of the Tuscarora in the early 1700s was particularly cruel in that white men had at first treated them with dignity, formed treaties with them, and purchased their land for the early settlements, New Bern being a primary example. To have some men like Lawson and de Graffenreid treaty with them as equals, while others like Able Ward and One-Eye Benny treated them as mere commodities in a business venture, was literally beyond the comprehension of the Tuscarora. War would ultimately follow, for no man in any culture will watch his women and children be stolen from him without putting up a fight. That war, when it erupted, would all but wipe out New Bern, and the North Carolina Colony.

Martin and Johannes got no real answers or ideas for increasing their business from their first visit to Mallard's Tavern, but they did both enjoy it. They quickly discovered that their initial fears about sinful temptations were unrealistic. They could take one dram if they wanted and merely say no to the allure of the soiled ladies, so there was no real danger to their souls there. Also, they both felt they knew more about what was happening in their city if they spent an evening or two at Mallard's Tavern each week. They built that into their routine, without upsetting too much the daily Bible readings each evening.

Of course, they, like everyone else, believed the recent troubles ended with the capture of Cary. The former governor had been shipped to London, and that was that! These two never envisioned an uprising by the savages, and they certainly never wanted to go to war again. However, history once again, was not to be so kind to them or the other settlers in this new city. The New Bern Militia would be at war in less than six months, and the town and the outlying settlements would pay dearly. Blood would soon flow freely along both of the twin rivers that cradled New Bern so comfortably in their watery arms.

On that first evening in Mallard's Tavern, however, none were aware of that terrible future. Instead, they were truly entertained around eight that evening, just as Martin and Johannes were getting up to leave. The betting had predicted it. Archie snored loudly one final time, rolled to his left a bit, and then with a quick turn fell directly into the fire. He came up both awake and with his buckskin breeches smoking and he cussed about that fall for almost a week!

# Chapter 2
# The Tuscarora Massacre
*Injun' Bashing In the Carolina Wilderness*

The Tuscarora War was the first and only Indian war that ever took place in North Carolina, and it should have never happened. Some people have alleged that the whites cheated the Tuscarora in trading or stole their furs outright. Others say it was a territorial matter with the settlers in the new city of New Bern taking more of the hunting grounds of the coastal tribes. Still others say the cause was slavery. As great philosophers have observed about many civilizations throughout history, the root of all of these potential causes of war is greed, and ultimately that was the curse of almost every early settlement on the North American Continent. New Bern was to be no exception to that rule.

Within a week of that August evening at Mallard's Tavern, both One-Eye Benny and Able Ward were headed up the Neuse, with more rope than the two had ever seen before. They were slavers, and they would need all the rope to tie up the slaves that they intended to capture from the Tuscarora. That captured stock would then be shipped to the plantations up in Virginia or the other colonies. The two slavers shipped out early on a Tuesday morning in the *Abraxas*, a twenty-five foot, open hulled sloop which Captain Brice had ironically named after an obscure Egyptian God, the God of both good and evil. These two took three other men with them on their first slaving venture up the Neuse.

Captain Brice had sent along one of his most trusted slaves, a large black man named Dunker Tim. No one could recall any reason for that name, but Dunker Tim it was, and he was at the helm of the *Abraxas*. Before parting, Captain Brice told One-Eye that Dunker Tim could be trusted with firearms and that he knew how to handle the small sloop well in the coastal waters. While none at that time would ever have admitted it openly, Captain Brice trusted Dunker Tim much more than either One-Eye or Able, the two white-trash crackers who his friend and partner Toby Mallard had placed in charge of this expedition.

The other two men on that cruise up the Neuse were new to the New Bern settlement. They were the type of rough, uncouth men that throughout history seem to end up moving from one seaport to another. New Bern was only a year old in August of 1711, but ships arrived regularly with cargoes from the Caribbean, Virginia, Charleston, Philadelphia, or even Europe and routinely disgorged the roughest, most vulgar men in the world. In short, New Bern was a colonial seaport village and consequently, it attracted more than its share of trash.

For that reason, the settlers of New Bern were wary of these men who roamed the seven seas. At that point, some twenty-eight families lived in the town, and there were only seventy-seven families in the whole of Bath Province—a territory reaching from twenty miles north of Bath down to the Cape Fear River. New faces were instantly recognized as such in that small community.

Boris Lefkin was a young man who had jumped ship in Charleston, South Carolina and made his way up the coast through the inland sounds in a flotilla of three coastal sloops, loaded with cloth, pins, iron axes, hinges, glass, and other higher end items for trading in the new settlement. Any such items that could reach the docks in New Bern demanded a stiff price in coin, when it was available, or deerskins which by then, had become the main currency in the town. At times, tobacco was also used as a medium of exchange. Lefkin had one doubloon that he'd kept sewn into his breeches since shipping the Spanish Main with the famous pirate, Calico Jack Rackham and his cutthroat band the previous year. He also had a twist of dark dried tobacco, and the tobacco was enough to purchase a willing woman at Mallard's Tavern for a thirty minute time slot. That was the early afternoon fee. It would increase, of course, as the evening approached. He even had some tobacco left over for a dram or two of the cheap local whiskey.

Lefkin had reached New Bern only the day before and was looking for something to do until his skipper picked up enough trade items to make the run back down to Charleston. Lefkin's name belied a Russian heritage, but he'd been a sailor for so long that he really didn't remember much about his first twelve years in Russia. He'd shipped out while still fairly young, with some rough men and the quality of his companions had not improved much over time. Still, he'd never been a slaver before. With that said he was big and mean and seemed to be able to handle himself well in a pinch. One-Eye looked him over at Mallard's and decided in less than a minute that he would do.

Thomas Pate was an Englishman who had shipped out of New Providence with various privateers for years. A privateer operating under a Letter of Marque from one king or another was merely an armed ship that was free to "privately" raid the shipping of enemy nations. When the wars ended and the warring nations made peace, the privateers were supposed to stop seizing ships on the high seas. Most didn't, of course, and from that point on they were merely called pirates. A new, robust, essentially ungoverned seaport town like New Bern was sure to attract more than its share of men like Lefkin and Pate, though the two had met for the first time at Mallard's Tavern in New Bern. Both Pate and Lefkin liked the general lay of the land.

For example, the very first evening right after these two met over a dram, the proprietor of that tavern introduced them to One-Eye Benny, who said he needed a few strong men for a sail upriver and hired them both on the spot. In only a few more minutes, the two men watched him hire another new man named Able Ward.

That bit of tavern "theater" was entirely for the benefit of the new men. Able Ward and One-Eye had been partners for years in various nefarious enterprises, and everyone in these parts knew it. Still, these two sailors were new in town so they didn't, and One-Eye thought that he'd better put a "plant" among the new guys. Therefore, as he'd explained earlier to Able, he'd pretend to hire Able in the tavern that very night. Then maybe these new men would confide in Able if they got any greedy ideas about turning the tables on One-Eye when they sailed up the Neuse. Convoluted to be sure, but One-Eye, Able, and even Toby Mallard correctly guessed that both Lefkin and Pate were pirates who would steal the last coin from their own mother if they could get away with it. In short the two new men were not to be trusted. Rough, uncouth, mean, strong, and dishonest, those two guys were exactly right for slavers.

Within two days the *Abraxas* was heading up Contentea Creek, a tributary of the upper Neuse. Sailing upriver can be long and tedious with the current against you all the way, but the broad, lazy Neuse was never known for strong currents, and Dunker Tim knew what the hell he was doing. When the sloop rounded a bend in the creek, about a mile or so out of the main channel of the Neuse, One-Eye noticed a smaller creek branching off to the left, and he knew in a flash that he'd found his base camp.

Now, both One-Eye and Able had a general notion about where King Hancock's town of Catechna was but neither had ever been there. They were sure it was further up Contentea Creek, which put them within walking distance of the Tuscarora town. To One-Eye and Able, the small creek looked to be as good o' location as any for a base camp. These two wanted to get close, but not too close, to Catechna, and then lay up along the outbound trail. They figured they could literally grab the Tuscarora right off the wilderness path.

In planning their strategy back at Mallard's over the last few days, they had determined that three or four men could lie in wait beside a well traveled trail and waylay the Tuscarora near one of their villages where the savages would not expect it. While Tuscarora had been captured and sold into slavery before, such captures were fairly rare, and most of that dirty business had taken place in the Albemarle, the northern counties of the North Carolina Colony, much closer to the Virginia settlements. Even then only one or two savages had been taken at a time, and there was always a question in the minds of the Tuscarora as to the fate of those who had "gone missing." Were they set upon by bear, killed by wolves, taken into slavery by the Catawba from the head of the Neuse, or had they been taken by the smelly-pales in Virginia?

Now One-Eye and Able proposed to go right to the hornet's nest and take a dozen or so strong warriors and a few strong young women for breeding stock, sort of like high volume slaving as it were. Further, if the first snatch and grab worked out well, One-Eye and Able Ward intended to do it again, what with a nearly endless supply of savages and each of 'um worth a fortune in deer skins right here under their nose.

To accomplish the capture of the savages, they set a base camp well away from the capture location, and there they left most of their supplies and their small sloop hidden well up the smaller creek. After only one night setting up the base camp, they traveled on foot for almost a day until they intersected the main trail into Catechna where they planned to trap some slaves.

Now the capture plan, what One-Eye called an "Injun Trap," was simplicity itself. Four men would hide just off the trail with two on each side of the trail about fifteen or twenty feet apart. Then they would wait for one or more Tuscarora to pass. Children were of little interest, and were allowed to pass by unmolested as were most women, or any group larger than three savages. However, when one, two, or three good prospects came along, one of the slavers, the one at the far end of the Injun Trap, would step into the trail, hum a tune and begin to dance a jig.

Any sailor in those days could hum a thousand tunes and dance a respectable jig or maybe even a hornpipe, music or no music. Both One-Eye Benny and Able Ward could cut quite a rug too. They figured that the antics of a man dancing in the trail in the middle of the wilderness would be enough to puzzle the savages for two or three critical seconds, and during that time the other men would spring the Injun trap by jumping into the trail behind the savages and clubbing them senseless with a three foot stick of hickory wood.

One-Eye called that part "Injun bashing," and it bore an amazing resemblance to modern baseball, but Babe Ruth had nothing on these foul slavers when it came to swinging a stout piece of hickory. In all fairness, it is easier to hit a human head that is perplexed by the antics of a crazy smelly-pale, and is therefore not moving, than it is to hit a baseball traveling along at ninety miles an hour. Still, the principle is the same, and in each instance, the savages went down like a sack of flour dropped into a wagon!

The slavers then tied them fourteen ways from Sunday, and hauled them back to base camp. By the end of the first day, they had five men and two women of child bearing age in the group. All of the slaves were bleeding from their head wounds, but that didn't matter much, since all they had to do was sit there calmly in their own muck for the next two days. They could grunt all they wanted, but the tight rope gags in their mouths prevented them from making too much noise. If they made noise for any period of time, One-Eye or one of the others would give them another whack with the hickory stick. Once in base camp, the slavers put even more ropes over them, and tied them to a large tree, upwind of the camp. They didn't even let the savages go to the bathroom, so within just twenty-four hours these savages stunk to high heaven, nestled tightly together there in their own urine and feces.

In just forty-eight hours nine savages had been collected, but one had not fared well after the Injun bashing. Lefkin had hit him pretty hard, and he bled out and died within an hour of the hickory beating. One-Eye and Able merely pulled him a mile or so off the trail and left him there to feed the bear and raccoons that evening. A full grown black bear can make the meat of a man's body disappear totally in just a couple of days, and a pack of wolves is even quicker. One-Eye and Able figured that nothing would ever be found of that poor savage and they were right.

The slavers needed one more good morning to capture several more savages. Their goal had always been twelve slaves in the first batch, delivered in reasonable condition to Captain Brice's Trent River dock. With a number of slaves already tied up at the base camp, one of the slavers had to stay there on guard, and this time it was Lefkin's turn. Thus, Pate, One-Eye, Able Ward and Dunker Tim made the march back to the main trail to catch two more savages.

On this morning, however, things didn't go as planned. The first savages down the trail were a group of fifteen painted warriors and they were clearly livid! Even if one didn't know savages, and both One-Eye and Able fancied that they did, one could have seen clearly that this batch was up to no good and were out seeking a fight. King Hancock and the others in the town had noticed that something was going on and that their kinsmen were going missing all the time, so they had sent a war party out to investigate. The slavers let that group run completely by, but it set their minds to working, and fairly soon they decided to get the hell back to base camp, and then get on back down the Neuse to New Bern.

They were lucky though, and managed to literally bump into two younger savages who were stalking a deer on the way back to their base camp. These two Tuscarora boys were between thirteen and fifteen and each would bring a good price, so One-Eye jumped into action. Now, One-Eye was savvy if nothing else, and when he saw this prime slave stock in the trail, he pretended to offer trade goods to them by placing his musket at their feet. No sooner had they looked down to examine it than Dunker Tim and Pate Injun bashed 'um good, and within ten minutes those two were hogtied and being hauled down the trail toward the base camp. Dunker Tim carried one and Pate carried the other.

This brought the total number of slaves to eleven, and with an irate war party rambling around the area and the Tuscarora catching on to what was happening, One-Eye figured that count was good enough. They loaded the sloop in fifteen minutes flat, and left for New Bern. With Dunker Tim again at the helm, they were out of the creek and under full sail in the main channel of the Neuse River within thirty minutes, and this time they were sailing along with the flow of the river.

Only thirty-six hours later they were at Brice's dock along the Trent River, having passed the docks of New Bern an hour before. By then, the slaves stunk even worse but Brice had Gideon and his other black slaves handle that problem in a rather straightforward manner. Without untying the savages the blacks strung them on a rope and dunked them, one at a time, in the Trent River until they smelled a bit less ripe. Then, the whole lot was untied one at a time, while one iron collar was fitted around their neck and another around their right ankle. Each collar was locked on and through the neck collar a chain was inserted that bound all of these eleven slaves together. They would travel all the way into the Virginia Colony wearing that same chain, five days more in the same open sloop they sailed in previously. On that day at Brice's dock however, they were placed in the lower level of the barn, and their legs were chained to the barn support posts. Finally, Captain Brice placed a guard in the barn to watch them during the night.

The very next morning, Dunker Tim, One-Eye, and Able shipped out on the same sloop, with the same batch of slaves, bound for Williamsburg in the Virginia Colony. Brice gave both One-Eye and Dunker Tim simple instructions. "Sell the lot of these savages for a reasonable price, and buy as many strong, black field hands as you can. I need two young wenches for breeding, and don't come back with less than eight slaves total. Don't buy savages (meaning Native Americans). They don't wear well in this climate."

Thus, did the slave trade begin in New Bern, not with black stock but with red. Long before blacks were imported directly into New Bern, this trade in Tuscarora slaves would nearly bring an end to this city, almost before it began.

Lefkin worked with One-Eye and Able Ward on a couple more slave trips up the Neuse, before shipping out of New Bern in 1714 on a three-mast square rig bound for the sugar islands of the Caribbean. Ultimately, he probably ended up involved in the African slave trade. His name would have been lost to history had William Brice not taken such meticulous notes, which he used to assist in his employment decisions for his farming operations. Brice noted that Lefkin worked hard and didn't steal too much around the farm. His note indicated he would hire him again, if the opportunity arose. Apparently it didn't. Once Lefkin shipped out of New Bern, he disappeared from history and nothing more is known of this man.

Pate, on the other hand, hung around New Bern for a number of years, working various ships or odd jobs in the settlement. He eventually acquired a small section of land in the colony to the south of New Bern along the White Oak River—no one seemed to really understand how—and became a fisherman.

In later generations, the town of Swansboro would grow into a small city on land once held by Pate and his descendents. Members of that family were pure watermen and seemingly became part and parcel of the swamps and marshes of this watery, flowing land, harvesting their livelihood from the Carolina sounds, bays, and rivers by fishing, shrimping, and oystering the waters of the Carolina coast.

Many Pate family descendents still live in those parts and still fish along that coast today. The very next time you enjoy some delicious shrimp from the Swansboro docks, or a fine soft-shell crab that could only be harvested in the Carolinas, you might pause a moment and consider who caught that delicacy. There is piracy afoot, all along that crystal coast, far out into those endless sounds and marshes, in the salty coastal air, and in the very blood of many living in the Carolinas, even today.

{Author's Note: Jesus and I both wanted to comment on the tone of this text. Slavery in all forms was inhumane in every sense, and the rough, cruel humor in the previous section of text is not intended to diminish that harsh reality in any way. Rather, this was written to highlight that complex world. We wrote this together and wrote it "in the vernacular" in order to show to the degree possible the mindset of the slavers themselves. Had anyone listened to Toby Mallard, One-Eye Benny, and Able Ward plan their slavery expedition, or describe their "Injun Trap," they would have heard the harsh, inhumane, gallows humor presented here. Indeed, the slavers in that period, would have laughed about their task, as dirty, smelly, and tiresome, but not cruel in any way that really mattered. After all, in their view, blacks had no soul and the Tuscarora were mere savages. For these men, slavery was a business that might have become their livelihood had Native American slavery worked over the long term. History records that such slavery did not work. Native American's simply died too quickly of the many diseases from Europe, for which they had no immunity, and within a generation, black slavery would overshadow slavery of the Tuscarora in the Carolinas.

Throughout this period, the men who actually engaged in the dirty work of slaving, men who captured slaves from the forest, or traded them, or actually bound them, shackled them, shipped them, and sold them, were certainly not paragons of moral virtue, but neither were they intentionally cruel men, at least not in their view. Rather the entire system was cruel, and it was a cruelty based both on racial prejudice and economics, not on malicious cruelty in and of itself. After all, if these men had practiced cruelty for cruelty sake, the value of their stock would go down.

Men like One-Eye and Able Ward were uncomplicated men out to make a buck in a way that was then, perfectly legal, if not wholly respectable in the community. While nearly impossible to understand today, by the standards of those days slavery was acceptable, and it is decidedly foolish to apply today's sensitivities to yesterday's belief systems. History judges all men harshly including we ourselves, and who knows what practices we engage in that with the passage of time will seem inhumane from that highly critical, future perspective?

Such writing would be presumptuous at best, if Jesus and I hadn't found several letters that document these attitudes, two of which came from our own family, carefully guarded for scores of years by Granny Bender. In fact, Captain Brice was also an ancestor, since one of his several daughters married one of the Benders in later generations. His papers and these two family letters, not to mention several other sources that Jesus found, demonstrate all too clearly the mindset of those rough slavers. In this mindset, lay the basis for centuries of slavery.

With that said, Jesus and I were both pleased to learn that our ancestor, Martin Bender, was not a slaver. Benders did own slaves in New Bern, and later in both Pollocksville, North Carolina, as well as in Leesville, Tennessee. Still, there is no evidence of Benders being slave traders or breeders. However, Captain Brice did employ slavers at various points, and there are several letters from slavers describing their "stock" for sale. One described how Tuscarora slaves during this early period were captured in the wilderness. Most of the documents existing today pertain to black slavery of a later period, but many things were the same, and slavery is still slavery at any point in history. Such distinctions as these, I'm sure, mattered not one whit to the slaves themselves. They simply longed for their freedom.

In retrospect, I felt honored to have explored that topic so deeply with my friend Jesus, given his color and mine. I think that, perhaps, we both grew in our understanding a bit. Suffice it to say that slavery was an ugly business that dehumanized everyone involved, and was clearly a shameful period in our common history. In the early history of New Bern and the Carolina Colony, that cruelty of slavery quickly led to the greater cruelty of war.}

## *Making War on New Bern*

King Hancock, Chief of the Southern Band of the Tuscarora, was viciously angry, as he suspected more and more that his people were being stolen by the smelly-pales. Indeed, any leader would be horrified by that suspicion and prompted into bold, decisive action, when his people are targeted and snatched from their homeland. The toll of captured Tuscarora mounted over that year, and family records found in a shoebox in Granny Bender's closet show that Captain Brice alone sent at least three "shipments" of Tuscarora slaves into Virginia for sale in the fall of 1711. Others in the Albemarle, Bath, New Bern, and some of the yet-to-be named settlements such as Trent Mill had been doing the same for several years, though probably to a lesser degree. By the summer of 1711, the Tuscarora decided they could no longer tolerate this treatment, and a massacre would be the result.

King Hancock first consulted with the headmen from the other Tuscarora villages along the Pamlico River, the Neuse, the Trent, and the White Oak Rivers. He pointed out that the smelly-pales were not only stealing the Tuscarora, but were literally making war on themselves. Again, this dumbfounded the Tuscarora who valued tribal ties above all else. The Tuscarora were aware of the rift that separated the Quaker Party from the Anglicans, and the Cary Rebellion was in full swing in June of 1711. Several Tuscarora scouts had watched the major battles at Daniel's Plantation and the Pollock Plantation, where the smelly-pales had used their large thunder logs (cannon), and fire-sticks (smoothbore muskets) to kill each other. King Hancock had even been approached by Cary and invited to make war on the smelly-pales who followed the new fellow Hyde. It made no sense to the Tuscarora. What nonsense, what craziness was this?

Amid this chaos more and more Tuscarora were "gone missing." While it is not known exactly when King Hancock made his decision for war, it must have been sometime after Cary was captured, since the Tuscarora made no aggressive moves during the Cary Rebellion itself. However, over the next three months in New Bern, colonists experienced a harsh, hot summer with very little rain. The mosquitoes were as thick as a blanket and seemingly the size of small birds. They tortured the colonists endlessly, as only Neuse River mosquitoes can. Between the Cary Rebellion, the bugs, and the drought, the year old settlement at New Bern was experiencing difficult times, and those difficulties would only get worse when King Hancock finally determined that he could no longer tolerate the smelly-pales in his wilderness. He would attack and either kill them or drive them all back to the Virginia Colony.

Before he attacked however, he traveled north to speak to the headman of the upper Tuscarora, King Tom Blount. Blount lived along the Chowan River in the Albemarle region of the Carolina Colony. He had dealt with the smelly-pales much longer than had King Hancock, since he lived so close to the earlier Virginia Colony, and the smelly-pale settlements along the Albemarle Sound. King Hancock sought out Blount to discuss a Tuscarora strategy to eliminate the smelly-pales from the Carolinas.

While King Hancock was by all accounts an honorable man, an honest man, and a fine warrior, Blount was the opposite. He was known to be a man with somewhat fluid morals, to put it mildly. In fact, he managed his affairs among the northern Tuscarora villages by either duplicity or simply by eliminating his competition. He was more than willing to sell some of his own people—his personal enemies—into slavery to the smelly-pales, and he had done so for at least a decade prior to the establishment of either Bath or New Bern. Once, he even sold a troublesome wife into slavery. For ten deerskins, he unloaded her to a rugged Virginian smelly-pale with only four teeth in his head. Ten deerskins wasn't a bad price for a loudmouth troublemaker of a wife. While intermarriage between whites and Tuscarora was not as widespread as such marriages would later be with the Catawba and the Cherokee tribes, there was some mixing of blood, and more than a few Carolinians today have Tuscarora genes in their family tree. In at least one Carolina family, those genes were initially purchased for ten deerskins.

Some historians suggest that the real roots of Native American slavery in the North Carolina Colony stem from these tribal political shenanigans among the Tuscarora tribe itself, rather than the outright capture of Tuscarora slaves by white slavers. While interesting, that proposition has the advantage of being totally impossible to prove or disprove at this point. It is known that, when King Hancock approached Blount with the suggestion that all Tuscarora make war on the smelly-pales throughout the North Carolina Colony, Blount listened carefully and then declined to unite the tribe in that endeavor.

King Hancock knew the measure of Blount, and never seriously suspected to receive any help from that foolishly immoral man. Still, protocol among the Tuscarora demanded that he attempt unified action, and now he'd done so. He was now free to protect his people as he saw fit, and that meant war all along the Carolina frontier.

### A Messenger of God

It was about this time in the early autumn of 1711, that a messenger of God, Josiah Russell Ipock, came to the growing city of New Bern and strangely enough this prophet was personally invited. In point of fact, two families of Ipocks had traveled with the original group of Germans to the new settlement arriving in April of 1710. However, the patriarch of one of these families had managed to misspell his surname when signing on for the voyage to the Carolina Colony, a phenomenon that was not uncommon in the centuries prior to public education. Thus two versions of this surname appear in the historic records. Still, the Ebecks and Ipocks were essentially the same broad family originating in central Germany, and both names appear in the historical documents associated with the early New Bern settlement fairly frequently.

Because the first harvest in New Bern during the fall of 1710 looked so promising, a man named Franz Ebeck had written to his brother in Germany and invited him to join the settlement. That correspondence took an interesting trip, characteristic of those times. First, the letter traveled via a small coastal sloop from New Bern to Charleston where it waited for two weeks before being taken into a mail packet bound for Europe. Once that mail packet was full, it was loaded on board a three-mast Brigantine for the trans-Atlantic trip to Scotland. Arriving in port there, the letter along with many others sat in storage for four weeks waiting until enough mail was collected to make loading it cost efficient. It then became part of another mail packet bound for Danzig, Germany that was placed aboard another coastal freighter, a much smaller brig, for the trip across the North Sea into Europe. From there it was a quick overland route of only one hundred and forty-five miles, and because of the well known German efficiency in such things, that trip took only two weeks. All in all, that letter arrived in a fairly quick time frame for that day, only three and a half months after it was mailed at the small hut that then served as a customs house next to the New Bern docks.

The minister, Reverend Josiah Russell Ipock, arrived in New Bern in the Autumn of 1711, almost a year after being invited to town by his brother Franz Ebeck. While the settlement had a small log church that was nominally Anglican, it had no minister as yet, and Sunday services were led by members of the congregation. Johannes Simmons had led several meetings himself, as had many other Germans in the single year since the sanctuary on Middle Street had been completed. While Johannes seemed to stumble a great deal while speaking in English, particularly if he was rushed or nervous, in German his prayers were grammatically correct and truly inspirational, so he led those Germans in services from time to time. In those days, ships along the coast brought many passengers of all faiths and any visiting minister that happened to travel through was immediately invited by de Graffenreid to lead the services for the entire community the following Sunday.

Reverend Josiah Russell Ipock was a fiery minister indeed! He was as staunchly "reformed" in his outlook as he could be, being a nearly rabid follower of Anabaptist tradition, which placed him more in tune with these Germans than with either the Quakers or the Anglicans that dominated politics in the colony. Still, he could and often did, deliver soul wrenching sermons on any topic that struck his fancy. He could make his followers cringe in fear at the might of the Lord, and while his sojourn in New Bern was fairly brief, he impacted that colony with at least one of his several sermons.

On his third Sunday, his message was focused on the many diverse sins he saw in the colony itself. His view of religion was certainly more focused on the vengeful, judging God of the Old Testament, and like Martin Bender he preferred his religion straight up, with no apologies to anyone. He never minced words and he took the liberty, after being in town for two entire weeks, to condemn anyone and everyone he chose, since he believed that God had singled them out specifically for chastisement. He selectively identified the threats to God's work as he saw them, casting an unwavering eye on Mallard's Tavern as the seat of most of the evil in the new city. He paid particular attention to the host of drunken sailors that managed to roam the docks at the end of Broad Street, and all along South Front Street by the placid Trent River.

Sitting in the service that day, were Martin Bender, Johannes Simmons, his wife Margaret, and their two children Christina and Katheryn. Archie Carmichael was there, though no one understood why, and he sat behind several leaders in the community such as Sheriff Jack DuVal, Captain Brice and his family, and Baron de Graffenreid himself. The Foscues from downriver rarely attended church, and only a handful of farmers from outlying farms were there. However, several sailors who apparently sought a life other than their normally harsh, rum-soaked existence were in attendance sitting in the back. Most of the German craftsmen living in the small town itself were in attendance, so the small log church was filled and almost everyone in the settlement heard this fiery message from God.

After vivid condemnation of most things fun—drinking, whoring, betting on the local cock fights, racing, or betting on turkey shoots, etc.—the Reverend Ipock launched into a most surprising condemnation of slavery. He had clearly been influenced by Quaker thought on that point since that band of religious deviants had always been staunchly anti-slavery, but he arrived at his condemnation of the peculiar institution after some judicious reflection on the habit of slave holders to find sexual release with their slaves. In his view any such relaxation was sinful. Of course, one might have expected such a condemnation since sex was involved, but then the Reverend stepped over the bounds of propriety when he announced that anyone selling, capturing, or holding slaves would be condemned by Almighty God, not because slavery was wrong, but because it led to so much sin in other ways. Slothfulness, the cruelty of capturing slaves among the savages, drunkenness, sexual pleasure with slave women, enjoyment of the many "hunts" for runaway slaves, all were openly criticized. This sermon led to extreme discomfort among many in the congregation, if not downright agitation. This preacher had clearly stopped preaching and was now meddling in their personal affairs!

In short, the Reverend Ipock saw slavery as breeding many sins, and condemned it as a practice routed in both lust and greed. His voice thundered, as he shouted from the pulpit, "The New Bern Colony, conceived wholly in greed and founded in so much blood, will most assuredly be cursed by our benevolent Deity, damned for all eternity by Almighty God!"

His mighty voice was heard all across downtown New Bern, and even some of the sailors sleeping off a drunken stupor on the floor of Mallard's Tavern two blocks away were awakened by that shout! Such was the power of the Lord in this man's spirit.

Needless to say, he was never asked to speak again, since so many in the congregation held slaves, and some, like Captain Brice trafficked in them to a degree. Even de Graffenreid had negative things to say about this "upstart, ill-educated minister, who apparently didn't realize that slavery was condoned by God, and was governed by principles put forth in the Bible itself."

The Reverend Ipock, certain as only an Anabaptist can be that he had done God's work, remained oblivious to the growing criticism for the next few days. However, his brother Franz saw the writing on the wall, and encouraged his brother Josiah Russell to consider taking his ministry up to Bath where, among the Quakers, his welcome might be a bit more cordial. He left within three days of that ill-timed, if accurate sermon.

In that fashion did the Reverend Ipock impact New Bern, by introducing a question into the minds of many that they had not considered before. Most of the German immigrants at that time did not own slaves, but the earlier English settlers in the area surely did. Moreover, many Germans worked right beside slaves, including Martin and Johannes, who typically had several slaves from the Brice or the Foscue Plantations working in their shop on orders for barrels from those two large agri-business concerns.

In the Simmons cabin, this sermon occasioned several active discussions of slavery. That very Sunday after the evening Bible reading, Margaret herself spoke up. "I am not certain why the Reverend Ipock found so much to criticize in our colony. We build here a new city, and we have property here that we would never have been allowed to hold in Germany. Does he not understand that? How can he condemn everything we try to do here?"

Johannes took up the thought. "I certain am what not means he condemns us all, but he wrong to condemn our slaves!"

Katheryn, ever seeking the opportunity to state her opinion, responded. "Oh, Father. Your English is still very poor. Don't you see? He was not condemning slaves but was condemning slavery itself. He was condemning all those who hold slaves or benefit from the work of slaves. He feels that holding slaves is wrong, since it leads to sins of the flesh, and other things."

That interesting point is often overlooked today. Much of the early opposition to slavery was not the moral outrage we feel today at the thought of viewing humans as chattel, but rather the concern for the sins slavery was destined to cause. Absolute power over anyone will, at some point, lead to abuses of the less powerful, and men in all periods of history have recognized that fact. Indeed, slavery was first criticized in that light. The lust angle was just an added benefit that made folks listen more to the sermon. Still, for many early opponents of slavery the fundamental wrong of slavery as viewed today, was not even an issue.

Johannes could not seem to grasp this concept however, since the Bible clearly allowed slavery, and in his view, even provided rules for slave behavior as well as for the behavior of slave masters. He stated this as clearly as he could to his family, and he then read one of those Bible passages in Colossians that slave holders the world over cite as the basic Christian guideline for slave behavior.

*"Servants, obey in all things your masters according to the flesh; not with eye-service, as men-pleasers but in singleness of heart, fearing God."*

Margaret however, held a different view, knowing the types of behavior that slavery might lead men to, and feeling truly sorry for those whom she considered the weaker sex. She pointed out that slavery of either blacks or savages did indeed result in less honest labor on the part of men since slaves did much of the work. Further, she agreed with the Reverend Ipock that slavery could indeed lead to unbridled lust. In fact, much to the surprise of both Johannes and Martin, she described in some detail the sin she witnessed so often as sailors slipped into the small framed whorehouse that stood right behind Toby Mallard's Tavern. She then launched into an amazingly accurate description of the several available women, among them two black slaves, and one Indian, a Catawba woman that Toby had purchased from the Tuscarora.

Johannes was shocked beyond belief, and he stupidly stammered out the first question that popped into his mind. "Margaret! How you could such things know?"

Margaret looked at her poor husband with what can only be called a loving and tolerant restraint. Her response was more cutting by virtue of the calmness in her voice. "I am a woman and a wife, Johannes. I am not an idiot."

At just that moment, Martin looked at Katheryn, and saw in her eyes the same look of gentle distain he saw in Margaret's face. He realized then in an instant, that women often understand the desires of men better than men themselves, and that they share many such secrets among themselves, seemingly with no words spoken at all.

In only a moment Margaret smiled lovingly and reached out to her husband. "Poor Johannes, do you not understand yet?" She then took the Bible and selected a passage in Romans that foretold the danger of seeking lustfully for the flesh. She read quietly for her family.

*"For they that are after the flesh do mind the things of the flesh, but they that are*

*after the Spirit mind the things of the Spirit. For to be carnally minded is death, but to be spiritually minded is life and peace in Christ."*

Margaret continued. "Johannes anything that leads one to sin is sinful, and we must always take care to avoid the lures of the Evil One." For her, that concluded the matter.

Neither Katheryn nor Martin expressed any further opinion on the question of slavery that evening, but both knew that there was some disagreement between Johannes and Margaret that could lead to problems. Martin favored slavery, as did most of the New Bern settlers, and thought that the Reverend Ipock should pack up and go, which is exactly what happened only several days later. However, as Johannes' business expanded, he and Martin both worked more and more frequently with slaves in the cooper's shed, and they both heard the horrid terms of the day—niggers, darkies—terms that have been used to dehumanize men and women for thousands of years. Johannes had even considered purchasing a slave himself for work in the cooper's shed, though he could not at that time afford such an extravagance.

In point of fact, nothing further was said on the matter at all that evening, since Johannes decided to pray and therefore close out the discussion. However, just as the prayer was almost completed, one of those family distractions occurred that always occasioned much laughter in that joyous German home. Max, the overly passionate family dog had lain quietly just beside the warm hearth, but he chose that precipitous moment to hump Katheryn's leg, and thoroughly shocked her when he mounted while her eyes were still closed, just as the amen was said.

### Visitors to the Tuscarora

On that same evening, after concluding his several visits to several other Tuscarora towns, as well as the towns of the other tribes along the Carolina coast, Hancock returned to Catechna. He was quite disappointed with the cheap hyperbole and phony antics of the leader that the northern Tuscarora insisted on following, but he had made his decision for war, regardless of the choice of King Tom Blount. However, as soon as he entered his hometown he was told he had visitors, two distinguished smelly-pales from New Bern.

With Cary's Rebellion over, and the harvest such as it was, coming in, de Graffenreid and his surveyor Lawson determined to seek a more direct overland route to the Virginia Colony. At that time the North Trail was the only real overland option for travel to Williamsburg and the other, older cities in the Virginia Colony. While that trail snaked around the larger rivers such as the Pamlico and the Chowan, it also crossed the innumerable creeks that lace through the coastal hinterlands of the Carolina Colony. Those hundreds of fords made the North Trail all but impossible to use after a hard rain. In short, when the water was high, no trade goods or livestock could move to the markets near the larger population centers in Virginia.

Water travel was always an option that worked very well for tobacco, corn, pitch, and other farm or forest produce. However, shipping livestock was very expensive, because feed as well as cattle, goats, or hogs would need to be freighted as well. In that environment de Graffenreid and Lawson sailed up the Neuse, using the same route that One-Eye Benny and Able Ward had used so often, to seek a better route to Virginia. These men hoped that the Neuse was navigable for its full length, and they suspected that it eventually headed northward toward the Virginia Settlements. In their quest to seek a better trail they ran instead, directly into a war.

King Hancock had already talked among the other headmen of the neighboring villages of the Tuscarora and he had planned a strategy with his warriors. What was worse, he had confided in King Tom Blount, a Tuscarora leader that he did not trust. He was sure that his plans for battle might be leaked to the enemy, so when he found these leaders of the smelly-pales on his doorstep in September of 1711, he was not sure he should let them live. In fact, he was absolutely sure that some of those he had confided his plans to would warn these men, thus endangering his battle plan, since many of the warriors had established good trading relationships with the smelly-pales. In short, someone was sure to talk, and King Hancock knew it.

What really frightened King Hancock however, was the weaponry. He was not overly concerned with the fire-sticks since some of his warriors had recently acquired those, even though most still hunted with bows and arrows. What did worry him were the logs that thunder. His warriors had seen what the thunder logs could do in the recent fights at the plantations along the Pamlico and Chowan Rivers, and if even some of those stories were true, the thunder logs had to be avoided at all cost.

King Hancock knew that he needed surprise in this battle. He wanted to attack the smelly-pales when and where the thunder logs were not around. Thus, when Lawson and de Graffenreid showed up in his village, he offered them the hospitality of the longhouse and he would talk with them to see what they desired, but as soon as he was told of their arrival, he decided not to let them escape.

Sitting on the three-legged stools scattered around in the longhouse, Lawson and de Graffenreid sought to make a bargain, and were using the same interpreter—Two-Nose—that Cary had used only three months previously. Two-Nose remembered that the previous conversation had not gone well, but at least the longhouse smelled slightly better than before. While the livestock were very much in evidence, the scalps of the Catawba had long since dried, and thus emitted no odor though they still hung beside the ridgepole as before.

Lawson was much more of a frontiersman that de Graffenreid would ever be since he had lived in the Carolina Colony for several years prior to the settlement of New Bern, and had learned much that this rough frontier had to offer. Lawson had traveled more in the Carolinas than any other white man, and he knew the other whites in the area like Cary and Brice, as well as the traditions of many of the local Indian tribes along the Carolina coast, such as the Coree, the Meherrin, and the Tuscarora.

De Graffenreid had sought the services of Lawson specifically because of that knowledge, and it was Lawson who selected the site for New Bern. Lawson had negotiated with the Tuscarora and had purchased land for the settlement. He had presented several muskets and twenty blankets to the headman of Cartouca, the Tuscarora village at the union of the Neuse River and the Trent that became New Bern to get him to move his people upriver, thus making way for the new settlement. He felt that he could surely secure the help they now sought from King Hancock.

Because of his expertise, Lawson took the lead in this negotiation, and thus he was speaking first in the longhouse that evening. Reaching toward the bundle carried by a black slave he retrieved the gift that was required to begin the negotiations. Then he carefully laid three muskets before King Hancock along with three blankets as he spoke. "King Hancock. We know of your wisdom and your knowledge of the Neuse River and this wilderness, and we seek your help. We bring these gifts to honor you, and ask that you lead us to find a better way to the Virginia settlements. Our North Trail is long and curves around all of the great coastal rivers, and we have to cross many creeks. They are difficult for our wagons and our cattle to cross after a heavy rain. We seek a straight trail from the head of the Neuse to the north."

Lawson was quite pleased with his complete yet concise request. He looked directly at King Hancock, which was exactly the wrong thing to do given the Tuscarora habit of showing respect by downcast eyes. Lawson was also grinning broadly since he believed that put the Tuscarora at ease. In reality it merely made him look silly. He had cautioned de Graffenreid to do likewise throughout the discussion, so both sat in the longhouse, grinning from ear to ear, and therefore looking incredibly stupid to the much more serious minded Tuscarora headmen that were assembled that evening. Lawson didn't realize any of those subtleties however, and was busy complimenting himself on his ability to understand the savages. He would have been absolutely shocked to learn that at that precise moment, King Hancock was deciding exactly how he would die.

Two-Nose translated the statements rather directly. "King Hancock. These smelly-pales bring a gift to you and seek your help to find the other smelly-pales to the north. They do not like the North Trail, and worry about wet feet in the creeks. They seek another route."

King Hancock had heard the request and understood the English just fine, but the translation gave him time to think, and he, as always sought every advantage when dealing with these deceitful smelly-pales. However, several of the other tribal leaders in the longhouse on that day did not have command of English, so the rough translation delivered by Two-Nose did do some good.

King Hancock, as well as many of the other Tuscarora present, realized immediately that any new trail that would avoid the numerous rivers and creeks along the coast would have to be located much further inland, and thus deep in the hunting grounds of the Tuscarora. For this warrior tribe, the loss of hunting grounds was always a critical concern, and was, in fact the very reason that the Tuscarora were almost always at war with the powerful Catawba, the tribe that dominated the central and westerly regions of North Carolina at that time. Even if King Hancock had not already determined to make war on these smelly-pales along the coast, he would not have been able to grant this request, since loss of hunting grounds was equivalent to taking food from the mouths of the children of his tribe.

The Tuscarora, while warlike and quick to take offence, often showed a good sense of humor. They joked with each other frequently, many times poking fun at the smelly-pales and King Hancock was no exception. Given the stupid grin on Lawson's face, King Hancock decided to mock him and thus began to grin back at Lawson, which looked completely absurd to the other Tuscarora, some of whom began to giggle a bit. Then, while smiling inanely at Lawson and de Graffenreid, King Hancock offered them a pipe full of tobacco. After they and he had taken a breath of tobacco, he spoke. "These smelly-pales are like old women, who cannot cross a creek without falling in!" And he smiled more broadly, as the other Tuscarora giggled a bit more. Several laughed outright causing Lawson and de Graffenreid to wonder what had been said.

Then King Hancock realized that he had to say something that could be translated for Lawson, so he said, "Two-Nose, tell this smelly-pale idiot that they may have their new trail, and that I will send scouts with them to show them the headwaters of the Neuse."

Two-Nose dutifully translated, and Lawson silently congratulated himself even more, while continuing to grin.

After a brief pause, King Hancock bowed and smiled at Lawson again, and continued, but this time his words were only for the Tuscarora in the longhouse. "Do not translate these words, Two-Nose, but all Tuscarora present must know that we will never let these filthy smelly-pales take more of our land for their trails. They build cabins and destroy trees wherever their trails go." At that comment many Tuscarora in the longhouse chuckled outright, and then cast their eyes down.

With the negotiations moving along so nicely, both Lawson and de Graffenreid were quite pleased. De Graffenreid was so ecstatic with the idea of a new North Trail that he reached back to his slave for more gifts, and took out three iron axes, which he then placed before King Hancock. He then said to Two-Nose. "Tell King Hancock that we appreciate his help and give him these axes as our thanks. Also tell him that we would like to leave in the morning tomorrow."

Two-Nose translated again for King Hancock. "These smelly-pales say thank you and will leave in the morning."

King Hancock, looked quickly into the faces of the other headmen and warriors seated in the longhouse. "Tobacco!" he said. "More tobacco for the pipe, and bring in the barrel of rum for our guests!" With that statement, he gestured grandly with his arms. "We shall have a celebration this night for our guests, since these smelly-pales do not realize that they will never leave Catechna alive. We will kill them tomorrow, and will not have to endure their smell any longer. Our warriors will enjoy eating their hearts in victory!" He spoke those harsh words with the broadest grin imaginable on his face, and the other warriors in the tribe laughed outright. Revenge is indeed sweet when it is wholly unexpected, and these smelly-pales were clueless as to the fate that awaited them. To put the matter simply, King Hancock had seen too many of his people go missing.

Two-Nose was savvy enough to know what to translate and what not to. He merely said to Lawson, "The Tuscarora King wishes to give a party tonight in your honor." In his translation, he did not mention the menu item King Hancock had discussed.

The Tuscarora now filed out of the longhouse into the cool autumn evening, with de Graffenreid, Lawson, and their slave in tow. They walked through the village toward the creek and on the bank of that lovely stream, they settled around a large fire that had been built in the center of the gathering grounds. Here would be their celebration.

First the women of the tribe brought dried meat, cooked wild turkey, and dried fish, a selection of grapes and nuts, as well as cool water from the river to refresh the men, and everyone ate with great relish. After eating, the tribal drums began a slow steady rhythm and a few warriors began to dance around the fire, sometimes slowly, in groups of only three or four, and sometimes more actively, with many more dancers. No women joined in the dance on this evening. This surprised Lawson, since he had seen savages dance, both men and women, in his earlier travels through Tuscarora country. However, unknown to the smelly-pales, this was a celebration of war and conquest and those actions, like the dance that evening, were the endeavors of men.

De Graffenreid, Lawson, and the one slave they had brought along to manage the trade goods and paddle the canoe merely sat by the large fire, as the first two got wonderfully drunk on the barrel of Jamaican rum that had come into the Carolina Colony via trade with the Virginia settlements. The whites watched the dancing for hours, and only then did King Hancock offer one of his several wives to both Lawson and de Graffenreid to enjoy for the evening. The leaders of the Tuscarora were known to occasionally practice polygamy and hospitality demanded the provision of such relaxing entertainments for one's guests. However, both visitors declined any serious sex play, since neither could perform at all well after so much drink. In fact, both Lawson and de Graffenreid soon fell asleep where they sat.

King Hancock had one of his wives cover each of them with a deer skin blanket. Only de Graffenreid's slave was sober, since he didn't trust these savages, and had forgone any of the rum. Still, after a bit more time even he fell asleep. They had planned on moving upriver the next morning, but the Tuscarora realized even if these smelly-pales didn't, that these visitors were not likely to survive another day.

## Infiltration

As Martin and Johannes worked through that autumn of 1711, the town of New Bern continued to grow. Ships were now coming into the docks every week in New Bern, and there really were docks along both the Trent and the Neuse waterfronts by 1711. The cooper's shed was a growing concern, and now had five other workmen, two of whom were black slaves owned by Captain Brice. In fact, the shed was no longer just a shed, but had doubled in size and now had stout walls made of strong wood beams that could support hanging tools or drying barrel hoops. It occupied a long stretch of South Front Street, just across the road from one of the five piers that now reached far out into the Trent River. At least one pier always had some type of ship tied to it, and a number of men were now working along the docks unloading trade goods or loading pitch or other outbound freight.

While the odor of fish seemed to permeate the docks themselves, since fish was sold at the foot of the first pier, the cooper's shed across South Front Street always smelled of hickory shavings. Someone was always hacking away at a barrel stave or hoop, or shaving the wood to assure a tight fit for the barrel, and Johannes barrels were known to be among the best.

Johannes and Martin shared the duties of management, since both could fell trees, carve staves, form barrel hoops, or direct others. Johannes was a master cooper, and Martin only an apprentice, but the young man was as good as his word had been on that first day on the shores of New Bern. He did work hard and learn quickly. Johannes, by this point, could trust him with almost any task and rest comfortably assured that the job would get done well. Martin was the type of apprentice, or employee that every boss dreams of having, someone Johannes could depend on.

One day, a young Tuscarora boy wandered into the cooper's shed. He spoke broken English and immediately turned to Martin, having quickly recognized that he was the boss. Johannes was out taking an order that afternoon, so the savage glanced quickly at Martin, then cast his eyes downward and said, "I need job take here. Work soon here? Work you?"

English was quickly becoming the most frequently used language in the city, since all of the original Germans strove to master it, and the more recent Swiss immigrants knew that language already. The savages had a bit more trouble, but most were at least understandable. This boy wanted a job, and even with the archaic syntax of this young Tuscarora, Martin found he could understand him. The boy could not have been more than fifteen or so, but he was big and wanted to work. Only yesterday Johannes and Martin had discussed bringing on more help, to fell trees and bring in the wood. That job was not a skilled labor position, and any strong back would do. The orders for barrels seemed to keep coming in, and even with the relatively poor harvest that summer more help was needed in the cooper's shed as well as on the lumbering team. Martin hired him immediately. His name was Otter.

Word had spread about the recent rebellion, and while Cary had been shipped off to London, there were still smoldering resentments over that fight. The Quaker Party had all but gone underground and that peaceful religion was to have less and less influence in the colony from that point on. However, hatred grows when nothing else will, and the numerous followers of Cary hated the followers of Hyde with a passion. Unfortunately, this infighting stopped any meaningful legislative discussion cold. The entire colony seemed to be on hold, with very few appointments being made for government positions. No land could be legally acquired, even though immigrants landed each week in the new city, and their first question was usually, "Is there any land for sale around here?" They all wanted what had been denied them in Europe.

When they were told they couldn't buy land, most of these new settlers merely marched out into the wilderness near some of the earlier settlers and began to fell trees and clear fields. Settlements grew up from nothing, or grew larger along every river and creek in eastern Carolina. Both the Trent River and its main tributary Mill Creek were mostly settled at that point, and farms were created everywhere seemingly at once, resulting in towns that would subsequently be known as Washington, Trenton, and Jacksonville. All grew as settlements at first usually around a grist mill along one stream or another and without any name or any official recognition whatsoever, since the legislature still meeting in Bath was all but paralyzed with political infighting and even existing settlements could not receive a charter or a name. Such was the sad state of affairs in the colony, but even in the toughest of times, life goes on, as it did for the Simmons family, and their apprentice, Martin Bender.

As the autumn of 1711 began to turn a bit colder, Martin would lead his group of four lumbermen into the wilderness for the fine hickory or oak that was to become the barrel staves for Johannes' barrels. It took many men to fell an old-growth hickory, or a chestnut, or oak or any of the other fine hardwoods offered by the forests of the new colony. When the pitch-men harvested pitch for various waterproofing applications, including treating the hulls of the wooden ships of the day, they sought out the pine in the forest and thus were working with a much softer, more pliable wood. Also, they didn't have to cut the tree down, but rather merely skin the bark a bit and then hang a pitch-bucket beside the tree to catch the sap. That sap was perfect for waterproofing ships, and caulking between the timbers in the hull.

In contrast, Martin and his small band of lumbermen sought out the older hardwoods and that meant that much more labor was required by their team of lumbermen. They had to drop a tree, and that was much more involved than merely harvesting pitch. Normally, Martin would locate one or two good trees within a few hundred yards of each other, and get two men working on each tree, chopping with their axes on either side. When plantation owners needed barrels for their goods, they often told Johannes that his men could harvest trees from the plantation itself, thus saving any cost for the wood. In that fashion the coopers got their preferred woods and the plantation owner got rid of some of the toughest trees to get rid of, and thus he eventually got new acreage cleared. Even with a strong hand, and an iron axe working on both sides of these old growth monsters, it still sometimes took a day or more to drop the heavy lumber, and even more time to skin off the branches, and cut it into movable sections that an ox team could tow back to the cooper's shed.

On any given day, Martin usually got his men started out in the woods, and then rode the one available mule back to New Bern to help Johannes in the shed itself. He'd check with the lumbermen in the forest later at the end of the day to measure progress, or if they were working far from town, he would bring them a hot lunch and inspect their work then.

Sometimes on those days, as he rode his mule from the woods, he would spot a deer or wild turkey to shoot for the stew pot. Every hunter knows that deer instantly recognize the gait of a man walking in the forest, and the deer then flee, most often without being seen. However a mule, cow, horse, or any other four footed animal can walk right up on a deer with impunity. Martin used that strange fact to kill much game in 1711.

In addition to the mule however, Martin had another important advantage. He had talked Johannes into purchasing one of the newly made rifles that in five or six more decades would come to be known as Kentucky rifles. These weapons were far superior to the smoothbore flintlock muskets of that era. German gunsmiths, many of whom had immigrated to Philadelphia or Boston, had created a rifle that seemed designed specifically for the frontier which in 1711 was the wilderness around New Bern. As those rifles became more popular in the 1750s and 1760s, when the frontier had moved west into Tennessee or Kentucky, those amazing weapons would acquire the name they would carry for eternity, Kentucky rifles. Not a single one was ever built in that state.

Unlike smoothbore muskets of 1710, these new rifles had grooves inside the barrels that resulted in a bullet spinning rapidly when fired. Much like a well thrown football, that spinning action gave a bullet a somewhat longer range and much greater accuracy. Most of these weapons were fifty caliber, meaning they fired a fairly large hunk of lead, and they had barrels between forty four and forty six inches long which increased the accuracy even more. A skilled shooter could hit a target at two hundred yards, whereas the older flintlock smoothbore muskets were accurate for only thirty to fifty yards. The earlier versions of the Kentucky rifle became available between 1700 and 1710, and Martin was the second person in New Bern to acquire one, since Captain Brice had purchased one only a few months before. Based on his knowledge of the forest, his mule, and that superior rifle, Martin got many more kills than some of the other younger hunters who had none of those advantages.

From Johannes perspective, the mule, though costly to maintain, meant that Martin, his most trusted man, could do much more for the business. Further, the new and relatively expensive rifle meant less frequent purchases of meat, a commodity that was becoming more costly in New Bern in the autumn of 1711. With the new rifle Martin could kill more game for the family table. Thus, Martin moved around the outlying plantations and farms in the New Bern and Trent Mill area more so than almost anyone else in the colony. That flexibility of movement was probably why Martin was the first white man to discover that an Indian massacre had begun. However, at the same instant that Martin became suspicious that foul deeds were afoot, John Lawson was being tortured to death by the Tuscarora.

# *The Death of John Lawson*

Lawson awoke that morning because he had to pee terribly. He opened his eyes and immediately wished that he hadn't. His head pounded from a severe hangover. The rum those savages had served that evening had been as good in quality as anything to be found in Mallard's Tavern in New Bern or anywhere else in the colony. Lawson knew that he had surely drunk too much. His head was killing him and he had to urinate so badly that he felt he had to move immediately or risk peeing all over himself, even though his hangover seemed to have paralyzed him somewhat. At first, he couldn't seem to move. Then, upon waking up a bit more, he was shocked to recognize that he really couldn't move! His hands had been tied behind his back and around a post in the middle of a circle where the savages danced only last evening.

Lawson thought that he must still be dreaming, so he jerked against the ropes. However, when he did, his head throbbed even more and the ropes cut into his wrists, which woke him up completely. He immediately became enraged and shouted at de Graffenreid and the slave, both of whom were tied, back to back, to a post nearby.

"Baron!" Lawson shouted. "The savages have put me in a truss, and I cannot get free!" Lawson squirmed and his shouting brought a couple of Tuscarora guards to his side immediately. These were two of the younger warriors who had danced the previous night. While they had showed great deference to the visitors last evening, this morning their faces showed only contempt.

Lawson was enraged and could not believe this bondage was intended. He shouted at the savages, "Let me and the Baron go immediately or I shall bring an army and destroy this entire village." Then he turned back to de Graffenreid, and shouted again. "I say, Baron. Can you get free? I think we should flee this city immediately and march back here with an army to teach these filthy swine a lesson!"

De Graffenreid, much slower to awake than Lawson, was finally opening his eyes and becoming aware of the situation. He was completely terrified as well as angry, but unlike Lawson he managed to hold his tongue. That restraint is probably what saved him.

By then King Hancock himself had been summoned and was calmly walking out to the dance area, where the visitors were only then becoming aware that they were his prisoners. His demeanor and calm gait enraged Lawson even more, and perhaps Lawson felt that he needed to show de Graffenreid that he, for one, knew how to deal decisively with savages.

"Untie us this instant you filthy, disgusting savage, you son of a whore!" Lawson shouted. He was beside himself with anger, and would have killed

Hancock that instant had he not been totally immobile, sitting there with his hands and arms tied firmly behind him around the stout pole. "Where's that damned Two-Nose?" He shouted, while looking around the Tuscarora village. Then he looked back at Hancock, and shouted even more loudly. "I need my interpreter! This goat loving, pig-faced sodomite savage is dumb as a post! He cannot understand a damn word I say. Hell, he couldn't find his own mother's teat without a map! Two-Nose, where the hell are you? I need my interpreter!"

Of course, King Hancock understood the entire diatribe and it clearly made him even angrier than previously, though the meaning was somewhat vague, since he was not well versed in English curses. While he enjoyed both swine and goat well roasted, he was sure that such was not the meaning of Lawson's ill chosen phrasing, and having one's mother's private parts mentioned in a curse doesn't go over well in any society on Earth.

One can only imagine the surprise Lawson must have felt when Hancock, calmly spoke in passable English, and told Lawson of his fate. "Shut up your cursing you foul fellow, or you will surely die today. Your English town will be destroyed within a fortnight, and we will be well rid of you filthy buggers forever." King Hancock used that phrase, "filthy buggers" since he didn't know the English word for smelly-pale at that time. One takes one's curses where one can and King Hancock was somewhat limited in that area, but he had heard many of the English smelly-pales use that term "filthy bugger" in just such a fashion before.

"You will be held here in this village while we kill your people, and when our warriors return, you will be roasted in our victory dance. When we eat your heart, your village will be no more, and we will have our land back!" That phrase was enough to shut Lawson up, at least for a moment or two.

The Tuscarora generally practiced neither human sacrifice nor cannibalism, but on occasion, various woodland tribes including those in the Carolinas would roast and eat parts of their enemies, believing that for a warrior to eat an enemy heart gave him strength in warfare. When warriors came in with the bloodlust that battle so often brings, such sacrifices were not wholly unknown. Hancock, at that moment, had just such a fate in mind for Lawson, de Graffenreid, and the slave, but within only a few more moments, Lawson's anger got the better of him, and he began to shout again.

"You swine! You speak English, yet you deceived me for these many years! You filthy bugger!" Lawson didn't realize he'd repeated Hancock's own phrase, and he was now so angry that he forgot totally that he would live or die at the mercy of the warrior chief before him.

"When did you learn our language?" Lawson asked, knowing the question was both irrelevant and somewhat stupid at this point. He continued babbling, by trying again to insult Hancock. "What matter of man can kill another when he cannot defend himself, you swine! Untie me, I say, or we shall return and destroy you and this village!" Clearly neither Lawson nor de Graffenreid was going anywhere, but Lawson had run out of insults to hurl at Hancock by that time, and that was all he could think of to say.

Still something in that curse must have struck home, for it was at that exact moment that King Hancock ordered his warriors to remove de Graffenreid and his slave from the dancing grounds. They were roughly picked up by the arms and led away to the far end of the village, where they were tied to the support post in the longhouse in which the negotiations had taken place the previous evening. Sitting there, back to back with the post between them, they listened for the entire day to Lawson's awful screams.

Understanding torture in this historic period is a part of understanding these warriors. For torture in that day was, on certain occasions, viewed as a test of strength and will. The Tuscarora were a warrior society and such societies throughout history have devised many ingenious ways to inflict pain and thus test the worthiness of their warriors. The powerful Aztecs in Central America, would stretch a human captive across their alter and cut his chest open with an obsidian blade, removing his still beating heart to appease their blood-hungry gods. They always observed the manner and demeanor of the one slain, and judged his worthiness by the quality of his courage at the instant of his death. Of course, that painful death was reserved for sacrificial victims or war captives and did nothing to strengthen the individual warriors of the tribe.

In contrast, the nomadic Indians of the great American plains devised a tortuous test of strength and endurance that would be punishable by law today, yet the warriors in those tribes willingly submitted to the cruel act. During the religious service referred to as the Ghost Dance, several tribal members would insert skewers under the breast muscles of warriors, who were then pulled aloft by ropes attached to the skewers. The other end of the rope was attached to a tall pole in the ground, and they were thus suspended, with their body weight pulling against the skewers, while their compatriots spun them around the central post. This torture was as painful as anything ever devised by man and many warriors had their muscles ripped from their bodies when they fell, but the warriors volunteered for it knowing that surviving it would make their personal power, their personal "medicine" much stronger. For many warrior tribes, to survive torture was to pass a test of will, and prove one's bravery and value to the tribe.

By 1711, the Tuscarora were the strongest tribe along the southern coast and they were feared by all of their enemies. Their warriors were strong and brave and each had undergone the intentional infliction of pain in various forms in order to build strength. One method employed by this tribe, as we have seen, involved inserting wooden splinters the size of toothpicks under the skin all over the body and then lighting those wooden splinters afire one by one. The wooden splinters would burn off the skin and some muscle tissue underneath, causing great pain. Warriors had to endure this without crying out, since the defense of the tribe might very well depend on a warrior's strength or his ability to endure such a horrendous pain. Like many such physical tests, this torture could easily lead to death and a more horrid death is difficult to imagine. This was to be Lawson's cruel fate at the hands of the Tuscarora.

Lawson realized none of this and his screams throughout that day and into the evening suggested that he never understood how the torture might have been endured, by viewing it and experiencing it as a test of will. Rather, he felt the burning of his skin repeatedly, smelling his own flesh as it was consumed by the small flames, and just as one sharp pain became a dull grinding ache, the savages would light a few more of the wooden splinters embedded in his flesh. This torture never ceased. He screamed, hour, after hour, after tortuous hour. His cries were an absolute horror to hear, as de Graffenreid later testified.

He did not die well.

Had Lawson shown bravery, it is possible that King Hancock might have spared him at some point. No smelly-pale watched Lawson's death, though, so who can know? In fact, little is known ultimately about how he died. It was rumored around the Carolinas that King Hancock finally got tired of his screams and slit his throat with his own razor just to shut him up once and for all. All that is known is that some time after dark, the screams stopped. An ominous silence then settled over the Tuscarora town.

Within only a few minutes, Hancock walked into the longhouse with his several warriors beside him and there he spoke to de Graffenreid. "Your villages will be destroyed and you will be held here until the warriors return." He then looked at de Graffenreid to see if he would put up a fuss like Lawson.

De Graffenreid was still tied to his slave, sitting there in a small pile of his own feces, since neither he nor the slave had been allowed to move anywhere during the day. Still, in the overall smell of a Tuscarora longhouse, the fecal odor merely added a heavy though slightly different aroma to the odiferous mix, and de Graffenreid considered that discomfort fairly minor, compared to his pending death sentence. More importantly, de Graffenreid had considered the matter all day, and realized that he lived or died at the mercy of this warrior chief. At that moment, he was merely grateful for the opportunity to bargain for his life, and he wanted to make the most of it.

"Great King Hancock. King of all the mighty Tuscarora. Killing me and this miserable slave will do nothing for your people, but if I return to my village with several of your warriors, I can provide you with twenty muskets to use against the

Catawba to the west."

De Graffenreid paused at that point, to give the King a chance to speak. When Hancock said nothing, he realized that at the very least, he had the King's attention so he continued. "Your warriors will use those muskets and they will be able to capture many Catawba and sell them in Virginia. You will have every advantage over them, since they use only the bow and arrow."

Hancock merely grunted, and left the longhouse. However, within only an hour he returned and began the negotiations in earnest. He looked at de Graffenreid, and merely said, "Fifty muskets!"

De Graffenreid knew he could not get fifty muskets. To do so meant he would have to raid the muskets designated for the New Bern Militia, and collect many more from families in the settlement, families who would never give up their guns willingly. Still, he was ecstatic to be negotiating at all and to merely agree with Hancock's first offer, would be an insult to the King. "Great King," he said. "There are not that many muskets in all the Carolinas. I will provide twenty muskets, and powder, lead for shot, and twenty blankets, that your wives will stay warm in the winter. That is all I can do."

Again, Hancock said nothing, so de Graffenreid continued. "I will provide these things for King Hancock, but I must get these from the new village on the Neuse River, so Great King Hancock and his warriors must not destroy New Bern or the outlying farms along the Neuse, the Trent, or Mill Creek." In this fashion, while sitting, bound, and under threat of death, de Graffenreid bargained to save the lives of the early settlers of New Bern. History to date has recorded no greater example of bravery in any colony of the British Crown, yet not many today even know of this historical event. De Graffenreid continued. "You may make war on those who take your land in Bath or in the Albemarle, but not on New Bern or my Germans!"

Ultimately, King Hancock agreed to spare a direct attack on New Bern or any of the outlying settlements that painted the letter "N" on their door. The N indicated that those on that farm had settled at the same time as the Neuse River settlers in New Bern. None of the settlers on any of the outlying farms ever knew of this arrangement, so other than New Bern itself, none were spared from the horrendous attack when it came only one day later. In the longhouse, Hancock never indicated any final agreement to this smelly-pale. He concluded the negotiations merely by grunting, as if in disgust, and walking out.

De Graffenreid did not know his fate and he was held captive for another five days, but he was then allowed to leave with his slave. They left the very day that the warriors returned, and they saw many white captives, mostly women and children, being led into the village of Catechna. De Graffenreid knew then it was to be all out war.

Hancock never inquired about the muskets since after the massacre he really didn't expect to receive them anyway. De Graffenreid did send thirty blankets to the king's village within only a few months however, sending them back with one of Hancock's own sons who had been captured in battle. Perhaps King Hancock thought that his son was worth more than the muskets. Meanwhile the massacre and the terror of the Tuscarora dominated all the settlements of the Carolinas.

## *The Massacre Begins*

The fateful date of 9/11/01 commands attention all over the world today. Likewise, Americans all know of the dastardly attack on Pearl Harbor on December 7, 1941. However, in the first several hundred years of the North Carolina Colony, the "date that would live in infamy," the date humbly remembered around family firesides for generations, often resulting in fear and heartfelt prayers each year, was September 22, 1711, the day the Tuscarora struck.

The Tuscarora Massacre was a well planned, highly coordinated attack that began at dawn throughout all the settlements of the Bath and New Bern areas. Only the settlements much further north in the Albemarle were spared. The attack was carried out with forethought and a dastardly cunning only the savages could have mastered and it left many smelly-pales dead without ever realizing what was happening. The Tuscarora had, wisely, infiltrated the enemy gatherings by slipping into the villages, farms, taverns, and trading posts of the smelly-pales. On that morn, they began to interact or work exactly as they had done for the entire previous year. These warriors were familiar sights around New Bern, the Foscue Plantation, the Banks farm, Bath, Trent Mill, and on the various other farms where they routinely labored, and for all outward appearances, things were perfectly normal. Then just after dawn, they struck.

The young Tuscarora working with Martin and Johannes, the savage named Otter, was a good example. When Martin led his four lumbermen into the forest just before dawn that day, he assigned Otter and a large black slave owned by William Brice, to chop down a very large oak that Martin had noticed previously. Then he took the others, another of Brice's slaves, and a free white man, further up the ridge to another of the large oaks on the Brice plantation, since Brice had ordered more barrels and was supplying the wood himself. Martin had just left his second two man team beside the second oak. He had mounted and ridden only fifty feet or so when he looked toward the first tree. From the height of his mount he could barely see over the slight ridge and he was surprised to see Otter bending over something on the ground, and seemingly extracting a hatchet. The hatchet looked bloody!

While Martin didn't know exactly what to make of that, he was sure that it had nothing to do with felling trees so he dismounted quietly, tied his mount to a small pine, and removed his Kentucky rifle from the sling on the mule's side. The weapon was loaded of course, since unloaded guns do no one any good in the wilderness. He needed only to put a bit of powder in his flash pan, and he was ready to shoot, if need be. He did that without even thinking about it. Leaving his mount, he thought he would move toward Otter quietly, to see what was happening, so using his woodland and hunting skills, he slipped soundlessly into the brush. Before he moved more than ten feet however, he saw movement off to his left and immediately realized that Otter was now stalking the other two lumbermen.

Seeing no mule nearby, Otter must have assumed that Martin was long gone and that killing these other smelly-pales would be easy. Yes, the Tuscarora even used that term, smelly-pales, for black slaves, though the "pale" didn't really describe blacks all that well. Within only thirty seconds, Otter was in striking distance, and emerged from the trees wailing a high pitched warrior's screech, similar to the sound that would, in a much later war, become known as the "Rebel Yell!"

The lumbermen barely had time to turn around and see this savage from hell charging forward and the one closest to the screaming warrior was sure that he saw his own death in that terrible, clearly bloody war hatchet. Otter closed to within ten feet of that man with murder on his mind but the lumberman didn't move. Of course, the lumberman was holding an iron axe, a tool that was as fearsome as any battle weapon ever devised by man, a weapon that had been used on battlefields since time before memory. Still, he did not even realize that fact. He stood there paralyzed with fear, totally unable to move. He knew he was about to die under a fearsome hatchet swing toward his head but then a fifty caliber rifle shot, a noise unlike any other sound in the world, cut through the warrior's screech and broke the terror. Otter crumpled in death, falling to the ground immediately before the lumberman with a large gaping hole in the back of his skull. Martin, with poised practiced aim, had hit the savage in the middle of the forehead, scattering his grey matter like a thick morning mist, leaving what was left of his brain glistening through the large exit wound in the back of his skull and thus open for public viewing.

The lumberman immediately pissed in his breeches, just as Martin emerged from the brush holding a smoking rifle. Martin looked at the man he had just killed, and automatically began to reload his weapon. Then looked up at his lumbermen, and asked the inevitable question, "What the hell is going on?"

The lumberman didn't answer. He had fainted. He fell first against the old oak he'd attacked previously with his axe, and he then scraped the skin on the side of his head as he fell limply to the ground while unintentionally dragging his face along the rough tree bark. Within a minute or so Martin had slapped him several times, to bring him around, and then he and his two remaining lumbermen went looking for the black slave at the other oak tree. What they found was disgusting. Not only had Otter killed the man but he had then cut the head from the body completely, and that would be one of the milder bodily mutilations on that fateful day.

Martin and his two remaining men hurried across the several miles of swampland to the Brice plantation house, where they heard other similar stories from fleeing families. Within only an hour or so of the beginning of the attack, the Brice plantation became a garrison, as did other plantation houses all through the Carolinas. Historians have documented as many as thirteen other such locations where groups of settlers gathered together to withstand the attack of the savages during the first few hours of that dark day. These garrisons became a refuge of sorts for those lucky enough to escape the initial carnage. Most of the folks in the outlying farms and distant settlements did not.

### *Wrath of the Tuscarora*

We, today, think that we know terror, with visions of aircraft crashing into buildings, or explosions in dusty cityscapes. We should realize however, that we are not unique. Our ancestors knew the same horror, the same terror, on the day the Tuscarora struck. The attacks made no sense to these Germans and other settlers, and this violence seemed to come out of nowhere. The murder of John Koonce was typical of the atrocities.

John and his family owned a farm along Mill Creek, just a couple of miles distant from Trent Mill, land that is today owned by a descendent of Martin Bender. John was in his newly cleared field along Squirrel Branch when his hired man, a Tuscarora the family had long known as Porky, murdered his employer. Porky's Tuscarora name, while unpronounceable in either English or German, sounded roughly like Pequato, and meant "finder of bear." His name quickly became Porky, which was at least, pronounceable by these Germans who were still struggling to learn English anyway.

Porky worked for about an hour that morning before daybreak, beside John using a pair of oxen in the field. They were trying to remove a large tree root from the center of the field that John and his ten year old son, Willie, had cleared during the previous winter. As Willie stood nearby waiting to help, John bent over to check the harness on the oxen. Just then the sun peeked over the tree line, and Porky grabbed a nearby axe and drove it deep into the back of John's skull while he screamed a terrifying war-hoop!

Willie was horrified at that image, but he was not immobile. He ran screaming toward the cabin followed closely by Porky, who had extracted the axe and was chasing the boy, clearly intending to murder the rest of the family. Willie's terrified screams and the war screech of the Tuscarora warrior were enough to let Willie's mother, Charlotte May, know that something horrible had happened, and she did what all frontier women did at moments like that. She grabbed the loaded smoothbore musket that always hung on two pegs above the fireplace. Such muskets were kept instantly ready for any frontier emergency from wolves, to bear, to savages, to murdering drunks that might wander by. Before Willie could reach the cabin across the field, Charlotte May was standing in the door, taking steady aim at the savage chasing her son toward the cabin, as both Willie and Porky jumped across the corn rows.

Willie ran as if hell were following him and when he got within twenty feet of the cabin, he looked up and stared straight into the business end of the family firearm. The thought of that gun in his mother's hands terrified him even more than the bloody savage that had just killed his Pa. Still, thinking like a much more mature man, Willie jumped to the side, thus giving his Mama a clear shot.

Porky never knew what hit him. The force of the fifty caliber lead ball caught him full in the chest, picked him up, and tossed him backward for several feet. He bled profusely, and died within a minute. Charlotte May never saw any of that since the kick of that powerful, black-powder weapon sent her sprawling backward across the packed-dirt floor of the cabin, where Willie found her only moments later. By the time he had reloaded the musket, his Mom had packed up the two year old and was ready to travel. They had no clue what might be taking place, but they wanted to get to the safest place they could, so they headed down the Mill Creek path hoping to reach Trent Mill, where a blockhouse fort stood for just such emergencies. Charlotte May carried a side of salt-cured ham in one arm and her baby in the other, while Willie carried the loaded smoothbore musket and led the family livestock, one cow and a couple of goats tethered together. They did go by the field briefly to say a quick prayer over the body of John, but they didn't remain to bury him. They gave not a single thought to the body of Porky, and both of those men were dragged off for a wolf feast that very night. The wolves throughout the Carolinas were well fed during the three days of the Tuscarora Massacre.

As Charlotte May and Willie passed the cabin of another Mill Creek farm family, the family of Eugene White, they saw that the cabin was on fire, and several bodies lay in the yard. They noticed no livestock, though several chickens were calmly pecking the ground. They didn't stop.

When they arrived at the blockhouse, they saw a large gathering of livestock, as if others were also leaving their farms and carrying or driving whatever they could. In only an hour, a group of thirty-two survivors, most of whom were women and children, crowded the blockhouse grounds. When Franz Tuber, the miller, suggested that they retreat as a group up the trail to the town of New Bern no one objected.

There was some talk among the crowd of searching the other farms along Mill Creek and further up the Trent, but that was considered too risky. Among this group, only eight males were present, and that included several eight, nine, or ten year old boys such as Willie who, in a pinch, were considered old enough to carry a weapon. There were twenty-nine muskets in the group, since some of the other women had brought along any weapon they could find. In fact, in frontier country like Trent Mill in those days most of those women could shoot pretty well, when necessary.

Still, there was simply not enough manpower to consider any rescue mission for others. After a brief discussion, the group decided to stick together and not send anyone to the outlying farms. Those settlers would be left alone, and most would not survive the day.

Under the overall direction of Tuber, however, the group did decide to check all the farms that happened to be along their route. By noon on that desperate day, that group was moving along with their livestock on the twelve mile march up Island Creek Trail from Trent Mill towards New Bern.

They did find four more stragglers along the way. One young woman named Katie Elizabeth Griffin was gathering wild grapes in the woods, and thus was not at the cabin to be killed, as her husband had been. She had her baby with her, and she had hidden, terrified and alone, in the woods along the trail until the group from Trent Mill passed by. Two black slaves that had been leased out to a tobacco farmer named Jacob Dillahunt also joined the group a bit further on, though they never explained how they came to be alone on the trail. On any other day that would have caused some question, but on that fateful day, no one even asked.

The group passed eleven cabins scattered along Island Creek Trail on the south side of the Trent River, but virtually every cabin raged with the fire of Tuscarora anger, and bodies had been strewn about like chicken feathers after a fox's sneak attack. In some cases, even the livestock had been slaughtered. The Tuscarora had learned the advantages of keeping livestock over the last year, but in the blood lust of that massacre some warriors had simply destroyed everything that moved.

The same story of massacre and mayhem played out repeatedly all along the Neuse and the Pamlico Rivers further to the north, as survivors banded together and headed for any location they thought might provide some measure of safety. The Trent Mill group traveled almost ten miles without encountering any Tuscarora, and then they came to the rickety bridge over Brice's Creek. Just as they crossed that bridge Captain Brice rode up to them on his stallion, and demanded to know who they were. Various survivors had been streaming into his plantation all day, so he knew that an Indian massacre was well underway.

Tuber replied to his question, simply saying, "We are from Trent Mill, and the savages have slain many!"

Brice nodded his head, and gave his orders. "Put your livestock in the corral yonder by the barn, and then find a place for your families to sleep in the barns or the pack house. All men and boys with firearms report to me on the porch of the big house in thirty minutes. You are now members of the New Bern Militia." He then rode off.

Within an hour, Charlotte May Koonce was helping a number of women watch the children who had been collected, while other women were firing up stew pots or cooking beans. By evening, over one hundred and twenty men, women, and children, were encamped at Brice's plantation, and many were now calling it Brice's Garrison. Martin and his two remaining lumbermen had reached the garrison by ten in the morning, and within twenty minutes a couple of young boys came rushing in with their mother astride a horse. She had suffered a severe head wound. That family lived only a mile off to the east of Brice's Plantation along the Neuse, and the father had been killed early in the day. When their Tuscarora hired hand had tried to kill the mother, the two boys, aged ten and thirteen, had fought him and wounded him with a shovel, creating a deep gash in his neck. With their pa dead in the field, the boys took their wounded mother to Brice's where she too, died later that evening. Scores of children became orphans on that desperate day.

By that point, another mother had arrived with a similar story, and Captain Brice feared he was to be swamped by women and children. When Martin and his remaining lumberman spoke of getting into New Bern, Brice exploded in a shout. "You can't leave these women and children here! They need the protection of the New Bern Militia!"

Captain Brice knew that Martin would heed that call, since he'd seen the measure of this young man only three months previously in Cary's Rebellion. The lumbermen were an unknown since he didn't know these men personally, but if this young man Martin had confidence in them, Captain Brice decided he would too. It was at that precise moment that the New Bern Militia began to respond, even though only two official members of that militia, Martin Bender and Brice himself, were actually present.

"Martin, you will take ten men and set guards at each corner of the plantation buildings." Captain Brice ordered. "Do not leave any men exposed but post them inside the buildings themselves. Make certain to place at least four of them around the livestock pens. I have already sent my slaves out to gather all of my livestock into the nearby enclosures."

Martin knew that he had the services of his lumbermen but those men had no weapons, and even with arms from Captain Brice's own armaments, the obvious problem was where to get men! Before he could speak however, Captain Brice, ever determined, anticipated his question. "We'll use these boys here," and he pointed to seven young boys, ranging in age from ten to fifteen years. He then continued, and his next words shocked Martin completely. "We'll have to arm the slaves."

Now giving slaves firearms was considered a final option, even in that distant time. Fear of slave uprisings was common from the earliest period onward in colonial history, and slaves having arms was a truly terrifying thought. While many individual slaves hunted for their own food, typically only one slave had the use of a firearm on any given day, and that slave was always required to turn in the weapon at the end of the day as well as give an accounting for each shot taken.

Further, the slavery of those early colonial years was a bit more intimate. The large slave plantations of the cotton era, plantations holding hundreds of slaves, were still in the distant future. In 1711, even the Brice plantation, one of the largest in the Carolina Colony, owned only eighteen or so slaves, and Captain Brice knew all of his slaves personally. He cared for them well, and was quite willing to trust most, if not all, with a weapon in order to deal with the turmoil with the savages.

Dunker Tim was a perfect example of such a slave. He had fought in Cary's Rebellion, and acquitted himself well. He could even be counted as a leader of the other slaves. Within only an hour, Captain Brice had found firearms for all of his thirteen male slaves, and they were acting under direct orders from either he or Martin, as were twelve other men and boys who had marched into Brice's Garrison with various groups from the distant countryside. Thus, at two in the afternoon, twenty-seven men and boys prepared to defend over eighty others then present in Brice's Garrison. Within the next couple of hours, however, that total number would increase to a hundred and forty nine. Included in that number were fifty one men and boys, including Martin and Captain Brice himself, ranging in age from sixty four down to ten. Each would carry a weapon, and each was now a member of the New Bern Militia.

## New Bern Defends Itself

By the next morning, across the Trent River in the city of New Bern itself, word was coming in from various farms that the Tuscarora were attacking all along the twin rivers, the Trent and the Neuse. Some survivors had drifted into town with tales of cruelty, torture, or bodily mutilation that would make any man weep. Johannes closed the cooper's shed, and was about to take his remaining men out to find Martin and his lumber crew, but the local leader, Sheriff Jack Hughes DuVal, had ordered all of the roads closed and no one could leave the city limits. Militiamen were called out and told to bring their weapons. They were quickly assigned in groups of seven or ten to guard the incoming trails on each side of New Bern, as well as the ferry landings across both the Trent and Neuse Rivers. No bridges had been built at that point over either river, and because of the distances involved in each case, a small ferry was all that was available. Everyone in the city was preparing for war, though no one knew what was really happening.

Margaret was helping prepare food for the militiamen stationed around the town, since those men would not be allowed to return home for some time. Katheryn was beside herself with worry, and cried openly to her mother. "But Mother, how can we help Martin and his men if we can't get across the river to find him?"

There was no answer possible for that question, with the Tuscarora in complete control of the countryside. The family, like many families in the town that day, did not know if their loved ones were alive or dead. They knew not Martin's fate, much less the fate of the other lumbermen in his party. No word had been received from across the Trent River at all, and no one even knew if Trent Mill or the Brice Plantation had been attacked. No word had come from Governor Hyde or the legislature at Bath, because Bath, like New Bern, was fortified and feared imminent attack itself.

Katheryn was hopeful for Martin's safety. She knew that he had a fine weapon and the skill to use it well, as well as a mule for escape if that became necessary. She knew that he could hold his own in woodland skills and that he had faced battle before and met that challenge. Still, she, Johannes, and Margaret all worried about him. The Tuscarora were killing everyone, and those savages could kill him with an arrow or a war hatchet before Martin even realized that they were upon him. Katheryn in particular fretted more with every minute. She longed for nothing more than to see him coming down the street with his mule and his new rifle, and she found herself looking outside the cabin frequently hoping for that first sight of his return. She was to be disappointed that day, as well as the next.

In multiple war parties, the Tuscarora rampaged for two full days, then three, stealing whatever they could, murdering, torturing, and dismembering many. While the savages never attacked New Bern itself in force, they did attack within sight of the city. One farmer, a man named Tanner Askew, had decided to remain in his cabin since he was only a half-mile from the city trail to the settlements along the Neuse to the west. His cabin was built near the trail and fields had been cleared between his land and the New Bern settlement, so the guards along that trail had an unobstructed view of his farm.

On the morning of the second day of the massacre, those guards saw a party of perhaps twenty-five Tuscarora warriors emerge from the trees along the trail, and within only a minute or so, Askew, his wife, and his two sons opened fire on the savages. Some of the guards at the trailhead wanted to run to the cabin and help fight off the savages, but without a commander at that location, the men decided their post could not be abandoned. One militiaman pointed out the obvious fact that the fight at the Askew farm could be a trap for the entire New Bern Militia. There could be a hundred more savages in the tree line just waiting for them to emerge and leave the trail into town completely undefended.

The Askew family would have to fight alone, and the fight did not go well. In only a few minutes, one of the savages managed to get to the side of the cabin and toss in a burning torch. It must have hit a whale oil lamp or a pot of cooking oil, since the rear of the cabin seemed to burst into flame almost immediately, with flames coming out the side door and the single rear window. In only a few more minutes the guards saw three figures, they looked like Askew, his wife, and one son emerge from the cabin, which was by then almost totally engulfed in flames. The family headed for the small barn just across from the cabin, but never made it that far. The man was cut down by arrows almost immediately, and the son was wounded, but the woman was captured by savages who then began to rape her repeatedly in the yard, while in full view of the guards at the western end of town. Her screams were horrific. They left her alive in the end, and two members of that guard unit went to fetch her when the warriors left. She made it back to New Bern barely alive, but she died within only twenty four hours of the attack.

{Author's Note: Only a couple of decades later, the fields around that burned out Askew cabin would be purchased by the government of Craven County, and that ground eventually became the location for one of the early hospitals in New Bern, St. Luke's Hospital, which was located on George Street and Broad. Few today know of the bloody history of those acres, or realize that death under what is now the parking lot of that building, had initially come not from the lingering passage of New Bern's older citizens, or the mistakes of impatient doctors, but from the arrows of the Tuscarora on that very ground. Those reflections should cause us a moment of pause today, and perhaps a bit of reflection on the sacrifices made to create a great city, and ultimately a great nation along these twin rivers. Here the Askew family died, in their attempt to build a life for themselves and create a new city.}

## *Attack at Brice's Garrison*

Over at Brice's Garrison, the Tuscarora attacked directly, by charging the barns and the plantation house on the afternoon of the first day. Captain Brice had organized a defense in depth, as soon as men began to stream in, and the later hours had given him time to refine his defense plan. Captain Brice himself led the battle, with around twenty men located in the plantation house itself. When the attack came, a steady coordinated fire spewed from the smoothbore muskets in that building. Dunker Tim took charge of fifteen armed slaves and they were assigned to the spring house, and along a ditch between the smoke house and the several slave cabins to the left of the plantation house itself. These men were separated and thus could not control their fire or coordinate their shots or their reloading with each other. Still, they were all experienced hunters, who could shoot well and they held their own.

Across the yard to the right of the plantation house stood the barn and behind that, the livestock pens. Martin was now in command of fifteen men in that barn. Some men were much older than he, but Captain Brice had addressed the group on that point forcefully and he left no doubt who was in charge. "I saw the measure of this young man in the recent rebellion, where time and again he showed himself worthy of command. No one in the New Bern Militia would hesitate in the least to follow him into battle, and no one within this Garrison shall show hesitation either. You will obey the orders of this young man as if they were my own. If any man does not obey those orders he will be acting in defiance of the New Bern Militia in a time of war, and will be subject to charges. In fact, damn it, I'll shoot the bugger myself!"

With that excited shout ringing in the ears of the men, Captain Brice gave his orders to Martin so all could hear. "Sergeant Bender, take these men here, and set a guard at the far end of the livestock pen. Place the rest in the barn and pack house, with most seeking firing positions in the hay loft. Partner your men together, so that one fires while his partner reloads. Kill the enemy when they attack the main house, and watch for an attack from the back of the barn. Support the men at the end of the livestock pen. You realize that those men guard our food supply. Put your best men there."

As ordered, Martin took command, and led his group across the yard into the lower level of the barn. There he divided his men by pairs, and gave them their

# Brice's Garrison

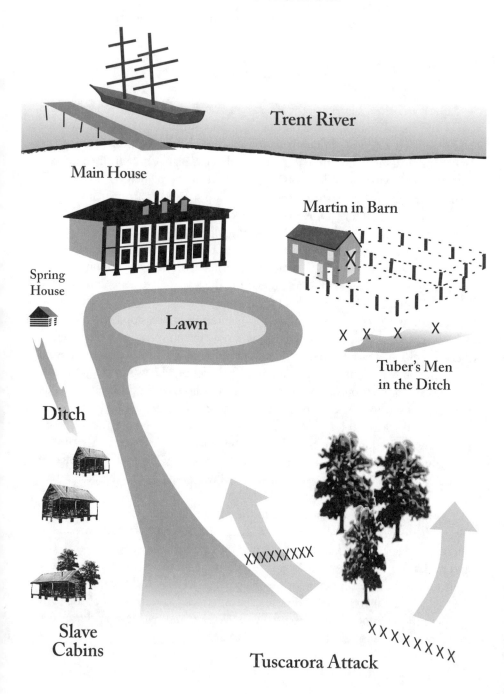

orders. He placed six men under command of the miller, Mr. Tuber from Trent Mill, at the far end of the livestock pen, with the orders to protect the livestock at all costs. He let them know that they would receive support fire from the second floor hayloft in the rear of the barn, just across the livestock pen, since everyone figured that the Tuscarora would attempt to make off with the livestock.

He then placed the others at every door and window in the barn, placing as many upstairs as he could manage, and talking with each of them about their specific areas of responsibility, their fields of fire, and the need to coordinate fire with their partner with one reloading as the other one fired. In that fashion, at least one member of the pair would always have a loaded weapon. In particular three men were told to fire out of the upstairs hay loft opening in the rear of the barn, and thus support the men across the livestock pen. Martin placed young Willie Koonce in the upper hay loft. Willie still clutched his father's musket, and seemed rather determined to fight well. Martin told him to fire directly in front of the window, when the savages reached that point. After all the orders were given, all of the men did what every soldier who has ever gone to battle has done—they waited.

An hour later, they were still waiting. By then, Martin was leaning on the frame of the open door at the front of the barn, seeking targets in the tree line that had yet to materialize. He'd already walked among his men once just to give them courage, and to check to see if they remembered their fields of fire. As he leaned on the door frame he noticed a spider whose web nestled between the frame and the side panels of the barn, and that brought a smile to his face. He remembered another spider on the ship that brought him to New Bern, and his reflections that the spider on that small coastal freighter had a home whereas he himself did not on that fateful day. Had that really only been eighteen months before? To Martin, it seemed a lifetime, and in many ways it was. While a boy had emerged from the small ship after that voyage, a seventeen year old man, fully confident and capable, with previous experience at war, now stood in this barn ready to serve his militia unit and defend his home. He commanded other men who were much older, but had no experience in combat. In short, he was a tested man, and as such a proven man. Both his men and Captain Brice were depending on him to lead.

The Tuscarora approached for the attack around four in the afternoon. No thunder logs were in evidence, so the warriors advanced down the main trail toward the main house, but when they got to within forty yards, fire spit from every window, every barn door, and every ditch on the entire plantation. The first wave of approaching savages was halted almost immediately, since they had only a few firearms. Most of their warriors were using bows and arrows, or war hatchets, so they had to get much closer to the smelly-pales to actually inflict any harm. In contrast, the whites all had smoothbore muskets, and Brice as well as Martin had the new Kentucky rifles. The fire from these weapons was horrid, and in only a few moments the savages retreated a bit back up the road.

Martin had personally fired four times from the front door of the barn, and with his new rifle and his experience hunting he couldn't miss. Once he saw that things were under control in the front, he dashed up the ladder to the upper floor and hurried to the rear of the barn. Sure enough, the Tuscarora did have a small contingent approaching the livestock pen from the tree line behind the barn, but he could only see ten savages. Martin was certain the men at the far end of the livestock pens could manage that force, particularly supported by the men in the barn. Martin did take one opportunity to fire at one savage from that lofty perch out the back of the upstairs hayloft, and sure enough, one savage fell to the ground. "Give 'um hell, men, or they will surely give it to you," he shouted as he flung himself back downstairs to check the fighting in the front of the barn.

Once the Tuscarora had time to regroup and mutually build up each other's courage, they swarmed in again from the front. Again, the musket fire brought many down, some within only thirty feet of the big house steps, but the deadly fire from three sides stopped them once again. As Martin moved through the barn again he passed by Willie Koonce, and the boy shouted to him, "I got one Sergeant Bender! I saw him fall!" Willie was very proud of himself, that day, and justifiably so. In the next decades, he would eventually father nine children, each characterized by a fierce family pride, and that great Koonce family would farm along these twin rivers for over three hundred years.

The savages, by that point, had realized that they were up against a large armed group of men who were well led. They abandoned their wounded in the yard, retreating again just out of range, where they remained visible for the rest of the day. They did not attempt another attack directly on the garrison that day, but Captain Brice expected them to come again during the night. However, he was wrong. The savages showed no further signs of aggression at Brice's Garrison on the first day, and apparently abandoned that area during the night.

At the end of the first day, only four of the men at Brice's Garrison had been wounded, and two of those were fairly minor wounds. Mr. Tuber had taken an arrow through his calf muscle in the lower leg that had punched all the way through without striking the bone. For some minutes during the close of that battle, he fought with the arrow sticking clear through his leg, looking like the arrows comedians would use hundreds of years later to place around their heads as comic props. After the shooting stopped, Mr. Tuber broke the arrow in two and extracted the wooden portion that was still in his leg. He then screamed at the top of his lungs, as Charlotte May Koonce poured whiskey into both ends of the wound. He had the presence of mind to stick the arrowhead in his pocket.

The Tuber family living along the White Oak River three hundred years later still cherish that historic if unusual family heirloom. It proves that their ancestor helped build this colony, and it is a source of great family pride!

One of Brice's black slaves had received a much more serious wound in his chest, from an old flintlock musket, carried by a nephew of King Hancock himself. The ball was too deep to extract, and the man would either live or die depending on his own body's defenses. He was coughing blood by the next morning, and died later that day.

At dawn, Martin, Captain Brice, Dunker Tim, Mr. Tuber, and several others sat together on the front porch of the big house and discussed their options. Most of them had managed to catch some sleep the previous night while others maintained watch, but none were well rested. Still decisions had to be made and these men stood to that task. The Captain, always aggressive, wanted to ride out and give battle to the savages wherever they might be found, but others including Martin had advised caution. Brice was wise enough to listen. In particular, Martin pointed out that they did not know what might be happening elsewhere and that they should coordinate their plans with those in New Bern.

At seventeen, Martin was now a seasoned fighter and had learned much of the wisdom of war from his several battles. Coordinated attack or defense always worked much better than emotional surges hither and yon, and one should know at all times where one's enemy was and what they were likely to do. That reasoned thought is why Martin had been the first to recommend that he, Johannes, and the others advance to the tree line in the fight at the Pollock Plantation, and that cool, clearheaded planning during a battle had distinguished Martin from that moment on.

Everyone had offered their advice that morning on the porch, and the conversation had begun to wane. It was clear that Brice would be needed to command the garrison, so he could not leave. However, they also needed to alert New Bern, find out what was happening, and seek assistance if any were available. If they sent a messenger however, the savages could run him down, or kill him on the trail as he passed by, and they all understood that dilemma. They had already rejected the idea of moving all of the survivors in mass to the settlement, since the many women and children, not to mention the livestock, would slow them down. For all they knew a whole army of Tuscarora, a thousand or more warriors, might be lurking just outside of New Bern itself! It was quickly decided that they should remain at the garrison since that was a good defensive position. Still, how could they get a message into the city and coordinate a plan? At that precise moment, at many other makeshift garrisons all across the Carolinas, other men were asking the same questions and making the same tough decisions.

Brice then noticed his hay crop in the distant field bend under a relatively brisk, gusty wind and he smiled as that gave him an idea. He made his decision and, as is the case with any good commander, it was both creative and unpredictable.

"Dunker Tim." Captain Brice shouted. "How would you like to go for a nice pleasant sail?"

Dunker Tim looked at his master for a moment, as if he were crazy. Then he caught on, and grinned broadly. "Yes, Suh! That would be mighty pleasant today, Suh!" The others merely stood there dumfounded, at least until Captain Brice spoke again.

Brice smiled at the men, and then continued. "You and Sergeant Bender will take the *Abraxas* from the dock yonder and sail across the river to New Bern. The savages shouldn't be able to catch you with the wind coming up." While the distance to the New Bern docks was around three miles by river, all on the Brice Plantation had always used the phrase, "across the river."

Brice continued. "Martin, once there, you will seek what help you can, and return here. The trip should take no more than five hours to get there and back, even with an hour or so on shore."

Within only a few minutes, Dunker Tim, Willie Koonce, and Martin Bender began what turned out to be an uneventful sail down the Trent to the docks at New Bern, where they were met at pier one by One-Eye Benny and his ever-constant companion Able Ward. They were immediately rushed to the end of pier two where another, larger vessel had just landed. There Sheriff Jack Hughes DuVal was coordinating plans, in the absence of anyone with greater authority.

The Sheriff was initially inclined to dismiss this ragtag group, as nothing more than, "A nigger slave, and two kids in a sailboat," until One-Eye Benny spoke up.

"Sheriff, sometimes I don't know beans from bacon, but this here boy is one to listen too!" He pointed to Martin and continued. "He's the one what led men to the tree line to stop Cary in that scrape up at the Pollock Plantation a couple months back."

One-Eye paused just then to spit his tobacco chew towards the dark acidic waters of the Trent River, waters that exactly matched the color of the tobacco wad. In those days, a man's spittin' was viewed by all as a measure of his wisdom and experience, and all such efforts were judged on both trajectory and distance. One-Eye hit the river about two feet from shore, giving him a total distance of just over six feet. He'd clearly earned his reputation as one to take note of! He continued.

"Wouldn' a believed it myself, hadn't I been up in the spring house watchin' it all, at Pollock's that day. I'd give 'm an ear if'n I was you, Sheriff."

Martin then presented his report to DuVal, who immediately saw the wisdom of maintaining the garrison at Brice's, since that would protect the southern flank of New Bern itself. However, when Martin asked about men and provisions that might be sent to Brice's Garrison, he was told flatly, "We have no food or men to spare."

Martin didn't press the point however, since it seemed that Brice's was provisioned about as well as New Bern itself, at least in terms of food. He did request and receive one small barrel of gun powder, and some lead for making musket balls. He was made to sign for them and promised to return any unexpended supplies to the city after the conflict was over.

{Author's Note: Martin Bender, a 17 year old boy, signed his name on that ledger on September 23, 1711, as if he were a man. Right under that signature he proudly wrote, Sergeant, New Bern Militia, Brice's Garrison Station. Other men were made to sign that same ledger as they received weapons, powder or lead for making shot on that same day, and of the eight who signed on that day, only five could write their own name. They were all Germans. The others signed with a large X, while Sheriff DuVal wrote their name out for them. The ledger has been preserved among the historic records now stored in London, England, with a copy on loan to the state government in Raleigh, North Carolina, a city that did not then exist.}

Martin, Willie, and Dunker Tim continued to stand around on the docks, to gather what information they could, and in a few minutes Johannes came in with a report from the far end of the settlement, where some Tuscarora had been spotted. The two embraced, and Martin told Johannes of the treachery of Otter, the Tuscarora brave that he had hired for the cooper's shed only three weeks previously. The two decided to take lunch together at the cabin, and both Willie and Dunker Tim tagged along.

As the cabin door opened, Katheryn, now fifteen years old, had been watching the approach through the window, and she again flung herself into Martin's arms, this time surprising neither Martin nor Johannes. Her words rushed out as she held him.

"Why have you not been home? Oh God! Did you not know we were worried sick? Mother was praying all night and Christina cried herself to sleep! Where have you been? Oh God, I have worried so, and here you are as if nothing has happened! Why are you not fighting here with the militia? We want you here!"

Max even came to attention and offered a low growl at Dunker Tim, since he was always a bit prejudiced against blacks. Johannes quickly eased the scene a bit, when he said. "Calm yourself, Katheryn and tell mother to serve us a meal, girl. We are all hungry men! Anything in the stew pot is fine, but we have little time!"

Katheryn replied, "Mother is across town, serving men at the far guard outpost. She didn't know you were coming."

Johannes merely said, "That is fine, Katheryn. You may serve the meal."

The stew pot was brimming over since many women were helping to feed the militia as they manned the guard outposts. Within only a moment, Katheryn and Christina, who had come rushing in from gathering eggs outside, had wooden bowls and spoons on the table, utensils that Martin and Johannes had carved only a year before. Katheryn was ladling out a fine potato and ham stew, filling each bowl to the brim, while Christina poured cool water to refresh the men.

Dunker Tim then did a strange thing. Without sitting down, he picked up his bowl of stew, while saying a kind "Thank you, Miss Katheryn. It sho' do look mighty good." He then turned to go back outside. No black slave had ever eaten in the presence of a white man on the Brice Plantation.

Martin noticed this and immediately guessed what was happening. His voice cut through cabin. "Dunker Tim!" All present were held breathless by that commanding voice, and Dunker Tim froze on the spot.

Martin took only a second to find the right words. He then spoke, again in the loud commanding voice. "Any man that fights by my side will always be welcome at my father's table. Please sit here. You have many things to tell Father about the battle, that I didn't see myself." Martin then gestured to the bench directly beside himself.

"Uh, Thank you, Suh!" Dunker Tim replied, not really knowing what to do. Then he nodded graciously. "Thank you, indeed, Suh!" He said as he walked back to the table and sat right beside Martin.

Just at that pivotal moment, Johannes said, "We shall give thanks." As always, he prayed in German, and thus with flawless grammatical precision.

*"Father, the savages are upon us and we fight to defend our city and our land. Help my strong son, here..."* Here his voiced faded away, as he looked up at Martin, who met his gaze proudly. Johannes paused a moment longer to gather his emotions, then continued. *"Help my son in his battle across the Trent River, and help me in mine here in New Bern. Be with your servants here and in the settlements, and bless all who sit with us today and sup at our humble table. We all worship in your name, and we all seek your grace. Let us defend ourselves and our homes, and let us be strong in this fight that we might accomplish your mighty works on this Earth. Amen."*

Everyone then ate for a few moments in silence.

Martin began to speak of the atrocities he had heard described, but a cautious look from Dunker Tim, and a quick glance toward Johannes convinced him that those cruelties should not be discussed in front of the women. He described instead the battle at Brice's Garrison the previous day, while Katheryn and Christina listened with wonder at horrific happenings. Dunker Tim took Martin at his word and added his perspective of that battle.

Soon Johannes departed to return to his guard post, taking along several helpings of the stew for Toby Mallard and his other compatriots at his posting. Martin, Willie, and Dunker Tim headed for the piers to return to Brice's Garrison. Martin did notice on that walk that Dunker Tim, unlike before, now walked right beside him, and that surprised him a bit. Why had he not done so before?

## *The Extent of the Massacre*

Prior to leaving New Bern on that day, September 23, 1711, Martin stopped by to speak to the Sheriff again, and there he heard more horror stories as several others who had just arrived in the city made their reports to the Sheriff. In each case Sheriff DuVal refused to send either men or food supplies to any garrison outside of New Bern, but he did release more gun powder, which was not in short supply. It was at this point that Martin began to learn the extent of the massacre.

A rider named Jake Antoine, had ridden out on the day of the massacre from Bath to alert New Bern and the other scattered farms to the danger. He had reached as far as the head of the Chocowinity Bay some twenty miles away from Bath and thirty miles north of New Bern before running into a fight. At the edge of that bay where the town of Washington would soon spring up, Antoine found a settler, John Porter, his family fighting for their lives against fifteen Tuscarora and Coree warriors.

Now Jake Antoine was tall and thin, but he was a rough-cut sailor, though some would call him a pirate. That meant that that he always carried several loaded firearms and in situations of known danger, he packed even more. He could shoot very well indeed, as he showed on that fateful day.

He later stated that he rode into that fight with no less than twelve loaded firearms on his person. When he rode headlong into the battle, Porter could see six pistols worn across his breast which he drew one by one, fired, and then calmly tossed aside, since all pistols of that day were single shots. Some in Bath would later say that the notorious pirate, Blackbeard stole this same idea from Jake Antoine himself, as Blackbeard always went into battle with six loaded pistols worn across his chest. At Porter's farm that day, Antoine also had five loaded muskets, each hanging in a separate scabbard across his horse. Thus, muskets stuck out in every conceivable direction, and he even had one small pistol in his boot. He never drew that small gun, but several of the loaded muskets did command attention.

Jake rode headlong into that battle looking just like a porcupine!

It took this rugged man only a moment to determine exactly where he needed to be, and with Porter and his wife, Eunice both firing from the cabin, Antoine circled behind the savages and then rode his horse directly at their rear. The Tuscarora had hidden behind a woodpile, so Antoine sought shelter at the edge of the barn to their rear, dismounted, and continued to fire on them from behind.

These Tuscarora had not infiltrated into the farms or settlements. Rather this batch was a raiding party, dressed in full war regalia, and many wore face-paint around their eyes, a circle of black around one eye and a circle of white around the other. When they turned around in alarm to face Jake, he merely "aimed for the pretty painted circles!" At least that is how he reported it later.

The Tuscarora were now receiving fire from not only several windows in the cabin, but also from this hell-hound porcupine-looking demon behind them. They scattered, running quickly to the woods where they disappeared. Jake had fired all six of his pistols, and four of his muskets by then, and nine savages lay dead or dying in the yard, most behind the woodpile. Porter hurriedly packed his family and Jake into his small sailing sloop, a ship only nineteen feet long, which was then further burdened with Jake's horse, two cows, a mule, and three sheep. They headed for Bath. However, when they heard musket fire, they thought that Bath was also being attacked, so they sailed wide across the river, and right past that town. They then decided to sail around the bend for New Bern, where they arrived on the afternoon of September 23, the day after the first attacks.

Like the other survivors, they had seen numerous burning cabins, and a number of mutilated corpses along the route. Even prior to arriving for the fight at Porter's farm, Jake had come upon a massacred family lying beside their burning cabin. The man had been dismembered—his arms and legs cut completely off and tossed to one side. A dead black slave lay nearby, with both his right hand and his head severed from his body. Just at the edge of the yard, Jake noticed an unborn baby who had been cut from the stomach of the young wife. It now hung by the umbilical cord in a tree where it had died quickly, but the savages had cruelly left the young mother alive to bleed to death. She had crawled several feet towards the tree, as her intestines unwound behind her on the ground. Jake found her there barely breathing, and still crawling towards her now dead child hanging in the tree. He took one look at the horrid wound in her gut, and with no words to her whatsoever, he took out a pistol and put a lead ball into her brain, ending her suffering.

{Author's Note: Frontier warfare is never pretty, never nice. The flowery descriptions of bravery from politicians, generals, ministers, or dictators notwithstanding, war is horrid and incredibly ugly in all its manifestations, and this frontier war in the Carolinas was to be no different. It was clear on that first day that atrocities were commonplace. They were eventually perpetrated by both sides in this struggle as they typically are in such warfare, but the Tuscarora certainly outstripped the smelly-pales in cruelty on that fateful September day in 1711.

However, if we condemn the actions of the Tuscarora because they seem extreme to us today, then we are insulting that powerful warrior tribe as well as embarrassing ourselves by our infantile understanding of history. To state again, the Tuscarora were warriors in a tough, demanding warrior society, governed by stringent and unforgiving warrior codes. When they saw their own people gone missing and discovered a few bodies of those who had been "Injun bashed" what should anyone have expected of them? In their view, the more horrible they could make their initial massacre of the smelly-pales, the less likely they were to continue to be attacked by the crude slavers, and least we forget, they accomplished that very goal with this massacre. This war did indeed stop the enslavement of the Tuscarora and other Native Americans in the Carolinas forever.}

In all, around one hundred and thirty settlers lost their lives on the first day of the massacre though the actual number may be much higher. Who can ever know how many outlying farms were attacked and totally destroyed? Attacks came throughout the territory of the southern Tuscarora towns, though true to his word, King Tom Blount and the northern Tuscarora never joined in the fighting. For that reason, the various militia groups in the Albemarle were extremely cautious about joining in the fight. They wanted to keep the northern Tuscarora out of the conflict as well as maintain their trading relationships with those northern Tuscarora villages that followed the leadership of King Blount. While not overtly admitted at that time, the politicians in the Albemarle really didn't mind having the Bath or New Bern settlements chastised a bit by this Tuscarora attack, since that merely resulted in more trade for those in the Albemarle.

When Martin, Dunker Tim, and Willie reported back to Captain Brice, Jake Antoine and his horse came along. Jake was determined to ride through all the southern settlements, warning everyone, as he'd planned to do when he left Bath, and ride he would. Captain Brice was eager to hear all that they had learned. As he listened to the report, which took Martin over two hours, he quickly realized two things. First this was not a single raid, but rather a full scale, highly planned, well coordinated attack on almost the whole colony. In noting the locations of the settlements that had reported in to New Bern (and many had not reported in by the end of that second day), Brice could determine that many different raiding parties had been involved so he realized, even if the others did not, that this was to be an all out Indian war.

Next, it was apparent to him that Sheriff DuVal was over-matched by the circumstances as well as his new leadership responsibilities. While the Sheriff could calm a few drunks over at Mallard's Tavern when necessary and make sure the betting was square at the weekly cock fights around town, he was not a man to lead the city in troubled times. Thus, Captain Brice did what effective leaders have done throughout history when confronted by incompetence in leadership positions. He merely assumed command of the entire New Bern district, and rather than seek orders from Sheriff DuVal, he began to issue orders to Sheriff DuVal!

That same evening Brice sent Martin and Dunker Tim back across the river with orders for the Sheriff to call up the New Bern Militia. Of course, that had already taken place, but Brice did not realize it at the time. They were ordered to muster the next day at noon in the town square bringing provisions for a ten day engagement, where he, Captain Brice, would take command and lead a raid into Tuscarora Country. Martin was told to deliver those written orders personally to Sheriff DuVal and then return immediately to Brice's Garrison that night.

Brice also dispatched Jake Antoine to ride to South Carolina, report the Tuscarora War, and seek the aid of the South Carolina Militia. Jake was allowed to rest his horse for the day, but he was admonished to be gone at dawn the next morning. Finally, Captain Brice dispatched Porter in his sailing sloop to Williamsburg in Virginia to let them know of the war on their southern border, and to seek help. Like Antoine, Porter was ordered to leave at dawn.

The next day, both Antoine and Porter were indeed dispatched on their separate missions, and Captain Brice prepared his ragtag group of untrained men to depart for New Bern. It was a six mile walk, so he thought he could leave at eight and make it by noon into the town though he would have to cross over the Trent using the ferry. He'd summoned Martin at seven in the morning to his breakfast table, and given him some disappointing news.

"Sergeant Bender. You have acquitted yourself well in my command both here and at the fight at Pollock's Plantation. While I want every good man with me on this foray, I also need to consider the defense of both New Bern and this important garrison. I need not tell you there are many women and children in both locations."

Captain Brice took another bite of his sausage and continued. "Of course, the town has many older men who are unfit for a march, but can stand guard duty in the town, so defense there will not be a concern. However, this garrison will require a military presence."

Martin didn't like where this discussion was headed, but he held his opinion until this respected leader finished with his point.

When Brice saw that silent respect from this young man, his opinion of the boy increased even more. "I need you to take command of this station, while I am taking the fight to the Tuscarora. I do not think you will be attacked again here since the first attack was not successful, but we do need to maintain some sort of strength here. I'll take all the free militiamen with me, and pick up more in New Bern. I'll also take most of the weapons, but you will have command of fifteen slaves from this plantation, as well as five of the younger boys. You also realize that a number of the women can shoot. We have more firearms than men at this point, and all the powder either of us could need, so there will be no scarcity of those items."

Here Brice paused, and then showed his maturing abilities in leadership. He did not order, but rather asked, if Martin would take command of Brice's Garrison under the conditions he had described. "Will you, Sergeant Bender, accept this temporary command of Brice's Garrison, and protect the settlers here?"

Martin nodded, and said, "I will, Sir."

Brice said, "Splendid! I'll leave Dunker Tim here with you. I know every slave on this plantation will obey him completely, so he should be of help. You and he get along well, I believe?"

Martin nodded at that, as Brice continued. "Very well, I'll depart within the hour. Please see if you can get this gaggle of untrained men into some sort of marching formation by then will you?"

Again, Martin said, "I will, Sir." He then left the Captain to his breakfast.

## *An Unexpected Attack*

Captain Brice rode out at the head of a column of thirty-eight men from Brice's Garrison on the morning of September 24, 1711, leaving little for defense of the garrison. Nevertheless, within fifteen minutes Sergeant Martin Bender had organized his defense in depth, given that he had few men to work with. He figured that the Tuscarora might still find the livestock an appealing target, so he placed four men, all black slaves who were good hunters and thus good shots, at the far end of the livestock pen once again. He supported these with three of the younger boys in the upper floor of the barn hayloft, ready to fire down on the savages from that area. He would again command the forces in the barn, so he also assigned three slaves and two of the boys to that post.

Dunker Tim was put in charge of four other slaves in the spring house, with three more in the ditch near the slave cabins. Martin gave Dunker Tim specific orders to circulate from one post to the next during the coming battle, if indeed a battle was to come their way. Martin knew that this completely exhausted his forces, but he had determined that those posts were much more heavily engaged in the previous attack than were the men in the plantation house itself, so he put all of his forces in those locations, leaving the plantation house itself defenseless in his initial plan.

When Dunker Tim heard the battle plan and noticed the deficit of men, he said, "Suh, they's no more slaves nor boys to fight up in the big house. What you g'oin do?"

Martin smiled to Dunker Tim as he looked directly over his shoulder and called out a question to one of the women. "Mrs. Koonce, have you ever fired a musket before?"

"Damn, sure have, Sergeant Bender!" Charlotte May replied loudly. "Killed me a savage just the other day, out in the field! Hunted with my man before too! I can shoot pretty fair, and I'd sure love the chance to prove it!"

Martin smiled knowingly. He still had his women! Nine women said that they could shoot fairly well and most of them had lost a family member, a husband or a son, to the Tuscarora only two days before. No group of women has ever been as eager to get into a bloody scrape as this batch of frontier hardened, pissed-off Carolina farm gals, and Martin proposed to use them. He really didn't believe they would be attacked again, but he needed these women since he had no one else for defense of the plantation house and necessity does indeed foster invention, particularly in a battle where all could easily lose their scalp, their life, or both.

The women Martin Bender armed that day ranged in age from fourteen to forty-nine, but the really angry ones like Charlotte May Koonce, seemed a bit on the young side. They would garrison the plantation house itself and Martin ordered them to defend it to the death. The women didn't balk at that extreme order at all. Certainly every single person at Brice's Garrison that day believed that a fighting death was preferable to capture by the Tuscarora.

Martin also stole another idea. He adopted the concept of multiple firearms that he'd heard Jake Antoine describe the previous day. Thus, with seven muskets left over after each of the slaves, women, and boys selected their weapon, Martin made sure that his best shots received two muskets. They were ordered to keep both loaded and ready.

The Tuscarora had not withdrawn totally from the area. When they left after the previous battle they had stationed two of their younger warriors near Brice's

Garrison to keep an eye on things. King Hancock's nephew, who was leading this particular raiding party, then took his force back towards Trent Mill to see if any survivors had escaped into the forest, or if any livestock was still around that might be worth stealing. One of the young warriors found him later that morning, so the Tuscarora leader knew of Brice's departure from the garrison only two hours after Captain Brice and his militia rode away.

About the same time that Brice reached New Bern and began to prepare his militia force to head up the Neuse into Tuscarora Country, that raiding party of Tuscarora was quickly heading back to Brice's Garrison thinking that it was mostly disarmed, if not wholly abandoned. At this point, the blood lust was satiated for most of the warriors and they were now more interested in gathering spoils from the farms and settlements they attacked. Many warriors were burdened with iron axes, stew pots, firearms, and other items stolen from various farm cabins.

By four o'clock on September 24, the Tuscarora were again surrounding Brice's Garrison, and while they could see several slaves with weapons in the ditch at the far end of the livestock pen, they could not see any other defenders. Martin had ordered that all livestock be brought into the barn save several cattle in the pen. He hoped that this would cause the enemy to think that most of the livestock had been taken to New Bern itself. It wasn't much of a ploy, but it might give the enemy a moment of pause, and causing one's enemy to stop for even a few seconds in a battle can be advantageous at times.

He'd also given the slaves at the far end of the livestock pen rather strange orders. They were to fire their muskets only once and then run back to the safety of the barn, leaving the three cows still in the pen for the Tuscarora to take. He didn't mind sacrificing a few cattle if it slowed down the savages some.

The Tuscarora didn't disappoint. At around four-fifteen in the afternoon, they moved into position and launched their attack. This time they paid a bit more attention to the livestock pen than before even though it was now comparatively empty. They put eighteen of their warriors on that attack position while the rest rushed the plantation house through the front yard just as before. Within only a minute of the first shots, Martin had detected the relatively light attack on the plantation house from his location in the front of the barn. In fact, the savages had fallen back to the tree line after only one volley, leaving four wounded in the front yard. This suggested two things about the battle, and both were critical.

First, with a light attack here, there would be a more serious attack somewhere else this time around, and Martin correctly guessed it would be behind the barn in the livestock pen. Next, the retreating savages here left Dunker Tim and his men with no targets at all to shoot at and thus wasted them entirely.

Martin acted immediately to address both problems. He grabbed the nearest man beside him—who turned out to be a twelve year old boy named Brantley Stephens, and shouted, "Run yonder to the spring house, and tell Dunker Tim to bring four of his slaves and come runnin' to the barn. I need him right here, right now! Go! Run!"

The boy took off toward the spring house like the devil himself was behind him, and Martin watched only for a moment to make sure he hurried along. Then Martin turned to find out what was happening in the back of the barn. He skipped the climb to the upper floor, and merely ran back through the lower floor of the barn which was now crowded with livestock. He jumped over one sheep in route. He reached the back door and looked out. Sure enough, three of the four slaves from the other end of the livestock pen were running for the barn door hell bent for leather, but Martin noticed that each still clutched his weapon and his powder horn! He nodded at that fact, proud of the courage shown by those men, knowing well that they would need those weapons before this was finished. In his mind at that point, they had become his men, not niggers or slaves, but his men. Still, he didn't stop to think of that at the time. They were in a bloody scrape to the death, and these men had shown courage by following orders to fire and then retreat. Martin didn't pause to consider the horrid fate of the man that had been left in that ditch.

Twelve Tuscarora were right down behind those men with their war hatchets raised, and one savage in the tree line was taking careful aim with a matchlock at the back of one of Martin's men. When Martin saw that, he stopped immediately tossed his Kentucky rifle to his shoulder in one fluid motion and fired. The savage went down without firing his musket, just as the men made it into the barn.

As they passed, one of the other men in the door fired, but apparently missed, since no savages fell after that shot, and Martin voiced his thought out loud. "We might have to fight these sons' o' bitches here in the barn. Get out your knives!" He'd used a curse in that sentence, and that surprised him for a moment. He'd heard it at Mallard's Tavern, but he'd never before used it himself. In fact he'd never cursed at all before but still, it seemed to fit right then.

Just then however two of the running savages stopped and grabbed the tether of the cows that Martin had left in the pen, thus taking those warriors out of the fight. That aspect of Martin's plan worked, but it still left ten blood-crazed Tuscarora warriors charging towards the barn, war hatchets ready, only fifty feet away. Neither Martin nor any of the other men huddled behind the barricade in the door had any time to reload their empty weapons. Martin leaned his rifle aside, and pulled his knife from the scabbard on his belt. He thought to himself, "I've never been in a knife fight before!" He then shouted to his men, noticing this time around with instant clarity, that he didn't see them as slaves or niggers anymore. They were his men! That thought hit him like a lightning bolt, but didn't distract him for even a second. He shouted, "Get yourself ready men, and we'll fight 'um right here in the barn!"

At that moment Martin saw something move just beside his right eye, and then his head seemed to explode with a giant noise! The explosion right next to his ear stunned him and for a moment he thought that he was surely dead. A cannon must have gone off, and he felt hot lead pass his ear as his hair flew forward from the blast. He jumped to the side, away from the massive explosion. But no cannon were here? What the hell?

His thoughts raced! Maybe a musket had exploded. Dunker Tim must have run to the barn with four or five men right down behind him. Maybe all had fired together somehow. No, not loud enough. A musket must have exploded. Martin figured that is what deafened him, but that much noise from five muskets? It can't be!

The Tuscarora were decimated in the barnyard. Of the ten charging warriors, all but two were now on the ground wounded, and those two were already running flat out for the trees as two others led the cattle away. The wounded savages who could crawl or hobble headed for the forest too. No threat there, at least for the moment. Martin didn't realize it but he automatically began to reload his Kentucky rifle as he turned to see what the hell Dunker Tim had fired or what had blown up behind him that made so much damn noise.

And standing two feet behind him, he saw the very eyes of death. How in hell did they get behind him?

He stared into the most hate-filled eyes he'd ever seen in his life, and it made his blood run cold, as time froze to a standstill. His heart turned to stone, as he looked into those cold, calculating, nearly feral eyes, a shark's eyes before the kill, a snake's eyes. There they were smothered in smoke, the harsh acrid smell of black powder stinging his nose. He was terrified! Every face, every eye looked just the same. Surely this was Satan himself come up from the depths of Hell to fight at Brice's Garrison. Martin was paralyzed for a moment, as he stared into those cruel, cold eyes of death. God they were harsh, but then…

Then the moment was gone as Charlotte May Koonce nodded to him, and calmly lowered her smoking musket.

The rest of the women did the same. They stood together in a line just behind Dunker Tim's crouching men in perfect volley-fire position. They had shot their weapons along with Dunker Tim's men right over the heads of Martin and the others. Thirteen muskets fired together really do sound just like a small cannon! They must have run to the barn right behind Dunker Tim, and there they stood, proudly surveying the deaths they had caused. Revenge for these women was terribly sweet! He looked at each of them, one by one. At that moment he understood.

Amy Charlotte White, twenty two years old, her husband and son both dead on the farm at Trent Mill;

Julia Whittey, forty two, one son killed and her only daughter stolen by the savages, her husband rode now with Captain Brice and the militia;

Katie Elizabeth Griffin, fifteen years old, her husband killed at their farm on the Trent, their first son only two months old;

Anna Martin, thirty-nine, her second husband now dead on their Neuse River farm, and their seventeen year old son rode with the militia;

Isabel Brice, daughter of Captain Brice was fourteen years old that day;

Laura Helen Banks, thirty-one, husband dead at their farm along the Neuse, one son and one daughter captured by the Tuscarora;

Eunice Colleen Carmichael, twenty nine, the wife of Archie Carmichael, who rode with the militia, was expecting in less than a month;

Lois Jarman, forty-nine, husband dead, and her sixteen year old son now rode with the militia.

Martin shook his head in wonder, and then had the same thought as before. No group of women had ever been as hungry to get into a bloody scrape as this batch of frontier hardened, pissed-off Carolina farm gals! Martin would never think of women as the weaker sex again, and he had learned at that point in his young life a great wisdom that some men never acquire. From that day forth he promised himself that he would never, ever, take a woman's emotions lightly again. He lived by that wise rule for the rest of his days.

{Authors Note: These women are certainly women to be honored. The names of these remarkable women were duly recorded by Sergeant Martin Bender on that same day when he'd assigned each one of them a musket. While women fought in many frontier scrapes over the next two hundred years in the Carolinas, this was the only time in history that women were officially recognized as serving in the New Bern Militia or any other militia in the colony. Those names, Charlotte May Koonce foremost among them, have been preserved throughout history, initially in the London records for the Carolina Colony and later in the state archives.

Those old documents reflect much of the tale of New Bern, but they also necessitate some quiet reflection. For these are the women of New Bern and of the Carolinas. These are our sisters and our mothers, the women of which all Carolinians are bred. We are fortunate, indeed, to have inherited these genes, and we owe them great honor and humble appreciation. For as much as any man, these women, and thousands of others like them, built this city, this state, and ultimately the nation that we enjoy.

The same must be said of Dunker Tim and his band of black slaves. Much of this nation was built on the sweat, the strong backs, and the shoulders of black men. These very same black men fought valiantly when they had to, and their fight represented more than merely saving their own hides. Of course, any of those blacks would have suffered the same fate as the white women and the boys, had the Tuscarora won that day at Brice's Garrison, but that alone is not the sum total of why they fought so courageously. Rather, they, like young Martin Bender, realized that building a settlement, a city, or a new nation is both tough and demanding. They fought like demons on that day, fighting for a better world on this new continent. They realized the ultimate worthiness of that goal and even with society at the time treating them so poorly, they still fought for it.

Jesus and I read of this fight, a victory by slaves and women in a rough frontier struggle, and we were amazed at these people! On the shoulders of men and women such as these was our city, our state, and our nation built, and today we find that our nation holds nearly limitless possibilities for us, because of their labors and their sacrifice.

Ultimately, from this fight at Brice's Garrison, and thousands of similar struggles through the years, a nation emerged which still promises peace, fairness to all, and respect for the human dignity of all men and women. These men and women, black and white together, created that dream for us all, and if our nation has not lived up to those ideals as yet, the fault is certainly ours and not theirs. These women and men, slaves and free alike, could have done no more.}

Dunker Tim took four men and killed any savages that were still alive in the field. They dumped those bodies, as they had those from the previous fight, into Brice's Creek, which emptied into the Trent River. Those Tuscarora, like Martin's own father a year earlier, washed down the Trent and the Neuse, finally feeding the crabs in the marshes and swamps of the Carolina coast.

Brice and his militia stayed in the field between the Neuse and Pamlico Rivers to the north of New Bern for several days, and fought one brief engagement with a force of three hundred Tuscarora. Given that number, Captain Brice considered it prudent to withdraw and his militia did so in an orderly fashion. They spent a few more days burying more farmers and their families on scattered farms, but by then they had ascertained that the Tuscarora had withdrawn to the west. They buried bodies where they found them and noted who was dead and who may have been captured by the savages. The final toll ranged between one hundred and thirty to one hundred and fifty dead, with perhaps as many as fifty-five or more captured as slaves of the Tuscarora. Those captives were mostly women and children and many never returned. Some probably lived out their lives as slaves in other tribes far to the west, the Cherokee or the Catawba with whom the Tuscarora occasionally traded. No count of the dead could ever be entirely accurate, given the extreme mutilation of the bodies, but one thing is certain. Every man, woman, and child throughout the Carolinas believed the dead were much more fortunate than the captives of the Tuscarora.

For reasons never disclosed, Captain Brice did not receive additional militia units from the Albemarle; those troops simply never arrived. Brice had deduced that between five hundred and a thousand warriors were on the rampage, and he knew that his much smaller force of less than a hundred was not likely to be effective against that number. The militia had muskets and most of the Tuscarora were still fighting with war hatchets or arrows, but numeric superiority is always important and sometimes critical in frontier war. Brice was wise to change his initial plan. Retribution would come to be sure, but it would come later.

Within a week, the Captain had returned to Brice's Garrison. He then dispatched Sergeant Bender in charge of a ten man mounted unit to scout the settlements to the south by marching down the Island Creek Trail and scouting around Trent Mill. Again, that militia group buried those they found, those not completely eaten by wolves. They recorded the names of those settlers who they did not find; then they returned to Brice's Garrison. At that point, with the initial danger past, the New Bern Militia was allowed to go home but was told to be ready on a moment's notice, if needed.

## A Different Home Coming

Martin returned to the cabin on October 3, 1711 completely weary, and as always riding his mule and carrying his Kentucky rifle. He'd told his lumbermen to report for work at the cooper's shed the next morning, when he and Johannes could take stock of things and determine the next work orders. He dropped the reins to the mule in the yard without even attempting to tie off the animal since he was just too exhausted. He then walked into the cabin. Margaret and Katheryn were both there, but this time Katheryn did not run to fling herself into his arms. Rather, she calmly looked him in the eye and said, "It is good to see you home Martin. After you have rested a bit, perhaps we should talk."

Martin noticed Margaret smile to herself as Katheryn spoke, and he had no clue what either Katheryn's soft words or Margaret's smile might mean, so he merely headed for the wash pot hoping that the water was warm. He'd been looking forward to the opportunity to throw his arms around Katheryn since he'd left Brice's Garrison that morning. He wanted to squeeze that marvelous young German girl again as he had done only twice before, but that didn't seem to be in the cards at the moment. Instead, he removed his shirt and began to wash up a bit, as Margaret ladled out a bowl of stew and put some fine dark bread on the table. Neither Johannes nor Christina seemed to be around, so he ate for the next few moments in silence. However, he did notice that Margaret's smile was still in evidence, though Katheryn herself seemed to be the epitome of serious propriety.

After a few large mouthfuls, he asked, "Mother, has Father been home?"

Margaret smiled, "Yes, Martin. The men continue to guard all the roads out of town, but the number of guards at each trail has been reduced. Johannes is home every evening for supper and Bible reading, but some nights he has to go back for guard duty. I believe he will be home all night tonight."

Martin said, "That is good. I should like to see him this evening. I have missed our Bible reading in the evenings, though some of the men with me at Brice's Garrison read the Bible some."

Katheryn then asked, "Has anyone seen or heard of the Tuscarora? Are Captain Brice and the militia after them?"

"They seem to have gone back to their villages in the west. No one has seen any of them, including those who were working at Brice's Plantation, since the massacre." Martin paused, considering how much to tell these women, and then he remembered that remarkable moment in Brice's barn when he'd seen death in the eyes of those farm women. He immediately decided that women, unlike men, could stand almost anything, so he continued sharing his thoughts.

"There has been no news of any further mutilations and the Tuscarora do seem to be gone. Some of those at Brice's Garrison were talking about moving back up the Trent River to their farms in Trent Mill, but Mr. Tuber, the miller, talked them out of that idea. They all decided to remain at Brice's for a few days more, until something is done about the savages. No one knows if the massacre is just a single massive raid or if they are coming back."

As usual, Martin's straightforward thought had cut to the heart of the matter. In those days after the initial massacre, no one knew what was happening. Governor Hyde wanted to take action but at least half of the legislature was still supporting former Governor Cary. In fact, some of the sitting legislators had circulated a petition to the king to free Cary as soon as he landed in London, stating that the entire Cary Rebellion had been one big, legislative misunderstanding! With those feelings still running strong in Bath, no legislation was likely to pass, and the members couldn't even agree on whether or not to ask for help from South Carolina and Virginia! The North Carolina legislature was more than willing to have the citizens of the colony undergo another massacre at the hands of the Tuscarora, but they could not find it within themselves to agree on a plan of action, even in the midst of war. At that point almost two full weeks after the initial massacre, the only official calls for help that had been sent were those ordered by Captain Brice, on the second day of the uprising, and as it turns out, one of those pleas for help would ultimately bear fruit.

In October and the rest of that fall, the citizens of the North Carolina Colony remained in the various garrison plantations around the state or in the two towns, Bath or New Bern. Martin could go home since his home was in one of the few strongholds, but many others like the miller Mr. Tuber, Charlotte May Koonce and her son Willie, and all of the other settlers of Trent Mill, were marooned for a considerable time in the garrisons, left there essentially to rot by their own paralyzed government.

"Martin!" Katheryn said, rather loudly. "Have you heard a word Mother has said? It seemed as if you were somewhere else and not listening at all!"

Martin smiled at Katheryn since that was all he could do. He had indeed been elsewhere, deep in his thoughts about the crisis, and he had no idea what had been said in the cabin. Through all time in all cultures, such are the ways of men; when in thought, they ignore what they often perceive as the babbling of women.

Katheryn continued, "Perhaps we should take our walk now, since you seem to have eaten at least half of the stew pot." As she said this, she smiled at him, and held her head to the side in a way that always warmed his heart. Here, at last, was the joking, laughing girl he so longed to hug.

Martin stood. "A walk to take the air would be wonderful. Perhaps we should walk down to the docks and see what news …"

"No!" Katheryn interrupted, quite firmly. "I don't want to know the news. We'll find out all of that later when Father comes home. Right now, I just want to walk." With that, she began to put on a shawl since the autumn air was becoming more brisk. "We shall walk to Union Point to look at the joining of the rivers. That always fascinates me."

Even today one can stand at Union Point in New Bern and watch the two rivers refuse to merge their waters for some distance. That mystery has been the occasion for many couples over the years to contemplate their own friendship or perhaps more. Some have called it Lover's Point, perhaps because it is so beautiful or perhaps the rivers themselves inspire that appellation. It seems that after a firm attempt to remain independent, the rivers do ultimately join, just as truly great relationships foster both independence and yet yield eventually to ultimate union.

Martin and Katheryn walked side by side, and did not touch initially during their stroll toward the point. Katheryn kept looking toward the river and Martin had the distinct impression that she was in deep thought—which perhaps meant that this was to be an important conversation, though he did not yet know the topic.

"Hello Sergeant Bender," came the cry from the general area of the piers. Charlotte May Koonce and her son Willie were walking across South Front Street toward them, and Willie had shouted the greeting. "It is a fine day, and I'm glad to see you here!"

"Good day to you Mrs. Koonce, and to you Willie," replied Martin. "I did not realize you had come into town."

"My sister lives just down the way on Hancock Street, Sergeant," Charlotte May said. "We decided we would remain with her rather than at Brice's Garrison for the next few days. Captain Brice has been more than gracious and we certainly owe him our lives, but housing and feeding that throng has surely been a trial for him."

"I'm sure," said Martin. "Mrs. Koonce, may I present Miss Katheryn Simmons, the daughter of my master, Johannes Simmons." Martin then turned to Katheryn, saying, "Katheryn, Mrs. Koonce and her brave son Willie here fought off the Tuscarora at their farm, and Willie served in my company at Brice's Garrison. He is a fine shot, and served well in the militia."

Katheryn bowed slightly, and smiled. "It is wonderful to meet the two of you, but introductions are not necessary." She looked directly at Mrs. Koonce, saying, "Mrs. Koonce, I am sorry for your loss, but your bravery, as well as the courage of your fine son here, have been the talk of the entire town." At that Katheryn bowed once again, and continued. "It is certainly my honor to make the acquaintance of both of you. And I do hope you managed to keep my friend Martin here out of too much trouble."

Mrs. Koonce smiled delightedly, proud to be recognized and also proud that her son was likewise recognized. "Miss Simmons, it is certainly our pleasure. I can see what a joy you are to your family, and now I understand why our brave Sergeant Bender was so quick to return to New Bern, since here he would have the delight of your company. Having a young lady friend seems to be preferable to battling the Tuscarora it would seem."

Katheryn smiled at that statement, but Martin blushed openly. He didn't really think of Katheryn as his "Lady friend," and was somewhat taken aback by the comment. Both Katheryn and Mrs. Koonce were quick to notice, since women do notice those things. They looked toward each other and smiled as if sharing some secret. Even Willie was grinning from ear to ear, joining in at the expense of his Sergeant.

"Do not let us keep you, Sergeant." said Mrs. Koonce. "I'm sure you and Miss Simmons have many things to discuss at Lover's Point." She emphasized that last phrase a bit too much for Martin's comfort, "But I do hope to see you around town from time to time."

"Certainly, Mrs. Koonce." Martin then turned to the ten year old, and said, "Willie, you will muster with the militia here in New Bern, yes?"

Willie looked very proud to be asked. "I will, Sergeant. I will see you at the drill this coming Saturday."

"Fine," said Martin. "See you then. Good day, Mrs. Koonce."

"Good day, Sergeant. Good day, Miss Simmons."

As they continued their walk, Martin could not help feeling that Katheryn was smiling a bit more now. As they walked on, she opened the conversation. "It seems you are a man of some importance now. You are Sergeant Bender, and everyone, even Father, speaks of your bravery. Something about leading men into the trees towards Cary's men, I think."

She'd said the last, as if mocking him in some way, but then Martin realized she wasn't joking, but rather exploring his actions, inviting him to speak. He didn't know what to say, but he felt he should try to explain his actions, the actions that had caused so much comment. "I thought we could prevent some of Cary's men from getting to the shore, if we went to the trees and fired on them. That was all."

Katheryn looked at him and smiled coyly. "Ah, but to think like that when they are shooting at you. I understand the cannon were quite loud that day. Father says that is the difference."

Martin remained quiet. How could one describe one's thoughts or one's decisions, motivated as much by fear as anything else, in the midst of a battle?

"What do you fear, Martin?" Katheryn asked. She had shocked him with that question; she seemed to have read his mind.

Martin continued walking slowly along the river thinking, but after a moment, he answered. "I think I fear getting taken by the Tuscarora." Here he wondered again if he really should share his thoughts with this girl, really share his experiences. Then he decided that he must as they walked on slowly, and Martin never even realized that Katheryn had already taken him by the arm.

"We found terrible things, Katheryn, after they had destroyed a farm, they did terrible things to the family, the bodies."

Katheryn seemed, strangely enough, to want to hear something else. "No Martin, I have heard all the stories. I don't mean that, I think I... well, I think I mean, what do you fear about me?"

Martin was surprised by that question. He'd never thought that way about her before, and he quickly said so. "I do not fear you! I, uh, I rather enjoy you. I like you a great deal!"

As they walked on he collected his thoughts, and in his mind for just a flicker of a second, he remembered those feminine eyes of death, the feral eyes of Charlotte May Koonce and the other women, those wonderful, marvelous women, at Brice's barn. They were women who had risked everything and had lost much, but still they fought on. Then Martin thought that he knew what to say.

"I fear not being as strong as I should be, or perhaps not as strong as I must be for this city, for this wilderness. I want to be as strong as, as those women in Brice's barn. This place, this new city, will demand much of us. I fear not having enough, not being enough, or maybe not being strong enough."

Katheryn looked at this young man, feeling he was almost there, almost opening up to her. She wanted him to be open, wanted to know him, to know and to share his deepest thoughts. She started to encourage him to say more, but then she wisely held her tongue, waiting while he took the time he needed.

Martin was looking far out to the distance, far across the Trent River as they walked toward Union Point. He wanted to explain it better. He wanted to explain it all, so he tried again. "When we fought in Brice's barn, I thought I might be killed by the Tuscarora. I had fired my rifle and all of my men had fired." Here he reflected again, that in his mind those men were not slaves, not blacks, not niggers any more. They were just his men, his companions on the field. In his mind they were fighters, just like he himself was a fighter. They had shared war, and lived through it all together, so they would always be his men, his compatriots. Some, like Dunker Tim would ultimately be his friends.

He continued speaking, "We were all unloaded and I drew my knife, but I do not know how to fight with a knife. Any of those savages could have bested me and killed me or killed us all. I thought that they would, but then the women came, and the slaves came, no, my men came, and they fired." He knew he wasn't making himself understood, but he knew he had to continue. "They all fired together, and they saved me. They fought like demons. Mrs. Koonce looked like a demon! But they were there, right where they had to be, fighting just like they had to fight. They were strong like they had to be."

He collected his thoughts once again, knowing he could not explain it well but knowing that he still had to try. "They were there, and they were strong, those women, when they had to be. Just like my men, like Dunker Tim and the others. They were my men, and not slaves that day, when we fought together, and they were strong. They had to be strong for that fight, and when they had to be, they were."

He felt completely emotionally exhausted at that point, but he thought he had explained himself as well as he could, save one final point. "Perhaps I fear not being strong, or not strong enough for this place, this city. Perhaps I fear not being strong enough for you."

Katheryn looked up at him, without speaking. She felt that she was seeing into him in some new and profound way, as she walked slowly with her arm locked in his, both of them walking toward the joining of the rivers. She had heard everything that he had to give at that moment. She spoke as they walked on, saying exactly what he needed to hear. "Martin, you are strong and you will be strong, when you need to be. Father says that you are. He says you have always been. I am sure he is right."

They walked only a few steps further and found themselves standing at the very union of the rivers. They stopped and looked out at the distance, with an arm behind each other as they faced the merging waters. They saw the color line, the Trent always dark and acidic, the color of dark tea, and the Neuse, broad, brown, and muddy. As always, the waters refused to join near the shore but out in the distance, reaching toward Pamlico Sound and the distant ocean, they finally merged.

Silence.

Katheryn would always be much wiser than Martin in affairs of the heart, and her German blood made her bold, direct, and practical. She understood many things, though she was only fifteen years old on that day. As they stood at Union Point still looking out at the twin rivers, without even facing each other, she voiced the thought for both of them.

"Martin. I believe that you should kiss me now. Please kiss me, Martin."

So he did.

# Chapter 3
# The Tuscarora War
## *The Barnwell Expedition*

The Tuscarora War is best understood as a three phase war; the Massacre, the Barnwell Expedition, and the Moore Expedition and aftermath. After the massacre, the citizens of New Bern and the Carolinas huddled desperately together in Bath, New Bern, and the numerous garrisons scattered around the Pamlico River, the Neuse, and the Trent. Almost all commerce in the colony came to a standstill, as all were afraid to leave the fortified areas to harvest pitch or to hunt, fish, or farm. The survivors were clinging to hope for help from the more established colonies of South Carolina or Virginia. Virginia proved to be utterly useless throughout the entire period, but South Carolina had a vested interest in helping the new colony to the north. As it turns out, they had Tuscarora in their back yard too!

Jake Antoine had covered the distance to Charleston in only five days, and once there, he had done his job well. During the massacre itself, Captain Brice, with no governmental authority whatsoever, had dispatched Antoine to ride cross country to Charleston in the South Carolina Colony and report the attack, while seeking whatever help he could. Within three days of his arrival there, Major Christopher Gale, a messenger sent secretly by Governor Hyde also arrived by sailing ship. The governor still could not get the North Carolina legislature in the Albemarle to act, so he'd taken it upon himself to send a messenger to informally plea for support. Gale had specific though secret instructions to secure assistance. He was to promise the South Carolina governor anything necessary in order to get the help that the North Carolinians so desperately needed!

Based on that blanket authority, and the vivid descriptions of the massacre provided by Antoine and others, Major Gale worked on the emotions of the South Carolina governor. He promised that if South Carolina could put a military force in the field the North Carolina settlements would provide support for them, and that the Albemarle Militia would join them at the Trent River near New Bern. Gale, being from the Albemarle region, an area that had not been attacked by the Tuscarora, could speak for the Albemarle Militia, but he had no knowledge of the New Bern Militia at all. For all he knew it could have been wiped out completely in the initial days of the massacre.

Of course governments never act quickly and the inevitable deliberations took some time, but South Carolina finally did come through and appropriate some funds for "defense of the colony." In the context of the Tuscarora uprising of 1711, that term "defense" essentially meant "fight the battle in North Carolina rather than South Carolina" since the Tuscarora held territory in both states. Thus, a mixed force of South Carolina Militia units and savages from coastal tribes in the South Carolina Colony was raised to march to North Carolina and end the Tuscarora War. It was believed at that time, that the best forces to use against savages were other savages, who presumably knew the frontier style of fighting. Also, warriors from various tribes could usually be bought for the cost of the spoils from such a frontier campaign. Those warriors often held long-standing grudges against warriors in other tribes, and were usually more than willing to fight, believing such things to be a rite of passage for all warriors. Therefore, these animosities stemming from decades of inter-tribal warfare made recruitment into such campaigns relatively easy. So a combined militia and Indian force was gathered over the next several months, and the North Carolina Colony was to provide provisions for this army. An untested man, Colonel John Barnwell, was chosen to lead those forces, when some funds were discretely slipped into the pocket of the governor of the South Carolina Colony.

Barnwell was a lanky man, who stood a bit taller than usual in those days, topping out around six feet, two. He was very thin for his height so his clothes seemed to hang limply from his tall body giving him the overall look of a scarecrow too long in the cornfield. He also had an annoying habit of turning his head to his right, away from the person he was speaking to, and then looking back at them with his eyes cast toward the left. While that resulted from a hearing loss as a child in his right ear (he always turned his left ear toward the person he was speaking too), that habit did not win him many friends among the New Bern citizenry. To top that, he spoke in a high-pitched voice that led some to question his age, while others cast aspersions about his general sexual orientation.

His father had purchased a leadership rank, a colonelcy, for his son only two months previously, and everyone knew about this means of appointment. In fact, Barnwell had no military skills whatsoever, save for the fact that he'd recently read a book on battle tactics by some obscure French general or another. Suffice it to say that he was not wildly admired in the Carolinas, even before his campaign against the Tuscarora.

Still, within two months, he was leading his army, fifty militiamen from Charleston and five hundred Yamassee Indians from the coastal regions south of Charleston. The savages with Barnwell were promised many Tuscarora slaves, guns, and whiskey if they fought well. In any such overland march in those days, many savages deserted the army as they came across other interesting things to steal, but other savages usually joined the frontier army as it moved through, seeking to plunder towns on down the line. The later additions included some Creek warriors, some of the Cape Fear tribe, and a number of Catawba savages who had long been the enemy of the Tuscarora in North Carolina anyway. The overall size of the force remained relatively stable.

Barnwell arrived at Trent Mill on January 19, 1712, and despite the promises by Gale, he found no men, no food, and no guides to lead his expedition. Mr. Tuber, a miller, seemed to be something of a local leader, so Barnwell conferred with him. However, Barnwell quickly ascertained that he had heard nothing of any Albemarle Militia in the area. In fact, Mr. Tuber indicated that most of the farmers in the area were now repairing their farm implements for the next planting. However he did indicate that most of them were still spending their nights in the village of Trent Mill, in Brice's Garrison, or in other garrisons, and not on their outlying farms, since some Tuscarora were still believed to be in the area. Tuber also stated that no further murders of whites had taken place during the last three months since the September massacre. Much of this information was of no use whatsoever to Colonel Barnwell, since it didn't indicate where the enemy was, nor did it provide relief from his men's hunger. At the end of the conversation, however, Tuber did provide one piece of advice of value to Col. Barnwell. He suggested that Barnwell ride a few miles further on, and consult with Captain Brice who had led the New Bern Militia during the massacre. Based on that advice, Barnwell left his force encamped at the farm of Mrs. Charlotte May Koonce, while he rode on to Brice's Garrison.

On January 23, 1712, these two gentlemen sat together by a warm fire in Brice's plantation house. While they both had the pedigree required in high English society at that time, the two couldn't have been more different. Brice was a seasoned, successful plantation owner, and a veteran militia commander. He had grown much in his command skills over the last year, since he, like many in the New Bern Militia had fought both in a rebellion and an Indian massacre, and two wars in one year would help any leader grow in his leadership skills!

Barnwell, on the other hand, was in command, because his father, a wealthy plantation owner in Barbados, had chosen to purchase a small plantation in the South Carolina Colony and put his son in charge. The opportunity to purchase the Colonelcy came later. In short, Barnwell was a man who had much to prove and he saw leadership in this campaign as one way to make his mark.

Brice's slave Gideon brought tea, and served them, just as these two, very different men began their talk.

Col. Barnwell, in that high squeaky voice looked sideways at Captain Brice and said, "I am not certain what I shall do. I have amassed an army and come at the invitation of the North Carolina governor, but I have neither provisions for my forces nor an enemy to fight! Have you a recommendation for me?"

Brice didn't like this tall thin man, and felt that his voice was most irritating. Still, one took help where one could, so he took a sip of his tea to give him time to gather his thoughts. Then he spoke. "We shall certainly have to teach the savages a lesson. They cannot attack the settlements of the Crown with impunity, and I do imagine that old King Hancock knows he is in for a thrashing!"

"That is well and good, but still doesn't help me feed my men! How can a governor in need of assistance not help those who have come to help him?"

Brice merely smiled to himself, realizing that he could never explain to this South Carolina man the total paralysis of the North Carolina leadership. Clearly those idiots in Bath or the Albemarle had made some commitments to Barnwell and were not prepared to fulfill them. Not only that, the governor had failed to inform anyone in New Bern that this force from South Carolina was even on the way!

On the other hand Brice reflected, he could help this young upstart with some of his problems, and perhaps create for himself an ally for the future. Even with his high-feminine voice, this man was a gentleman and would eventually be influential in South Carolina. He might be helpful one day. Brice decided to try. "I say, Barnwell, why not treat your savages like hogs?"

Col. Barnwell was taken aback by the suggestion, and was mildly offended. "Like hogs did you say? Indeed! These men, even the savages, are my allies sir, and I intend to treat them well. I am afraid I do not understand what you mean."

Brice smiled at his guest. "Oh, Barnwell, I'm having a laugh at your expense. Do forgive me for not being clear." Brice took a bit more tea, and then continued. "You have over five hundred savages from South Carolina with you. Is that what you said?"

"Yes, Indeed! They are mostly Yamassee from upper Florida, with some Catawba and others thrown in."

"Indeed," said Brice. "And did these savages come for the spoils they might acquire in this campaign? Muskets, scalps, axes, and such?"

"Of course!" replied Barnwell. He was sure these questions were leading somewhere, but he was not sure where. "Yes. That is the hope of my government, that these savages can acquire spoils that will justify their time, and that the governor will not have to pay for this expedition at a later date. That is often the way we acquire our savages for these campaigns, and the North Carolina settlements were supposed to provide provisions."

Brice agreed. "Indeed. Well, clearly that has not taken place, so perhaps you should let your men run free through the area and scavenge for a time. What?" Brice made a broad gesture to the west. "Send them out there! Give them, say ten days, and turn them loose, just like our local farmers do with their hogs! What say ye? What could it hurt?"

Barnwell was catching on. "You mean, let them scavenge for themselves, and then report back? They would have to fend for themselves for that time?"

Brice said. "Just like hogs in the local woods. Farmers turn them out all the time, and they fend for themselves. They'll eat anything! When our farmers need to butcher one, they set out food. A lure, you see, and it brings them back in!" Brice paused, and again took a sip of tea, before he continued. "Treat your savages just like hogs, and you won't have to feed them. You can order them to return in two weeks, lure them in with a fight that will begin then, and they'll return, I'm sure! Perhaps help will arrive by then!"

Barnwell was voicing his thoughts openly now. "Why do you recommend two weeks? Do you think the Albemarle Militia will be here in two weeks? Will provisions arrive?"

Brice found himself warming to this young, irritating, and brash fellow so he decided to be completely honest with Barnwell. "Unfortunately Barnwell, I do not. I think Governor Hyde will not be able to persuade our legislature to take any action. We are essentially paralyzed you see. However, when your savages return, I can activate the New Bern Militia. It is a smaller force, and is not as seasoned as the Albemarle men, but it is a fighting force, and we will take the field beside your army and thrash the Tuscarora, once and for all!"

Barnwell was warming to the idea, but still exploring the implications of it or possible problems with it. "But Captain Brice, if we set these Yamassee loose for two weeks, these savages will surely wreck havoc on the entire area!"

"But my dear Colonel," Brice said, as he smiled and once again, gestured to the wilderness in the west. "Isn't that exactly what we want them to do?"

So the strategy was born that would allow the five hundred Yamassee warriors from South Carolina and northern Florida (which in those days, meant the area that would soon become the Georgia Colony) to forage for food, cattle, horses, or anything else they could steal, as long as it was stolen from other savages. Thus, began a two week period that still stands as the single biggest crime wave in the history of North Carolina. Barnwell pointed his Yamassee to the west with strict orders. "Steal nothing from whites, but take what you need, and report back here in two weeks." Of course, stealing nothing from the whites was not a problem at all, since no whites lived anywhere to the west, and therefore, the Yamassee looted only the villages of other Indians. Further, this strategy also helped solve Barnwell's other problem. Now he had only to feed his fifty militiamen, and Captain Brice even helped with that!

In that fashion, on January 24, Barnwell turned loose his Yamassee warriors on the western tidewater and central section of the North Carolina Colony. Word was also sent to the New Bern Militia to muster for a thirty day campaign, on the morning of February 7, 1712. The Tuscarora were soon to learn the high cost of killing white settlers in the King's Colonies, and most of the Yamassee thoroughly enjoyed their two week crime spree.

## The Battle of Narhantes

By February 10, Col. Barnwell led three hundred, seventy-five Yamassee warriors, fifty Charleston Militiamen, and sixty-five men of the New Bern Militia, under the immediate command of Captain Brice into the wilderness. This force moved along on the north bank of the Neuse River toward the heavily fortified Tuscarora town of Narhantes. This town was not the home city of King Hancock, but was nevertheless a Tuscarora stronghold and it was located only twenty-two miles to the northwest of New Bern, while Catechna, Hancock's home town, was over thirty miles away. Further, rumors were circulating that the Tuscarora had armed Narhantes and created a series of blockhouse type forts around it, making it a border stronghold. Col. Barnwell thought it advisable to destroy Narhantes first, and then move on to Catechna to capture or kill King Hancock. There was even some hope that Hancock might be captured at Narhantes, thus ending the war even sooner.

Narhantes was an open village with no surrounding palisade walls. In fact, the various longhouses in the town, the fields, and the horse corrals were scatted along the banks of the Neuse for almost a mile. Barnwell quickly observed that the Tuscarora had indeed constructed a series of blockhouses around the town, some were merely fortified log cabins, while several had an internal set of two blockhouses, surrounded by a small palisade wall of stout logs. Several of these were clearly still under construction, and were thus of little concern to Barnwell. In fact, none were sophisticated fortifications such as one might have found on a European battlefield of those days. Still, stout wooden walls can be quite a barrier when no cannon are available to pound them down, and Barnwell's was one of the most ill-equipped expeditions in history. He didn't even have food for his forces, much less heavy armaments. However, given the overwhelming ambition of this young man, that didn't deter Col. Barnwell in the slightest.

Barnwell sat astride his horse beside Captain Brice, and several subordinates discussing a plan to attack the small town. While no official ranks existed in the New Bern Militia since the legislature could not make that type of appointment while in its state of near paralysis, the New Bern Militia had essentially created its own leadership. Captain Brice was in command of course and serving as his lieutenant was Toby Mallard, the proprietor of Mallard's Tavern. Lt. Mallard had acquitted himself well in the recent massacre, serving as second in command to Sheriff DuVal in New Bern. On this particular expedition, the Sheriff had remained in New Bern to keep order and take command there should the need arise, but Toby was free to go, and did so, over some objections from his wife. Even with the New Bern Militia gone, there were still many older men in New Bern who were customers of the tavern not to mention the occasional shipload

# Battle of Narhantes

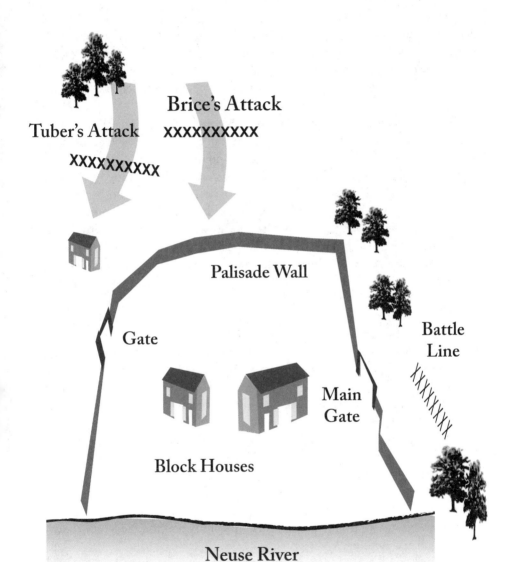

Tuber's Attack
xxxxxxxxxx

Brice's Attack
xxxxxxxxxx

Palisade Wall

Gate

Battle
Line
xxxxxxxx

Main
Gate

Block Houses

Neuse River

of thirsty sailors. When he'd been called up, he determined that he would go, and leave his wife to run the tavern. Even in the midst of war, taverns are prone to do quite well financially.

Serving under Lt. Mallard were five Sergeants; Johannes Simmons, Martin Bender, Archie Carmichael, Franz Tuber, and Ernst Franks. Each of these men had shown leadership in various battles previously either in Cary's Rebellion, or against the Tuscarora during the massacre, so others in the militia would submit to their command. Each commanded a squad of twelve militiamen, except Tuber who commanded seventeen militiamen from Trent Mill.

The palisade wall around the targeted blockhouse was about one hundred feet long on the east and north, with the northern wall curving back toward the river. The wall on the west was about fifty feet long and the enclosure was open to the Neuse River on the south side. The palisade itself was made of strong hardwoods and was approximately five feet high, so the Tuscarora could stand behind the wall and shoot over it. Unlike many such palisade walls, this enclosure had no ditch or moat outside of the wall, since the construction plans for all of the other blockhouses precluded using labor for that purpose. However, two blockhouses had been constructed inside the palisade, thus providing several layers of defense, and multiple firing positions on several levels. Each blockhouse stood around twenty feet high and had firing holes on two stories on each of the four sides. Only thirty feet or so separated the blockhouses from each other. Of course, savages in the higher floors of those blockhouses could shoot over the heads of the warriors at the wall, which was only fifty feet distant, with bows and arrows, matchlock muskets, or the newer flintlock muskets that had been stolen by the Tuscarora in the massacre only three months previously. Another blockhouse of some concern stood to the rear, and outside of the enclosed palisade wall, approximately three hundred yards away.

At this moment, Brice, Mallard, and all the Sergeants were waiting for Barnwell to describe his plan of attack. All were mounted, though most of the sergeants were on mules rather than horses. Barnwell rode a bay, but Captain Brice of course, rode his stallion. Sitting there in a circular group, Martin could not help but compare the two leaders, and wish that the Captain rather than this lanky scarecrow from South Carolina was in command. Still, he held his own council and said nothing.

Barnwell took a final look at the section of the town they could see, and made his decision. In that high pitched voice he spoke, making most of the others recoil visibly. "I believe the enclosed area at this end of the town is the strongest of the blockhouses, and we shall attack that first." He now addressed Captain Brice, since he knew not the names of the others in the group. "Captain Brice, I would like a force of ten men to form along the tree line just north of the encampment, and that contingent shall place fire on the second blockhouse. We do not want savages from there engaging our forces over here, what?"

Brice replied. "Sir. Do you propose to attack the nearest encampment and the next at the same time?"

Barnwell replied, "I do not, unless we are fired upon from the second blockhouse. Otherwise, we attack each fortification in turn. Please disperse your men to the north and the east in a battle line, and support them with the Yamassee."

Martin cringed when he heard that term, battle line. Overall he'd done fairly well hiding behind trees, in barns, or shooting from depressions in the ground during his first few battles, and it just made no sense to him to stand in a pretty little row in order to let your enemy shoot at you more easily. Still, such battle line tactics were the military practices at that time throughout Europe, so every would-be commander in the new world like Barnwell mindlessly decided to follow the pattern. Again, Martin did not speak, but he did make eye contact with old Archie Carmichael sitting across the circle, and it was quite apparent that Archie had the same thoughts as he.

Brice replied, "Very good sir!" Then he paused to think the matter through, changed the battle plan slightly, and issued the orders. "Sergeant Tuber. You shall take your men from Trent Mill and place the second blockhouse under fire, but do not fire unless you are fired upon. You are there merely to protect our other forces from attack from that blockhouse. I see no savages there presently, but there may be a contingent inside, so when they fire, you may attack and destroy them. We need ten minutes for our plan to unfold, so if the battle is not joined within fifteen minutes of the first shot, you shall charge that blockhouse and attack it. Render it useless, and kill anyone you find. Then rejoin with the main attack on the fortified encampment at this end of the village, attacking this fortification from the west."

Mr. Tuber, a miller who had never been a Sergeant before merely replied, "Yes sir."

Of course, Brice knew of this man's relative lack of experience, which is why he placed him at the only spot on the field that was not likely to see heavy action. Then Brice continued. "Lt. Mallard will lead Sergeants Carmichael, Bender, and two hundred of the Yamassee warriors and approach from the east. That is open terrain, and the militia should form a battle line forty yards from the palisade wall and bring fire on the fortress. Once the battle is engaged, fire for five minutes on the enclosure. Then use the Yamassee and charge the wall at least once. However do not sacrifice your warriors or your militia needlessly in further attack. Your job is to draw the fire of the enemy in your direction during the initial part of the battle, so approach in battle line but disperse into cover after the initial volley and continue to bring fire on that wall."

"Sergeants Simmons and Franks will accompany me into the woods to the northwest of the enclosure. We will wait until the firing to the east begins, and then we will wait an additional five minutes before we attack from the northwest. If we are lucky, we'll be able to approach those lower walls and only then will we bring the remaining Yamassee forward. Perhaps we can boost some of our men and some of the warriors over the top before the Tuscarora realize we are there, particularly if Lt. Mallard can command their attention! Once inside the palisade, we will open that gate on the western end. You Sergeants, Simmons and Franks, will assign your men in pairs now and determine who is to go over the wall first. Do not let the men decide that question. You must make that choice in each pair, and give it to your men as an order. I do not want a debate society formed at the foot of that wall!"

At that bit of levity, each of the men in the circle laughed, including Barnwell.

Brice continued. "We shall take the next twenty minutes to get our formations into position. I am sure that old Hancock knows we are here, but he cannot know our plan. Explain everything carefully to your men in the next few minutes, as you prepare. They need to know what is expected of them, and when. God speed to you all." He then turned to Col. Barnwell. "Did you wish to add anything, Sir?"

Barnwell spoke only briefly. "That should do nicely, Captain Brice. With you in the tree line to the northwest, I believe I shall accompany Lt. Mallard."

"Sir! It will be my honor sir!" Mallard said.

Barnwell looked in his direction but did not speak. It was clear that he agreed entirely with Mallard's assessment on that point!

### The Best Laid Plans…

In virtually every battle in history, a moment comes when the battle plan fails, and the texture of the battle changes drastically. Perhaps the battle situation is not what the commanders expected, or factors impacting the battle such as the weather change, or to put it gently, men simply screw up. This battle, however, was to be the exception to that general rule. The militia approached the palisade from the east and engaged the Tuscarora, thus drawing all of the warriors behind the palisade to the eastern wall, just as Brice had planned. Those militiamen under Lt. Mallard, fired one volley then took cover behind trees and stumps or behind a small creek bank that offered some protection. In several minutes, Lt. Mallard ordered a charge and the Yamassee rushed the wall, under the covering fire from the troops led by Martin Bender. Some got close enough to use their bows and arrows, but others did not. The charge faltered thirty feet from the wall, and the Yamassee retreated in good order. Fortunately, that charge had the intended effect. It distracted the Tuscarora.

Within the first five minutes of the battle all of the Tuscarora were firing on that group, which made life hell for Martin Bender initially. However within two minutes he was comfortably sheltered behind a large oak tree some twenty-five yards from the east palisade wall. He was within range of the arrows of the Tuscarora on the outer palisade wall, but not the savages in the upper story of either blockhouse within the wall. Of course, many of the Tuscarora in the blockhouses had old matchlock muskets, and these weapons were deadly out to fifty yards or so. Still, Martin was about as safe as one can be in a battle. From that vantage point he calmly loaded his rifle and fired at any savage head that popped up over the wall. He killed several that way and thus contributed something to the overall battle plan.

When Captain Brice saw the firing concentrated toward the east, he used hand motions to order his militiamen to advance on the palisade wall from the northwest. As he hoped, his men approached the wall without drawing direct fire. He also noticed that the blockhouse in the distance still appeared deserted. While that meant that Tuber's militiamen were not in the fight, it also had the effect of giving Brice, and not Barnwell, control of that reserve force. By this point, Captain Brice was savvy enough in warfare to know he would probably need them. He still held over a hundred Yamassee, Creek, and Catawba warriors in reserve also.

Brice's men moved as one, but to a man, they realized the advantage of surprise, and they did manage to attain the wall while receiving only sporadic fire from some of the Tuscarora in the blockhouses. Apparently, it was just as Brice had suspected. Almost every Tuscarora within the enclosure had run to the eastern wall to engage the men there, including some who had initially been stationed in those blockhouses. While neither Brice nor Barnwell knew the strength of the opposing force, they were sure that their enemy could not outnumber them in that single fort, and so they attacked with confidence. With most of the militiamen now just outside the palisade wall, Captain Brice ordered the warriors forward, where the militiamen, working in pairs, calmly tossed them over the wall. By this time the Tuscarora had caught on to the threat and were sending some of their forces from the east wall to meet the enemy now entering the courtyard, and the first Yamassee inside were killed almost immediately. However, that became a moot point, when one of those warriors opened the western gate from the inside and let in all of Brice's militiamen and the other Yamassee and Catawba warriors.

It was pure terror. Hand to hand combat began just inside the palisade wall, with ancient enemies kicking, screaming, shouting, stabbing, cursing, gouging eyes, swinging unloaded muskets, war hatchets, or wooden clubs. Knives flashed and smoke poured over the enclosed courtyard inside that small palisade wall. With Tuscarora bringing fire from both blockhouses on the smelly-pales and enemy warriors in the yard, and Tuscarora running from the eastern wall to join the battle, the savage fighting became more brutal minute by minute.

Nothing today can come even close to viewing a hand-to-hand Indian knife fight. The Catawba and Tuscarora had been bitter enemies for decades, and both warrior societies championed skills with arrows, knives, and war hatchets. The terror inside that palisade wall was horrendous, as forty odd, man-to-man fights broke out all at once amid the acrid smoke emanating from all of the muskets firing in the courtyard. Over a hundred warriors whirled and contorted in every way conceivable, bending, flipping, somersaulting, and doing movements that would make modern gymnasts swoon with envy. Of course in the battle, the beauty of the movements was merely accidental; the purpose was to kill.

By this point, Johannes had charged into the enclosure leading his men, but even he, a man who had seen the horror of war in the charge at the Daniel's plantation, was shocked at the flying blood, exploding brains, the smoke, and the horrid wounds he witnessed in that enclosed circle of hell. While watching the horror, he continued to load his musket and fire, and thankfully, none of the Tuscarora came to meet him with a knife. He did see that his men and the friendly savages were overcoming the Tuscarora in the enclosure, but they were paying a terrible price. The muskets in the blockhouses were taking a deadly toll, so he shouted for his men to follow and he charged toward the small door in the lower floor of the nearest blockhouse. With seven men right behind him, he reached the outside wall of the blockhouse and pressed his back against the wall where those in that blockhouse could not fire on him. Of course, the Tuscarora in the other blockhouse could, so his men were still under fire, and one was severely wounded at just that moment by an arrow in his lung from the other blockhouse. He paused just long enough for his men to reload their muskets. They were sure to need that firepower when they charged through the door into the hell that awaited them.

## Hell in the Blockhouse

He shouted to the men still with him, using his native German. "Are you ready? Put your knives in your teeth to get to 'um quicker," and he did so himself. With his knife in his teeth, he could say nothing further so he nodded to his men and charged. With his men behind, he ran through that dark, small opening.

Any veteran of house to house warfare will agree that fighting multiple enemies in an enclosed room is absolute terror itself, since death is so very immediate. In that blockhouse Johannes met his own private hell. He immediately saw four savages in the lower floor, and he knew in that instant that one of them would probably kill him. Each was firing out a different side of the blockhouse and each turned to face him when he entered. Two seemed to have loaded muskets, and two others pulled knives from their belts, as they tossed aside their bows. Each of those four was bringing their weapon to bare on him alone.

He fired his musket into the gut of the Tuscarora brave on the opposite wall, one with a musket who was the easiest target to hit, then Johannes jumped to his left, as he tossed his musket away and grabbed his knife from his teeth. He backhanded the savage that he saw standing just to his left, as that warrior began to turn more toward him. Johannes then stabbed him in the side with the weight of his entire body behind that knife. He buried the knife up to the hilt, and even felt that his hand had partially entered that bloody, gaping wound. That savage was surely dead. Within only a second Johannes had shot one Tuscarora brave and buried his knife into the side of another. Johannes immediately heard explosions as other muskets went off, as other militiamen behind him fired into the savages still standing on that level. In less than two seconds it was over and the lower floor was cleared. Every Tuscarora on that level was dead on the dirt floor.

One of the militiamen, the one immediately behind Johannes, had been gut-shot, and was bleeding slowly, lying on the dirt. However, five more were still in the fight, and two of those were reloading their muskets, and looking with some trepidation at the wooden ladder in the far corner that led to the upper level of the blockhouse. Going up that ladder meant death for sure, yet these men knew that they would have to do exactly that.

Johannes quickly retrieved his weapon and began to reload, as his men paused to look at him. He merely gestured to the ladder and two men who had not been engaged on the lower level began that fateful climb. By then four more militiamen had entered the blockhouse since the fighting in the courtyard was winding down.

Without thinking, Johannes ordered. "Those with loaded muskets, up the ladder. Kill at least one savage and drop back down. Let the next man take your place, but tell him which way to fire before he climbs."

That strategy seemed to work in a fashion. While no one wanted to go up that ladder, the men took turns poking their heads up and taking a quick shot. Some drew out their single shot pistols for that work, and those weapons were much more appropriate for that task than the more cumbersome muskets. In less than a minute the six Tuscarora warriors in the upper level were all dead. Of course by then three more militiamen lay dead or dying at the foot of the ladder, each wounded horribly in the head or face.

More men entered the blockhouse at that point, since it was safer in there than remaining in the courtyard where they were still under fire from the other blockhouse. Men took positions and began to fire across the courtyard toward the other blockhouse, and thus the interior became increasingly smoky. Still, in the dim light and smoke, Johannes noticed something strange on one of the dead Tuscarora warriors near his feet, lying on the dirt floor. His knife had been buried deep in that warrior's body, but when Johannes extracted the knife it tore the deerskin shirt a bit, and Johannes saw.... What was that?

Tits?

Johannes looked closely at the chest of the dead warrior. That couldn't be, could it? He cut the deerskin a bit more with his knife, correctly guessing that this savage was past caring.

His discovery confirmed it; tits. He'd stabbed a woman to death on the lower level of the blockhouse.

By then another contingent of militiamen and Yamassee warriors was clearing the other blockhouse, so the firing in Johannes' immediate location waned. As it turned out, Sergeant Tuber led the attack on that second blockhouse, and did an admirable job, as had Johannes Simmons. Altogether, the entire attack took only forty five minutes.

The enemy dead were stacked in a blockhouse which was then burned. In summarizing that battle, Col. Barnwell estimated, and Captain Brice confirmed, that about one hundred and fifty Tuscarora had been positioned in that palisade and the two blockhouses. A number of them had escaped however, through the open gate after the fight in the courtyard. In all fifty-two enemy warriors had been killed, and that included eleven women who had been stationed in the blockhouses. Those women, in particular, had fought like demons. The militia and the Yamassee together had taken thirty-nine Tuscarora as prisoners. Those Tuscarora would be sold as slaves in Charleston by the Yamassee within the month.

Barnwell's losses among the militia were only seven killed and twelve wounded. However, the Yamassee losses were higher, though they were never reported. Also, many of the wounded would die later, since many of the wounds were head wounds, particularly among those who fought in the blockhouses.

The militiamen realized with trepidation that there were still eight other blockhouses to clear in this one community, but only an hour later, they were ecstatic to find that the Tuscarora had abandoned the entire village and all of the blockhouses. This battle, at least, was over.

There were two unfortunate results of Barnwell's victory at Narhantes. First,

King Hancock himself was never in the village, so any possibility of catching or killing the Tuscarora leader and thus ending the war early was thwarted. Also, with this victory in hand, the warriors that made up most of Barnwell's forces merely grabbed the spoils from every single cabin and blockhouse in Narhantes, and headed back to South Carolina to sell them. To add insult to injury, they even stole the prisoners as spoils of war and led them into slavery. Of course, Barnwell himself had wanted to do the same thing, hoping that such a slave sale would offset the costs of this venture for the state of South Carolina. Still, his forces had suffered a significant reduction in strength and he had many other villages to destroy.

As the blockhouses burned with scores of bodies inside, his high pitched voice was heard over the battlefield, again making everyone in earshot cringe. "I say. I believe that does it for this nest of vipers, and what a jolly good show it was! What?"

Captain Brice merely looked at this youngster and smiled. Barnwell's uniform, a highly tailored knit wool of his own design, was seemingly clean enough for parade review before the Queen, and Captain Brice could not help but reflect that this pretentious sod had never even been close to the battle! Brice, in contrast, had been in the thick of almost everything, including the battle in the courtyard, though he'd missed the horror of the indoor fights to clear the two blockhouses. Sergeants Tuber and Simmons had commanded those two attacks.

Still, Brice had led from the front, and had a serious wound to show for it, a cut just above his right eye, that left blood trickling down his face and onto his blouse and topcoat. Within a day, someone in the New Bern Militia coined the term, Blood-Eyes, for their Captain, which became both a nickname and a mark of honor, not only for Brice but for every member of that militia force. One could hear that appellation whenever Captain Brice led the men in all future engagements. "With Blood-Eyes leadin' us' we canna be stopped!" While the captain pretended displeasure at such a nickname, in truth, he reveled in it. The name suggested that he had attained that most desirable of goals for any leader who proposes to take men into combat. His men knew he was a fighter, and they now felt like he was one of them!

Perhaps that's when the trouble started. Because of that wound, it was determined that Captain Brice should take a guard of ten men, and lead the wounded back to New Bern. Without Captain Brice in support during the next engagement, the "Scarecrow from South Carolina" would be in sole command!

Sergeants Martin Bender, Johannes Simmons, and Archie Carmichael were perhaps, the first to seriously consider the implications of that. These men had helped load the wounded onto several two wheeled carts for the trek back to New

Bern. The carts had been brought along to carry the possessions of the settlers that the Tuscarora had stolen three months earlier in the massacre, but with the Yamassee and the Catawba slipping away with much of that booty, the carts could be used for other purposes. Lt. Mallard, who had also received a glancing wound in the side from a musket ball, was ambulatory but was nevertheless ordered back to New Bern along with Brice and the others. As he helped organize the loading of the wounded into the carts, he looked as his Sergeants, just before departing and spoke in a low voice. "Keep your men in line, and your heads down. Fight well, like I know you will, but don't let that damned scarecrow from South Carolina get the good men in the New Bern Militia killed!"

There was no response that could be made to that, so Johannes speaking for all of them simply said, "Get yourself to New Bern. Soon to tell them we'll back quickly."

## A Surprise or Two in Catechna

With many of the buildings in Narhantes still smoldering that evening, and the squad with the wounded already decamped and on the trail to New Bern, Barnwell asked his Sergeants to sup with him, so Bender, Tuber, Simmons, and Carmichael sat with several leaders of the Yamassee and one minor chief of the few remaining Catawba around a fire. As soon as they finished eating some deer meat they'd found in one of the long houses in Narhantes, Barnwell shared his plans. Again Martin cringed at that obnoxious, high pitched voice.

"Gentlemen! Our men have provisions from this fort that they can eat, but those will not last long. It is time to move on to Catechna! On to Catechna, I say! King Hancock must be there, and I want that savage's head!" Barnwell hoped to inspire the men with bold statements such as this, but to the men who actually did the fighting such blather in Barnwell's high-pitched voice seemed merely stupid. They all wanted Hancock dead, since that would probably mean the end of the trouble with the Tuscarora. Still, there was just something irritating about the high, squeaky voice of this man, and the sideways, birdlike way he looked at anyone.

Hearing nothing from his subordinates, Barnwell continued. "Have your men ready to leave at dawn. They may make fires for cooking tonight if they choose, but not in the morning. We move at first light for Hancock's town. We'll have to go upriver a bit to cross the creek at the next ford, but then we head southwest to catch those buggers once and for all! I shared these plans with Captain Brice, so the authorities in New Bern and Bath will know our intentions, and will know of our victory here!"

Martin had the distinct impression at that moment that Barnwell considered the last point to be the most important of those two, but he would never voice such thoughts aloud. As the men stood, he merely shared another brief look with the other sergeants, as if to confirm Lt. Mallard's earlier caution; we can't let this idiot get our men killed! In the morning, it was on to Catechna!

While the two day trek across the wilderness was generally uneventful, their arrival at Catechna held a surprise. The village was abandoned completely—the long houses empty of anything of value. But just across Contentea Creek, King Hancock had built a fort and moved the entire village inside. Like Narhantes and most of the Tuscarora towns, Catechna was a scattered village, and the long houses were dispersed around fields as were the corrals for the horses. The village was simply much too large to enclose, so Hancock had done the next best thing and had created a fortress to defend. The palisade walls around Hancock's Fort were nearly a hundred and fifty feet on each side, and three blockhouses, similar to the two story enclosures in Narhantes, had been built inside. The walls enclosed one hundred and thirty battle hungry warriors, though Barnwell did not realize that at the time. Still, it was apparent to all that taking this Tuscarora fortress promised to be even more of a challenge than Narhantes.

Thus, at around three thirty on the afternoon of March 5, 1712, Barnwell considered the new task, and he wasted no time issuing his orders, crude and undeveloped though they were. "We'll attack with an envelopment by placing men on three sides and bringing fire on them. The Yamassee will be divided equally among the Sergeants, under their command, along with the militia. Then we'll storm the gate in the westernmost wall!"

Martin Bender and Archie Carmichael were to take their forces and attack the western wall near the gate, while other groups were assigned to other sections of the palisade. Each commanded ten or so militiamen and well over one hundred Yamassee warriors. Barnwell stated, "I'll remain with the men on the west, to attack the gates at the appropriate moment."

They began to move at once, and were ready in just over five minutes. However, just after the Sergeants got their men into place, King Hancock demonstrated another tactic that none had anticipated. Just before Barnwell ordered the firing to commence, a high pitched scream was heard from inside the fort. The sound was horrifying, sounding like some demon from hell, and it managed to terrify all who heard it, but before Barnwell and his men could consider what it might entail, the gate cracked open a bit.

Out came a white woman, obviously one of the captives from the massacre the previous September. Her skirt was torn, her hair uncombed, her face was bloody from various beatings, and her bloody, bruised breasts were exposed for all to see, in the fashion of the savages. The gate was shut immediately.

"Don't shoot or they'll kill my babies!" She shouted, above the obvious sounds of torture. At just that point, another terrified wailing began inside the fort, and the woman shouted again, "They'll kill my sweet babies if you shoot!"

Archie grabbed the woman, who immediately went limp in his arms, but continued to cry, looking around to determine who might be in charge. "They say if you shoot, they'll kill them all. They'll kill my babies, if you attack!" She looked around the circle again, but she kept repeating the horrible ultimatum of King Hancock. "They'll kill us all! They say they'll kill everyone if you shoot. Please don't fire on the fort!"

Again, the screaming coming from at least three separate voices within the fort seemed to confirm the woman's statements. One man, actually a sixteen year old boy whose father had been killed in the September massacre the previous fall, shouted, "Dirty savages!" He immediately fired at a head exposed above the palisade wall, and began to reload. Several other militiamen likewise fired.

Barnwell's high pitched voice cut through the screams and the scattered firing. "Hold your fire until I command you! Hold your fire, I say!"

Martin realized then the one advantage of such a high pitched voice—it could carry over other sounds! Still, he quickly reflected that this was the only leadership advantage the scarecrow had shown thus far.

One more militiaman fired, and Barnwell continued. "Hold your fire, I say! Do not fire, until commanded!" With that second command, the firing stopped altogether, but not the horrid screams from the several torture victims inside. As described by Barnwell after the fact, "Those cries and lamentations were heart rending sounds and would terrify any man no matter how seasoned in battle he might be."

Barnwell was aware that he was losing control of his army, so he shouted to the fortress walls. "I say! Let loose the captives, and do not harm them further. We are willing to talk with your leader."

The tortured screams of the victims continued for a brief time as all listened in horror, but in a minute or so, they seemed to trail off somewhat. They did not stop completely. The gate again opened, and a second woman emerged shouting, "Don't shoot! Don't shoot! I bring a message!"

By the time she reached Barnwell she had stated the proposal from King Hancock in no uncertain terms. "I am Mrs. Ebeck, and I have five children in the fort. There are many captives there, captives of the Tuscarora. Their chief says to leave now and no one else will be tortured. Please, you must leave or he will torture my children!"

As Barnwell questioned Mrs. Ebeck, she confirmed she had been captured the previous September, and that her husband was dead. All of her five children were now captive in the fort, though none had been tortured as yet. Her twelve year old daughter had been raped several times over the last months, and Mrs.

Ebeck watched one of those horrid episodes. Still the girl had already survived that, and might even live through this, if only they were not tortured to death in the next few minutes! She indicated that "perhaps twenty-five whites" were in the fort as hostages and potential torture victims.

At that, the first woman asked, "What of my son Stephen? Is he alive?" The answer was apparent on the face of Mrs. Ebeck. "I am sorry," was all she could say.

Soon, even the cries of the final torture victims stopped, and there was silence. Barnwell convened a hasty meeting of his leaders. None but he were officers, but all were more seasoned in battle. They sat on logs in a circle so they could all see each other. They each realized that they had a tough decision to make.

Archie Carmichael spoke up first. "Hell! Let's storm the place, and get as many as we can. We got to! How can we do anything else, with those savages holding twenty-five of our women and kids in there? Who knows what they'll be doin' if'n we leave um' with our women?"

Barnwell seemingly agreed, saying "Quite right!" Then however, he shut up, since he wanted the opinion of his subordinates. He was proving to be more of a leader than Martin or the others had given him credit for, at least in that sense.

Tuber spoke next. "I'm mad as hell too, Archie, but we didn't come way out here to get women and children kilt!" He spat his tobacco chew on the ground at that point, and looked back at the other Sergeants. "I'll fight as quick as the next man. Hell, I already have, but we still got to think of them women and children in there! They'll die if we attack, and there ain't no way we can get into that there fort quick enough to save 'um."

Johannes spoke next, and in spite of his English, his thoughts settled the matter. "My wife? My daughters? I want not in fort to be killed." He then paused just a moment to clear his thoughts. "We Hancock catch next week, next month, when he wives and children not hold!"

At that moment, one of the men standing just outside the circle, Josephus Bell, spoke. He was known to be a good shot and a good hunter. He was a terror to the deer and bear population along the upper Trent River and "Little Hell Branch." He was not expected to speak since this was a meeting of officers, or Sergeants as the case may be, and he was neither. Still, Josephus figured he had a right to talk, and talk he did. He was fifteen that night, when he spoke up for his family.

"My Ma was caught last fall in the massacre. I'm here for her." He then spit his chew, much as he'd seen his own Pa do for many years. "Pa's dead, kilt in the field. But my Ma, I don't know about." He paused again, and every Sergeant and even Barnwell realized this man's ultimate right to a voice, even when he was supposed to have none. "If'n it was my Ma in there, and I recon' it might well be, I'd want her to have a chance. Ain't nothin' wrong with catchin' ol' Hancock next month! I'll damn sure be lookin' for him the rest of my life. I ever catch him slippin' up a trail somewhere, I'll cut his throat myself." Here he spit again, and the dramatic effect couldn't have been stronger. "Yea, I'd want Ma to have a chance. I recon' we ought to head on back to New Bern, for a time. Maybe Ma and those others can live a while longer."

The matter was decided by that lone voice of reason. Barnwell and his Sergeants had decided at that very moment, what experienced combat leaders have long known; when hostages are at risk, tread lightly.

Martin, however, had another, more refined idea. He spoke up. "Col. Barnwell. We should negotiate."

Barnwell was intrigued with this, but not certain what Martin meant. "Continue Sergeant Bender."

"We should ask for half of his hostages now, including the five kids of Mrs. Ebeck, and the others that have been tortured, if they're alive." Martin paused at that point, and closed his eyes in thought. He was trying to guess what Hancock was up to. Thinking like one's enemy is always an advantage, and that became apparent as he shared his thoughts. "Right now, ol' Hancock's in there hoping we take his terms. Why? Why does he need us to agree to this? Why did he send out Mrs. Ebeck, here? Maybe he's nearly out of shot for those few flintlock muskets he's got, or maybe there ain't no food in there. Anyways, he wants us gone, and since we can't attack while he holds our people, let's oblige him, but first we negotiate. We try to get something from him!"

Barnwell thought he saw a way out of this quagmire that might salvage a bit of his honor, so he asked. "What did you have in mind, Sergeant?"

"Let's agree to leave, but first offer him some shot and powder for half of his captives. He can get that shot and powder anyway from any one of fifty farms within twenty miles of here, but we might just get a few more of our folks safe." Martin paused, then continued. "I don't see that we loose nothin' by trying that."

Barnwell then shocked the entire group by adding an original idea that, as it turned out, was quite reasonable. "We'll ask for half of the captives now, and then we agree to depart, as you suggest. However, we'll make return of all captives held by the Tuscarora part of the deal. They'll have to bring them to Bachelor's Creek near New Bern in, say ten days." Barnwell didn't add his real reasoning that evening. He didn't wish to be criticized for leaving a battle while hostages were still at risk, so he included the return of all captives in the deal.

Within thirty minutes, the deal was struck, pretty much as Martin outlined. A truce was negotiated that promised to end the hostilities once and for all. Hancock got some powder and shot that he could easily have captured anyway, and he agreed to no further attacks against the settlers. In exchange, he gave up twelve captives, including all five of Mrs. Ebeck's children and Mrs. Tina Bell, the Ma of Josephus Bell. Hancock also agreed to turn over twenty-two more captives in ten days at Bachelor's Creek. With the truce thus concluded, Barnwell and his army were moving away from Fort Catechna less than an hour later.

However, Barnwell didn't return to New Bern. Rather, he retreated only seven miles from Catechna and there he had his South Carolina Militia construct his own fortification along the banks of the Neuse River, some twenty-five overland miles from New Bern. After construction, he held those militiamen and the Catawba warriors to garrison that fort, and once again sent his remaining Indian allies savaging in the countryside of North Carolina since he still had no food for them. He hoped against hope to receive the supplies soon that North Carolina had promised for his expedition.

He named that fortification, Fort Barnwell, in honor of himself, since he was convinced that his actions had both punished the Tuscarora and ended the conflict! He planned to stockpile food and supplies in Fort Barnwell, and use this fort as a supply depot and a stronghold against the Tuscarora if necessary, to ensure the truce.

{Author's Note: Interestingly enough, the remains of that earthen fortification can be seen today, along the banks of the Neuse River about twenty miles by river from New Bern. Those now shallow earthworks are the only physical remnant of the entire Tuscarora War in existence today. However, a historic marker stands beside the nearby highway to briefly tell the story of that fort, and a delightful, small North Carolina village in that area has born the name, Fort Barnwell, for almost three hundred years.}

## The Blood Flag

Barnwell decided that he could not feed the New Bern Militia any easier than he could the Yamassee, so with a ten day respite anticipated, he sent them home to New Bern. Martin and Johannes had been in town for only one day, most of which they slept. That evening they went to Mallard's Tavern right after supper to hear what news they could. They expected the talk to turn to the attack on the Tuscarora village, but instead the talk quickly turned to pirates, always the curse of any seaport town.

Two sailors sat at a table, and one was talking with a crowd of patrons. Archie Carmichael was already drunk and asleep by the fire, once again perched on two legs of the same three legged stool, but no one paid him any attention that night. The sailor doing most of the talking was named Pate, the very same

Thomas Pate that had bashed savages with One-Eye and Able Ward only one year previously.

In a port city like New Bern, even a one-time pirate could get a job on the many coastal freighters that hauled pitch and tar to the larger shipyards everywhere on the east coast, so Pate had been shipping on a brig with a cargo of naval stores. Only two days before it left the docks of the Brice Plantation, sailed down the Neuse, across Pamlico Sound and out through Beaufort Inlet, bound for Charleston. Just as Martin and Johannes entered, they heard the beginning of Pate's tale.

"We was still within sight of the inlet itself when we spied a fast frigate. Thought she was sailin' on down the coast we did, and I never seed so many men on a frigate before, but she stood well out to sea and with a goodly wind in her sail we knew she'd sail on by right smart. We tacked to get sea room and lost speed. Just about then she turned and bore down on us as her gun-ports flew open! Every one o' them damn cannon looked mean! They was six pounders and she was sportin' twelve big guns on her starboard as she closed. She catched us for fair, in only an hour, then she hailed us with a cannon shot from her quarter deck, right across our bow. Then we seed the Jolly Roger going up!"

{Author's Note: No one today knows how that term, Jolly Roger came to be associated with pirate flags. Some speculate that, because almost all of the early pirate flags were bright red, the French had labeled them "joli rouge" or "pretty red." These were also called "bloody flags" or the "blood flag" and pirates used that harsh red color and blood imagery to strike fear into the hearts of potential victims. Traditionally, red flags meant that no quarter would be given to any who resisted, so the use of that flag meant pirates would kill all who fired on them. Others say the name is a derivative of "Old Roger," a term then used for the devil. Whatever the origin, the term applied to all pirate flags even though most pirates later developed their own stylistic flag.}

Toby Mallard saw how interested his patrons were in Pate's story, and he knew a good entertainment when he saw one, so he said. "Ye gets a free rum if you tell the tale." Pate grinned wide enough to show all three of his remaining back molars, and said "Thank 'ye!" as all in the tavern settled in to hear.

"Our Captain, Jacob Oliver, ain't no fool so he looks at the wind, shakes his head a bit, and then hove to. He had no chance you see?" Pate looked around at his audience, and pointed to a twist of tobacco on a nearby table.

Melvin Thigpen gladly smiled and shared his tobacco with Pate, who bit off a goodly chew. Toby moved a cuspidor closer to the story teller, but didn't really expect that it would get much use. Pate continued his tale.

"They come along-side right smart and before they even begun to board we knew it was Blackbeard himself. His Jolly Roger's black as night, and sports a skeleton and a spear pointed to a bloody heart, ya see? We seed it flappin' in the breeze." Pate took another sip of his rum. "First we seed Blackbeard's Claw up on the quarterdeck, the ol' bastard Christopher Blackwood, himself, lookin' all mean and disappointed. He's the son o' bitch that leads Blackbeard's boarding party, ya see, 'cauz he can fight like ol' Roger himself! He was real pissed that he didn't get no fight out of us!"

{Author's Note: For several years Christopher Blackwood had indeed led Blackbeard's boarding parties, since he was an accomplished swordsman and was even more deadly with a cutlass or a pistol. He was called "Blackbeard's Claw," by every sailor on the seven seas, and was almost as large as Blackbeard himself. He was a mean, cruel cutthroat, and thus held the perfect qualifications for his job!}

Pate continued, with his audience in the tavern spellbound. "Then we seed the man himself, coming up from his cabin and mountin' the steps up to the quarterdeck, like some fine potentate! His hair was black as coal and his eyes was mean lookin' and they was dark too! He was bigger than the Claw, and had a dozen loaded pistols hanging across his chest. He looked mighty fearsome."

{Author's Note: In that particular, of course, Pate was lying outright. Blackbeard himself said he never wore more than six pistols on his chest, and it would be nearly impossible to mount twelve.}

"He had his long hair in braids with ribbons tied in each, and his head was smokin' from the matches he sported under his hat. He were a fearsome thing, but all he did was kindly thank the Captain for lowerin' sail, and then he inquired about our cargo."

The crowd was getting more and more excited, and Thigpen felt emboldened. He asked, "What were ye shipping? What was in your hold?"

Pate warmed to the question. "Now, that is the question ain't it? Truth is we was carryin' nothing that any self-respecting pirate would even want! Forty heavy barrels! A load of pitch can be had for not much effort, and while it was all gathered up in barrels and ready for stealing, it wasn't worth all that much. No, maybe ol' Blackbeard thought we was carrin' something else, like a load of tobacco or maybe some slaves, or some deerskins for sale."

Martin and Johannes looked at each other with the same thought. If that ship carried pitch for the larger shipyards in South Carolina, they had probably made the barrels for that cargo!

Mallard himself asked the next question, even as he poured drinks for two farmers who had just entered the tavern. "Was Captain Oliver carrying any mail, or gold, or coin on board?"

Pate shook his head. "Nothin' I knows about. He carried only his paymaster's money for the crew of ten at the end of the voyage; nothing special. Blackbeard stole all o' that, a' course!" Here Pate took a sip of his rum, and looked at the rapt audience conspiratorially. "Want to know what I thinks?"

A loud voice was heard from the back. It was Sheriff Jack DuVal. "Hell yea, you damn fool! That's what we're all hangin' around here for! It ain't because we like you or your confounded blubberin' for damn sure!"

The entire tavern had a good laugh at that rude comment, including Pate himself, then he continued. "I see our fine Sheriff is well into his cups tonight, but hell, ain't we all? No matter. What I thinks is somebody let ol' Blackbeard know to raid that very ship!"

Thigpen was the first to object. "Why in hell would he be interested in a load of pitch? It has some value but not much, compared to other cargo. Why steal that?"

"Here's my figurin' on the matter," Pate paused dramatically, and then continued. "If ol' Blackbeard himself was in cahoots with someone who let him know when to hoist a ship, he'd usually steal only the best, right? Wouldn't he want to cover that up, see? So's nobody would know that he was bein' protected or even tipped off when a good cargo was sailing from the New Bern docks!"

The crowd generally agreed that was logical and most began at that moment to think of Governor Hyde, and the rumors of Hyde's protection for Blackbeard. Thigpen continued his question, "So you think Blackbeard took that ship and that load o' cargo just to confuse matters a bit?"

Pate continued. "I do! As I see it, he'd want to steal a few ships that weren't of much value and lift the cargo anyway, just to keep his sources hidden!" Pate then paused and took a large sip of his rum. Mallard quickly poured another shot into the pewter mug for him, and thus encouraged him to continue, which Pate gladly did. "Well, that's what I think. Still, it could'a been more simple. Maybe Blackbeard was layin' just off the inlet and waitin' to take the first ship passin' by."

Thigpen continued his questions. "Did he board ya?"

Pate answered. "Yep! First, Blackbeard himself ordered all our men to the top deck, and we all got up there right smart, Captain Oliver too! Then about fifteen of 'um came on board with the Claw in the lead while the others held us under their guns, with a swivel cannon pointed at us from the riggin'. Then I seed someone I knowed from right here in New Bern!"

Sheriff DuVal was the loudest. "Who did you see, you ol' bastard? If he's on land he's mine to hang!"

Pate replied, "Calm down Sheriff. He for sure ain't on land, but I seed him, I did! Ol' Black Jambo, that nigger slave from the Foscue Plantation. He come along, right on board with the others. He was carryin' a cutlass and helped the crew carry away the cargo, stowin' it below decks on Blackbeard's frigate."

Thigpen put in his opinion. "That slave was always trouble. See how easy he tamed his own kind? And he was mean too! Hell, he was a bigger slaver than One-Eye Benny, here! Need to watch a slave like that! He'll double cross you every time!"

One-Eye Benny, sitting right beside Thigpen, added his thoughts. "To hell with you, Thigpen! Still, seems like I did hear that Foscue has a reward out for Black Jambo alright. He run off about six, maybe eight months ago, but there was some talk that maybe the Tuscarora got him."

Pate chimed in. "I heard that too. But he was damn sure standin' there on *Queen Anne's Revenge* right behind the Claw with Blackbeard himself." *Queen Anne's Revenge* was the name Blackbeard had chosen for his frigate, and he never explained why he selected that name.

Pate concluded his tale. "I tell you, as God is my witness, Black Jambo may have been a mean-ass slave, but now he's a mean-ass pirate! And that damned blood flag has, for sure captured one of it's own! He's a pirate and he's shippin' with that demon from hell, right now!"

{Author's Note: Historically many slaves did chose to join pirate ships when presented with the opportunity. It was widely known, even then, that on pirate ships, those slaves became free men, and like all other pirates aboard, they then had a voice in what the ship did, where it sailed, and what ships it attacked. As strange as it may seem, one way to freedom for slaves in those decades was chosing a life of lawlessness aboard a pirate ship, and many, like Black Jambo, chose that life. Given their alternatives, who could blame them?}

Sheriff DuVal then continued the questioning. "So why didn't you join him, Pate? I'm sure he probably asked ye!" While Sheriff DuVal was fishing for information with that question, it was often the case that pirates invited the crews they captured to join them. Many seamen did.

"Come on Sheriff," Pate grinned showing all three of his remaining teeth. "An honest working sailor like me?"

The entire tavern exploded with laughter, including the Sheriff. All knew of Pate's unexplained and dubious past, not to mention his proclivities toward dishonesty whenever it suited him. Flustered not one bit, Pate continued. "Besides, he didn't need us! Our small brig would' a only slowed him down. The ship was no use to Blackbeard at all, so he didn't need us and he didn't need our ship. He' weren't concerned about what anyone would say, with a frigate armed to the teeth! She was a beautiful ship too! 'Course, we all know that the governor ain't likely to run out and catch him in these waters!" Again, the crowd laughed at Pate's humor. "Naw. Blackbeard merely let us go our merry way, and told us to make sure we talk about how nice he is, a kind man ya see! But only to those that don't shoot back!" All laughed loudly again, in the cozy warmth of Mallard's Tavern.

To Martin and Johannes, while the story did seem a bit funny, it also seemed sad, in the sense that it conflicted with their deep sense of fairness. In some ways, it seemed an offence against God. The pitch and tar that had been stolen, did belong to someone, in this case to Captain Brice, and even though it was no great loss, it was still a loss, and they objected to it. Stealing was against the commandments, and as Anabaptists who held the commandments as sacred, they did not find humor in defying God's law. Moreover, they were unnerved that so many in the tavern did! Further, the hints or outright suggestions that Governor Hyde, a man they had actually fought to support, was dishonest enough to take bribes for protection from a notorious thief like Blackbeard deeply offended their Germanic sensibilities. They fought for an orderly world in which a man's pay was determined by his work, and in which stealing from another was wrong. Many in the tavern that night didn't seem to realize that, including even Sheriff DuVal!

Both Martin and Johannes left the tavern after Pate finished his tale, with a sense of uneasiness about their new home. They knew that a rough frontier required rough men. They had fought often enough to realize that simple fact, but still they wanted to believe in their efforts as more than merely making a living constructing barrels. They wanted their new city to mean something, maybe the right to work hard and earn the fruits of one's own labors, or maybe the right to own land and other things in New Bern they could have never owned in Germany. Maybe this new city meant having one's property protected, or maybe the right to worship God as one pleased. Overall, that evening at Mallard's Tavern seemed to argue against those hopes, and it generally left a bad taste in their mouths. Their religious beliefs, and that hope for a better future drove these Germans, since realistically it was all they had. That same night both Martin and Johannes prayed deeply about their discomfort.

Neither realized it at the time, but in only a few short years, they would have an intimate taste of piracy. First, however, they still had to deal with the Tuscarora.

## *A Fractured Truce*

As it turns out, both the white frontiersmen and the Tuscarora would break Barnwell's truce. March 15, 1712 came and went with no sign of the Tuscarora or their other captives. In fact on that date neither Barnwell nor the Tuscarora showed up at Bachelor's Creek, as demanded by the terms of the truce. Barnwell was deathly ill and had moved to New Bern to recover, so he'd sent Sergeant Simmons in his place. The Tuscarora headmen and King Hancock never showed up at all nor did any representative.

The citizens of New Bern and the entire Carolina Colony were all viciously angry, not at the Tuscarora who were expected to act like savages anyway, but at "that damned South Carolina scarecrow," meaning Barnwell, for believing that savages would honor the truce at all. Many still hoped that their own family members were captive with the Tuscarora, rather than dead and drug away by bear or wolves during the massacre, and Barnwell's stupidity in believing he'd put an end to the uprising, they viewed as naïve, if not completely absurd. Barnwell took some time to recover from his illness, and had to defend himself from his sickbed at the Brice Plantation.

He was almost apoplectic. He shouted to all who would listen, white and slave alike, "How could any man of honor sign a truce and then totally disregard it?" His complaining got so bad, that Brice's personal manservant, Gideon humbly asked to be relieved of the responsibility for tending to his needs, and none of the female slaves would willingly go anywhere near him. Thus, Dunker Tim had to care for Barnwell during the final days of his recovery.

Of course, King Hancock was not a man of honor, in the sense that Barnwell meant. Rather, he was a courageous leader of a fiercely competitive warrior society, fighting desperately to preserve his tribe and their way of life. He would use any means at his disposal to win, and none can blame him for that. Ultimately, it was a fight he would lose.

Once Captain Brice visited Barnwell in his sickbed, and that was the only brief conversation these men had during that period, since Captain Brice was quite busy organizing the New Bern Militia for another venture against the Tuscarora. Brice spoke first. "Hello, John. I hope your recovery is going well!"

Barnwell responded, again in that irritatingly high voice. "I say, Captain. I do appreciate your concern as well as your hospitality during my illness. I suppose I could have remained at Fort Barnwell and recovered there, but I am afraid I could not have escaped my duties at the fort." Barnwell sighed. "Of course, with my name and my honor dragged through the mud by every bloody beggar and near' do well in the colony, one might wish for a Tuscarora arrow in the heart instead of a quick recovery."

"Come now, Col. Barnwell. It is not as bad as all that. That rabble is to be ignored! They still call me Blood-Eyes or some such nonsense! Damn the buggers to hell, I say!" Of course, Brice was lying since Barnwell really was universally hated in the Carolinas. Still, sometimes lies have their usefulness, and Captain Brice needed this South Carolina Scarecrow, well, strong, cocky as usual, and back at the head of the South Carolina Militia again.

Brice continued. "Some believe you did the only thing that could be done, with that torture going on in Fort Hancock. Who knows but it might have worked?" Brice had thus lied again. Barnwell had indeed failed and everyone knew it. He had tried the one tactic that meant no more immediate torture for the captives, in order to free those and the other hostages, and it had not worked, so he was hated by almost all in the Carolinas. He didn't realize that sometimes to stop a bully who is committing horrendous unspeakable acts, one has to strike and strike hard. Other times one simply has to kill, but Barnwell had done neither at Fort Hancock in early March of 1712. Thus, he stood condemned.

As things stood on March 15, 1712 King Hancock still held between twenty-five and thirty hostages who had no hope of rescue until the South Carolina Militia was functional and on the march once again. Further, Hancock could still attack the outlying settlements at any time. Almost everyone considered the scarecrow from South Carolina a failure in every sense of the term, and that alone tore at Barnwell's heart.

Still, a man only fails when he allows himself to do so. He may be down and universally chastised by his fellows, but that does not mean he has failed; it only means that he is hated. It is not the man who is knocked down that fails; it is the man who does not get up that is the failure.

In that regard, Barnwell showed much more character than history has given him credit for. By March 18, 1712 he was out of bed, and only two days later he was astride his horse heading back to Fort Barnwell. There he would organize his Yamassee, who had been ordered to report back to Fort Barnwell on March 15, and then he would strike the Tuscarora again, without mercy. He had ordered that the New Bern Militia under Captain Brice join him at the fort, ready for battle on March 26, 1712.

During that long ride Barnwell intentionally hardened himself against the pitiful "cries and lamentations" of the tortured captives. Surely Hancock would try the same ploy again, but this time Barnwell was determined to ignore those cries. There would be no cessation of hostilities. He would attack Hancock's Fort, kill Hancock himself, and thus end the madness once and for all!

When he arrived however, he found many of his Yamassee had reported back, but finding no food or supplies, they had left once again. Some had said they were headed home back to South Carolina. Barnwell could not believe it but the North Carolina legislature, meeting in the Albemarle, had still sent no supplies or powder at all for his men! Once again, he could not feed his army! He did a hasty count, and found that he had only one hundred and twenty four of his Yamassee warriors at the fort since many had found nothing to eat and had simply left.

Despite that devastating setback, Barnwell still did not lose conviction. He had over a hundred of the most experienced warriors in the Carolinas and he had his South Carolina Militia, a force of forty-five whites. He also knew he would soon be joined by Captain Brice, and the New Bern Militia, which would bring his forces to something over two hundred. That would have to be enough.

It took some time for Captain Brice to collect the New Bern Militia, and he was a bit late in arriving. Still, he was on the way and he'd sent word to Col. Barnwell that he and the New Bern Militia, seventy-five men strong, were coming. That was good news for Barnwell to receive. Further, Governor Hyde had sent a rare direct communication to Barnwell that arrived on April 1. It indicated that the North Carolina legislature had finally acted to provide food and supplies to his hungry army. Based on that support, Hyde explicitly directed Barnwell to continue his attacks until Tuscarora power was broken in the Carolinas.

Barnwell figured correctly that it would take quite some time to get supplies from the Albemarle to Fort Barnwell, and that he should not wait until they arrived. Still, tears rolled down the face of the scarecrow from South Carolina, as Blood-Eyes rode into Fort Barnwell on the evening of that spring day, April 6, 1712. In his wake marched a determined looking group of men, ranging in age from ten to fifty-seven, and unlike the raw untested Germans who only a year previously had marched to the Daniels Plantation for their first experience in battle, the New Bern Militia on that April day in 1712 were confident, cocky, and battle hardened.

Brice rode in the front looking resplendent on his stallion, the very picture of an English colonial leader. Lt. Mallard and Sergeants Simmons, Bender, and Carmichael rode immediately behind and they all looked determined. That young fellow, Bender looked somewhat less regal than the others, riding along on that old mule, and he apparently had no less than four muskets sticking out from his saddle in every possible direction. Another was slung across his back, for God's sake! Still, he, like all the others, was a battle tested man, and Barnwell knew he had leaders he could depend on.

He commented to one of the Sergeants in the South Carolina Militia, "No uniforms, little discipline in the ranks, and no organization apparent at all. Still I have never seen a more beautiful army than this! Don't they look splendid! With our Yamassee, and these Carolina roughs we cannot be beaten!" Barnwell was correct in his assessment. While there were more experienced armies at various points around the globe on that spring day in 1712, none had seen more recent fighting or more hand to hand combat than this group of very determined Germans, who, to a man, were now seasoned frontiersmen.

Captain Brice was aware of the impact of his arrival on Col. Barnwell, and managed the moment with his usual nonchalance, as he rode up to report. "I say, good evening Col. Barnwell, I do hope that we didn't miss your party!"

Barnwell merely smiled and responded in that high voice, "Not at all Sir! In fact, I do believe that on the morrow, I'll use you and your militia to full advantage! I do so thank you for coming! Perhaps you could join me in an hour, after you refresh yourself?"

Brice smiled at the scarecrow, thinking, he may become a leader after all. "I'd be delighted, Sir!"

Before he could do so, both leaders were surprised when another detachment of thirty-two frontiersmen marched into Fort Barnwell, only a few minutes later, and asked to speak to the Colonel. These men were from a garrisoned plantation that stood on Chocowinity Bay twenty miles up the North Trail from New Bern. While they had seen no fighting since the massacre itself they were ready to do their part, and had heard that Col. Barnwell was gathering his army at Fort Barnwell for a march against the Tuscarora.

In the predawn darkness of April 7, 1712, Col. Barnwell led his mixed force against Hancock's Fort. On that day, he commanded one hundred and twenty eight warriors who were mostly Yamassee from South Carolina, seventy-five men of the New Bern Militia, under Captain Brice, thirty-two frontiersmen from Chocowinity Bay, and various other white stragglers who had drifted in during the night, bringing his non-Indian contingent to a total of one hundred and fifty four. This army of two hundred and eighty-two proposed to attack the Tuscarora stronghold of King Hancock.

The palisade walls around Hancock's Fort had not been reinforced or changed in any way that Barnwell could detect, during the month since the previous attack. Of course, the three blockhouses inside still stared back ominously at the attackers from behind those stout walls. By dawn Barnwell's force had surrounded the palisade and begun firing at any warriors who popped their heads above the walls.

At first, Barnwell rushed his Yamassee warriors to the wall near the exposed gate, with covering fire from the frontiersmen. The frontiersmen all had muskets or rifles and could thus provide supporting fire, whereas many of the Yamassee carried only bows and arrows or war hatchets, and could not do the same. Barnwell sent them forward toward the walls twice on that first morning of the battle, but even with covering fire from a hundred and fifty guns, the Yamassee took casualties. Those initial charges did little good.

Captain Brice then suggested a more subtle strategy to Barnwell. "I say, old man, perhaps we should fire the walls!" Barnwell liked the idea, since it at least was something novel, so he ordered members of the South Carolina Militia to form a troop of ten men and set the palisade walls ablaze. They sent several riders on horseback to Fort Barnwell to retrieve some jars of bear grease, some whale oil, and anything else flammable they could find. An hour later, while the Yamassee charged the wall near the gate, once again under the covering fire from over a hundred rifles, ten men hauled the flammables to the wall opposite the Yamassee attack and tried to set that wall on fire. Of course, that was easier said than done, since strong, stout, and more critically, *green* hardwood doesn't burn all that well, and this tactic accomplished little other than the unintentional waste of the whale oil for the few lamps in Fort Barnwell.

Of course, any formal army in the world at that time would have attacked the walls of Fort Hancock with cannon. A few well placed shots from a respectable six inch smoothbore gun would have reduced those walls to toothpicks, and probably could have destroyed the blockhouses as well! Further, cannon could be found all over the Carolinas at that point, since almost every ship mounted two or three and pirate ships mounted many more. Cary had even managed to acquire some during his rebellion the previous year! Still, neither Col. Barnwell nor Captain Brice had seen fit to acquire cannon for this battle, so the walls stood there, day by day, mocking the best laid plans of Col. Barnwell's army. Another charge by the Yamassee the next day did nothing further, and the attack settled into a siege of Hancock's Fort, with each side sniping at the other, and neither making any real progress toward victory.

To make matters worse, Hancock was much better prepared for a siege engagement than was Barnwell. Any military leader knows that in siege warfare, supplies of food and water are at least as critical as a goodly supply of ammunition. In the sieges of Petersburg and Vicksburg during the American Civil War or the siege of Stalingrad in World War II, food and water were so critical they actually became mediums of exchange, and were much more highly valued in those cities than money itself during the actual siege. One cannot eat money, and in siege warfare it often comes down to a question of who has the largest stockpile of supplies. King Hancock, with no formal military training at all, had foreseen this very possibility while neither Col. Barnwell nor Captain Brice had. Thus, King Hancock had ordered his Tuscarora to stock Hancock's Fort with water, dried meat, salted fish, and all the ammunition and arrows possible. He knew that unless the smelly-pales brought the large thunder logs, he could sit behind his stout oak walls, eating and drinking those supplies for several months, and he hoped that the smelly-pales would get hungry during that time and merely go away.

As it turns out, that is exactly what happened. Barnwell still could not feed his army, and promises of coming supplies notwithstanding, his men were starving. He sent riders to New Bern and Bath to demand that food and ammunition be sent immediately. He sent both frontiersmen and Yamassee warriors into the Carolina wilderness to hunt for deer, bear, rabbits or anything else that could be eaten by two hundred and eighty-two hungry men. None of these actions produced enough food to change his situation, and on the tenth day of the siege Barnwell was forced to arrange another truce with King Hancock.

By the end of that day, April 17, 1712, Barnwell, having no real authority to do so, signed an actual peace treaty with the Tuscarora. However, just before the meeting, King Hancock fled the fort, and his subordinate negotiated with Barnwell. That treaty like the previous truce, called for the return of all hostages held by the Tuscarora, as well as the return of any livestock or other items stolen from Carolina farms. It stipulated that the Tuscarora abandon the land between the Neuse and Cape Fear River to the south, as well as surrender King Hancock himself. Everyone except Barnwell believed that the document was as worthless as the previous truce for which Barnwell had been so maligned, but Barnwell still felt he had no option but to sign the damn thing and withdraw his army to New Bern where he at least hoped to feed his men.

Upon hearing of the treaty, Governor Hyde nearly had a heart attack! How could the Scarecrow from South Carolina dare to defy his direct order to carry the battle forward, when he knew supplies were on the way? He and many in the legislature, now meeting in the safety of the Albemarle, were considering bringing charges against Barnwell, but that reaction was mild compared to the reaction of the folks at Mallard's Tavern in New Bern. They were discussing hanging the scarecrow outright!

Over the next two weeks a few somber voices of reason could be heard. Captain Brice, who had been on the battlefield with Barnwell had seen the critical nature of the supply problems and he defended Barnwell doggedly to all who would listen. Even Col. Pollock in the Albemarle had some kind words for the scarecrow. "Had Barnwell not come to the aide of our colony, the Neuse, Trent, and Pamlico settlements would have been deserted, as well as a great deal more of the country." These two leaders, Brice and Pollock, had earned the respect of Carolinians all across the colony, but their voices were simply drowned out by the overwhelming, if unjustified, anger at Barnwell. Some folks seemed to hate him more than their enemy, the Tuscarora. With those vile voices ringing in his ears, Col. Barnwell simply decamped from the docks of New Bern and headed back to his plantation in South Carolina, where he claimed he had saved North Carolina from the savages!

Of course, Barnwell's departure from the Trent River docks on May 11, 1712 did nothing to help feed his hungry Yamassee warriors, and they were as Toby Mallard observed one evening in mid May, "Some damn mad savages!" Those warriors had found few spoils in their battles thus far, and few had collected a single scalp! Over a hundred Yamassee warriors still stood to muster in Fort Barnwell in early May, and with no commander on the scene other than some Sergeant of the South Carolina Militia those Indians deserted in mass, the very day they heard that Barnwell had left for South Carolina. Throughout late May, June, and July of 1712 the Yamassee, and a few Catawba again swept through the Carolina countryside stealing whatever they found worth taking, this time stealing from whites as well as from the Tuscarora villages they encountered. Carolinians would have been much wiser, and much better off, had they showered Barnwell with praise and then sent him packing along with his Yamassee warriors, but that was not to be. For the time being, the Carolinians still had the worry of a second Tuscarora massacre, along with the real threat of having one's entire livelihood stolen by the hungry Yamassee. Again, Toby Mallard, ever the bard of New Bern, and a font of great wisdom sat in his tavern one evening and summed it up. "If'n these damn Yamassee is here to help us, then I recon' the cure is pretty 'nigh as bad as the damn disease!"

Barnwell, having been completely vilified in North Carolina, cared not one whit! Once at home in Charleston, he worked doggedly and made a huge success of his plantation, and eventually founded an important family in that influential colony. Neither his sideways look nor his high pitched, irritating voice was a genetic trait, so his progeny suffered not from those characteristics. Barnwell himself came to be respected in those parts for having saved the North Carolinians from total destruction by the savage Tuscarora, a perspective which in retrospect is historically accurate.

When all is said and done, history must conclude that this scarecrow did well for himself. He came to the aide of his neighbors when called to do so, and won a decisive victory at Narhantes. If the North Carolina settlements didn't meet their obligations to him, he certainly did to them. While he didn't destroy the Tuscarora, he did hurt them, and kept them in check for almost a year, when the North Carolinians themselves could do neither. In fact, this man had never failed in any meaningful sense, and he deserves much more respect than he has received. No matter what life brought his way, no matter what trials—starvation, lack of support, or the harsh criticism of his fellows—he simply kept coming. Anyone in any age, who can accomplish that, is indeed a man of substance.

## *Yellow Fever*

Unfortunately for the North Carolinians, Barnwell had never been provided with the resources needed to finish the job against the savages. The power of the Tuscarora was still unchecked in the area between the Trent and the Pamlico Rivers. Various raids on outlying farms still continued, and while the Yamassee would steal you blind, many of the Tuscarora raids continued to result in murder or even vile mutilations of the bodies of the smelly-pales, as King Hancock continued in his attempt to drive the invaders out of that region of the colony.

Still, Hancock was fighting a war in the only way available to him. He had neither the armaments nor the manpower to attack New Bern or Bath outright, and while his terror tactics were intentionally cruel, he nevertheless must be viewed as a typical, if calculating leader among the various warrior tribes along the coast. His overall goals were not unreasonable, given his perspective and experiences. He was not seeking revenge by that point in the autumn of 1712, nor did he seek to eliminate the smelly-pales from the entire North American Continent, as would many Native Americans in later years. He merely wanted the area between the Pamlico and the Trent Rivers reserved for his tribe, and he thought he could at least accomplish that goal. By the summer of 1712, he almost had.

However, at just that moment, an epidemic broke out that, strangely enough may have saved the North Carolina Colony. A bout of yellow fever placed a very capable man in a senior leadership position, and good leadership often makes a profound difference in any historical period.

Yellow fever is a viral disease and often struck in the Carolinas with no warning, a curse that lasted well into the twentieth century. The disease was and is born by mosquitoes and maims many, while killing between fifteen and fifty percent of the victims in any given year. In September of 1712 that disease, merely by the happenstance of one mosquito, found as a victim one Edward Hyde, Governor of the Carolina Colony. That hungry little bug changed history.

Now, all true North Carolinians take great pride in the extreme size and amazing dexterity of our mosquitoes. When one lives in a land of beautiful lakes, slow meandering creeks, rivers, sounds, bays, and huge lowland swamps, one will inevitably live with mosquitoes and absolutely nothing will ever change that fact! Joking about these pesky little bugs is the only real option, and most Carolinians understand that and thus relish that time honored past-time.

A Texan was out on a horseback bear-hunting trip near Catfish Lake with a North Carolina boy. They sat by the campfire one evening while the Texan loudly bragged that Texas mosquitoes were so big he'd once seen one swallow a bird! The Carolina boy said not a word, but he did turn on a flashlight and that drew in a mosquito that buzzed around a bit, and then flew off, carrying away the Texan's horse!

The Tuscarora were the first to live in these parts, and they had the same thoughts on mosquitoes as we do today. They are one of only a few Native American Tribes that actually created a legend to explain the mosquito.

*"One time there lived a giant mosquito, bigger than a bear and more terrifying. When he flew the sun could not be seen and when he was hungry, he would fly into camp and carry off a warrior or two and pick their bones clean. Many warriors tried to destroy the beast but their arrows fell off him like dew off a leaf. The Chief and the Conjuror prayed together to the Creator to help them destroy this animal. They sang, and they danced, and they prayed all night. Then a giant Bat and a large Spider heard their cry for help, and decided to have pity on these poor, miserable human creatures.*

*Bat came down from the sky looking for the monster Mosquito to battle with him, and Spider spun a huge web to try and catch him. The great Mosquito knew that he could not beat Bat so he decided to fly away, and he flew so fast that no one could see him. He was faster than lightening, and the only sound was the wild zooming of his wings, but Bat flew behind him just as fast. Mosquito flew all around, over rivers and creeks and even to the great mountains, and over the ocean, and to the large lakes in the north, but Bat flew with him.*

*When the sun was going down, the Great Mosquito turned to see that Bat was still with him, coming nearer, and that is when he flew into the huge web of Spider. The battle was short and the monster Mosquito was destroyed. His blood spattered and flew in all directions, and a strange thing happened. From the blood, were born many thousands of small mosquitoes with sharp stingers. They flew away in all directions, and still attack warriors and all of the animals. It happened long ago, but to this day along our rivers and streams, we have thousands, no, millions of mosquitoes, and Bat still hunts them at night, and Spider still spins a web to catch them. A Tuscarora warrior should never harm Bat or Spider, but rather thank them for helping kill our mosquitoes!"*

On September 3, 1712, a few die hard mosquitoes flew around a group of human creatures up in the Albemarle. That evening Governor Hyde was entertaining a group of Virginia gentlemen at another plantation home of Col. Thomas Pollock. They sat in the cooling evening beside the Chowan River as the senior house slave, dressed in his finest black suit, brought them fruits, sweetmeats, and other delicacies, and served them some fine French brandy that Governor Hyde seemed to favor.

At that moment, Hyde was speaking to Pollock alone, on the porch about the continuing problems in the paralyzed government. "I know not what action to take, Col. Pollock. These damn Quakers still undercut my every move, and will not vote a shilling to help rid us of either the Tuscarora or the Yamassee. The settlers in New Bern are still hungry, if not starving but they fear going into the woods to hunt, and no crops can be planted until next season."

Of course, by that time, most of those who were still called "The Quaker Party" were not really Quakers. The religious die-hards of that group had left the colony when Cary had been sent into exile in London the previous year. Still, many in government opposed Governor Hyde's policies for a host of reasons. In particular, they opposed sending any help to the upstart settlements of Bath and New Bern.

Hyde continued. "You should hear their comments in the legislature, Col. Pollock! 'Why should those damn Germans be allowed to create a major port that will take the place of the Chowan River? Why were those upstarts allowed charters for those towns at all?' It is most distressing, I say!"

Tom Pollock listened to the complaint. He'd heard it all before from Governor Hyde, and had, by this point, determined that Hyde like Cary before him was a blithering idiot. In Pollock's view, this damned governor could barely wipe his arse in the outhouse without legislative direction and approval! He certainly knew nothing about leading a colony. Like many members of the genteel aristocracy in the Carolinas, Pollock wondered why the Lords Proprietors continued to select these fools for leadership when many who lived in the colony itself knew its problems much better, and would do a much better job governing; he himself, as one example! Pollock was wise enough to smile at the self-serving nature of that thought, but that should not suggest that he didn't believe it with every ounce of his being!

He turned back to Hyde, just in time to hear again, "I really don't know what to do! I've appealed again for help from Virginia, but they do nothing to help us, and …" here he swatted his left elbow with his other hand and shouted, "Damn these mosquitoes! I say, is not there a single plantation along this river that isn't a nest of them!" Hyde didn't realize he'd just insulted his host, but then again such things slipped by him frequently, and Pollock merely smiled again, thinking, "I wish those bugs would simply fly off with this infantile bugger!"

This was the single mosquito that changed history.

Three days after the party, Hyde was indisposed. He actually failed to attend the legislative committee meeting that was planned in order to discuss support for fishing limitations to be placed on the Coree Indians, so white fishermen could harvest oysters more readily. More importantly, he missed a meeting at the Chowan River docks with the privateer Edward Teach, and he was forced to let his secretary, Tobias Knight, manage that meeting without him.

The next day, Hyde had a fever, a headache, and experienced multiple chills. He also noticed a bruise on his thigh, but he didn't remember bumping into anything. He was bleeding under his skin and didn't realize it. He had the signs of the first stage of yellow fever, and didn't realize that either.

The disease next progressed in Governor Hyde, as it does in many victims, though a period of "black vomit." Governor Hyde coughed up a dark concentration of his own blood. His chills become more pronounced and his nausea resulted in not-eating for a period of days. Thus he was losing strength. The governor was completely incapacitated by September 10, and slipped into a coma that evening. That coma, at the very least alleviated his suffering, and resulted in a more merciful death than the governor would have had otherwise. He expired on September 12, 1712. Hyde had been the governor of the North Carolina Colony for just over a year, and in that short time had presided over both a major rebellion and the first two stages of the Tuscarora War. Things are never dull in the Carolinas!

Fortunately the death resulted in some movement in the government. On September 13, 1712, Col. Thomas Pollock was nominated as the acting governor of the North Carolina Colony, by the other legislators. A few of those gentlemen were heard to remark that no one should let the Lords Proprietors in London know of Hyde's death, least they send over another idiot. Most legislators felt that Col. Pollock would do a splendid job of governing, and he did.

His first decision, though an unannounced decision, was to ignore the legislature entirely. He even came up with a scheme to disband them for a time, and as strange as it might seem, it worked! Speaking to the entire body only a week later, in late September of 1712, Pollock pointed out that the legislature had met almost continuously over the last ten months, trying to keep in touch with the actions of the Tuscarora and Barnwell's expedition. Then he suggested a "brief respite." Pollock recommended that various committees continue to meet and make recommendations to him as needed, but he strongly felt that the legislature itself should take a much deserved recess. Surprisingly, there was no opposition at all!

With that pesky democratic body out of the way, Col. Pollock did what he did best, he took command. He immediately sent for King Tom Blount, who was the titular leader of the northern Tuscarora. When they met at the Pollock Plantation, Pollock carefully thanked him for keeping his followers out of the war, and then immediately blackmailed the reigning King of the Tuscarora!

By simply considering what his enemy desired, Pollock was able to identify the real reason that Blount had refused to join with King Hancock. Blount and his savages traded much more with the Virginia settlements and those in the Albemarle, than did the southern Tuscarora and King Blount, by not joining in the war, was acting to preserve that trade. Pollock was smart enough to use that leverage to motivate King Blount to help put an end to the conflict.

First, Blount was told to find King Hancock. In short, if trade was to continue, the notorious Hancock had to be delivered along with all white captives of the Tuscarora, and the scalps of the other hostile savages. In return, trade would continue and Blount would be declared King of all Tuscarora in the Carolinas! Thus, did Pollock make King Blount a deal that the King could not refuse!

Hancock was delivered to Pollock's plantation within a week, where he was summarily hanged in an old hickory tree beside the Chowan River. That tree still stands along that river only ten miles north of Edenton, North Carolina, and today it is known as the "hanging tree" though no one other than King Hancock was ever hanged there. No "scalps of the other hostiles" were ever turned over to Pollock or any other authority, but a number of captives were. Two weeks after Pollock blackmailed King Blount, eighteen captives, mostly females and children, stumbled in to Fort Barnwell where they identified themselves as Tuscarora captives. King Blount sent Col. Pollock a message in which he indicated that no other captives were held by the Tuscarora in the North Carolina Colony, and that was probably true as far as it goes. However, over time, evidence mounted that almost a score of whites and several blacks were sold as slaves by the Tuscarora to other tribes to the west, including the Cherokee, the Catawba, and the Creek during that timeframe. The Tuscarora were, after all, businessmen who knew the value of a slave, white or black.

In one sense, however Col. Pollock's decision to take a firm stand with King Blount had an adverse effect. By capturing and handing over King Hancock, King Blount had angered many of his own followers, and attempting to take away their newly captured white or black slaves angered many more. By late October in 1712, many of the leaders of various Tuscarora villages who had followed Blount were beginning to pull away from his influence, and some had even sanctioned raids against white farms in their territory. Thus, from the perspective of Pollock and the legislature, the war continued, even though King Hancock was dead.

At that point, Pollock fired off another request to South Carolina, since Virginia had been no help at all, requesting the support of a militia force of "a thousand savages from any tribe" to be led by a contingent of white officers. Col. Pollock, acting not only as colonial governor, but with the implicit authority of the North Carolina Colonial Legislature, again promised that the North Carolina Colony would provide food and munitions for this expedition, just as his predecessor Governor Hyde had done. Pollock's official communication explicitly requested any white leader other than Col. John Barnwell. In an unofficial letter that accompanied the request, Pollock made his opinion more clear, when he wrote, "Should Barnwell return to this colony, there is no doubt in my mind that he would be summarily hung!"

The South Carolina Governor got the none-too-subtle message. Again desiring to address the uprising while it was still confined to the North Carolina Colony, the governor agreed in October of 1712, to mount another expedition, and this time a man with serious military training, Col. James Moore would lead.

### The Moore Expedition

Unlike the previous expedition led by Barnwell, the South Carolina Governor had chosen the right leader for this foray into the hinterlands of the North Carolina Colony. James Moore was the type of no-nonsense man that colonial militiamen would follow into hell if need be. He rode straight in the saddle, and looked a man in the eye when he spoke! He was decisive in battle and in command decisions, and if he was a bit abrupt with his subordinates, he considered that his prerogative as commander of the army, and to hell with what anyone else thought!

In early December of 1712, Col. Moore led his army into New Bern and sat down to sup with Captain William Brice at the Brice Plantation. When Col. Moore asked about the provisions for his army, Captain Brice had to give him the news that, just like before, no provisions had been delivered. Thus, Col. Moore immediately confronted the same problem that had driven Barnwell to make two bad truce agreements with the Tuscarora. Absolutely no food was available for his nine hundred man army!

Col. Moore exploded into a string of curses that would make any sailor of that day proud! The rage went on for some minutes, and only the essentials are presented here.

"By God, the rascals! Damn them all to hell!" Col. Moore shouted, as his brother, Captain Maurice Moore, and his other subordinates cringed. Captain Brice merely looked on with cautious distain.

"They promised food, delivered none, and now they expect me just to conjure up bacon and beans for nearly a thousand hungry savages as if by magic? By God, I'll kill them! I'll cut their filthy heads from their damned shoulders! I'll throttle the lot of them!"

Col. Moore's army, like Barnwell's the previous year, was made up almost entirely of warriors from various Indian tribes. Of the eight hundred and fifty savages with Moore, three hundred were Cherokee from the South Carolina Cherokee villages, fifty were Yamassee from the coast, two hundred were Catawba from the interior of North and South Carolina, and the remaining three hundred represented eleven smaller coastal tribes. Col. Moore had only fifty white men with him from the South Carolina Militia, including his brother, to command this diverse group of warriors.

Captain Brice was scared to even suggest any possibilities to this enraged man, so he merely poured more wine and observed silently as the cursing went on. Brice could see that Moore understood his desperate situation. If Barnwell could not manage to feed less than five hundred savages, Moore could clearly not feed eight hundred and fifty, but unlike Barnwell, Moore decided immediately what he would do.

"I think that Barnwell and his savages stole from the wrong damned enemy! By God, the enemy is in the Albemarle! To Hell with those… (Several quite extensive curses are deleted here because, at this point Moore uttered a string of invective that should absolutely never be seen in print. He referred explicitly and in a rather foul manner to Acting Governor Pollock's extremely rude sexual acts with Governor Pollock's esteemed mother, his dog, and various barnyard animals, while also casting similar aspersions toward the rest of the North Carolina Colonial leadership!). "If that despicable lot will not feed my army, then I'll deposit my starving army on their damn doorstep!" He managed to increase the volume of his shout on the last point, which truly amazed Brice not to mention all of the others in the room. "I'll have my savages take the food right off the fine china on the damn dinner table of the governor himself, and those…" (More curses are deleted here, and this curse was even longer and more vulgar than the previous effort!). "They will then, by God, feed my army or they'll have nothing to eat themselves!"

Moore's anger never abated, and he was as good as his word! He moved his army out of New Bern the very next morning at dawn, heading not for the fortified Tuscarora towns only thirty miles away but for the larder of the leadership of the North Carolina Colony which was over ninety miles up the North Trail along the north bank of the Albemarle Sound! Being a considerate man, he did have the forethought to send a messenger to Acting Governor Pollock informing him of the pending arrival in the Albemarle of his nine hundred man army of hungry savages. While the text of that message has been lost to history, it would have certainly been one of the more impressive messages of its type, and had to have been some version of the common theme, "Guess who's coming to dinner!"

Suffice it to say that food was on hand for the army when they arrived in the Albemarle. In fact, Col. Moore enjoyed the hospitality of his Albemarle hosts so much that he absolutely refused to move the army again, until he received firm confirmation that food, munitions, powder, and the other necessities of war had in fact, been delivered (not sent, mind you, but actually delivered) to Fort Barnwell near the Tuscarora fortifications along the Neuse River. He let his strong feelings on the matter be known to all of his hosts in the Albemarle region, and they, without exception, hated him even more than they had hated Barnwell the previous year!

Of course, most such large deliveries of food and munitions take considerable time, but throughout late December of 1712 and early January of 1713, Moore and his nine hundred man army were eating the plantations in the Albemarle out of house and home! The army butchered cattle whenever they needed to with little regard for ownership, and they collected chickens daily from any farm within twenty miles. Few deer were left in those woods, and not a single wild turkey could be found in that region for years! Under those circumstances, the food for the army was gathered in record time, and was shipped via coastal sloop into the Pamlico and up the Neuse to Fort Barnwell in central Carolina quite quickly too! Moore was always as good as his word and on January 17, 1713, he decamped, leaving the Albemarle, and headed to a freshly resupplied Fort Barnwell.

Col. Moore's army arrived at Fort Barnwell on January 20, 1713, where he was cheered as his officers and white troops came through the gates by none other than Blood-Eyes and the New Bern Militia. Martin Bender, Archie Carmichael, Franz Tuber, Lt. Mallard, young Willie Koonce, Dunker Tim, and all the rest were there to greet Col. Moore, and many reflected that like their commander Captain Brice, this man Moore looked fit to command an army. Johannes had taken ill, with the most recent bout of yellow fever, and while it weakened him considerably, he never developed symptoms past the first stage of that disease. When Martin left the cabin on January 18, 1713, Johannes was already recovering, but was still too weak to join in this muster against the Tuscarora.

Captain Brice jokingly shouted to Col. Moore as Moore rode into the fort. "I say, Col. Moore, every member of your staff seems to have gained a few pounds with your recent trip to the Albemarle! I trust they fed you well? What?"

Moore merely smiled at the taunt, as he dismounted. "Indeed they did, Captain. Indeed they did! It is wonderful to see you and the New Bern Militia here! Perhaps now we can finish this bloody business. I have the army, the provisions, and now I need to see the enemy in my sights!" Moore dismounted, but before he had even set foot inside the small cabin that served as the command center for the fort, Moore ordered his scouts to seek out and observe Fort Hancock which lay only seven miles away. Moore, of course, knew of Barnwell's efforts in that region the previous autumn, and he realized that while Barnwell had attacked that fortification twice, it had never fallen. In fact, Fort Hancock had withstood a ten day siege! Col. Moore wanted to get an initial impression of what he might be up against.

Within a day his scouts had reported back something strange. Fort Hancock had been completely abandoned, but a much stronger fortification had been built several miles further away along the same creek, and near another Tuscarora village called Neoheroka. It was to be this city and this powerful fortification that Moore would strike.

## The Troy of the Carolinas

In building Fort Neoheroka, the Tuscarora had constructed one of the largest military fortifications ever seen in the Carolinas! They had created a masterpiece of frontier defense for the early 1700s. The strong palisade walls were made of heavy oak, backed by two feet of earth, and more oak, and they were higher than the walls at Fort Hancock. Here the walls stood over eight feet in height, and held walkways on the inside so warriors could stand on the parapets and shoot, while those in the enclosed courtyard were protected. Further, the walls were irregular in shape and while this holds no real military advantage, it at least prohibits one's enemy from clear communications. It is far easier to say, "Attack the west wall," than to say, "Do you see that second curved projection of the palisade wall near the third small tree slightly to the left of center? Attack that!"

But this fortification presented many more challenges than merely irregular walls. Over an acre and a half of ground was enclosed by those walls, and at strategic points all along the walls as well as behind them in the enclosed courtyard itself, no less than eight separate blockhouses were constructed. Again these were two story affairs that allowed warriors to shoot over the walls from the top levels, but these blockhouses were larger than the previous efforts, and had many more slits through which warriors could poke rifles or fire arrows. Close examination of one blockhouse showed four rifle slits in each direction meaning that sixteen warriors could shoot from the top level of that one blockhouse alone!

The enclosure also housed a number of cabins, as well as what appeared to be caves that allowed warriors to move from blockhouse to blockhouse without exposure. These caves were really ditches that had been covered over with heavy logs and then two feet of earth, and they were visible from the outside, only as mounds of earth that ran from one critical location to the other. There was even an enclosed passageway that led down to an extension of Contentea Creek, which would allow the savages to get water without being exposed to enemy fire! This was, by far, the most impressive fort the Tuscarora ever built, and if Fort Hancock was provisioned to withstand a siege of one or two months, Fort Neoheroka presented the uncomfortable possibility of successfully withstanding a much longer siege.

Moore, when he saw this fortification only two days later, could not help but admire it. As a trained military man he knew his military history, and he sought from that resource a most apropos comparison. "My God! These are the hallowed walls of ancient Troy, transported into the Carolina wilderness! They are impregnable! We shall certainly need a well developed attack plan to breech those walls!"

After Col. Moore returned to Fort Barnwell that day, he disappeared completely into his quarters. Before slamming the cabin door, he ordered pen and writing paper and said that anyone who should disturb him would suffer immediate execution! He then told Captain Brice to manage things within the fort and keep observers stationed near Fort Neoheroka. He even ordered a guard placed at the door to his cabin in Fort Barnwell, and since Brice wanted to use trusted men for that duty, Sergeants Martin Bender and Archie Carmichael were ordered to pick one man each and stand by that cabin twenty-four hours a day. Brice specifically ordered that at least one of the Sergeants was to be there at all times, day or night!

Inside of that small cabin, Moore didn't bath, he barely ate, he requested water or rum only rarely, and he soon looked as bedraggled and uncivilized as some of the Cherokee warriors he'd led to the fort. He pissed only off the rear porch of the cabin when necessary, and used the outhouse rarely, quickly returning to his cabin while speaking to no one. Martin and Archie would occasionally enter the cabin and stoke the fire with more hickory wood, and then they would then leave without saying anything to Col. Moore, who either sat by the fire, or worked on his small table creating an attack plan that he considered worthy of Fort Neoheroka. Other than those two, no one in the fort came within twenty feet of Moore for that entire time. Even Captain Brice and Moore's own officers were ordered to stay away.

On the afternoon of the third day, Moore did something he had not done at all for over nearly seventy hours. He spoke. More accurately, he began to shout.

"Sergeant! Bring me a wash pot, and water. Bring me hot water! See that my second uniform is well pressed by the slaves, and have Captain Brice and all of my officers and senior Sergeants meet me at the covered horse shed in one hour!"

Martin was the sergeant on guard duty at that moment, so he came rushing in to the cabin at the first sound of that shout and realized only when he arrived and looked at the stinky man before him that he'd missed most of that multiple order. He simply said, "Sir?"

He was terrified for a moment, as he stood there. He hoped that Col. Moore would repeat the order without Martin having to request it, for the temper of this man knew no bounds and his curses had already taken on the aura of legend! The two simply stared at each other for a few seconds, and then Col. Moore did something else entirely uncharacteristic and wholly unexpected. He smiled! Then he laughed outright at the perplexed young Sergeant before him, and said "What's the matter, my young friend? Did you miss the orders entirely?"

Martin merely stammered, "Well, Sir, I… uh…"

Moore merely waved his hand as he interrupted, "Never mind, we'll start with a warm bath. Yes, I think a bath, first. Prepare that, if you please."

"Yes Sir!" shouted Martin with a smile on his face. He was to be spared that legendary temper of Col. Moore! Martin literally ran to the porch to get the slaves to prepare warm water for the bath, but Dunker Tim, unlike Martin, had heard the orders the first time they were shouted. He seemed to hang around Martin much of the time, and often helped when he could. He was already rushing to bring over a large metal washtub, and he shouted at two other slaves to fetch pitchers of hot water from the cook shed. Col. Moore would get his bath in record time!

At that moment Martin was so relieved he could have kissed Col. Moore's feet! He like the rest of that army, would have gladly followed Moore into hell itself right then. That feeling was quite fortunate, since within two days Martin and the others would have to do exactly that! They were going to march on Fort Neoheroka!

## *The Plan of Attack*

To any military man, the plan that Col. Moore had developed was indeed a thing of beauty. In some ways it was simplicity itself since the first phase mainly involved a coordinated attack in force from only one direction. However, Moore's plan was not dependent upon massed charges into fields of deadly crossfire, as were many single axis attacks. While many military leaders seemed to prefer massed charges in those days, Moore knew that such a tactic would cost way too many lives. Instead of sacrificing his army in charges against that Troy-like wall, he would, instead use construction! An axe and hammer would be his weapons!

Even Martin, with no military training at all, yet having a world of experience in various battles, could see the advantages of the tactics Moore's plan envisioned, and Martin was sure that the plan would have the effect of sparing many men's lives, possibly his own. Moore's plan involved no less than six major construction projects, and he would have his men undertake those building jobs immediately. In fact, with the hammer and axe being by far the most important tools on that battlefield for the next month, Moore even imported many workers from both New Bern and Bath to help with the building. Those men were older and were not in the New Bern Militia, but they could dig, they could fell trees, and they could build! Of course, this resulted in over three hundred additional mouths to feed, during the cold month of February in 1713. In turn that necessity resulted in another interesting communication to Acting Governor Pollock.

Now Col. Moore was no fool, and he knew that Governor Pollock hated him thoroughly for parking his hungry army in the Albemarle throughout the coldest days in January. For that reason, his communication took on a tone that Col. Moore believed to be a humorous diatribe.

*Thank you, Governor Pollock, once again for the warm hospitality and the gracious provisions you afforded me and my army in our recent social visit to your plantations. We have also noted the many foodstuffs sent more recently to Fort Barnwell, and we appreciate them as well. Unfortunately, we shall now have to request several more items…"* (Later, the governor's secretary, Tobias Knight, stated that Acting Governor Pollock actually gasped as he read that line!) *"… that are required under the present circumstances. We shall need one hundred and fifty axes, seventy five hammers, fifty saws, and two thousand nails immediately, in order to construct bastions which will allow us to envelop and then attack Fort Neoheroka. With those*

# Battle of Neoheroka

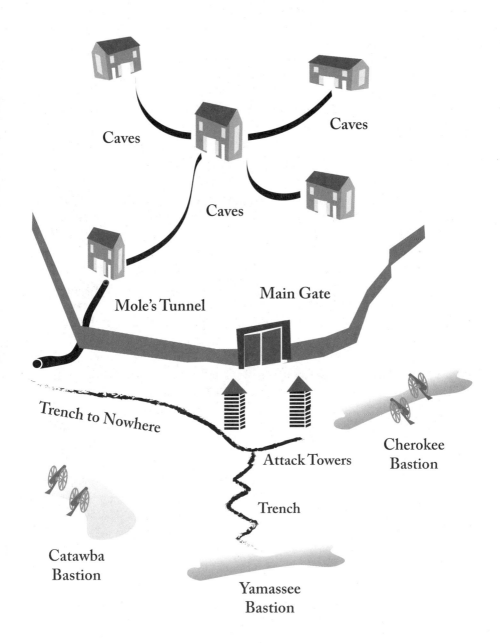

Caves

Caves

Caves

Mole's Tunnel

Main Gate

Trench to Nowhere

Attack Towers

Cherokee
Bastion

Trench

Catawba
Bastion

Yamassee
Bastion

*implements, along with the slaves and white labor force I have conscripted from the local towns, I have every anticipation of success. Should I not receive your confirmation that these items will be shipped to me forthwith, I shall decamp my army and once again, come calling in the Albemarle! I do hope to see you very soon!*

*Your Honorable Servant*
*Col. James Moore*

Amazingly, the hammers, nails, and axes were delivered to Fort Barnwell in just over a week, by several guards and a contingent of twenty-five slaves from Col. Pollock himself, who simply asked, "Where do we go to work?"

Eight hundred and fifty warriors of Moore's army chopped trees nearly scalping the land near Fort Neoheroka of all hardwoods, while the whites and their slaves, led by those who were knowledgeable in construction, dug holes in the ground. The plan initially involved construction of three batteries, which were essentially earthen forts approximately sixty feet in front, and tapering on the two sides to an open rear. However, to dig those within a reasonable range of Fort Neoheroka, the men had to have protection from musket fire from the fort walls. In order to accomplish that, Moore had several sections of wall built of a lighter wood approximately ten feet by six feet, and those were placed on what amounted to large sleds. Thus, those portable ten foot walls could be moved into position between the planned excavations for Moore's bastions and the walls of Fort Neoheroka. They protected his diggers.

Moore had even devised a complicated pulley system that allowed Moore's oxen to be shielded behind a nearby tree line, while they, indirectly moved the walled sleds into place, thus exposing only a series of long ropes to musket fire from the fort. With four of those ten foot sections in place end to end, Moore's "Army of Moles" as the men soon dubbed themselves, could dig the first bastion with impunity. After only a week of preparations, the bastion was ready, and the Tuscarora watched as the walled sleds were pulled away toward the location of the second bastion. As they were slowly moved, the walled sleds revealed an earthen bastion, approximately sixty feet long in front, with earth on three sides, and a wall of hardwood along the front facing Fort Neoheroka. That bastion on the right of Moore's attack line was called the Cherokee Bastion and would be manned by the Cherokee.

After that bastion was completed, Moore called for his brother and Captain Brice to join him. When they arrived he simply pointed to two other locations on the field, and said, "There and there. Two more bastions, gentlemen, if you please. I shall return in a week!" He then called for his horse and rode off alone toward New Bern. No one knew why.

Two other bastions of similar size and construction were built, approximately four hundred feet apart, taking another twelve days. The Yamassee Bastion anchored the center of Moore's line and the Catawba Bastion was constructed on the left. In the Cherokee Bastion and the Catawba bastion, Moore placed his surprise, four cannon that he had procured from a frigate that had the misfortune to be docked along the Trent River in New Bern at the wrong time.

Only four days after he left the field, Moore had simply shown up at the docks in New Bern with Sheriff DuVal in tow and said to the Captain of the frigate, I'll need four of your cannon and four good gun crews. The poor captain had no real choice in the matter, and Col. Moore simply handed him an IOU, against the treasury of the North Carolina Colony, saying, "I'm sure Governor Pollock will make good on those funds, the very next time you dock in the Albemarle. Good day!"

Once again, less than a month after this, Acting Governor Pollock found another reason to hate Col. Moore!

The cannon were transported in four wagons pulled by oxen to Fort Barnwell and then placed in the bastions around Fort Neoheroka. These were light three pounders, carriage guns which meant they were mounted on movable wooden platforms and fired solid shot three pound balls. Powder and cannonballs were also shipped in the carts. These were not the large six pounders Col. Moore had hoped to acquire, but he believed they would help some. Johannes, who was now feeling better, volunteered to drive one of the ox teams to the battlefield, and thus joined in the subsequent fight if not the main construction effort.

However, the line of three bastions was only the beginning of Moore's construction plans. He envisioned a wonderfully direct attack plan that originated from the center of that line in the Yamassee Bastion. From that covered location, Moore again set his men to digging! Excavating a zig-zag trench that was seven feet deep, and four feet wide, Moore's army of moles approached the walls of Fort Neoheroka, without ever coming under direct fire. When they reached a spot only twenty-five feet from the walls, these men buried large poles in the ground, rigged their pulley system to them, and once again began to tug at the walled sleds, which moved ever so slowly toward the Tuscarora fort. With those walls again in place, this time only twenty-five to thirty feet from the walls of the opposing fort, the men began to build a set of two large "Attack towers." These two towers were really blockhouses that hovered over the end of the trench and were facing the fort only twenty-five feet away. They both stood higher than even the blockhouses within the fort. From those two new blockhouses, the white militia and any slaves that were known to be good shots, could fire directly down into Fort Neoheroka.

{Author's Note: It is hard to imagine today, that massive military constructions such as these were ever a part of the North Carolina tidewater landscape, and many might find these descriptions difficult to believe, but such is the rich history of the Neuse River basin. Even those living in nearby cities such as Grifton, Goldsboro, Greenville, Kinston, New Bern, and Washington know not of these large military constructions, and many a deer or bear hunter along the Neuse River or Contentea Creek has probably walked over the locations of these fortification many times, without ever realizing it. Of course, wood and earthen forts do decay quickly in the moist climate of this region and very little is left of these constructions today. Moreover, three hundred years is a long time by any standard. Today, a lonely highway marker stands on Highway 11 North of Kinston, talking vaguely about some victory over the Tuscarora nearby in 1713, but that alone is a poor remembrance of this rich history. It is sad somehow that these places are not more treasured. Let us never forget that men of many colors—red, black, and white—died on that ground, fighting in a desperate struggle for their varied ways of life. In retrospect, each of those men deserves our thanks, and our honor, but today we do not even know their names.}

With his three bastions, Cherokee, Yamassee, and Catawba ready, and his two massive attack towers in place, Col. Moore discussed the final aspects of his attack plans with his senior leadership, and his field commanders. He had not placed these aspects of his plan on his initial battle maps, with the specific intention that these aspects of the plan were to remain secret until the last moment, even from his senior staff. One could never tell if any of his commanders might be captured by the savages, and then tortured to reveal the attack plans, so on some things Col. Moore kept his own council.

However, it soon became apparent that the good Colonel was not quite finished with his "army of moles" just yet! No one could figure out the reasoning, but Col. Moore had them digging trench just behind the two attack towers heading out to the west and then taking a sharp turn leading essentially to nowhere! The men in fact began to call it that, the "Trench to Nowhere," until the good Colonel told them to shut the hell up about it! His army of moles grumbled a bit, but they did shut up and they kept on digging! Col. Moore himself directed their excavations, and told them to say nothing of their work on pain of death. They were still digging on the first day of the battle, and none of them understood, even then, exactly what they were doing or why.

## *The Attack*

All was in readiness, and on the morning of March 20, 1713, at exactly eight AM, a trumpet sounded from the Cherokee Bastion to signal the beginning of the attack. Within only seconds that sound was drowned out completely as four cannon fired their hot deadly lead directly at the walls of Fort Neoheroka. Just as Col. Moore had feared, the cannon accomplished nothing at all!

After that initial volley, as the gun crews struggled to reload all four cannon, one could have heard the sigh over a mile away as over a thousand men looked at that stout wall, completely invulnerable. Without exception they all realized that three pounders, while fearsome weapons to a ship at sea, represented nothing more than a rather loud knock on the door of this fort! The walls were simply too strong, and were backed by two feet of earth! Still, the cannon were there and it was a battle so Col. Moore ordered continued firing. He did instruct the gunners to concentrate on the one gate in the convoluted wall that faced his bastions. He knew, as did everyone there, that this particular gate, at some point, simply had to go!

Much more effective that morning was the fire of Kentucky rifles from the rifle slits in the three bastions. Martin and all of the other men with the newer Kentucky rifles, had been assigned to the three major bastions in Moore's line since the range of those weapons made hitting a target the size of a man's head on the parapets of Fort Neoheroka child's play. Those targets were only forty yards away. At some point after fifteen minutes of fire from the Kentucky rifles, a South Carolinian standing beside Martin in the Cherokee Bastion spontaneously generated a name that would outlive anyone on the battlefield that day, and he did it with an ill timed curse!

"Damnation!" he shouted above the din of the rifle fire. "Moore's rifles are doing some real damage to those dumb-as-dirt savages!"

{Author's Note: No one realized it at the time, but that term "Moore's Rifles" would catch on in popularity throughout the South Carolina Militia on their march back to Charleston. As most of the men in that militia unit equipped themselves with such weapons over the next decade, they chose to call themselves Moore's Rifles, and eventually the term became an official designation for that unit in the South Carolina Colonial Militia. They became some of the best sharpshooters in the world at that time, and fought sixty-five years later in the American Revolution under General Daniel Morgan, making quite an impact in various battles. In fact, the unit designation persisted well into the Civil War. The brigade known as Moore's Rifles, were sharpshooters in the Confederate Army by 1863 and acquitted themselves quite well in numerous Civil War actions. They distinguished themselves quite impressively with their accurate rifle fire on Little Round Top at the Battle of Gettysburg.}

In 1713, the Tuscarora were sure that their walls would protect them from fire, since they knew nothing about that new rifle or its range. They had only the muskets they had captured or purchased prior to the war, and they knew the effective range of those precluded effective fire from the bastions.

However, nothing spurs progress like a war, and by the time of this battle some forty five militiamen had chosen to arm themselves with the newer Kentucky rifles. Like Martin, they knew how to use them and their fire was deadly. That is when the wisdom of Col. Moore's battle plan became apparent. He had the men in the bastions fire at any target that presented itself using their longer range Kentucky rifles, while he continued to pound the gate with his cannon. However, he specifically ordered that none of his Indian allies or the men armed with muskets in the two attack towers fire until ordered to do so. He wanted to reserve that fire for a bit later.

Col. Moore was a gifted battle commander, for the same simple reason Martin Bender was; he knew how to think like his enemy! He wanted to give the impression that warriors on the courtyard inside the fort were not under fire. Of course, the Tuscarora warriors were not stupid, and they could clearly see the rifle slits in the front of the attack towers, but with no fire coming from that source, they continued to expose themselves in the courtyard with little regard for their safety. Perhaps the smelly-pales were limited in their ammunition or simply forgot to station men at those rifle slits. Of course, the bravado of the Tuscarora warrior, the desire to test oneself in the face of danger before one's peers, also worked against the Tuscarora that day, as Col. Moore had hoped it would. By thirty minutes or so into the battle with only the cannon and the Kentucky rifles from the bastions firing, the savages exposed themselves repeatedly in the open courtyard behind the walls. They would soon realize that mistake.

Men who were known to be good marksmen with smoothbore muskets, a weapon that had a much shorter range than the Kentucky rifle, were stationed in the top of the two attack towers. Those towers were only twenty-five feet from the wall and the courtyard beyond and from that range, it was difficult for them to miss anyone in the courtyard. Moreover, Col. Moore had given specific instructions for those men to work in groups of three at each rifle slit. In that fashion, one man would be shooting while two others reloaded. Since a smoothbore could be loaded and fired as many as five times in a minute, that meant that fifteen different shots could be fired from every single rifle slit in the two attack towers. With each tower presenting five rifle slits facing toward the enemy, an amazing rate of fire was generated! Nearly a hundred and fifty shots could be carefully aimed and fired over the walls at any savage in the inner courtyard, and twenty minutes into the battle, the Tuscarora did not even realize that danger!

Col. Moore had set up his command center in the Yamassee bastion, which was the central location in his line. From there he could see the impact of his rifles and the lack of impact of his cannon. About twenty minutes after Col. Moore ordered the firing to begin, he turned to Captain Brice and his brother

Captain Maurice Moore, and said calmly, "Would you gentlemen care to take a stroll?"

They both knew of Moore's penchant for choosing ill timed phrases and his absolute mania for secrecy. Neither responded, so the good Colonel merely smiled and turned his request into an order. "Do accompany me, please." To their surprise, he then headed not out the back of the Yamassee Bastion, but rather into the trench that zig-zagged toward the two attack towers. Those trenches were not covered, but they were deep and Moore had sent runners moving through them throughout the first minutes of the battle, sometimes on an errand no more important that reminding the men huddled in those towers to hold fire until ordered otherwise! He did that, of course, to conceal his own use of the trench when it became necessary.

The men in those towers had been left completely out of the battle up to that point. They were huddled together, sitting in the lower floor of the tower, with only a couple of lookouts in the top level, and by that time, they were pissed! They were getting tired of some idiot coming in every five minutes or so to repeat orders that they considered stupid anyway! Why couldn't they fight too? When could they shoot?

When Archie Carmichael saw another busybody coming out of the trench, just a uniform seen out of the corner of his eye, he spoke without thinking. "And what does that damn South Carolina idiot want now? He orderin' us to pee together or something? Why can't we shoot?" Only then did Archie turn to face not some lackey, but Captain Brice, his immediate superior and Col. Moore, Commander of the Army!

"Uh, sorry, Sir. I didn't see you there and, uh…" Archie tried to apologize, but was not allowed to.

Moore precluded him with his shout. "Gather around, gentlemen. Let's talk a bit!" As the fifteen men gathered, he continued. "Remember your orders to fire in groups of three. I want a high rate of fire from this tower. I think we shall find many targets in that courtyard, and I want a continuous fire on them throughout the day. Now line up in your groups of three, and I'll inspect your weapons." Col. Moore knew the weapons would be clean, loaded, and ready. He really wanted to see the men group themselves into firing elements of three men each. They quickly did so, and after that inspection, Col. Moore shared the next phase of his plan. "Gentlemen, you will move to the upper level, and when you hear musket fire from the other tower, you will open fire on the savages in the courtyard. Should you see women or children there, fire on them. These savages would do no less to your women and children. Good luck and good hunting!"

Without speaking further, the Col. turned back to the trench, and went immediately to the other attack tower to issue the same orders. However, rather than leaving that tower, he instead turned to the ladder leading to the higher floor and climbed up, with Brice and his brother right behind. They were followed by fifteen excited men with loaded muskets who were glad to join in the battle. Col. Moore took one quick peek out of the closest rifle slit, and sure enough, many of the savages were crossing the courtyard. He knew his musket men would have many available targets, and he was about to set them loose.

He then gave the order. "Men there are many savages to target. Pick one quickly and shoot to kill. Then move to your left and quickly away so the next man may have a shot. With the cannon firing and the rifles shooting in the bastions, I believe it may be some time before the savages realize we are now firing on them from this position."

With that, the musket men stood to their rifle slits, and the first five men fired, and moved to the side as they reloaded. Immediately afterward, Col. Moore heard firing from the other attack tower as well. The rate of fire was exactly what he had hoped for, and it did take the savages over a minute to realize that they were now under fire from the towers, since that noise was lost in the overall noise of the useless cannon. Soon it was an assured death for any Tuscarora to be seen in the courtyard or standing up to full height on the parapets of Fort Neoheroka! By that time, well over sixty savages lay dead or wounded in the courtyard, and Col. Moore's forces has suffered only five wounds!

Once the savages did realize the new threat, however, targets inside the walls became much harder to find. The battle continued with rifle and musket fire exchanged for several hours. The whites in the attack towers began to take more hits, since muskets fired from the parapets inside the fort could easily hit a three inch rifle slit only twenty-five feet away. However, after three hours of the exchange, Col. Moore replaced the musket men in the attack towers with others who could shoot, including some of his Cherokee and Yamassee warriors. Both Moore's musket men and his riflemen in the bastions were finding fewer targets at that point, and it was surmised that the Tuscarora were using their cave system.

The battle could have gone on in that fashion for many more hours, days, or weeks, but Col. Moore had several additional elements to his attack plan. At about three in the afternoon on that day, he determined to try a frontal assault. While his cannon had not dislodged the gate, they had collapsed one of the large hinges on one side, and Col. Moore thought that the gate might give way to a determined charge. He had previously had his builders fashion twenty ladders that would allow his warriors to scale the walls and hopefully open the gate or knock it down. He decided to use his Yamassee for that initial charge, and they would be led by his brother, Captain Maurice Moore.

Had Col. Moore merely charged the walls after the attack began, his

Yamassee and Cherokee warriors would have charged into a horrendous fire from the parapet walls, but at this point, Moore's rifles had cleaned off the parapets, and the muskets in the attack towers had killed many in the fort, and driven the rest underground. He thought the time might be right to test the walls and the gate, so he gave the order. Strangely enough, he then turned over command of the battle to Captain Brice, and disappeared once again. Brice thought this was crazy, but he knew the idiosyncrasies of this man and didn't question it, least he feel the wrath of that incredible temper.

At four o'clock on that afternoon of the first day, the Yamassee charged the walls. Captain Moore had divided his forces into five separate groups, each of which would carry multiple ladders to overcome the walls. Suddenly the cannon ceased their firing and that was the signal. Under the covering fire of Moore's rifles and the muskets in the attack towers, two hundred Yamassee warriors charged. They met only scattered fire from Fort Neoheroka, since any Tuscarora showing himself above the wall immediately drew the attention of Moore's rifles. The ladders were placed at the walls, and the Yamassee scaled them. The first Yamassee to top the wall were killed outright by fire from the several blockhouses in the courtyard, but then many managed to get over the walls, as the Tuscarora in the interior of the blockhouses reloaded their muskets.

As soon as those Yamassee warriors dropped into the courtyard, they ran like lightening to place their backs against the lower side of one blockhouse or another, since that was the only cover available. These savages had bows and arrows, as well as some older muskets, so they could return fire, but they quickly found that there was no real cover for them in that deadly courtyard. Even pressed against the lower outer wall of one blockhouse, they were still under fire from another, and the Tuscarora were picking them off quickly. Several of the Yamassee did manage to open the gate a bit, before one of the gate hinges broke away, leaving that heavy wooden gate only partially blocking the opening.

The Yamassee were hoping for an immediate charge of the remaining Yamassee and the Cherokee at that point, and Captain Brice, now in command, did not disappoint them. With that gate partially open, he sent three hundred more warriors into the fight. Many of those warriors died trying to get inside the gate, since the Tuscarora in the blockhouses concentrated their fire on that vulnerable point. Still others made it inside, and the battle progressed. With that many enemy now inside the walls, control of the blockhouse closest to the partially open gate changed hands. Captain Moore led that fight inside the blockhouse, and it was as horrid as Johannes' blockhouse battle had been the previous year. Captain Moore did suffer a serious arrow wound inside that blockhouse, and he carried that arrowhead in his left shoulder for the rest of his life.

As evening fell on the first day of that battle, Captain Brice ordered no further offensive operations. Rather he had his men consolidate their gains, and move to set up another all out assault the next day. He had the wall sleds brought up all the way to the attack towers, and his men could now use either the trenches or the portable walls as cover from the occasional musket fire from the fort. He posted a strong guard in all of the attack towers and bastions, and he moved two of his cannon up to the top floor of the attack towers, where he had men, using axes, create a firing hole large enough for the three pounder carriage guns.

At that point, the Tuscarora had suffered losses but were not nearly defeated. They were still in strong positions in their remaining blockhouses and their cave system, but the Yamassee and Cherokee warriors had opened the gate partially, and controlled one blockhouse near that gate. Throughout the night, only occasional rifle fire erupted from time to time, and most of Captain Brice's men slept where they were assigned in the bastions, the trenches, or the towers. Those in the interior blockhouse in the courtyard kept a stronger vigil, expecting a night counter attack but that attack never came.

### Colonel Moore's Next Surprise

Around ten that evening, Col. Moore appeared once again at the Yamassee Bastion, seemingly from nowhere, and inquired about Brice's dispositions for the night. After Captain Brice gave his report the Colonel seemed pleased. He then took a few minutes to see his wounded brother at the makeshift aid camp some two hundred yards behind his attack line, and while there, he visited a bit with the several other men wounded in the day long campaign. When he returned to the Yamassee Bastion, he smiled at Captain Brice, and then repeated his request of earlier in the afternoon. "Captain Brice, care to take a stroll?" Again, Brice had no clue what to expect, so he merely said, "Yes Sir," and grabbed a lantern.

Col. Moore continued. "Have three of your most trusted Sergeants join us on this stroll if you please. I shall need about thirty men."

Brice responded. "I know the leaders you want, Colonel. Please spare me two minutes to collect them."

In less than a minute, Brice had ordered Martin Bender and Archie Carmichael to join him in the Yamassee Bastion, where he spoke to Col. Moore. "Sir, these are proven men and can be counted on. I'll fetch Johannes Simmons when we pass the attack towers. He fights with a musket, you see."

"Indeed," replied Col. Moore, and he took off down the trench toward the attack towers. In less than a minute, Col. Moore, Captain Brice, Martin, and Archie paused at the trench to nowhere. Here Brice dispatched Martin to fetch Johannes. These men then followed Col. Moore into the trench to nowhere. They had heard rumors of this trench but had not traveled down it.

That trench led twenty-five feet out to nowhere, parallel to the walls of the Tuscarora fort, and then took a sharp turn. Anything beyond that turn had been kept secret from everyone on that battlefield throughout the entire time, and the army of moles had even been digging all through the first day of the battle. The reason for the secrecy was obvious to all, once they made that first turn. Within only five feet of that turn, the trench to nowhere became a tunnel, approximately five feet underground, and supported by wooden logs for its entire length. It was four feet wide, and almost four feet high, so those in the tunnel had to bend over to pass, but it was clearly large enough for an assault force. In fact, if Col. Moore's calculations were correct, the tunnel reached far under the wall of Fort Neoheroka and ended immediately under one of the blockhouses still held by the Tuscarora. For that Col. Moore was almost apologetic.

"As we dug this afternoon, I was not sure how far to go, and we had to miss the Tuscarora caves in the courtyard, you see. While the tunnel follows the same general direction as the last five feet of the trench, we cannot be certain exactly where it ends. The distance is almost fifty feet, and demonstrates that we are well under the parapets. I believe we are under that pesky blockhouse on the left." He then smiled at Captain Brice, and continued. "Perhaps we could make use of this entrenchment in the morning?"

Captain Brice, seeing the various possibilities, said immediately. "Indeed! I am certain that my men here can find a use for this tunnel! We shall greet the morning with a rather loud explosion, just at dawn I should think!"

Moore's full attack plan was now clear to all of these subordinates, if not to others in his army. It was indeed a thing of beauty, and included many elements;

1. Sled walls to cover his constructions,
2. Three bastions,
3. A trench system moving toward the walls,
4. Two attack towers,
5. Intentional withholding of fire from his muskets in the attack towers,
6. Use of cannon to cover the firing noise of those muskets,
7. Trench to Nowhere, and finally,
8. A tunnel under the walls.

Each of these elements had the result of sparing many lives in Moore's army, but as these few men stood in that tunnel, each realized that he was to lead an assault force in the morning, either through this tunnel or over the walls. None found this to be a pleasant thought, but they had seen enough death at the hands of the Tuscarora, that each was prepared to do his duty.

An hour later these same five men, Col. Moore, Captain Brice, and Sergeants Martin Bender, Johannes Simmons, and Archie Carmichael sat together around a small table in the Yamassee Bastion. By the light of a small whale oil lamp, they looked at Moore's attack plan, on which Col. Moore had now drawn both the trench to nowhere and his tunnel. He had labeled the trench by the name the men created only two days before, "Trench to Nowhere" but he also labeled the tunnel the "Moles' Tunnel." He wanted to honor his diggers who, for the first time in almost forty eight hours were having an uninterrupted sleep, rather than a two hour cat nap. The evening was quiet, as guards posted on both sides kept vigil. There had been no musket fire for almost an hour.

Col. Moore began the discussion. "Captain Brice. Have our guards detected any movement at all in the fort?"

Brice responded immediately. "Not a sound, Colonel. It's quiet as a church mouse in there."

Col. Moore reflected on that a bit. "Maybe they have planned a surprise we don't know about. Let's post guards at the rear of every bastion, as well as at the aid station, least other Tuscarora come calling shall we?"

Brice responded proudly. "Already done, Sir. I'm sorry I didn't mention it in my previous report. It slipped my mind."

Col. Moore then turned to his map. "Indeed! Well, gentlemen. Let's discuss how we might use the Moles' Tunnel, shall we?"

Johannes, like the other sergeants, wanted to get this part of the discussion moving, but he was still struggling to master English, and he could not frame the question as he wanted. With little preamble, and no concern for protocol, he began the meat of the talk that evening, and what came out of his mouth summarized the exact issue to be decided, even if it was not framed in perfect syntax. "Sir, are I think, are… we go over or under?"

Col. Moore looked dumfounded, thinking the man an imbecile, since he had never heard Johannes speak before and didn't realize his struggles with the English language. In contrast, Captain Brice grinned at this cooper turned soldier, who he had come to depend on so much. "I think what the good Sergeant means is, shall we breach the wall with explosives, and go above ground through the breech, or plant our charges under the blockhouse, and trust that they will open a clear path into the courtyard. Over the wall, or under?"

Col. Moore merely said, "Indeed. I'd like to hear the thoughts of each of you men, since you will lead the assault elements. We are placing ourselves into your undoubtedly capable hands, you see."

Archie was a hard drinking man and a simple farmer, but he was also a leader in the New Bern Militia. He, like all members of that proud clan of Scots, never withheld his opinion, whether it was requested or not. "I think we pack charges at the end of the tunnel, and blow the hell out of the blockhouse. We can then charge the gate same as them Cherokee did this afternoon. The explosion will confuse 'um a bit and our Cherokee are still in the interior of the first blockhouse and can cover us. We'll get more men in quicker that way."

Captain Brice then showed his military background. "I say, doesn't it seem that two holes in the wall are better than one? Let's ignore the blockhouse, and blow the hell out of the wall. Then we assault both openings."

Col. Moore presented the challenge to that tactic. "I'm sure we can successfully assault the wall after we blow it, but that leaves the rest of the tunnel as useless. The Moles will have done that last thirty feet of digging for nothing, if we merely blow the wall!"

Martin then stated the obvious conclusion. "Why don't we do both?"

The discussion then centered round that suggestion, and how to carry it out. It was decided that the moles would plant two small barrels of black powder under the blockhouse, and another two barrels under the wall. Col. Moore gave the order to bring up the powder, and when the moles passed by only a minute or so later carrying four barrels of powder into the trench, both Martin and Johannes recognized their own work. They had built those barrels as multipurpose barrels only a year previously. Obviously they had been shipped up to the Albemarle hauling something else, and then had been reused for the gunpowder shipment to Fort Barnwell.

They planned to light the fuse for the blockhouse charge first, and as it burned past the charges under the wall, the last mole would light a shorter fuse to those charges and run like hell for the end of the tunnel. If he could make it out, and around the bend in the trench, he should survive the blast.

At that point, the three Sergeants would lead their compliments of ten militiamen through the breech in the wall, and directly to the toppled blockhouse. After they cleaned up any opposition from that wrecked blockhouse, the remaining Indians in Moore's army would charge both the open gate and the opening in the wall. They could also bring cannon fire on the remaining Tuscarora blockhouses from their attack towers, and while the walls were stout wooden affairs backed by earthworks, the cannon could poke through the wooden blockhouses with relative ease since no earth backed that wood. Johannes, in particular liked that aspect of the plan, as the last thing he wanted to do in this life, was lead an assault on another blockhouse.

The next morning, Col. Moore gave the honor of lighting the fuses to a New Bern man, who was a miner originally from the Albemarle, Mark Roberts. He had been one of the army of moles, and had some experience with explosives and fuses, so he had been chosen to represent the moles and set off the explosions. He moved up the trench to nowhere at dawn, once Captain Brice had made certain that everything was ready. The dual explosions, one only twenty seconds behind the other, started the second day of the battle of Fort Noeheroka.

As the first explosion shook the ground, Martin looked up to see the tower immediately behind the wall lean drastically to the left, but then it hung there, as if suspended by some unseen rope from heaven for a few seconds. When the second explosion went off, the wall disintegrated creating almost a twenty foot breech, and Martin saw the tower behind fall to the ground. Before the smoke could clear, thirty men were running to that breech in the wall, and all of the rifles, muskets, and cannon at Col. Moore's disposal had opened up at once. The very ground shook with explosion after explosion, and smoke poured from the two attack towers, as the three pounders were fired at the next interior blockhouse.

Martin shouted to his troop of ten men, "Let's go!" and then took off running toward the wall. In the noise no one heard him, but they knew what was required and they followed. At his request, on that attack he led many of the men whose women had saved his own life in Brice's barn on the third day of the massacre. Julia Whittey's husband Ben was there running right beside him, as was Josiah Martin, and Lois Jarman's boy, Daniel. Martin had also asked for Willie Koonce to be in his group, but Captain Brice forbade that, urging Martin to take men who were somewhat older. Brice suspected that the battle might involve hand to hand combat at which a twelve year old like Willie would be at a disadvantage, and he shared that thought with Martin, who quickly agreed. However, Captain Brice did have to yield on one point.

Dunker Tim was running along behind Martin too. He had come at Captain Brice's order to help in the construction, but when the building was done he had asked Captain Brice to let him fight along beside Martin. "I can kinda' keep Sergeant Bender ou'n any trouble, don't ya see, Suh?" Old Blood-Eyes relented and had permitted his favorite slave to fight beside his favorite Sergeant.

This group ran flat out across the short distance from the trench to nowhere to the new breech in the wall, while a massed group of over a hundred Cherokee moved toward the partially opened gate at the same time. Archie Carmichael and Johannes Simmons also led groups of ten men right behind Martin's group. The Sergeants had agreed that Martin's group would enter the fort first, and that the others would follow. As soon as Martin got to the breech in the wall, he jumped a few scattered logs, and then ran immediately to the remains of the blockhouse, as it still smoked from the explosion. Martin saw movement under a log, and when a head popped out he shot into the Tuscarora face. His men were likewise cleaning up any living enemy from that blockhouse. Martin soon determined that enough of the blockhouse had remained together to provide a measure of safety behind it, since his men were not under fire if they kept their head down. He watched as the next blockhouse began to topple, yielding to the cannonade from the three pounders in the attack towers. Those damned little cannon were finally doing some good! Martin immediately saw the advantage to using those cannon to knock down the other Tuscarora blockhouses, so he grabbed Dunker Tim and sent him scurrying back to share his thoughts with Captain Brice and Col. Moore.

"Dunker Tim, get to Captain Brice, and tell him we have a location where we can fire a cannon on the rest of the blockhouses in the courtyard. We won't have to assault them if we knock 'um down with cannon, but I need one cannon right here at the remains of the first blockhouse, and I need it right now! Bring the gunners too! Run! Tell him to send me a damned cannon!"

Dunker Tim didn't hear the last part of that order, since he was already running across the courtyard to get the message to Captain Brice.

Col. Moore and Captain Brice heard this strange request together in the Yamassee Bastion less than a minute later, and Col. Moore was about to say no outright since he didn't want to risk the possibility of having his cannon seized by the enemy. Captain Brice however, persuaded him to listen, by saying, "Col. Moore, I urge you to let me take one of the cannon forward. I have fought with this young man Bender through several battles, and I've never seen an instant in battle in which his instincts were wrong. With your permission, I'd like to escort that cannon and the gun crew myself."

Moore had to pay attention to that request, since Captain Brice obviously trusted this young man enough to put his own hide on the line, and go right along with the gun! Within only five minutes one of the gun crews was moving a cannon from the Catawba battery into the trench and forward to the breech in the wall.

Of course, it took almost thirty minutes to get that gun moved and back into action, but once it opened up on the other blockhouses, it was apparent that the battle would move out of the range of the other gun in his bastions, so Col. Moore ordered the other cannon moved up, along with his entire reserve of Catawba warriors. He suspected he could carry the fort that very day thanks to his army of moles, and a fairly bright, if still young, Sergeant in the New Bern Militia!

The rest of the battle was bloody, but relatively straightforward. The cannon in the attack towers could hit most of the blockhouses in the courtyard, and coupled with the two cannon within the courtyard itself, they reduced the remaining blockhouses to splinters in just over four hours. When a Tuscarora warrior did reveal himself, over forty of Moore's rifles and hundreds of muskets in the captured blockhouse fired in unison. From that point on, the Tuscarora never had a chance.

Many did hide in the caves however, and for that Col. Moore had a simple solution. As a blockhouse was reduced, if a cave lay below, a couple of barrels of powder were placed at the mouth of the cave, and the entrance was blown up. Col. Moore intended to leave his opposition buried in those caves, but prior to the final blockhouse coming under fire, the Tuscarora surrendered. Thus, at least some of the Tuscarora in the caves escaped death below ground, though some were, no doubt buried in those caves, and their bones rest in that ground to this day.

By the end of March 22, 1713, Fort Neoheroka was a smoking ruin, and four hundred and eighty-nine Tuscarora were dead. Over four hundred surrendered, and were eventually sold into slavery by Col. Moore, as he and the newly named "Moore's Rifles" marched back into South Carolina several months later.

While Col. Moore did chase some Tuscarora raiding parties during those next months in 1713, the battle at Fort Neoheroka broke the back of the mighty Tuscarora Nation in the Carolinas for all time. Many of the remaining Tuscarora left the state to return north, and settled with a group of Indians that shared a common language. They became the sixth nation of the Iroquois Confederation in what was to become upstate New York.

Other members of that tribe continued to raid outlying farms for a period of two years, but King Blount and his group of northern Tuscarora would occasionally hunt several of them down and bring their scalps to the local sheriff for a bounty. King Blount's leadership over all the Tuscarora in the state was reaffirmed, and a small reservation was provided to them along the Pamlico River. However, that was later moved into an unsettled area on the Roanoke River, in what is now Bertie County, North Carolina, near the town of Windsor. Most citizens today do not realize that an Indian reservation ever existed in eastern North Carolina.

### *Martin's New Patron*

There was one more result of the battle at Neoheroka, and that was the fact that Martin now had a new patron among the leadership in the South Carolina Colony, a senior leader of the South Carolina Militia, and a future politician that would be among the leadership elite of that colony for the next several decades, Col. James Moore. In fact, prior to leaving the state Col. Moore had a conversation with Captain Brice about that young man. They sat on the veranda overlooking the Trent River on Brice's Plantation, where Gideon served them wine and fruit.

"This is an excellent wine, Captain Brice. Very nice."

Brice replied. "Thank you Col. It is French, I believe. It is certainly nice to have ships coming back to the New Bern docks again! While we have many advantages in our new colony, we still look to other colonies or overseas for the finer things!"

"Quite right, I should think. Quite right!" Col. Moore took another sip of his wine. "I appreciate you allowing my brother to convalesce in your home. It did him a world of good I should think, those few weeks here."

Brice was magnanimous. "Glad to do it Col. It is only fitting, I should think since he and you have done such a service to our colony. I trust he has arrived in Charleston?"

"Yes, indeed." Col. Moore responded. "I received word only last week he had arrived, fit as a fiddle."

"Ah!" said Brice. "That is good news, indeed."

Col. Moore took another sip of the wine. "I shall leave tomorrow on the sloop heading back to South Carolina on the morning tide. I've received orders to return to Charleston. It seems the city is having some problems with scoundrels on the high seas."

"Indeed?" said Captain Brice. "Pirates, you mean? Not Blackbeard!"

"Something like that, I believe," Col. Moore replied, "Though I've not heard that name mentioned."

"Nothing that a few ships-of-the-line cannot handle, I trust? Where is His Majesty's Navy?"

Here Col. Moore paused again. "It will be mainly a naval matter, I'm sure, but you know colonial government. Whenever there is any problem at all they call us! They always 'Call out the militia' whenever the legislature hiccups, or the honorable governor farts!"

"Indeed they do!" said Captain Brice, as both gentlemen had a good laugh, along with their wine. "Indeed they do!" Captain Brice gestured to have Gideon fill the glasses once again.

"I do have a request of you in that regard, Captain," continued the colonel. "I might need some small contingent of New Bern Militia for some of these new duties."

"Oh," replied Brice. "How so, Colonel?"

"It seems that there is a navigable river to the south, that has become a pure nest of vermin." Col. Moore said.

"Oh," said Brice. "You can't mean the White Oak, surely? It is barely the length of my arm! Hardly a river at all!"

"Oh, no! No," said Col. Moore. "The Cape Fear, much further down. Navigable for some miles from the sea, I've been told. Not a broad passage as is your Neuse River, but it is deep. Seems some of our illustrious brethren of the sea have taken to careening their ships there." Col. Moore sipped the wine again.

"Can't have a Port Royal here on the mainland, now can we!"

"Ah, the outdated relics of Queen Anne's War, indeed!" Captain Brice said. "I've lost cargoes to the buggers myself in these waters."

Col. Moore decided to pursue his point. "That river is technically in the southern part of the North Carolina Colony, and should I have to operate along that river, I would appreciate a liaison, and small contingent of the New Bern Militia to work with me. Perhaps you could furnish me with that Sergeant Bender, and a few men from time to time. What?"

Captain Brice was politically savvy enough to understand the request for what it was; a bold attempt to remove the government of the North Carolina Colony from the equation. He also understood the reasons for approaching the matter as a low key, informal request from one militia commander to another. Of course, Col. Moore had just assisted the North Carolina settlements in a profound way, with the Tuscarora. If he now assisted Col. Moore, he would have another important ally in South Carolina, in addition to Barnwell, with whom Captain Brice still corresponded. Brice, ever the wise politician could see no reason to be an obstacle to this plan, and many reasons to agree to the request.

"I do believe you will be quite satisfied with Sergeant Bender. He is one of de Graffenreid's original Germans, but has done well here learning the language, and learning a trade. Perhaps we should promote him in rank a bit?" Captain Brice made that last suggestion, to assess Col. Moore's reaction, and it was just as he suspected.

"Oh, I'm sure that won't be necessary. The man has little education and is quite young, though I am pleased to say his battlefield instincts were jolly on at Fort Neoheroka, just as you indicated!" With that statement Col. Moore had confirmed Captain Brice's suspicions. A promotion for Martin Bender above the rank of Sergeant would require action by the governor of the North Carolina Colony, and Col. Moore clearly wanted to avoid that! Captain Brice was now certain that Col. Moore had received instructions to make a low level request for militia assistance, specifically to avoid involvement of Col. Pollock, the acting colonial governor of the North Carolina Colony. Clearly, the governor of South Carolina suspected Col. Pollock of taking bribes from pirates, as everyone had suspected of Governor Hyde.

"No," continued Col. Moore. "Having the good Sergeant, and a contingent of, say fifteen men with Kentucky rifles will be sufficient, I should think. That man could shoot a gnat off a mosquito's arse at two hundred paces!"

"Indeed!" Said Brice, as they both laughed. "He can indeed! Wish I had a hundred more just like him!" Captain Brice sipped his wine again, then continued. "Well, when you need Sergeant Bender or any help from the New Bern Militia, any help at all, do contact me. I am sure that providing assistance to our neighbors in Charleston is the appropriate thing to do, and I can have them in the Cape Fear in a fortnight!"

"Thank you, Captain. Thank you indeed."

It would be several years, before Col. Moore took advantage of this discussion, but that day determined one aspect of Martin Bender's life. On that day, without even knowing it, Martin Bender had been "volunteered" as a participant in several more battles. He would witness history in a deep and profound way unlike any other North Carolinian in his day. He had seen many aspects of both Cary's Rebellion, and the Tuscarora War, and now he was to witness another colonial Carolina problem, piracy, and strangely enough several of his next fights would come on the high seas.

# Chapter 4
## Pirates of the Carolinas

Everyone has heard of the "Pirates of the Caribbean," through hundreds of movies and thousands of books, and that trifling little sea does deserve some grudging attention in pirate lore. It was after all, the early route of the Spanish treasure fleets and scores of Spanish galleons loaded to the gunwales with Mexican gold or Peruvian silver, saw their final hours of sunlight on that small sea before succumbing to one hurricane or another. However, the massive treasure fleets of the Spanish were becoming rare by the early 1700s, and most pirates turned their attention elsewhere. In those days, many of them sailed for the Carolinas.

The Atlantic Ocean itself is fifty times the size of the Caribbean, and that massive ocean held many more ships laden with rich cargoes to plunder. Further, every single one of them sailing from the new world had to travel along the Carolina coast to catch the favorable Gulf Stream currents that run just offshore from south to northeast and on towards Europe. The barrier islands of the Carolinas direct those winds and currents far out to sea. In fact, any third grader with a map can tell that those long string-like islands seem to jut out into the Atlantic like the elbow of some massive giant. The Carolina coast became both the Graveyard of the Atlantic and a perfect haven for pirates because of those islands and those ocean currents.

As citizens of one of the early seaport colonies, we might talk of the Caribbean a bit less and look to our own backyard just a bit more. Here, in the Carolinas be the pirates, and we would be remiss indeed should we overlook that interesting bit of Carolina history! Neither Martin Bender nor the Simmons family had that luxury.

The same shallow sounds and barrier islands that create the picture perfect sunsets today in the Carolinas, the very waters that made this beautiful coast so difficult to settle, also created that nest of vipers. If beach goers today admire the sun and sand, the endless miles of pristine Carolina beaches, or the sound of the surf gently probing the shore, the brethren of the sea, as the pirates fancied themselves, admired this coast for much different reasons. They could hide there, and they did so by the thousands!

While it is not widely acknowledged today, this beautiful Carolina coastline of shallow sounds, bays, and gentle meandering rivers was a major retreat for the brethren, second only to Port Royal, in Jamaica, and perhaps New Providence Island in the Bahamas. The only two seaport towns in the North Carolina Colony in 1715 were Bath and New Bern, and while history does not document every ship that sailed up the Neuse River to the New Bern docks in those days, it would be quite shocking had pirates not sailed up to those piers from time to time to peddle their stolen wares. The peaceful Germans and Swiss who settled New Bern, as well as the English who had previously settled in and around Bath, all interacted with pirates on a daily basis. The Simmons family was no exception.

Martin Bender was twenty-one in the year 1716, and for a young man who today would merely be graduating from college, he had already accomplished much in life. He was a veteran of two wars, Cary's Rebellion and the Tuscarora War, and not many twenty-one year old men can say that. He was a Sergeant in the New Bern Militia, and more importantly he had earned the respect of the men in that experienced fighting force. He was working towards a career, and had completed nearly seven years as an apprentice and journeyman cooper. He owned outright his original allocation of two-hundred and fifty acres of land along Mill Creek in the Trent Mill area just south of New Bern, though he did not then clear that land. He hunted there, however, as have his descendents for three hundred years.

By 1716, Martin Bender was an accomplished frontiersman, a great shot with his Kentucky rifle, and he could skin out a deer in less than an hour. Many of those skills had been picked up through uncounted hours, days, and weeks of hunting, tracking or fishing with Gator Jim, Dunker Tim, One-Eye Benny, or Able Ward. Finally, for various reasons, this young man had caught the attention of two influential patrons, gentlemen both, Captain Brice of New Bern and Col. James Moore of South Carolina. Both were to be quite influential in Martin's life.

Martin had also faced the uglier aspects of life. He had lost both of his parents as a young boy and while he had essentially been adopted by a fine family of German immigrants, he still felt quite alone in this world. As he watched the carefree play of Katheryn and her younger sister Christina in the cabin, he often longed for a sibling that he would never have. He knew he was alone, and in his early years he felt that aloneness.

He had also seen war, up close and personal, and he hated it. He had killed men and watched several die slowly and painfully in his rifle sights. He wanted no more to do with war or battles, but such was not to be his destiny. He was soon to face conflict again, and this time because of a loud-mouthed wife in, of all places, Barbados.

One day in early September of 1716, Captain Brice stopped his horse just outside the cooper's shed and shouted a greeting. Martin hurried out. Brice then gave Martin some rather strange orders. "Sergeant Bender. You will muster twenty men of the New Bern Militia and lead them south, past Trent Mill and Jackson's Tavern through the wilderness and all the way down to Cape Fear.

There you will place yourself and your men at the disposal of Col. Moore. You will leave in three days, and arrive at the mouth of the Cape Fear River in eight days. He is expecting you by then. My man, Dunker Tim will be your guide, as he has traveled before in those parts."

"Yes Sir!" Martin replied. "May I ask what we might be doing, or why we are going?"

Brice grinned as he considered his answer. "You are going south because of Stede's Shrew. It seems that some damned fool in Barbados cannot control his wife!" Captain Brice then laughed at what was apparently a private joke, while Martin merely stood there dumbfounded. "Tell your men to pack food for a thirty day period, which should be quite enough, I would think. You will be helping the good Colonel capture a nest of pirates."

"Yes Sir," Martin said. "Who will be in command?"

Brice looked at the young man before him and grinned openly. "Why, you will, Sergeant! Good hunting!" Then the Captain laughed again, as he rode away down South Front Street without having ever dismounted. Thus, in 1716, did Martin Bender begin his pirate hunting career.

That evening in the cabin, Martin told Johannes, Margaret, Katheryn, and Christina of the visit by Captain Brice. It had been several years since the New Bern Militia had been called into service, though they had drilled repeatedly once each month. Still, Martin was unsure of his role, given the cryptic orders provided by Captain Brice. Why would a Sergeant lead an expedition, when Captains or Colonels normally did? Who had ever heard of such a thing?

"What go did you have to?" Johannes asked, in his still broken English, meaning, why do you have to go? Margaret and the rest of Johannes' family despaired of Johannes ever learning to speak correctly, but they also realized that they themselves and the other Germans still spoke with a heavy accent. Their speech still sounded very different from Captain Brice, Mr. Foscue, and the other English that had settled in this area prior to their arrival. Still, their father was a valued member of the community, the best cooper in New Bern, and a leader in the New Bern Militia, so his language difficulties were ignored by the family and all in the new city, even when he led the local church service among the Germans. In fact, Johannes got tongue tied most frequently when he was nervous and spoke too quickly in English. He never had such problems when speaking German and many had noted that in prayer, as he communed with God, his syntax was flawless, and his prayers were truly inspirational.

Martin could not answer Johannes' question directly since he knew no answer. While seasoned in battle and a veteran frontiersman, political intrigue merely left Martin bewildered. He would have been quite perplexed had Captain Brice tried to explain the reasons that a lowly Sergeant should lead an expedition, under the command of a South Carolina Militia commander, to capture pirates on the Cape Fear River in North Carolina, that the colonial governor of North Carolina didn't want captured anyway! He merely said, "I go where Captain Brice orders me to go. He is a good man, and he is my Captain. I would just like to know why."

Perhaps it was the simplicity of that statement that moved Katheryn at that moment, or perhaps she merely wanted to make a gesture of some sort before her parents. She was eighteen years old that day, and had already turned down advances from other young men. It was considered unseemly to marry the journeyman in one's father's business, but she was by that point well past caring. She was already past the age at which most women married, and she simply knew that Martin was intended to be her husband, even if he didn't.

Perhaps she saw that he needed assurance at that moment. She was always a caring woman and she did know her man and recognize his needs, many times before he did. On the other hand, perhaps she merely thought it was time to do something! Of course, she and Martin had stolen kisses before, but never within view of Johannes or Margaret, and certainly never in front of the entire family. In the cabin, these two continued to pretend to be merely brother and sister.

Still, as Martin spoke, Katheryn determined exactly what she would do. Sitting beside him at the table, she slowly reached for his face, took his chin, and pulled him toward her. She had kissed him firmly, smack-on the lips, before either her mother or Martin knew what was happening! Johannes sat at the head of the table and concentrated on a chicken leg, well fried, so he had managed to miss the whole thing.

Margaret however, saw this horrid indiscretion, and was quite shocked! "Katheryn!" Margaret shouted. "What 'r ye a-doin' girl? Are ye daft?" A stupid question, since Margaret had just witnessed exactly what Katheryn was doing!

Johannes looked in shock at his wife as she screamed, and with a mouthful of partially chewed poultry, he tried to ask the obvious question, "What's happening?" Instead he got tongue tied yet again, and turned that question into one of the deeper philosophical observations in his life. "What happens is happening!"

Christina began to giggle at both her mother's shock and her father's English, as Max stood to attention by the cabin door and began to growl lowly, clearly aware that something had gone terribly wrong at the dinner table. Katheryn took control immediately. "We should read the Bible, and I know just the passage."

No matter how a parent may wish to chastise a daughter, it is difficult to do so when the daughter is seeking spiritual guidance from the scriptures. Margaret said, quite firmly, "Yes, Indeed! We shall do so now!" …to which poor Johannes responded, "What happening is to us here?"

By then Katheryn had retrieved the Bible from the shelf near the fireplace, and sat back down at the table. She looked for only a moment before finding the passage she sought, but she didn't read immediately. Instead she said, "Martin, you know of Jonah and the whale?"

Martin nodded.

"Then you know he did not go where God wished to send him at first, and then he was swallowed by the whale."

"Yes, Katheryn, I know the story well," Martin replied.

"But Martin, do you know the most important part of that story? It comes after."

Martin merely looked perplexed and was wishing for another kiss, but he knew that was not likely at that moment. Katheryn had a full head of steam and was trying to make a point, and no power on earth would sidetrack that effort! This young German girl was clearly, every bit as determined as her Mennonite mother had always been, and neither had ever known an ounce of humility.

Katheryn continued. "The most important part of that story is at the end. When God called Jonah the second time! Jonah goes, just as God wishes." She then turned to the Bible and read those simple verses that have emboldened righteous men for thousands of years, lifting some to heights of greatness through the ages.

*"And the word of the Lord came unto Jonah a second time, saying, arise and go unto Nineveh, that great city, and preach unto it the preaching that I bid thee. So Jonah arose, and he went up unto Nineveh."*

Katheryn continued her thought as she shut the Bible. "Do you see, Martin? Jonah had to go, and while he didn't go as he should have the first time, God is forgiving and He spoke to Jonah a second time, and Jonah did finally go! That's the important part, more important than the story about the whale. He had to go and he went, just as God told him to!" Here she paused, not sure she had made her point.

"Don't be like Jonah, Martin. Go where God tells you to go the first time!" In that simple statement Katheryn had summarized the very essence of Mennonite and Anabaptist beliefs, completely and perfectly. God spoke directly to each man and woman, and the righteous simply did as God commanded. It was an unwavering belief in simple, direct, very personal communication with God, unimpaired by priests, bishops, structured belief systems, or anything else. These Germans practiced and experienced an absolute, immediate awareness of God's will in their lives, and indeed, it was their ultimate responsibility to "Go where God tells you!"

Katheryn continued. "You will go to hunt pirates on the Cape Fear, Martin, because you must go. It is your job to go! You are strong and you will always go when you are called. You will lead because you must lead. You will go because you must go!"

With that statement, she began to feel much more confident in her actions, and perhaps she realized at that moment, that her words provided guidance for her as well as for Martin. She was commanded and convicted in that instant, and she would not waiver in a decision that she believed her God had only then placed on her heart. She again pulled his face toward her and boldly kissed him a second time, with no thought whatsoever about her parents who were still watching in abject horror. She then continued to make her final point. "Yes, Sergeant Martin Bender, You will go because you must go. You will lead, as God wills that you lead. That is who you are."

Here she paused just a bit, as if seeking a bit more courage, which she quickly found deep within herself. Her lower lip quivered only a bit as she continued. "But then you will come back to us, and when you do return, Martin Bender, then you will marry me!"

## *A Nest of Pirates*

Pirates were attracted to the waters of the North Carolina Colony like moths to a flame, and the inlets, rivers, and bays of the Carolina coast became a virtual nest of pirates. They came by the thousands. In retrospect, it is no surprise that an active, though lower ranking, leader in the New Bern Militia was, on occasion, called upon to root out these vermin. These beautiful Carolina waters offered rich prizes out of Charleston harbor and off the Virginia Capes, and coastal protection for pirates throughout the decades, in a variety of ways.

First, these waters of North Carolina were way too shallow for the British Royal Navy, the Spaniards, or the French Fleet to patrol. Whereas most pirates conducted their trade using small sloops or brigantines of one hundred to two hundred tons displacement, the mighty navies of the major powers in those days seemed to believe that bigger was always better. The larger ships of the famed French Royal Fleet as well as British "Ships-of-the-line" often carried from eighty to a hundred and ten heavy cannon aboard. These were usually carriage guns that fired a six pound solid shot ball. They each required a gun crew of four gunners to fire and were mounted on three gun decks on each side of the ship. These ships were built large to carry that much weight, not to mention a crew large enough to man fifty guns at once, since one only manned the guns on one side of the ship at any given time. The ship-of-the-line was bigger than anything else afloat with some vessels displacing eight hundred or even a thousand tons! Any of those massive battle wagons would dwarf the average pirate ship.

In fact, history records that no pirate ever commanded a ship that even approached that size and probably none ever wished to. The shallow sounds of the Carolina coast and the many islands in the Caribbean simply did not provide enough water under the keel for those large ships, and pirates sought ships that were much lighter and more nimble, not to mention much faster. They used ships that were smaller and would allow them to sail the shallow lagoons of the Caribbean islands and the sounds of the North Carolina Colony in order to hide from the powerful navies of the world.

Further, political protection was indeed provided to pirates in the Carolinas, just as the rumors in Mallard's Tavern suggested. Both Governor Hyde and his designated replacement Governor Eden provided safe haven in the Carolinas for pirates in exchange for a cut of the revenue. Acting Governor Pollock only served in that capacity for twenty-four months and there was never any evidence that he partook of ill-gotten pirate profits. However, by 1714, Governor Eden had arrived, and he clearly did! A careful search of the historical records has indicated that, in all probability, Eden not only earned money from Blackbeard, but may have notified him of particularly rich prizes that were departing various locations along the east coast. The First Secretary to the colonial governor of North Carolina during those years, the same thief and scoundrel that served Acting Governor Pollock, Tobias Knight, had arranged those nefarious payoffs directly with Blackbeard himself. That is why the famous pirate was able to move so freely in and around Bath or New Bern.

When Blackbeard came to New Bern, he generally resided in one of the rooms in the whorehouse behind Mallard's Tavern along East Front Street, and he seemed to prefer one of the black slave whores that Toby kept upstairs. However, in Bath, as we have seen, Blackbeard actually married a young girl and set up housekeeping for a time. To be both graphic and very direct, this man had big brass ones, and this turn of phrase does not refer to any preference Mr. Teach may have had for bright, brass cannon balls!

Next, the Carolina Colony presented few opportunities to enforce the laws against piracy. Pirates chose to operate along this Carolina coast much more frequently than any other colony on the North American Continent specifically because the relatively unsettled nature of this new colony prevented enforcement of law. Between rebellions and savage attacks from the Tuscarora, capturing pirates was not a high priority here. Pirates quickly learned that they were safer in Carolina waters than anywhere else on the eastern seaboard.

Further, the settlement of the North Carolina Colony, unlike any of the other thirteen original colonies occurred during the decades when piracy was increasing worldwide. Just about the time the North Carolina Colony was being settled a number of events in Europe led to a dramatic increase in piracy, a period between 1690 and 1730 that has been called the "Golden Age of Piracy." To understand this, we need to look a bit at Europe.

Many European powers in the late 1600s armed private ships and commissioned them as "privateers." These privateers were allowed to plunder the shipping of the enemy nations under the authority of a "Letter of Marque," which was essentially a "permission to steal" letter from one king or another. Privateers kept most of the valuable goods and property they stole, including the enemy ships they seized, and they paid a percentage of their profits to their king. At least they were supposed to. Some colonial power was always at war with another, so privateers were handsomely employed for most of those years in the late 1600s.

Unfortunately, all at once peace broke out all over Europe. In a twenty year period, two major wars ended. Both King William's War (1689-1697) and Queen Anne's War (1702-1713) came to a conclusion, and the many privateers who had been sailing against the shipping of enemy nations now found themselves in the waters of the new world with nothing exciting to do.

Now anyone who has ever studied either psychology or history will tell you that human behavior rarely changes at least in any fundamental way. While various persons can and do improve themselves from time to time, fundamental change of character is rare, and the privateers had grown to like their rather roguish lifestyle, funded of course by stolen booty. Almost without exception, they continued to capture ships, even though the legal basis for it no longer existed. In those decades a very large number of former privateers became pirates.

Some privateer captains had scruples and while continuing to take prizes, these few steadfastly refused to capture a ship from their own nation. Captain Benjamin Hornigold, sailing out of Port Royal, Jamaica, was one of these. For several decades during this period he took prizes from every nation on earth, except Great Britain, just as he'd done as a privateer. The vast majority of pirates however showed no such scruples and once the wars in Europe ended, they merely viewed the resulting peace as an opportunity to capture any ship on the high seas.

Peace in Europe thus generated a Golden Age of Piracy in the western Atlantic and Caribbean, more pointedly in Bath and New Bern, not to mention most other towns and cities on the eastern seaboard. Historians have estimated that upwards of two thousand different pirates operated along the east coast of North America during this period, with most of them spending considerable time in the Carolinas. Blackbeard, Stede Bonnet, Calico Jack Rackham, the list of famous scoundrels goes on and on. Even "Black Bart" Roberts, the most successful of all the pirates of that era took prizes off the Carolinas. He captured well over four hundred ships in his long pirate career, and according to historians between twenty two and twenty six of those sailed out of Bath or New Bern!

## The Brethren of the Carolina Coast

Several of lesser known pirates in the Carolinas are even more interesting than the pirates with more recognized names. For example, Captain Edward Low, and his ship the *Fancy*, captured several prizes in the waters off the Carolinas. He then sold his stolen goods right on the docks in New Bern. He was the first pirate known to have flown a black flag with a red skeleton on it, rather than the more traditional blood flag, so the flag that, today, means piracy worldwide, originated right here in the Carolinas. Captain Low was a vicious man and was known for his cruelty to prisoners. He tortured many while out on the high seas, but he himself was never captured. Some say he settled into a farmer's life near Swansboro, North Carolina where he had friends like Edward Pate.

The pirate ship *Happy Delivery* sailing out of the Albemarle under Captain George Lowther fired on an armed merchantman in June of 1712, just off the Hatteras Coast. However rather than turn tail and run, Captain Wade Honrine of the *Amy* turned to fight, and brought his ten cannon to bare on the pirate ship. That was enough to send Lowther and his band of cowardly pirates fleeing into the Hatteras Inlet were the *Happy Delivery* ran aground! The pirates scattered like rats into the forest along the coast. A year later this same crew was captured after taking several prizes off Charleston. They were tried, quickly hanged, and then buried in the South Carolina swamps below the high water mark.

Anne Bonny was, perhaps the world's first feminist. She knew she could do whatever any man could do, and she set out to prove it. She was one of several female pirates of the day, and she was as vulgar and as vicious as any male pirate afloat! When her crew boarded a prize, she fought like a demon, wearing trousers and a large red blouse, with a cutlass in one hand and a pistol in the other. This feisty Irish girl was raised on a plantation near Charleston, but she fell in love with a pirate, married the man, and together they went a-pyrating. She later sailed with Calico Jack Rackham until their ship was taken off the Carolinas. At that point, she was pregnant and though she was sentenced to death, she was spared the hangman's noose, because of her pregnancy. Some say she later escaped and settled in the Albemarle or southern Virginia. However, her lover, Calico Jack, and the rest of that pirate band swung in Charleston in 1718.

Less is known about the majority of the pirates along the coast of North Carolina. Newspapers were rare in those days, and none were printed in the North Carolina Colony at that point. The pirates themselves didn't make notes of their dubious adventures and no pirate ever kept an accurate ship's log! Creating a chronicle of one's crimes is never a good idea, so few pirates wrote anything at all about their voyages, and as a group, pirates tended to be illiterate ruffians anyway. In some cases, we have only names and a few scant facts from court records, but these are enough to document many pirates of the Carolinas.

John Brierly from Bath, a member of Stede Bonnet's crew, was hanged in Charleston for piracy in 1719.

Rowland Sharpe of Bath was a member of Stede Bonnet's crew, but he could prove he was forced to join that crew as a ship's carpenter against his will. He was acquitted in a piracy trial in Charleston in 1718.

William Lewis, Captain of the *Morning Star*, sailed from the Albemarle, and captured numerous vessels off Virginia and the Carolina coast. He was murdered by his own crew in his sleep aboard his own ship one night, because his crew believed he was "too intimate with the devil," as they later testified. He must have been truly scary for a band of pirates to think of him as frightening!

Caesar, a Negro and former slave from Bath, sailed with Blackbeard out of Bath, and was supposed to blow up Blackbeard's ship rather than allow capture. He failed, and was hanged with Blackbeard's crew in Virginia.

Israel Hands, sailed for a time with Blackbeard, but then retired in Bath. He was nevertheless captured on the streets of Bath and tried for piracy in Virginia. He was sentenced to death in 1722, but was later pardoned. He died many decades later, a beggar on the docks in London. Interestingly, his name was later used in a famous fiction novel about pirates, *Treasure Island*, by Robert Lewis Stevenson.

Emanuel Ernados sailed his small sloop from the docks of New Bern, but was captured and hanged for piracy in Charleston in 1725.

Black Jambo, a slave from the Foscue Plantation in Trent Mill, sailed first with Stede Bonnet, and later with Blackbeard. He was killed at Ocracoke Inlet when his ship was captured.

John Churchill was born in London, but sailed out of New Bern with Lowther. He was hanged for piracy on St. Kitts in 1722. A distant nephew of this man later achieved some minor degree of fame by leading the nation of Great Britain during World War II.

All of these pirates as well as many others found sanctuary in the Carolinas. Many other names were never recorded, and surely many of these villains, like Low and Pate, at some point cashed in their gains, bought a local farm, and settled down. This fact has led to the oft-repeated phrase, "Scratch a Carolinian, find a pirate!"

If a cowboy is the true measure of Texas, then pirates are the definitive characters of the Carolinas in this period. In fact, at least one major university, not to mention scores of high schools, took a pirate as their fighting symbol. Should your favorite division one team ever face East Carolina University on the gridiron, you should be prepared for a tough, bruising game. As those famed East Carolina half-backs fly past your defensive line, take a good look at purple flags fluttering all around you, and you'll see the face of Blackbeard!

It was into this maelstrom of pirate activity that Martin Bender was tossed in 1716. While not a man knowledgeable of ships and certainly not a sailor, Martin and a small contingent of the New Bern Militia would play a minor role in the capture of several of these pirates on the Carolina coast, though the reason for their role was somewhat convoluted, and deserves some consideration. You may have noticed a subtlety in the cryptic notes on court records above. While thousands of pirates operated along the North Carolina coast, not a single one was ever captured, tried, or hung by the colonial authorities there. Thus, neither Bath nor New Bern ever witnessed a pirate hanging! It was the older, larger, and more successful ports of Charleston, Baltimore, Boston, and the Virginia Capes that suffered the most from the brethren, and the authorities in those areas were not taking bribes from the pirates as were the North Carolina authorities.

Still, those colonial powers did not want to send their own militia into another colony without some cooperation from the colony that was the target of the operation, so they needed a "cover" that at least suggested such cooperation. With the blessing of Captain Brice, a few members of the New Bern Militia were often called on to help, and Martin Bender led some of those expeditions. The reason for his leadership is clear in retrospect; his rank was low enough that no one would care if he screwed up. In the broader colonial politics of the day, he was just unimportant enough for chasing pirates along the coast of the Carolinas.

Captain Brice had also been correct in that Martin's first action against a pirate resulted from a man whose wife nagged him without mercy. In fact, the story of "Stede's Shrew" and the Gentleman Pirate of the Carolina Coast is truly unique.

### Stede's Shrew

Stede Bonnet (pronounced Bone-nay') was a gentleman from Barbados, the first of the famed sugar producing islands of the Caribbean. The rich island soil made many families quite wealthy on the many massive sugar plantations in the mid to late 1600s, and some of these families sent their sons to carve plantations out of the Carolina wilderness. History shows that many early aristocratic families around Charleston had roots in Barbados. Of course, thousands upon thousands of African slaves were worked to death on those sugar plantations on Barbados and other Caribbean islands, earning a fortune for their English masters, and the system of labor intensive, agriculture-centered slavery on large plantations that arose in Barbados, was merely transplanted into South Carolina directly from the sugar islands. What we today envision as southern slavery did not arise on the cotton plantations of the Deep South. It, along with sugar and spices, came to these shores as an import from the sugar fields in the Caribbean.

Stede Bonnet was born of an older Barbados family and was highly educated and quite refined in his tastes. He was a gentleman, his wealth coming from his sugar plantation holdings near Bridgetown, Barbados. By 1708, he had completed service with distinction in the army and led a settled aristocratic life. He attended the same Anglican Church as had his father before him, and owned nearly two hundred slaves. The price of sugar in Europe had been excellent the previous year, making Stede even wealthier. Perhaps for that reason, in 1709 he chose to marry a pretty little sixteen-year-old wife. Everyone knows that pretty women can always help one spend one's fortune, and Stede wanted nothing more than his plantation, an easy plantation life, and a pretty wife to produce another generation of Bonnets. Indeed, all seemed right with the world, at least, until the day he got married.

The pretty little girl by all accounts turned into a shrew from hell immediately after the ceremony. She was as horrid and vile as any creature yet seen on Earth. According to reports of the house slaves, her temper dominated the mansion, and when she was "in such a fiddle" she refused to comb her hair or dress for the day. Rather, she roamed the halls of the large mansion in her sleeping gowns and generally terrorized the household! She cursed everyone. She threw things at Stede and anyone else nearby. She shouted, she pouted, she denied her husband her sexual charms, taunting him instead with stories of her passion for her previous lovers, and on occasion, she beat her personal slave, Matilda, without mercy. In one instance that is still discussed on the island, this creature actually beat poor Matilda so horribly that her face was disfigured for life.

The behavior of this young girl would have been more characteristic in the courts of Attila the Hun than in the upscale English society of Bridgetown in the early 1700s, and soon everyone on Barbados was talking about it. In truth this girl was crazy as a loon, and today she would receive in-depth psychiatric care, or perhaps be drugged into oblivion. However, in those days, she was mistress of the plantation and only her husband could discipline her, a task Stede refused to undertake. For some inexplicable reason, this man loved his wife, despite her bad behavior, behavior that, by any standard, was horrid enough to make any man consider murder. While that may have been an option for some it did not appeal to Stede.

This unsatisfactory situation went on for a few years and Stede apparently did demand his sexual pleasures from this creature from time to time, since three children were produced of this unholy union, their births duly registered in church records of the day. Still, the life Stede led left him quite unfulfilled and hell was a constant reality in the Bonnet plantation home. Meanwhile, Stede continued to manage his plantation and his wealth while he tried to determine what to do. Perhaps he should have put her out, or arranged an accident for her (surely the slaves would have gladly helped!), and we will never know why he didn't. We do know that he finally hit on an idea that left his fellows on that island shocked. He would go a-pyrating!

That phrase and that spelling "a-pyrating" was used even in the 1700s, to represent not only theft on the high seas, but a retreat from bland reality into a devil-may-care, freebooting existence, that promised to be quite pleasurable, if also quite short. The brethren knew their lives would probably end in a hangman's noose, but they also knew that they would know adventure and experience great pleasures, if not untold wealth, during their pirate experience. Most pirate careers lasted only three or four years before the hooligan was captured and hung or merely blown out of the water by one warship or another. Still, the life of the brethren was exciting and Stede wanted escape, so a-pyrating he would go!

He purchased a sloop of forty-five feet with his own funds, and in a clandestine business deal on a nearby island controlled by the French, he was allowed to acquire ten cannon. These included eight four pound carriage guns, and two swivel cannon which he mounted on his bow. He mounted four carriage guns on each side of the deck, and hired four gun crews. He then dubbed the ship *Revenge* which may suggest some subtle motivation related to his beautiful, though nagging wife. He paid a crew of experienced seamen, in advance to sail with him, and with seventy experienced men on board, he stole away with the tide one night in 1714, sailing out of Bridgetown never to return. He headed for the Carolinas.

Because of the "pay in advance" idea, Stede's crew functioned differently from virtually every other pirate band. First of all, every other pirate acquired his pirate ship by theft whereas Bonnet owned the *Revenge* legally. Further, he had already paid his crew, and both of these were unique among pirate crews and caused some problems at the outset of the voyage.

Pirates in those years generally operated on principles that can only be described as democratic in nature, a fact that shocks many today. Other than in battle, when the Captain's word was absolute, virtually every pirate crew voted on every action they took, including which ships to challenge, who to take as hostages, and which direction to sail. Such voting resulted in motivated crews, since all pirates had a say in almost all decisions. For some, like Black Jambo and the many other African slaves that joined various pirate crews, the shipboard existence offered much more control over their lives than would any existence on shore, even if they had been free men! For that reason many black slaves found their way into piracy on the high seas, where they, like all pirates, enjoyed shared decision-making. In fact, history has shown that pirate crews could and often did vote pirate captains out of their command, if they believed one of the subordinates could lead the crew to more prizes and more wealth.

Bonnet's approach had thwarted all such conventions and his men resented that. The attitude was palpable within only a few weeks of the start of the cruise. They wanted a new man at the helm, even though Bonnet promised them the same share of any captured booty as other pirate captains in addition to their pay. His crew was still not happy, and an unhappy crew of pirates can ruin your whole day!

To put the matter bluntly, Bonnet knew absolutely nothing about running a ship, any type of ship, much less a pirate ship. While he did manage to catch a couple of ships off the Carolinas and the Virginia Capes, prizes as they were called, his complete lack of shipboard leadership skills was apparent to all, including the crews of the ships he approached. Sailing with the man was an embarrassment for many in his crew and they resented it, even if he did capture a few prizes. In those days any idiot with a blood flag and a starter pistol could have made hundreds of coastal freighters heave too in the Carolinas, since there was no law to speak of in those waters anyway. History records that Bonnet was merely lucky for a first time sailor, taking four rich prizes in only seven days.

Off the Virginia Capes, Bonnet captured the *Trooper* a sloop out of Glasgow, and the *Endeavor* a Brig from Bristol. The *Young* from London, heaved too under his guns just off Ocracoke, and then sailing south along the Hatteras shore, he captured the *Turbes*, a larger sloop from Barbados itself. This was enough to stop the crew from voting this man out, as perhaps they should have done. He was, after all, capturing prizes that would make them wealthy. Also, they figured that Bonnet did own the ship and he had paid in advance for their services. The crew decided to let matters alone for a time.

Now, pirates didn't want to sell their ill gotten gains in the same locale where they captured those prizes, so Bonnet sailed south with his stolen loot. It was an interesting collection of items; one hundred-twenty rolls of calico cloth, ten ivory tusks from the African coast, forty hogsheads of sugar, ten kegs of gunpowder, ten hogsheads of tobacco, twenty-two barrels of fine rum, and a shipment of fifteen spinning wheels originally destined for the Albemarle. Stede had decided to peddle his wares in the Caribbean and then take shore leave and enjoy his profits for a time.

When he was on that voyage south, he pulled in to the Cape Fear River to take on some water and provisions, and it was a chance sighting by a lone bear hunter on the riverbank that resulted in the abortive Moore expedition to the Cape Fear River in 1716. The bear hunter, a man from Charleston, thought that Bonnet might be careening his ship in the Cape Fear which would take a month at least, so he informed the authorities in Charleston that pirates were encamped in the Cape Fear River. Those authorities immediately mounted an expedition, and requested assistance from the New Bern Militia.

Careening a ship in those days was an involved process that allowed sailors in the 1700s to clean and sure-up the hulls of the wooden sailing vessels of the day. Throughout history, a certain type of sea-born worm has attacked wooden sailing ships, boring holes in the bottom of the exterior hull planking. Barnacles build up on the hulls too, slowing the speed of the vessels. In order to clean these pests off, the ship had to be sailed to shore on high tide and anchored in shallow water. When she beached as the tide went out, she would be levered onto her side using long ropes affixed to the top of the mast. In that fashion a large portion of one side of the hull would be well exposed out of the water and could then be cleaned of barnacles and worms, and recovered with pitch. The ship would refloat on the next high tide, and as that tide retreated the ship would be levered in the other direction exposing the other side for the same treatment. Pirates careened their vessels much more frequently than anyone else, since a newly cleaned ship was a fast ship, and their lives depended on the ship's speed.

In this instance however, the bear hunter was wrong. Bonnet was not careening, but merely taking on supplies. He left that river in less than twenty-four hours, so twelve days later when Martin Bender and nineteen members of the New Bern Militia reached the Cape Fear, they were told by Col. Moore that the pirates were long gone and were then sent home, having accomplished nothing but a hard march through the Carolina wilderness. Stede and his crew of pirates were gone from the Cape Fear before the New Bern Militia had even left New Bern, so Bonnet's capture would have to wait until another day.

## A Night at Jackson's Tavern

This futile militia raid in 1716 did have two results, both of which impacted Martin Bender, directly, and one would cause him some degree of spiritual challenge. First, the services of a dark brown tavern whore taught him a bit about the techniques of love. Second, Martin Bender got married.

With the mission to find the pirates in the Cape Fear aborted, Martin and the New Bern Militia turned north to return to New Bern in late September of 1716. They made excellent time for the next two days on the rough Indian trail that would, ultimately become Highway 17. They then reached a small tavern just at the headwaters of the New River, only thirty-five miles south of New Bern just at dusk. While most of the men planned to merely camp again on the rough ground, the new tavern keeper, a large bald man named John Berry Jackson, saw an opportunity to make some money, and he offered a free dry place to sleep, if the militia commander would pay for twenty hearty meals for his men.

Jackson also insisted that Martin, the Sergeant and expedition leader, sleep in one of the rooms on the second floor.

Martin thanked him for the kindness and was about to decline, when Dunker Tim, seeing Martin's reaction, said. "Suh, this tavern keeper has offered to let all nineteen of our men sleep in the barn for free. Please don't insult this man's hospitality." With that thought in mind, Martin agreed to stay in the second floor room by himself. It was a minor decision that would ultimately change his life.

An hour later, the tavern keeper served all of the men a nice meal of deer stew, for which he charged the New Bern Militia only a pittance. As it turns out, John Berry Jackson was quite a deer hunter, and the local deer population suffered mightily at his hands. Like Martin, he had a new Kentucky rifle, and again like Martin, he could use it. On that first evening nothing was seen of this man's horrid character; he was merely a host and as a tavern keeper he was generous with the New Bern Militia.

As the men sat at the tables in the tavern, a young slave girl, with very large warm-brown eyes, brought the plates to the tables. Each was piled high with the hearty deer stew, and a large chunk of fresh-baked cornbread. The girl looked to be only seventeen or so and had a beautiful warm brown tint to her skin. The tight smock of calico that she wore accented her curves, seemingly heightening them each time she leaned across the table to place a plate before one fellow or another. She then retreated to the kitchen house out the back door, but quickly returned with a large bowl of steaming potatoes that she placed in the center of the table right beside a large chunk of butter. The men were all but drooling at that point, for two very different reasons!

Most of the men, Martin included, couldn't keep their eyes off this young girl, save for Dunker Tim, who was cautiously watching Martin's reaction to the girl. The men got very quiet the second time she came to the table, but then, Able Ward, who rode with the militia from time to time, opened his foul mouth and broke the spell. "Recon' be some o' our wives 'll have a high and mighty time, soon. They for sure be some leg-spreadin' once we reach New Bern again!"

Every man at the table laughed at that truth. When men return from war, Indian fights, or even an aborted raid where they didn't even find their pirates, they still manage to enjoy their wives, often with great vigor. Just at that moment, one of the rowdy guys at the other end of the table cupped his hands around the young girl's bottom. Martin watched that with envy and he was sure this girl could be had for only a deerskin or two, which caused him to smile. Given his character and his religion, he couldn't consider that option, but sometimes he surely wished that he could! In fact, he'd never before been with a woman, since both his faith and his family forbade that, but he did have dreams now and then about what it might be like.

Martin also noticed that for some reason, when that rough fellow grabbed the girl's behind, Dunker Tim tensed up. Grabbin' a gal was not uncommon in frontier taverns when a comely young serving wench happened by the table, but Dunker Tim clearly didn't care for it in this case. In fact, he was about to stand up and for a second, Martin sensed trouble, but then the girl merely smiled and moved away.

At just that moment, the tavern keeper called her. "Beatrice! Mind the stew pot in the kitchen now, and check back with our customers later." Clearly this was his way of removing the girl for a time. He'd used this strategy before when groups of men arrived at his door. He'd show her off a bit in one tight smock or another, and that always made the men hungry for her. Then he'd order her away on some pretext. It always worked, and he was now sure that he'd receive several offers of deerskins this very evening for her services, so overall he was quite happy as the evening moved along. Butter was placed on the table and the men ate heartily. Martin found himself thinking of getting back to Katheryn, and by then every man in the militia knew about his pending wedding.

Able Ward, enjoyed making his friends laugh, and his first joke had gone over pretty well so he thought he'd try again. "Well, I recon, they'll be a new wife soon as our Sergeant gets back in town! Now Sergeant, are you sure you be knowin' what you'll be doing? Do you want a few pointers from me and the boys, here?" At that, many of the men were grinning and slapping the tables saying "Here! Here!" Able continued, "Maybe we best let you practice a bit with that thar brown gal tonight?"

Again, the fellows laughed, and Martin along with them. Still, when the young girl came in again Martin more than the others found himself wondering what she would be like. A bit later, his interest grew even more. As Martin sat at the head of the table, she leaned between him and Able who sat just to his left, to retrieve a pitcher and refill it with water. Able cupped her bottom himself this time, and said something like "She's mighty fine, Sergeant!"

Martin, looked quickly to the other table, where Dunker Tim sat with young Willie Koonce, but Dunker Tim had left for the outhouse only a minute or two before, so he missed this episode. Martin was wondering why Dunker Tim would care about this slave gal, but just as he looked back to her, he saw that Able's hand was still caressing her bottom, and this time Beatrice was smiling! In fact, she was looking directly at Martin, as Able enjoyed her bottom, and she was showing no inclination to move away from Able's hand at all! She even seemed to back into it a bit! Desire exploded inside of Martin, as she continued to smile at him, with her bottom being massaged by another man. While it lasted only a few seconds, the smile remained. To Martin it seemed like hours of pleasure!

The spell was broken when a large mug of rum was placed before Martin, and John Berry Jackson shouted, "Everyone drinks the first round on the house. Gentlemen, here's to the New Bern Militia!"

Cheers were heard all around, and Martin picked up the dram, thinking, I'll not insult this fine innkeeper. One drink I can take!

As it turns out, one dram was all it took, but then again, the large mugs used in those days really did hold a considerable volume of hard Jamaican rum. Martin had never taken much rum before, but the toasts kept coming, and the young girl kept showing up with more rum from time to time, though strangely, Martin's mug was not refilled.

Later that night, the girl seemingly disappeared, and Martin continued to laugh with his fellows, and sip the rum that remained in his large mug. At some point, when it became apparent that the girl was not likely to reappear, Martin wandered up the narrow stairs to find his room. By then some of the men were drunk, having ingested several mugs. One snored so loudly that young Willie compared him to a jackass. Able, however had a more apropos comparison, suggesting he could outdo even Archie Carmichael's famously loud snoring in Mallard's Tavern!

Martin almost tripped into the "first room on the right," were John Berry Jackson had directed him. He sat on the bed and had gotten his breeches and his shirt off and was working on his undergarments, when the door opened quietly and Beatrice came in with a water pitcher, and poured some hot water into the wash basin on the wash stand. "Mr. John says I should treat you to a bath!"

Martin wanted to say that a bath would not be necessary, but he realized that his speech was slurred a bit, and Beatrice seemed to be ignoring him anyway. She ordered him to sit still, as she knelt in front of him and began to wash his arms and chest. The rag and the warm water on his shoulder felt good, and as she helped him bathe himself. She began to talk, softly. "There, there, Mr. Martin. Just relax now, and let me take care o' things. I'm here to make this bath feel good to you! Just let me take care o' things. Close your eyes and I'll take care of things."

As the bath continued, she moved behind his back, crawled on the bed behind him, and circled him with her arms to wash his chest. Her voice was soft and her hands were soft, and she seemingly knew just how to massage his shoulders and his neck to relieve his stress. As the bath continued, he felt her pressing into his back with her entire body. He began again to feel the most erotic pleasures in his life, and when she began to kiss his neck from behind he was lost.

He turned to her, and his lips found hers. Hers opened in a way that Katheryn's never had, and they explored each other with their mouth and lips as she pressed herself to him with only her smock between their skins. They lay back across the bed together and continued to kiss, as her smock seemingly crept off, up above her head. She lay naked beside him and his lips were on her face and her neck, and her breasts for what seemed like wonderful hours of pleasure. He kissed her again and again, and he didn't realize that she directed him, showing him what to kiss, and how to touch her, as she wanted to be touched. He didn't know that love could feel like this, nor did he realize that his clothes were now gone. As they made love, he felt her move toward him and moan slightly, and then he felt pleasures that he had only dimly imagined before.

They made love several times, each more exciting that the first, but each also more gentle, more relaxed. Then he drifted off to sleep, and a bit later, she crept away in the night.

The next morning just after dawn, Dunker Tim knocked on his door, opened it a bit, and said, "Sergeant? We's best get moving, if we want to make New Bern today." Martin got up and dressed quickly. When he came outside his men were already assembled, and while a couple smiled to themselves discretely as he came down the steps, no one said anything. Even Able Ward, who might have been tempted to make a crude comment, kept silent.

Many years later Martin finally learned why he'd been spared the typical round of crude jokes. Dunker Tim, that remarkable slave, who had managed to become Martin's friend, had threatened every single man in the New Bern Militia! "Ever any one of ya'll says one word to my Sergeant, about that particular night, and I'll cut you up so bad, so's even the Tuscarora can't find nary a damn part o' ya!" All knew that Dunker Tim and Martin had for some strange reason, become fast friends, and every single man in the New Bern Militia knew that in this instance, Dunker Tim meant exactly what he said. To a man, they kept their mouths shut!

Martin remembered his night of sin at the tavern often, and frequently felt some remorse, but he knew that he was not a captive of that sinful life. He even had some fond memories of that night, and he hoped that he could give pleasure to Katheryn as he felt he had to Beatrice. He never realized that Beatrice had been teaching him and guiding him all the while, but he did learn many things in that one evening without even realizing it. As for the sin itself, he prayed deeply over the next few days for forgiveness and in his heart, he was sure that God understood his sin and had already forgiven him. Only a month after he returned to New Bern, he felt ready to take a wife.

Katheryn was never one to be sidetracked by sudden changes in plans, so when the militia returned to New Bern much sooner than she or anyone anticipated, she merely planned her simple wedding a bit sooner. In keeping with Mennonite tradition, it was intended to be a simple affair, solemn and somber, as required by their stern, simple beliefs. One aspect of the celebration she didn't plan. Since the church held no slave balcony, Dunker Tim could not attend, but this remarkable man had devised a way to participate none the less!

As Martin, Katheryn, Johannes, and Margaret emerged from their home, each in their best clothes and looking quite dignified as they prepared to walk solemnly to the church for the service, a few friends of Martin suddenly materialized out of thin air, and joined the rear of the procession. Martin's hunting buddies, Gator Jim, Willie Koonce, Able Ward, and Dunker Tim, each in their frontier breeches, joined the line and to make matters worse, Able had brought along his fiddle! He began to play a "quick-time hornpipe," an English tune popular in those days that with the passage of time and the addition of lyrics would eventually be known as *She'll be Comin' Round the Mountain When She Comes!*

That particular song is not the most solemn tune for that type of occasion, but it did attract the immediate attention of almost everyone in New Bern. The majesty of the walk was further compromised, however when Dunker Tim began to shout his joy, right along with the music! As he walked along, more of a skip really, Dunker Tim negotiated the street, one side to the other, as he loudly hailed all who happened to be within earshot. "We have a fine weddin' today!" he shouted at the top of his lungs. "Sergeant Martin Bender is taking Ms. Katheryn Simmons today in the church house! Everybody come on and wish 'um well. Our Sergeant is getting hitched! Right now, today! Ya'll come on down to the church house!"

Margaret thought the quick fiddle tune and the shouting to be a bit unseemly, more appropriate for Mallard's Tavern than a Mennonite wedding. When she mentioned this, however, Martin grinned and simply said, "I am happy, and I do want everyone to know!" Katheryn merely smiled, and that was all the encouragement Dunker Tim needed!

He continued to serve as town crier, skipping across the street, and loudly shouting his joy, for the entire five blocks to the church, thus showing his love and respect for his friend. After a block he had even synchronized with the music, and was chanting in time!

*"Sergeant Martin getting' married here today! Yes Suh!*
*We has got ourself a weddin' here today!*
*Now come on to the church house, and see his pretty bride, our*
*Sergeant Martin getting married here today! Yes suh!"*

As they arrived, Able stopped his fiddlin' and Dunker Tim bowed them into the church. His final celebratory shout could be heard all over New Bern! "Best wishes to you Sergeant Martin, and to yo' lovely bride Ms. Katheryn! What a great day! What a great day, indeed, suh! We have a weddin' today!"

Martin Bender took Katheryn Simmons as his bride on November 14, 1716 at the Anglican Church on Middle Street in New Bern, North Carolina Colony. On that day, the Bender family, a family that was to enjoy a three hundred year history along these twin rivers in the Carolinas, began.

Most members of the New Bern Militia were present as were such notables as Sheriff Jack DuVal and Captain William Brice. After the rather loud arrival at the church, the wedding went off without a hitch, save one. At the precipitous moment the bride was presented by her father. Just as the visiting minister asked, "Who gives this woman to be married?" rather than saying the expected line, "I do" Johannes, excited by the moment, got tongue tied once again and turned that into a question, "Do I?" Everyone in the church smiled, and the wedding continued without missing a beat.

## A Few Drinks With the Boys

By the late summer of 1717, Stede Bonnet had seized several more ships and amassed another stolen cargo. This time he also had a ship to sell. Like most pirates, Bonnet allowed most of his prizes to go their merry way once he'd stolen anything of value on board, but on that second voyage he did keep one ship, the *Anne*, which he thought he could sell in the Caribbean. His sloop and that captured prize sailed on down to New Providence Island where he hoped to unload the loot and see what cash his stolen wares might bring. He had also lifted some gold coin from one of those prizes, but that didn't amount to very much.

His crew sailed into that beautiful Bahamas port happy on that day in 1717. The men were excited since they all knew what pleasures a port call could bring, and each knew he had a goodly share of coin coming! Every single pirate would get one share of the proceeds, except Stede, as the Captain, and the Quartermaster who received two shares each. The sail master, boatswain, and chief gunner each snagged a share and a half for their duties.

Most of these rowdy cutthroats would burn through those funds in New Providence in less than a month, drinking rum by the gallon, buying new clothes, and purchasing the attentions of the local whores, sometimes several at a time. That particular practice was not unique to New Providence, but it had originally developed there. It was called a "pyrate's welcome" since only the newly rich pirates could afford the luxury of several females at once, and what a fine pleasure it was, at least in a pirate's mind!

As this suggests, little financial discipline was exercised by pirates since they enjoyed spending their loot, and all of them expected to die quickly anyway. The myth of the pirate's "buried treasure" is purely a creation of Hollywood. Still, all in all, it promised to be a happy time in the ramshackle town that would one day be known as Nassau, as Stede sailed in, since two other pirate ships were also in port. Unfortunately for Stede, the Gentleman Pirate, he was about to meet a couple of rogues that were anything but gentlemen! It was on that very evening, that Bonnet was introduced to the most notorious pirate of them all.

In New Providence at that point there were at least nine taverns, and almost all were near the waterfront to catch the traffic of sailors coming ashore. Occasionally, a British ship-of-the-line would come to port and disgorge two hundred or so thirsty sailors. Other times a smaller Royal Navy frigate would stop by, but mostly it was pirates that came calling in New Providence, and all headed immediately to the taverns. This particular tavern was called the "Queen's Booty" though no one ever explained exactly what that name meant. It included the entire lower floor of a long two story building near the docks, which was complete with twelve large tables, a fireplace, and two spittoons that were frequently ignored, one in each end of the room. The whorehouse was upstairs, for convenience.

Bonnet did not know that Blackbeard preferred to drink in that particular spot, so the meeting that took place on that night must be considered merely a coincidence. Still, Bonnet would pay a stiff price for choosing that watering hole! Teach sat at a table with Blackbeard's Claw right beside him as always, and when Bonnet walked in, Teach took the measure of the man in less than a second. Like everyone else sailing the seven seas, he'd heard the stories of the man who ran away from his pretty, ill-mannered wife to go a-pyratin' and like everyone else he had little respect for that man! Here was the bugger in the flesh, all cocky, with only a few rich prizes off the Carolinas! Teach merely looked on as Bonnet strutted in, and then Blackbeard smiled knowingly at the Claw; they would toy with this upstart pirate!

Bonnet walked in with his chief gunner, sat at the first table he saw, and shouted, "I'll be buying the next round for all here. Our voyage has been good for us all!" He lifted his mug, as cheers sounded from the eighteen men already in the tavern, all of whom would get a free drink on Stede's coin. It was only then that Stede noticed a couple of massive fellows sitting at a table in the rear of the bar near the fire, and, yes, one did have a long black beard, hanging to the middle of his massive chest. Bonnet knew at that instant it was Blackbeard, and he felt somehow, as if he was in the presence of royalty!

Blackbeard merely raised his mug toward the puny man buying the drinks, and smiled at him. Again, he looked over this pitiful excuse for a pirate, pretending to be someone important and buying drinks for everyone. Then again, he thought, this idiot did have a couple of ships and some worthy cargo to sell. Had Blackbeard been a bit more into his cups, his mean streak may have shown itself there and then, but he'd only just sat down and didn't have a full load of rum as yet. He grinned at the Claw, and thought again that it would be fun to play with this pitiful man for a time. Never in the eons of time or in all the dark depths of the Atlantic did a more deadly shark ever circle its prey with such cunning!

Within a few seconds Blackbeard had decided what he would do. He waited until most had finished drinking their dram, and then he stood and shouted. "That's all the drinking on Captain Bonnet's coin ye be doing tonight! The next round I pays for, and it'll be a toast to Captain Bonnet! A worthy Captain has joined the ranks of the brethren in fine fashion, I says, with nine prizes in the last ten months. Here he is with many a good cargo and a ship to sell! To Captain Bonnet!" He hoisted his mug, and took a swig, to cheers all around, as did all the others.

Bonnet didn't know what to make of this, but it felt good to have the recognition of Blackbeard and his peers. He felt alive in a way he'd not felt for many years. He hoisted his mug, and took a dram with his fellows. It was good to be a pirate!

The Claw, then spoke, looking at Bonnet. "And will the good Captain be joining us then?"

Bonnet smiled, stood, and walked over to Blackbeard's table, as the Claw shoved a stool in his general direction. Bonnet sat down, the unsuspecting fish before the hungry, cagy shark.

The Claw, knowing well what his Captain had in mind, urged Bonnet on. "So tell us about catchin' the prizes!"

Stede, proud of the recognition from this notorious pair, was more than ready to tell of the capture of his several ships, and the three men talked for almost an hour, as the rum flowed freely. Both the Claw and Blackbeard himself asked pointed questions about how Stede chose to approach one or more of his prizes, leeward, or windward? With the Jolly Roger flying or hidden? Gun ports open or weapons concealed? Stede was more than happy to share his strategies and the stories of his victories.

After about an hour, when the stories seemed to be mostly over, the Claw posed a question that surprised Bonnet. "So, with your victory, you and your boys'll be staying here a while I expect?"

Stede hadn't really thought that far ahead, but he didn't want to admit that to these two new friends! "We'll enjoy the rum and the women for a while, I think, but then we'll be leaving on the tide in four or five days. I mean, how much can one man drink?" They all laughed at Stede's question. Blackbeard merely sat back and watched as the Claw did his work for him.

"Indeed," said the Claw, as he laughed at Stede's joke. "Indeed. We was plannin' on sailing along about that time, weren't we Captain?" The Claw looked at Blackbeard for confirmation.

"We were, indeed!" said Blackbeard. "Always sail with the new moon, I say. We be heading to the Carolinas!"

The Claw continued, "Maybe we should sail out together." He said, as if it was an idea that had only then occurred to him. He took a quick dram, and continued. "There's more prizes in the Carolinas and richer ones too in this season! Hogsheads o' tobacco is coming out soon, to ship to London. The traffic out o' Bath is light, but Charleston is always good shippin' and more sloops be shippin' from the Trent River docks in New Bern these days. The Chowan River in the Albemarle is good huntin' too!" The Claw gobbled down some rum and then continued his thoughts. "They's deerskins a plenty shipped out from the Trent River docks as well as the Albemarle, and those we sells in Virginia!"

Then, as the Claw paused, Blackbeard spoke up. "Every damn one of the bastards 'll be more likely to heave too with the brethren comin' on 'um from all sides!" Blackbeard laughed his deep throaty, laugh, and then took another dram, as did they all.

At that moment a girl of fifteen with flaming red hair came by, having been sent by the bartender with more rum. She filled the mugs at the table, and Blackbeard cupped her breast in his massive right hand as she leaned over the table to fill the mug of Bonnet. She merely giggled, as he said "I'll be having at thee later, my girl. For now, fill 'um all up again, for all here!" She gladly did so, much to the pleasure of the tavern owner who was carefully keeping his tabs on who bought which rounds for the whole tavern!

The drinking continued until nearly dawn the next day, and the men enjoyed the services of the several women, the young one with the red hair, a black wench, and several that were not so young and nubile. With the rum flowing freely it really didn't matter much to these men.

The general discussions of sailing together continued through the next several days, and after five mornings, when Blackbeard took his frigate and sailed out on the morning tide, Captain Bonnet and the *Revenge* went along.

Stede thought he'd made a deal with a fellow Captain to try their luck together along the Florida and Carolina coast, but Blackbeard had other plans. During their five day shore party, Blackbeard and the Claw had talked Bonnet into hanging on to the sloop *Anne* which Bonnet had captured previously. It had been fitted out with four six pounders on each side, and now sailed under the orders of Israel Hands. Only two days out of port, Blackbeard invited Hands and Captain Bonnet to his own ship for dinner, and then he had Bonnet placed in what amounted to "protective custody." He knew that Bonnet couldn't command a ship and sailing with him would be a danger to all, so Blackbeard simply forbade him to leave. He did not mistreat Stede, but rather simply told him to relax and enjoy the cruise!

This left Stede quite unhappy, but what could he do when he was out on the high seas on Blackbeard's ship, imprisoned by Blackbeard's crew, and with his own crew supporting Blackbeard? Less than an hour later, Blackbeard sent his chief gunner, Richards, to command Stede's ship the *Revenge*, leaving Blackbeard in overall command of a flotilla of three armed pirate ships, and some two hundred and eighty pirates! The Atlantic had never seen such firepower or so many cutthroats under the control of any single pirate Captain before, and it would not stop there!

## Blackbeard's Queen

Blackbeard's own ship was the largest ever commanded by the brethren of the sea. The *Queen Anne's Revenge* was a two hundred eighty ton frigate, and her three masts carried more sail than any other frigate afloat. It was fast for a ship of its type, very fast. As a gun platform she sported forty cannon and it is hard to imagine the terror one felt seeing Blackbeard's distinctive flag floating above all of those weapons, each one peaking out at your ship across twenty yards of open ocean! That single ship could blow any other ship in the Carolinas out of the water.

For heavy work such as ship to ship action, she carried twelve six-pounders mounted on carriages on each of two gun decks. The twelve gun ports on either the starboard or port side looked formidable indeed. Each of those smooth-bore cannons could poke very large holes in any ship then afloat, but Blackbeard wanted to do more than merely kill ships. He wanted to kill people.

For that, the *Queen* as he chose to call her, also had eight three pounders mounted on the quarterdeck. He used those for what he called "close work." Those cannon tended to be fired much more frequently than the heavy guns, simply because Blackbeard rarely fought an enemy that was serious enough to demand the attention of his full armament. In short, with his fearsome reputation, the skill of his gunners, and his version of the Jolly Roger floating high in the breeze, few chose to challenge him. Most ships tried to outrun him, and once they realized they couldn't, they merely gave up without a fight!

Should Blackbeard need them however he also had smaller swivel guns in the rigging and mounted on the forecastle. These were smaller cannon that could be manned by one sailor. They were anti-personnel weapons that most frequently fired many small iron pellets like a large shotgun. Unlike the other armaments, these guns could swivel, and fire in almost any direction. By firing five or ten of these swivel guns, he could sweep an enemy deck clean of his opposition.

Sailing alone, the *Queen* was formidable. With forty cannon and proven gun crews Blackbeard could attack even the largest merchantmen on the high seas, and he did exactly that from time to time. Off the Island of St. Vincent in the Caribbean, Blackbeard and the *Queen* took a large, well armed coastal freighter, the *Great Allan*. She was laden with a rich cargo of rum bound for several ports in the Caribbean but those thirsty lads had to do without, because Blackbeard's crew of cutthroats stole every barrel! After the cargo was transferred to the *Queen* all who wanted were invited to join the pirate band, and those that didn't were put ashore. The *Great Allan* was put to the torch. Blackbeard and his crew then partied for days on that rum, drinking as much as they could. They finally sold the rest in Bath for transshipment up to the taverns in Philadelphia. This large prize alone multiplied Blackbeard's reputation ten fold, but his next feat was wholly unbelievable!

A month after taking the *Great Allen* Blackbeard was sighted by a British warship, the *Scarborough*. The two closed on each other for a while in the Windward Islands, but Blackbeard pulled away when he saw that the *Scarborough* was not a merchant ship. The *Scarborough* gave chase but the captain did not initially order his gun crews to their guns, since the *Queen* had the wind and was a faster ship anyway. He was sure that he'd chase this cutthroat for a while, and would then lose sight of him overnight.

Blackbeard, by all accounts, stood on the quarterdeck, drinking rum while he led the *Scarborough* on a chase of two hours or so. When all realized that the *Queen* would soon outdistance the *Scarborough* completely, the unbelievable happened. Blackbeard ordered a tack to bring the ship back toward the man-of-war, and had his gun crews load cannon in his entire gun battery! This is the only recorded instance in history, when a pirate chose to fight a heavily armed British warship, just for spite! There was no possible gain Blackbeard could have been after, since warships carried no cargo and little coin. He fought the *Scarborough* that day merely to show that he could.

The *Scarborough* quickly unveiled her thirty heavy guns, even while Blackbeard's Jolly Roger was run up on the *Queen*. The British had known they were chasing one pirate or another, but when that flag was hoisted, they realized they were chasing the most deadly pirate of all! Blackbeard knew ships and he knew the winds; many in those days remarked that there was no better sailor on the high seas than this pirate, Blackbeard. He maneuvered carefully to keep his ship out of range until he could overtake the *Scarborough* on the same heading. Then he quickly closed for battle bringing his portside cannon to bare. The ships came abreast of each other and the heavy cannon roared to life bringing hell to each ship as fire, shot, and oak splinters flashed in every direction delivering instant death to many men on each side. The Royal Navy gun crews were the best in the world and drilled repeatedly while at sea to assure rapid, accurate fire, and quick reloading. Their cannon were reloaded and ready to fire before Blackbeard's, but not by much! Before the ships could even bare away, another salvo was fired by both sides. Shot raked the decks of both ships, and tore large holes in the port side of the *Queen* as well as the starboard side of the *Scarborough*. Blackbeard's ship now had many dead sailors and seven guns on her port side out of action. The *Scarborough* had lost six of her starboard guns. However, Blackbeard had more guns to loose, forty cannon to thirty on the *Scarborough,* and what was worse, the starboard battery of the *Scarborough* now held only nine battle ready cannon and gun crews!

Blackbeard then showed his seamanship, as he pulled past the man-of-war. The officers on the British warship thought, several hoped, that he might retire, since nothing further could be gained for the pirate from continuing the battle. However, they did not know the measure of this man. Blackbeard again turned to the British ship to bring his guns to bare, but like the cagy Captain that he was, he tacked quickly so that his starboard cannon would face the starboard of the *Scarborough* in a running pass in the opposite direction. In that maneuver, he exposed the undamaged side of his ship to the *Scarborough,* and his starboard battery still held twenty heavy guns! On that pass, his cannon attacked the damaged planking on the starboard of the *Scarborough* and the Scarborough could fire only her starboard battery of nine usable cannon!

The men on the *Scarborough* knew what was coming, and could do absolutely nothing about it! Cannon roared again on both sides, but twenty heavy guns facing a wounded ship does much more damage than nine guns facing undamaged oak planking. The result was inevitable; the *Scarborough* was doomed. After that run, the *Queen* pulled away, and Blackbeard's laughter was heard across the waves. It was apparent to all that Blackbeard could have sunk the *Scarborough* with only one or two more passes. Her main mast was down, limiting her maneuvering, and her starboard battery now presented only three cannon in battle ready condition. However, Blackbeard had made his point! He allowed the *Scarborough* to limp away toward Barbados for repairs where the men of the British Royal Navy would tell of Blackbeard's victory. For the first and only time in the history of piracy in the Atlantic, a pirate had bested a British Man-of-war!

After that engagement, Blackbeard's reputation knew no bounds, but more was yet to come!

# Blackbeard's Navy

With the *Queen* alone capable of such feats, the thought of Blackbeard in command of several ships shocked sailors all over the Atlantic. Having taken Stede Bonnet's *Revenge* and his captured prize the *Anne*, Blackbeard now sailed with three ships under his command. In the fall of 1717, just as these three ships reached the sea lanes along the North Carolina coast, a large brig named the *Trent* sailed into the open ocean coming from the New Bern docks. She belonged to a group of plantation owners and farmers near Trent Mill, and sailed under Captain Tim Morton. That day she was hauling twenty-five hogshead of tobacco bound for Virginia. As the brig rode the tide out of Topsail Inlet (what is today known as Beaufort Inlet), she tacked to catch the sea breeze from the southeast, and lost her way. It was then that Captain Morton spied a heavily armed frigate and two armed sloops with the wind in their sails baring down on her. The Captain was concerned, knowing that sailing anywhere in the Carolinas was dangerous, but he didn't believe that any pirate commanded a frigate and two smaller sloops. That was unheard of, so Captain Morton was not unduly troubled, at least initially. His brig was lightly armed with four pounders, two on each side and he figured that he could hold his own if needed. However, he changed his mind only a moment later, when the fast frigate turned toward him and hoisted the Jolly Roger!

Like most acts of piracy in the Carolinas, there would be no ship to ship fight that day. As Morton saw gun ports open on all three of his pursuers, he knew he stood no chance of escape. Any way he turned, one ship or the other would have the wind, and all were more heavily armored than the *Trent*. In only a moment, he struck his flag and hove too, hoping for mercy. His men were sailors, not fighters, and while they could fire his four measly cannon they had not done so in over two months—gunnery practice not being a high priority on most coastal freighters. The piracy on the high seas on that day would go unchallenged.

After Blackbeard relieved him of his gold, he asked if Captain Morton and his crew would like to join the pirate band. By then it was clear that Blackbeard was taking the *Trent* as one of his own so he would not have to unload her. Many of the men saw no problem joining the pirates, and one even recognized a former slave from the Foscue Plantation, Black Jambo.

While standing behind Blackbeard, Black Jambo grinned as soon as he saw that he'd been recognized. He then said, "Come, on my boys. Captain Blackbeard will treat you well!"

Some of the men decided then and there to become pirates, and of the *Trent's* crew of fourteen, nine sailed away with Blackbeard. However, the Captain himself refused, explaining to Blackbeard. "Sir, I have a family on the Trent River that I enjoy, and a small farm there. I would request that you allow me and the men that wants, to take the dinghy and paddle back into the inlet."

On that particular day Blackbeard was in a kindly mood and with one look at Captain Morton, he nodded yes to that request. Then he made a request of his own. "You'll be telling the Sheriff of New Bern that ye was set upon by Blackbeard and his mates, won't ye? Tell' um we be kind to those what don't require the attentions of our cannon in battle!"

To that request, Captain Morton replied, "I will, Sir!" Captain Morton realized that all pirates wanted to be feared, but that most really didn't want to fight, and Blackbeard's request made sense in that light.

Blackbeard continued. "We be sailing with the winds up to the Virginia Capes, and on to Boston. You tell's 'um that, too!"

Captain Morton and his remaining men were then placed in the dinghy and given four paddles, with which they had to cover four miles of ocean. By then the tide was turning, and they would make it back to the inlet. They paddled hard, and made it back into the Core Sound just before dusk, as they watched Blackbeard's Navy sail away to the northwest.

Pate had described the *Queen Anne's Revenge* exactly correct several years before at Mallard's Tavern. Blackbeard's frigate was indeed a beautiful ship and it was armed to the teeth, as Captain Morton reported the next week to Sheriff DuVal. Further when Blackbeard took the *Trent* that day, Captain Morton became the first seaman in the Atlantic to recognize something that would eventually send terror up and down the eastern seaboard. The *Queen* alone had more firepower than any other ship along that coast, but when the *Queen* and the *Trent* sailed together along with the two smaller ships that comprised Blackbeard's Navy, then the *Queen* and its master owned the coast of the Carolinas!

## The Siege of Charleston

Blackbeard has been described as many things over the years, and the reality of the man may at this point, be lost forever in his legend. His reputation has ranged from renegade to near saint. Some say he was the meanest cutthroat among the brethren in those years, and much evidence supports that. Others take a different view, and some even claim he was merely getting revenge on Queen Anne! By that reckoning Blackbeard served as a sort of Robin Hood figure, stealing from the wealthy, and selling his goods back to the lower classes at discounted prices along the Carolina coast. Some even claimed that Blackbeard had been one of de Graffenreid's settlers, and had seen firsthand, the abandonment of the colony to the wicked Tuscarora during those awful years of 1711 and 1712. In that version of the legend, this man of the sea was seeking revenge against Queen Anne for not helping those North Carolina colonists more. While no real evidence supports that idea, it would certainly explain the unusual name of Blackbeard's frigate, *Queen Anne's Revenge.*

Some things are known about this man. He was brave to a fault, and never shrank from a fight. In battle, he was deadly with his ship handling skills, his cannon, his personal armament of six pistols, and his slashing cutlass. He commanded his ships with a level of skill that made sailors of the day proud to sail with him, even those who had been forced into piracy. Finally, while he may have been many other things, history records that he was never a man to think small! When one commands a powerful navy, why seize a single ship when you can have so much more?

Rather than heading north as Blackbeard had indicated to Captain Morton, Blackbeard steered northeast just long enough to get beyond sight of Captain Morton's dinghy, and then tacked southward. Charleston was by far the largest port in the entire hemisphere in the early 1700s far outpacing even New York in terms of shipping tonnage, and it was here that Blackbeard pulled off one of the most classic thefts in the history of piracy. Here he besieged a city!

It is not clear if holding the entire city hostage was his initial plan. At first, Blackbeard's Navy merely lurked about just outside of the Charleston harbor and stopped every ship either inbound or outbound. If the *Queen* had the wind in her sail, Blackbeard would stop the ship himself, but if he was out of position, one of his other ships did the task. When he stopped an outbound ship he relieved them of their most profitable cargo, usually deerskins, slaves, gold, or tobacco, and then sent them on their way. He didn't bother the lesser profitable cargos such as pitch or grain. Inbound ships presented a problem however, in that he didn't want the authorities in Charleston to catch on too quickly to his presence. He'd steal what he wanted from those vessels, and then hold those ships for a time, because if they went into the Charleston port, they would warn other ships not to depart!

The plan worked for almost two weeks and Blackbeard had taken nine ships in that time, an unheard of feat for any of the brethren of the sea. One of them had been a passenger vessel, and had presented Blackbeard with some highly valuable hostages, including one member of the governor's own council, a mister William Pope! Another ship held fourteen slaves that would bring a pretty shilling in the Caribbean! Another ship held gold worth over six thousand pounds. At that moment, just with those several prizes, Blackbeard and all of his men were wealthy beyond comprehension.

By then however, the authorities in Charleston had noticed that not a single ship had crept up to their docks in over a week. For that busy port, such a lack of commerce for a whole week was unheard of! They sent a small sloop out to investigate, and when it saw four ships approaching, and counted almost a hundred guns among them, it scurried on back to port to confirm that pirates were about. At that point, the Port of Charleston, the busiest port in the western hemisphere, was completely paralyzed! Nothing went in and nothing came out. Six large frigates and two brigs were tied along the Charleston docks, their captains refusing to leave while pirates were off-shore in such strength.

Other men, lesser men, might have called it a day by then and retired to enjoy this booty, but Blackbeard was unlike other men. When it became apparent that no other shipping was leaving the harbor, Blackbeard decided to cash in his hostages for an even larger payoff! About that time, the Claw pointed out that his rum kegs were getting close to dry and his medicine chests were all but empty. Blackbeard merely said, "I fancy I know where we can find some medicines!" Within an hour Mr. Richards, who Blackbeard had placed in command of one of his ships, was dispatched with Mr. Pope in a small dinghy, and they were rowed calmly into Charleston by the Claw and Black Jambo.

When they reached shore, the Claw and Richards took Pope into a nearby tavern, and told the proprietor to "Fetch Governor Johnson!" When the governor of the South Carolina Colony arrived, they delivered their demands; gold worth five hundred pounds, four kegs of rum, and a list of medicines. Pope confirmed that the pirates held twenty-two hostages, many of whom were among the elite of Charleston. The terms of the deal were not negotiable, and they also included a warning. If the pirates were harmed in any way or if the demands were not met in two days, then Blackbeard would deliver the heads of all of his hostages, Pope's wife included, to the governor's doorstep. Then Blackbeard's Navy would sail into the inner harbor and destroy Charleston!

For two whole days, Black Jambo, the Claw, and Richards strutted through the streets of Charleston, drinking wherever they pleased, and enjoying many of the dockside whores. No tavern keeper had the courage to present a bill for any of those services, but if the truth be told, the whores didn't mind the pirates at all. With no other sailors coming or going, they had been getting quite bored, and the pirates at least tipped them fairly well.

Meanwhile the governor of the South Carolina Colony, so very powerful in his own colony, was absolutely powerless when it came to an enemy on the high seas. The legislature debated various responses, and while it took all of the two days, they eventually realized they had no realistic alternative. Nothing in their entire colony, and probably nothing in the eastern Atlantic could stand up to Blackbeard's Navy. London was keeping most of her ships-of-the-line in the Mediterranean, and if Blackbeard had wanted, he could have sailed into the harbor and used the eighty seven guns on his four ships to sink the ships at the Charleston docks and then level the entire city!

After three days, the medicines and the ransom were sent out to Blackbeard's ship, and true to his word, Blackbeard released his hostages. He had his men place them on Sullivan's Island in the middle of Charleston harbor, and then he calmly sailed for Ocracoke Inlet, his favorite hiding place in the Carolinas, leaving the Charleston authorities both humbled, and very, very angry! They would seek and ultimately get their revenge, but other pirates would pay that deadly tally!

### Bender Babies Arrive

The same week that word reached New Bern about the siege of Charleston, Kathern Bender went into labor, so Martin and Johannes both missed the news initially. Katheryn had gained quite a few pounds and was waddling around the cabin, looking for all the world like a sow on stilts. Martin, wiser now in the ways of women, merely assured her that she was lovely, and that he wanted to be a father as soon as possible. Johannes and Martin had built a small cabin for Martin and Katheryn right behind the original family cabin, since Johannes owned that adjacent land. In that way, Margaret could help her oldest daughter deliver the baby, and eventually help care for the child.

When the screams began, Margaret and Christina had the presence of mind to send Johannes and Martin both away, telling them to go to Mallard's Tavern, but nowhere else. They would be sent for when the time was right. Martin didn't want to go, but when he heard his young wife scream a second time, much louder than the first, he decided that he would be much better off in the tavern. Just as they walked in, the talk turned to the Charleston Siege. Sheriff Jack DuVal was speaking to Captain Brice at the table near the door, and Archie Carmichael slept off his liquor on the stool by the fireplace, resting on two legs just like always.

"What I don't understand is how that cutthroat Blackbeard got aholt o' so many ships! Damn his hide all to hell!" The Sheriff was always vocal when it came to crime of any type. "Why can't the Royal Navy catch that bugger? One ship-of-the-line would clean out that nest of vipers! Send those ships to the bottom of the Pamlico, I say, and would probably do well to wipe out most of Ocracoke and Bath too! Then we could send His Majesty's Navy on down to Jamaica and New Providence for the same treatment!"

Captain Brice took a sip of his rum, and added. "I hear one of those ships was heisted from the men in Trent Mill! Captain Morton indicated Blackbeard didn't sink his ship the *Trent*, but sailed her away. I'll bet the bugger has cannon mounted all over her by now!"

Johannes and Martin sat at a table behind Captain Brice, but Johannes wanted to get in on the discussion. "What is you say, Captain? What bugger is now got cannon?"

Captain Brice turned, "Ah, Sergeant Simmons! Sergeant Bender! Do prop up there and join us. We were just talking about the news from Charleston. Seems Blackbeard had laid siege to the entire port! He demanded some medicines and monies for his hostages! Got them too!"

Sheriff DuVal looked over at Martin and Johannes, and added his thoughts. "Those buggers in Charleston gave in to the cutthroat! Can you imagine! What sense does that make?"

Captain Brice didn't even try to address that question. He was thinking ahead. "Martin, it seems there may be a call for more assistance to capture these hooligans. You may be headed for the Cape Fear again!"

Martin responded. "I go, at your orders, Sir!"

Just then Toby Mallard came by. "Ah," he said. "Are you a proud papa yet, Martin? Didn't I hear a woman screaming her head off when I came past your cabin earlier?"

Martin merely grinned, and said, "Not yet. I hope to hear soon!"

Brice, who had not realized that Katheryn was expecting smiled and said, "Well then, my good Sir, can I stand you to a drink? In honor of your first son!"

Johannes and Martin both accepted, and Captain Brice bought them all a dram. As Toby filled the mugs the Captain offered a toast. "To this baby and to all future Bender babies! I'm sure this one will be healthy, and that many more will follow!" All drank to that toast.

Later that same night, on August 23, 1717 in the Bender cabin on South Front Street in New Bern, a healthy baby boy was born. Martin and Katheryn named their first child, Daniel Brice Bender, with that middle name chosen to honor Captain Brice. In the cabin, all was happiness as both the child and Katheryn were doing fine.

Johannes cried when he first saw his own daughter in the small bed feeding his first grandchild! Martin Bender joined him in tears at that moving sight. He was as proud at that moment as he had ever been, and over the next few days everyone came by to offer congratulations.

May Koonce and her son Willie came by the very next morning and brought a pie. Toby Mallard, Sheriff Jack DuVal, and even Captain Brice's daughter Isabel came to pay their respects. Dunker Tim stopped by several times over those early days, bringing some wild berries for Katheryn and Martin, and each time tickling the baby's chin, grinning all the while.

No one in New Bern realized it at the time, but that baby was Martin Bender's second son.

## *Hunting Advice in the Tavern*

Later that same week, Martin and Johannes were again sitting in Mallard's Tavern with One-Eye, and Able Ward. They were talking about hunting bear in the swamps below New Bern, since Johannes and Martin were planning to put in some meat for the winter. A few sailors were at a table in the other end of the tavern, and Toby Mallard himself was doing the serving, along with his wife. Normally, one noticed one or more of the whores helping out with that job—the Indian whore seemed to be a particularly good waitress—but none of them seemed to be in evidence on this evening.

Able said, "It was me, I'd sail on down the Neuse about five mile, and then catch that ridge that leads due south. After ten mile or so, it'll take you to a series of ridges, where Cap'n Brice is setting up a mess of tar kilns. They'll be cooking turpentine out'n those pines for a hundred years or more, and when they was goin' in they seed plenty o' bear sign!"

{Author's Note: Able was talking about a ridge that the bear hunters in the area know well, even today. It has been called "Tintarkle Ridge" for the last two hundred years or so, and many know it only by that name. The real name of that ridge, a name first used in 1717, was "Ten Tar Kilns" and that is exactly how many pots Captain Brice set up along that ridge, three hundred years ago to cook out his turpentine.}

"I guess that'd be about the best bet," said Martin. "Sure ain't much bear left along the Trent, with all the farmers clearing land and all. Recon' any savages be hidin' in that swamp?"

One-Eye chimed in at that. "No damn savages anywhere in the whole damn colony that I can see! Colonel Moore licked 'um good and sent 'um running!"

"Hope right that is!" Johannes said.

Able said. "You'll find your bear in those ridges, and you'll have some company. I hear Captain Brice has Dunker Tim and five other niggers living on the ridge with the tar pots."

Martin was a bit surprised by that last phrase. Dunker Tim had fought beside Able Ward several times with the militia, and those two had even crashed Martin's wedding, with Able playing the fiddle, while Dunker Tim danced along in the street! To hear Dunker Tim merely called a "nigger" caused Martin a moment of pause. Martin really didn't care for that term "nigger," but it seemed that everybody in those days used it.

Just then with a pause in the conversation, these men all heard one of the sailors at the other table, asked a simple question of Toby. "Where are the whores?"

Another grinned and said, "I want the big black one with the large…"

But Toby had already interrupted him. "Ain't no whores tonight. They is all engaged."

Silence! One could have heard a pin drop in Mallard's Tavern. No one could believe it! One-Eye was the first to recover and he asked the obvious, "Where are all your whores, Toby?"

Toby looked sheepish for a few moments, and then replied. "They has all been engaged."

One-Eye wasn't satisfied with that answer, and Martin began to suspect that he had planned on seeking a bit of fun himself later that evening. One-Eye continued, "What the hell is happening, Toby? Where are your damn whores? Is you a tavern or ain't ya?"

It was clear that Toby had to come clean. "I don't suppose it can hurt to let you know. Just about this time yesterday, Blackbeard's Claw come in here bold as the King of England himself along with two other guys, and told me he'd be taking my whores for eight whole days!" By this point, everyone in the tavern was listening!

"He paid in advance, and told me he'd get 'um back to me when they was done. I doubled what I usually charge, and even added in all the morning hours when whores usually sleep, but he paid smartly in doubloons and put 'um all in his sloop. They sailed down the Neuse toward the Pamlico about five o'clock yesterday afternoon."

One of the sailors off a brig out of New Bedford, piped in, "You mean you ain't got a single whore? No whores at all?" He was clearly brokenhearted, as both his words and his face showed his disappointment.

"Worse than that. Ain't nobody got no whores! The Claw said he'd already stopped by Jackson's Tavern on the New River, and they were goin' on up to Chocowinity Bay to pick up the whores there too. I'll bet they ain't a single whore to be had in the whole colony!"

Martin took note of the mention of the whores at Jackson's Tavern, and he hoped that Beatrice wasn't involved in this business. He didn't think of her often but when he did, he again asked forgiveness for his sin. Still, thoughts of her always did bring a certain warmth to him, as well as some fond memories.

One-Eye spoke up first, and merely said, "Well I'll be damned!"

"Not for any sinnin' you was a plannin' on doin' tonight you won't!" Able couldn't help but joke with his friend, and everyone in the tavern laughed at that, which pleased Able no end.

The laughter was so loud it even woke up Archie, who stumbled a bit as he put the third leg of his stool back on the floor. Then he shouted, "What the hell's so funny?" He managed to catch his balance though, and avoided falling into the fire on that particular evening.

## The Ocracoke Orgy

Toby was right. Sure enough, in the autumn of 1717 all through the Carolinas, the whores disappeared! Neither Bath nor New Bern nor any settlement in between had any comfort at all to offer the weary traveler. The Claw had rounded up almost every whore within a hundred miles and seemingly sailed away. As it turns out, Blackbeard had promised every pirate in his entire Navy, all two hundred and ninety six of them, a party. Rum was no problem, since one of the last prizes they took off Hampton Roads in Virginia was shipping fifty barrels of rum to several thirsty taverns in Williamsburg, and another twenty on up to Philadelphia. The party was set to begin in a week, after the Claw managed to acquire some companions. This is probably the only time in history that anyone ever tried with such diligence to corral all the whores in the entire colony, but it takes considerable female companionship for two hundred and ninety six pirates. Meanwhile Blackbeard worked his men like dogs, holding out the hope of a party fit for royalty, even as the Claw planned and coordinated the biggest "kegger" in Carolina history!

Meanwhile, the pirates had work to do careening Blackbeard's Navy. The men had been careening each of the ships Blackbeard had, and while the two smaller sloops were no problem, removing forty heavy cannon from the *Queen* took considerable time. By this point, the *Trent* was sporting twenty cannon herself, and all of that heavy iron had to be taken completely off the ship, before she sailed into the shallows, since that had the effect of raising her out of the water, which helped with the process. Careening one ship was a hell of a chore, but Blackbeard had the *Queen* and the *Trent* both grounded and rolled over on their sides, while his pirates scurried over them like ants running across the broad flanks of a couple of beached whales. One sloop he kept in the tides for a quick getaway should he need it, and the Claw had the other rounding up the whores.

No sooner had his men beached the *Trent* than a smaller brigantine named the *Diamond* sailed into Ocracoke Inlet on the tide. She was a fast ship, much smaller than the *Queen* or the *Trent* but her guns looked fearsome, until somebody recognized the ship as another pirate vessel. As soon as Captain Charles Vane saw the *Queen* laid too, he fired a cannon in honor of Blackbeard, and hoisted his Jolly Roger! He had come to the same inlet for the same reason, and within twenty-four hours his ship was laid on its belly just like the other two ships.

By the end of the week, all three ships were well cleaned and floated again, and just as the men restored the cannon, the Claw returned with no less than forty-seven whores, all of whom were terrified but more than willing to ply their trade. They'd been told that their masters or owners had already been paid, and also that these pirates had considerable coin still to spend. What they earned up here at the Ocracoke Orgy, they could keep!

History records this event only through folklore of the pirates themselves, and a few verbal descriptions from the whores some months after the fact. Fiddles played, everyone danced, poker and gin games kept all entertained, rum disappeared by the barrel, and forty-seven females never worked so hard for money in their lives! With a ratio of six pirates to one whore, the whores did duty that would make a union chief proud, as they shamed themselves repeatedly, all night and most of the day. The timing got so bad that after the first day, Blackbeard had the Claw limit each whore to only two men an hour, and even institute some sleeping rules to allow the girls a bit of a break. Still, as the men got drunk the girls got wealthy, and several slaves were actually able to buy their own freedom when this one week was over.

Governor Eden heard of the Ocrocoke Orgy almost three weeks after it was over, but he still called out the Albemarle Militia and the New Bern Militia to "sally forth and capture the pirates!" Some four weeks after the party was over, a hundred and fifty men converged on the empty beaches of Ocracoke Inlet in several small sloops, only to camp out for a day and then return home. More than one grumbled about the wasted trip, since all were sure that the governor didn't really want to catch Blackbeard anyway, and had merely sent them up there for show. Thus, did Martin Bender lead his second expedition against pirates, and both of those trips were abysmal failures.

### *Along the Cape Fear*

Martin's third foray to capture pirates was to be more successful that the first efforts. In the autumn of 1718, Captain Brice again appeared at the cooper's shed and indicated that Martin was to lead another raid towards the Cape Fear. "We have it on good authority that Stede Bonnet and the *Revenge* are really there this time. He careened inside the Cape Fear, ten miles or so upriver. You will take five men on horseback and get there within four days. You will have to travel fast and light, but Dunker Tim used that trail only a month ago, and says that it is fair going, even down below Jackson's Tavern in the swamps."

Again, Martin replied, "Yes sir! I'll will call the boys and leave today."

Captain Brice repeated himself, to make certain his favorite Sergeant heard the urgency. "Martin, pick four other men with good horses, men you can depend on. Col. Moore will be there in strength. I've received word he will have most of Moore's Rifles, over a hundred men, with him and you are merely there to support him, but take nothing for granted. Take good men with Kentucky rifles and pick men you can depend on in a pinch. You will have some fighting to do on this trip, I'd wager!" Captain Brice could not have then realized how fortuitous that last phrase was!

Within only four hours, Martin and his small contingent of men were mounted, and heading down the Island Creek Trail toward Trent Mill. Martin had a strong horse by then, a bay that he trusted and all of the other men were mounted too. Each was a man that was seasoned in battle, and Martin had fought beside each before, save one. Able Ward, Dunker Tim, Willie Koonce, and Gator Jim, all rode with Martin that day. Gator Jim didn't usually ride with the militia, and he'd never been in a battle with Martin before, but he happened to be in town when the call went out, and he knew those southern swamps better than any man alive. Martin had hunted with him often, and knew him to be the best man in the county with a rifle. Gator Jim agreed to the pay of two shillings a day for his services, so he was quickly invited along. Each man carried his own load of a heavy blanket, water, some parched corn, their Kentucky rifles, and any other weapons they could strap on, or tie to their mounts.

They would reach Jackson's Tavern by evening. Martin had planned to drive his men hard for two days, and then rest up some just before they reached the Cape Fear. He thought that he might see Beatrice again at the tavern, but he promised himself no more sin. He actually wanted to thank her, since he had now realized just how much he had learned in one blissful evening in her bed. That evening turned out quite differently!

After a hard day of travel, they arrived at the tavern on the New River just as the sun set. Martin indicated they would pull up for the night and hit the trail early the next morning. The men all went into the tavern where they sat around a single table. Three other travelers were already in the tavern, scattered around several other tables. If any of those other men thought it strange that Dunker Tim, a black slave was sitting with the white men in the tavern, they kept those thoughts to themselves. To put it simply, those five men from New Bern looked scary as hell, riding in with more weapons than any group of men would ever carry normally. Each had a look of calm, cool confidence, a look of quiet determination in his eye, and each looked like he could hold his own in a rough fight. None of the locals wanted to mess with that bunch of rogues, and one even suggested quietly to his friend that they looked like thieves. Such was the look of these, the select of the New Bern Militia.

Each of the New Bern men knew of this strange friendship between Martin and Dunker Tim, and each had seen Dunker Tim in a fight or two before. All were glad he was along with them, since they wanted good men beside them in a fight, no matter who he was or what color he might be.

John Berry Jackson greeted these new arrivals by placing a mug of rum before each one, and said, "You're here just in time for supper. I kilt a bear along the south bank of the White Oak River just three days ago, and she cooked up real good!" Then he shouted toward the back room, "Beatrice, bring stew and bread for five hungry men. I've already got the rum."

Each of Martin's men had been to Jackson's previously, and each was hungry to see the beautiful girl come in again in her tight smock. Able and Dunker Tim were curious to see what Martin's reaction would be this time. Dunker Tim was sitting right beside Martin and was looking in his direction. He saw Martin's short intake of breath when the girl walked in, but it wasn't for the reason he suspected. When Dunker Tim turned to look at this young beautiful girl, his blood boiled in an instant.

Her face was bloated and bruised, her lower lip was split on the left, and her left eye was injured and swollen almost shut. She had been beaten, almost to the point of disfigurement!

There was a stunned silence in the room, as every man watched this young girl, so very beautiful, yet so hideous after this beating. Martin's initial thought was that the pirates had been rough with this girl at the Ocracoke Orgy, only two months earlier. He quickly rejected that thought, however because those bruises were much more recent.

Jackson himself broke the spell, and his ill-advised bonhomie almost got him killed on the spot. "Got to show these niggers who's boss sometimes, or they'll begin to take advantage!" He clearly saw no problem in rough discipline for a slave girl that both served his customers and earned money for him in his whorehouse. He'd apparently overlooked the fact that a slave was one of his customers at that instant, sitting right at the table in front of him.

Martin was seething inside, and was trying to find some response to this horrid man, but just then Dunker Tim pushed his chair back a bit from the table, and Martin suddenly remembered his earlier flash of anger when some man grabbed this whore's bottom on the previous trip. Without thinking, he reached over with his right hand and grabbed the arm of Dunker Tim, to hold him down in the chair. Able Ward had grabbed his other arm at just that moment, so Dunker Tim merely sat back down. His stare alone, was almost deadly, as he looked at Jackson with cold calculating eyes.

Martin's thought was something akin to, "Oh hell!" He recognized that look. He had seen that very stare in the eyes of a bunch of women at Brice's barn many years before. Martin's next thought cut into his mind with crystal clarity; "Unless I get Dunker Tim out of here, Jackson won't live through the night!"

Just then, Martin caught a glimpse of Beatrice. She was behind Jackson, and was looking directly at Dunker Tim, and she seemed to be shaking her head indicating, "No!"

Martin didn't know what that might suggest, but he was sure he was saving

Jackson's sorry life by making Dunker Tim calm down. Martin spoke up before thinking about it. "Dunker Tim. While the boys eat, you and I will check the horses. Come with me!"

Martin stood, and Dunker Tim stood. Able Ward moved his stool back a bit, ready to stand in an instant if need be. For a moment Martin though he might have to man-handle Dunker Tim to get him to leave—a thought he did not relish—but after another harsh stare at Jackson, Dunker Tim turned to the door. He marched out of the tavern toward the barn, with Martin down behind him. Just as they left, they heard a baby begin to cry, and then Jackson's crude shout. "Beatrice, get that damn nigger baby o' yours to shut the hell up!"

It is interesting to consider Dunker Tim's unlikely status among these men, and situations such as this at Jackson's Tavern show that status rather starkly. Dunker Tim was a slave of Captain Brice, but he was clearly a trusted one, who was allowed to navigate the Captain's sloop, carry a firearm, ride alone to distant settlements on errands for the Captain, and fight right beside the white men in the New Bern Militia. The vast majority of slaves even in those early days of the colony were not trusted in any of those ways, and Dunker Tim's status must be considered relatively unique. He is mentioned not only in the diary of John Bender, Martin's son, but also in Martin Bender's own writings, which made their way into that diary, as well as the business papers of Captain Brice himself. Captain Brice paid a high tax for his ownership of Dunker Tim, as a highly skilled slave. By fighting beside these men in battle after battle, Dunker Tim had earned not only their trust, but also their friendship, most of all the friendship of Martin Bender.

However, friends or not, Dunker Tim was still a slave, and had no legal rights to speak of. While indentured servants like Martin could bring a complaint in the courts about mistreatment from their masters, Dunker Tim could not, and certainly Beatrice could not. Even on that very trip, Dunker Tim was fulfilling the role of a slave in one sense. He often stood in for Captain Brice on pirate hunting expeditions such as this, because any gentleman who wished to be excused from his required service to the New Bern Militia need only provide a trusted slave to fight in his stead. That practice, seemingly strange to us today, would continue throughout the long history of slavery in our nation, well into the American Civil War.

Had Dunker Tim raised his hand to a white man, even a contemptible one such as John Berry Jackson, he would have been instantly cut down by those others in the tavern that evening, as merely a rebellious slave. What was worse, even his own compatriots in the New Bern Militia thought slavery was merely an expression of God's world view. In fact, the status of a man, in those years, was believed by most everyone to be fixed and immutable, and clearly such prejudices held many men down in life. While not slaves, the men in that militia group were not aristocrats either. Martin himself was still considered an indentured servant to Johannes and Margaret, since most indentures in those times lasted for nine long years. None of the men in that five man contingent of the New Bern Militia would ever be considered a gentleman, as was Captain Brice, so no matter how well they served the militia or their colony, they would never be in the colonial legislature, or stand for office, even local offices such as the Sheriff of New Bern. Their place in society was fixed forever, but the most limiting status of all was clearly slavery. That fact was starkly clear from the color of the bruises on Beatrice's face.

Such thoughts were far from Dunker Tim's mind that evening. He merely wanted to kill.

Martin's harsh voice caught him in the middle of that thought, just as both entered the barn. "What the hell was that about?"

Dunker Tim did not waste time reflecting on his status as a slave. In that barn, with only the two of them present, he could talk to his friend. He'd earned that right by saving Martin's life in Brice's barn, not to mention several other times on several other battlefields. "Beatrice is my sister, Suh! I can't see her treated this 'a way."

Martin wasn't really shocked by that revelation. He really didn't know much about where Dunker Tim came from or who his family was. He merely stared at his friend, waiting. He wanted to get all of Dunker Tim's anger out.

Dunker Tim continued. "Suh, we's slaves, and I knowd that, but still that girl is my sister and I can't abide watchin' her whored out and beat just 'cause that skin-headed bastard gets into his rum! I'm gone kill him! I'm gone kill him deader than a witch's heart!"

That phrase was clearly unintentional, but an interesting turn of phrase none the less. John Berry Jackson was indeed bald, and was thus a "skin-head" as well as an overt racist and these two meanings were thus paired together that night. From a historical perspective, the use of that term in the papers of Martin Bender seems to have been the first use of the term "skin-head" in history. Why Martin Bender chose to write down the account of this event for his sons on this particular evening becomes clear later.

Just then both men were surprised, as another voice spoke up from the back of the barn. "Ain't the first time!" They both turned to see Gator Jim lurking in the shadow just outside the door. This man could move like a light wind, and one never knew where or when he would appear. He would seemingly materialize out of thin air, such were his stalking skills.

He spit a wad of tobacco juice, and continued. "I recon I get down here more'n you boys from New Bern. Hell, Catfish Lake is only fifteen miles over in the swamp. This girl gets beat right regular! I seed it before, when o'l Jackson gets his drunk on."

Here Gator Jim paused, and spit another wad into the dirt. Then he spoke his mind, like Gator Jim always did. "Recon a man got to do what he got to do, Dunker Tim. Even a nigger slave like you. But if'n you go against a white man when people seed it, you'll hang sure as the sun commin' up in the morning. And Cap'n Brice won't be able to do not a damn thing for ya, neither."

Here Gator Jim paused and seemed to be carefully considering his next words. "Course, if'n there was an accident out in the swamp sometime, when Jackson was huntin', well gator's 'll eat most any pile of shit, even a smelly ol' cur like Jackson." He took a moment and looked both Dunker Tim and then Martin in the eye, then he spit again. He'd said his piece at that point, so he merely turned, and headed back for the tavern.

Martin didn't like where this was heading. "There will be no killing and no accident in the swamp, Dunker Tim. We will think of something else." Both men looked at each other for a time, clearly at an impasse. No other options seemed to present themselves.

Finally, Dunker Tim spoke. "Suh, I can't leave my sister here. I knowed she a nigger slave, but she a woman with a babe, and I can't leave her here!" Dunker Tim paused a bit, as if considering something, and was about to speak when another shadow fell across the open barn door.

Beatrice walked in, holding a baby in her arms when she said, "Dunker Tim! Stop actin' a fool! Does you want to get us both kilt tonight?"

Dunker Tim looked at his sister for a moment. All the pain of all the slaves throughout history seemed to be etched clearly in his face. "Ain't right for no man to lift a hand like that to a woman with a babe, Bea. Even a nigger slave. Ain't right, damn it. Just ain't right!"

Beatrice looked back at him, "Don't go getting' loud now. Don't get yor' temper up! That only cause more trouble!"

Just then, Jackson shouted from the front room of the tavern. "Beatrice, bring more stew for these hungry men! Bea! More stew!" He clearly thought that Beatrice was in the kitchen house and not in the barn.

Beatrice, Martin, and Dunker Tim all stood for just a moment more, looking at each other. Then Beatrice said, "I gots to go now, but don't think no more 'bout doing nothing, you hear, Dunker Tim? I don't want no dead brother, and I don't want no more trouble, You hear!" She looked at Dunker Tim one more time, and decided that he had calmed down a bit. "Don't do nothing now. We'll talk after everyone asleep tonight." She left, and headed back to the house.

Dunker Tim and Martin remained in the barn alone. Neither said anything. Dunker Tim was trying to calm down. Martin was searching for some way out of the impasse, knowing that Dunker Tim would surely kill Jackson if given half a chance. Martin believed that Jackson deserved killing, but killing was wrong. It was the purview of God and not man.

Also, such a killing would lead only to Dunker Tim's hanging, and he could not bare that thought for his friend. He even found himself considering Gator Jim's suggestion about an accident in the swamp. However, he knew that such a thing was wrong by any moral standard, and Martin was nothing, if not a moral man.

They stood in the barn for a while, saying nothing. Neither could come up with any plan that ended well, and both knew that Dunker Tim would eventually have to do something, even if it meant his own death. However, Martin had the feeling that Dunker Tim would honor his sister's request and not commit murder openly, at least not that night. After thirty minutes or so they walked back into the tavern.

### Along the North Bank of the Cape Fear River

Stede Bonnet had his ship, the *Revenge* back under his own control again. He'd been all but a prisoner of Blackbeard for almost four months, but one day, as Blackbeard headed north to careen his ships once again he unexpectedly sent Stede to his own ship, and let him sail away. Within the hour, Stede had discovered the reason for Blackbeard's supposed kindness. The *Revenge* was so laden with barnacles she was slowing down the whole of Blackbeard's Navy. Blackbeard clearly felt he needed neither a poor sailor nor a slow ship to weigh him down, so Stede was allowed to sail away.

That meant Stede had to careen his ship quickly, least he be caught by one of the British frigates that sailed the coastal waters. While the royal ships-of-the-line were kept closer to Europe in case a significant war with France or Spain broke out again, the Royal Navy did send smaller frigates into these waters around the Carolinas. Some of those carried twenty or thirty heavy cannon and could put up quite a fight against almost any pirate ship afloat. Stede didn't want his slow, worm-eaten vessel to be his coffin, so he headed immediately to the Cape Fear to careen her and get her in fighting trim again.

The fates would bring several men together along that North Carolina River, in only a few more days. On the same evening that Martin and Dunker Tim stood in Jackson's barn pondering Beatrice's situation, Stede was sixty miles south of Jackson's Tavern, and his crew was finishing careening and caulking the *Revenge*. In only three or four more days, she'd be refloated, and her cannon restored. Then they could sail the Carolina waters for more prizes!

Eighty miles further south on that same evening, Col. Moore, the leader of Moore's Rifles of the South Carolina Militia, also prepared for battle. Unfortunately, on his last evening ashore, he ate a large mess of shrimp, a delicacy that he dearly loved. However several shrimp in that meal carried an unusually high bacteria count and within only six hours the good Colonel tasted his shrimp for the second time, as they traveled this time in the opposite direction in his digestive system. The shrimp were not nearly as tasty on that run though as they had been before, and after he tossed almost all of his dinner, the Colonel determined that he could not lead the expedition on the morrow. Like most of the other pirate hunting trips, he figured this expedition would probably arrive too late to find any of the brethren anyway, so he sent for his second-in-command and ordered him to take the lead on this foray to the Cape Fear.

For that reason, Col. William Rhett commanded this particular expedition to catch pirates. The next morning, he sailed in two sloops, the *Henry* and the *Sea Nymph*, out of Charleston Harbor, along with a hundred and thirty men, including the ships' compliment of sailors and sixty men of the Moore's Rifles Brigade aboard. Col. Rhett knew that a small contingent of the New Bern Militia was coming to assist him using an overland trail down from Jackson's Tavern. He really didn't expect much assistance from that quarter, since everyone knew that Governor Eden profited mightily from the pirates and would not be highly motivated to catch them. Still, Col. Rhett didn't worry much about that, since he didn't feel he would require much help. Each of his sloops carried eight cannon, and thirty of the world's best riflemen. If he did meet with the New Bern Militia, he planned to keep them well away from the battle.

As the evening at Jackson's Tavern turned out, neither Dunker Tim nor Martin got to speak with Beatrice again. When they went back into the tavern, Jackson and Beatrice had both disappeared, leaving several other slaves to serve the remaining men and clean up. After an hour or so, Martin made a point of bedding down on the tavern floor right beside Dunker Tim, just to make sure that he behaved himself. The next morning, Martin rousted his men well before any of them expected him too, and the New Bern Militia was up and on the trail before dawn with nothing to eat at all.

After they had been riding for only a few minutes, Martin rode up to the front of the line beside Dunker Tim, who seemed to be still seething. Before Martin could speak, Dunker Tim said, "Suh, I got bi'ness at that tavern when we comes back through. Now you knowd I do, and I don't want nobody in my way, when we comes back this way!"

Martin wanted to acknowledge that statement, but could think of no real response. He merely said. "Keep your mind on the fightin' ahead. It'll be rough. I'm glad to have you at my side again." They rode in silence, side by side for a few moments, both thinking about the numerous times they'd fought together.

Each was a warrior, honed in the skill of killing at that point, and while they were confident in their own skills, they felt stronger fighting together, because they each knew that they could depend on each other completely. Finally, Martin spoke. "I just sent Gator Jim and Able back to the tavern to fetch us some reinforcements. You leave him alone when he gets here!"

Dunker Tim merely said, "Suh?" He didn't have a clue what Martin was talking about, until an hour or so later, when three riders caught up with the others along the trail. Gator Jim and Able Ward were riding along as if nothing strange had happened, but Able led another horse by the reins. Atop that mount, sat John Berry Jackson all wrapped up in rope, with a very black left eye, and a knot the size of a small egg on his forehead. His hands and arms were tied about him and he couldn't even carry his reins. He had a rope firmly placed, gaggin' his mouth, and it was tied so tight he could only make gurgling noises, which was just fine with Martin since Martin really didn't want to hear what he had to say anyway.

As they rode up, Martin stopped and turned in his saddle. Then he stated in a solemn voice, "As commander of the New Bern Militia on this expedition, I have decided that we need an experienced guide to the Cape Fear. I have therefore ordered you to place yourself at the service of the New Bern Militia. You will guide us, either willing or unwilling."

In those days, with the Tuscarora War only a few years past, any militia commander could conscript anything or anyone he wanted in the North Carolina Colony, and while rare, forced conscriptions were not unheard of in those times. Typically this was done by an officer, but Martin was indeed serving in just that function on this expedition.

Martin continued in his formal statement. "Gator Jim will escort you and see to your needs and you will serve as my guide. You will obey all my orders on this expedition, and then we shall return you to your home and pay you for your services." Then Martin turned to Gator Jim and said, "Remove his gag, please, and if he behaves himself, untie him."

As soon as the gag was taken out of his mouth, John Berry Jackson did anything but behave himself. He let out a string of curses that would have made Col. Moore proud, and those curses of Col. Moore were now legend!

Martin listened for less than ten seconds, and with no let up in sight, he merely said, "Gag that son-of-a-bitch again!"

Gator Jim actually smiled as he tightened the gag once again, and whispered to Jackson as he did so, "Now, now. Ain't yo' Mama ever tell you not to talk like that?" He tightened the gag enough to shut up Jackson, such that if Jackson uttered more than a low moan, his lips and mouth would be cut by the ropes.

Dunker Tim smiled to himself, as he heard the cussing stop. He would be killing Jackson soon, and virtually every man in the New Bern Militia on the trail that day knew it. As it turns out, they were all wrong. Still, if any of the other men in that group thought that conscripting someone to guide them down a clear trail that most of them had traveled several times before was rather strange, they kept it to themselves.

### Pirate Battle on the Cape Fear

It was getting on toward evening on a cold autumn day, and the wind was high for the autumn, running from the west at almost twenty knots. Stede's ship, the *Revenge* had been refloated only that morning. His pirate crew of forty seven sailors was restoring the cannon, and had two mounted on the starboard and three on the port side. They had many more to mount, and were busy with their work almost four miles upriver from the mouth of the Cape Fear. In those waters, the banks of the river were still sandy or muddy, much like the other salt-water marshes along that coast. During most of the careening process ships were laid on their sides, so the masts were almost parallel to the ground, and they were well hidden in the marshes. However, the *Revenge* was now upright, and masts of sailing ships could be seen for miles over the low salt flats.

Just as evening came, the tide went out, leaving the *Revenge* again sitting on the bottom, and slanted at a twenty degree angle, as she came to rest with the new weight of the cannon aboard. It was at that moment, that the masts of Rhett's two sloops were spotted some distance away across the salt marshes. Rhett did not attempt to make it upriver against the tide, but he decided to prepare for a battle the next day. He knew he had a pirate in his sights; why would a merchant ship careen so far from anything or anyone? He thought at the time, that it might be Charles Vane, but any pirate would do. The whole of Charleston still seethed at the thought of being held hostage by Blackbeard, and any of the brethren captured would be held accountable for that humiliation, whether they had been with Blackbeard for that siege or not! Rhett and his men worked hard that night as they cleared their gun decks for action.

The tide would turn at midnight but no one wanted a night battle since none could navigate the dangerous, sandy shoals of the Cape Fear at night. The fight would take place on the high tide the next morning. Stede Bonnet and his pirate crew, like Col. Rhett and his men, spent the evening clearing the decks, restoring more cannon, and preparing for battle. Stede would try to force his way quickly past the two armed sloops and out into the Atlantic where his newly cleaned hull should allow him to outrun Rhett's ships.

With the tide rising around nine the next morning, the *Revenge* floated once again, and the pirates had managed to mount two more cannon on each side.

They had planted one swivel gun on the quarter deck, and ignoring the three inch guns still stacked on shore, they chose to mount more six inch cannon. The *Revenge* was now armed with four six-inch guns on the starboard, and five on the port side; that would have to do. Stede had told his men they would abandon any cannon still left on shore, when the tide was right in the morning.

Col. Rhett looked toward the pirate mast that was still a mile or so away, just in time to see the sails run up, so he hoisted anchor, and moved up the Cape Fear to greet the *Revenge* as she came out. Stede and his pirates proudly hoisted their Jolly Roger, but every sailor on that ship understood that they faced an interesting problem. They had the wind behind them and could make good headway, but the turns in the river channel prevented them from taking full advantage of the wind. Also, they were sailing toward the ocean, but against an incoming tide which slowed their progress. Col. Rhett had the opposite problems. He sailed with the tide but had to tack against the winds in a fairly narrow channel. Also, his goal was to keep Stede bottled up in the river, so he had to maneuver his ships to assure that Stede did not merely sail on past him.

As Rhett's two smaller ships approached within a half-mile of the *Revenge*, he chose to tack into the wind, loose headway, and turn to run in the same direction as Stede. By the time they finished that tack, each could bring their guns to bare on the pirate ship, and each opened with their port side battery. They sailed in the middle of the channel and hoped to run Stede aground on the sandy northern bank of the river. Stede knew this, as did every pirate on the *Revenge*, so he steered, as best he could toward the middle of the river, putting himself ever closer to his enemy.

It must have been a sight to see; a pirate battle; ship to ship fighting right on the Cape Fear! Two sloops under commission of the governor of the South Carolina Colony, fired on a larger pirate ship in the salt-marsh mouth of the river. The sloops each had their four port cannon engaged, and all of those were on the deck, but the *Revenge* was much larger, and had two guns mounted on the top deck and two on the lower, or 'tween deck. All twelve of those cannon cooked off every thirty seconds or so, and with little wave action in the mouth of the river, and the enemy ships in such close proximity, each shot tore large holes in the opposing vessels. Within only fifteen minutes, each hull facing the enemy cannon held numerous holes from cannon balls, and occasionally after penetrating the wooden hull, a six-inch shot would take off a man's head, or remove an arm or leg on the deck. Blood, gun smoke, and splinters flew everywhere on the decks and the inside of the ships. At some point, during this thirty minute running battle, the tide changed, but no one noticed amid the cannon firing. One of the members of Moore's Rifles, on the *Sea Nymph* was heard in either a shouted curse or heartfelt prayer, "Oh God, let me get one good shot with me rifle before they make a Swiss cheese of our ship!"

The battle went on for almost a mile, but then a shudder was felt in the hull of the *Revenge*, as she grounded on one of the many sandy shoals that complicate shipping in every river mouth in the world. Cheers broke out on the *Sea Nymph*, as she sailed on by and swiftly racked the *Revenge* with her port side cannon. Thirty members of Moore's Rifles had mounted the deck and were firing at any pirate stupid enough to show his head above the gunwales of the *Revenge*. Pirates who were not manning cannon, fired back, killing a number of the South Carolina Militia on the deck of the *Sea Nymph*.

While both the *Sea Nymph* and the *Henry* mounted only four inch guns, that size cannon ball still tore a respectable hole in the *Revenge* as each shot found its target. Men lay dead and dismembered on all three ships at that point, but no one had any time to find the corpses and toss them over the side in the running battle. With the *Sea Nymph* now past the *Revenge*, the captain of the *Henry* attempted to sail past the *Revenge*, which was now solidly grounded, and rake the pirate ship with her cannon. However, she had not sailed in exactly the same course as the *Sea Nymph*, and within a minute she was well grounded also, only eighty feet from the starboard side of the *Revenge!* Further, as those two ships grounded, each careened in the same direction, leaning to the port side, which was quite unfortunate for the crew of the *Henry*. While a twenty degree slant to port had the effect of hiding the entire deck of the pirate ship from the gunners on the *Henry*, the *Henry* leaned in the same direction, which had the effect of completely exposing her deck to the gunfire from the pirate ship!

Under those conditions, the remaining members of Moore's Rifles quickly recognized that the exposed deck was no place they wanted to be, so they retreated down the gangway of the *Henry* to the hold below. From there, a few could fire through the several portholes but they were firing upward and were not terribly effective. Meanwhile the *Sea Nymph* had turned to sail back upriver toward the action, but managed to ground herself on the opposite shore of the river, and she was out of the battle completely, at least for the time being.

The *Revenge* and the *Henry* continued to fire on each other with their cannon, and the hulls of each ship now appeared to be more hole than planking! Neither could do anything but wait out the five hour tide, and then see if there was enough lumber still nailed together to float! The pirates, in particular were feeling feisty, and shouted invitations to the militia to "Come up on deck and join the party!" The *Henry* would answer each taunt with either a cannon shot or some shouted curses of their own, and after a while each side began to conserve its powder and cannon balls.

The situation could have remained like that for the entire tide, but at just that moment, Martin Bender was ashore just abeam the *Revenge*, looking up in total

# Battle of The Cape Fear River

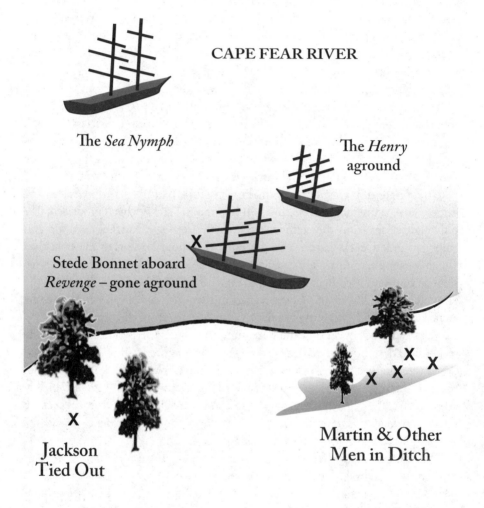

CAPE FEAR RIVER

The *Sea Nymph*

The *Henry* aground

Stede Bonnet aboard
*Revenge* – gone aground

Jackson
Tied Out

Martin & Other
Men in Ditch

disbelief at a large pirate ship obviously grounded only fifty feet from the tree he hid behind. What was even more unbelievable, the deck leaned in his direction, exposing every single pirate—it looked like it was forty men or more—to direct fire from his position!

Martin had left his men about a quarter mile down the trail, and walked forward with Dunker Tim, to look things over. He didn't want Dunker Tim out of his sight while Jackson rode along with the group all tied up and gagged. None of the men in his five man unit would have lifted a finger to save Jackson, had Dunker Tim merely pointed his single shot pistol at Jackson's head and pulled the trigger. Still, Martin didn't want that, and he had to make sure that Dunker Tim's head was in the right place. When you go into battle, you really should focus on that and nothing else.

Martin said, "Dunker Tim. Are you seeing this?"

"Looks like we's got mo' targets than we's got guns," Dunker Tim said. "Course oncet we shoot, they be shootin' back right quick, and they's ten of them to every one o' us!"

Martin continued to voice his thoughts. "With the deck slanted like that, they can't bring their cannon to bare on us. We'll have a load of muskets pointing our way though!"

Martin and Dunker Tim both knew they would have to bring fire on the pirate ship, and neither relished that possibility. Then Martin came up with an idea. "When they do realize we're over here, it would sure be nice if they were shooting at something else. We need to give them a target! Something else to worry about."

Dunker Tim though he knew what Martin was suggesting. "I'd like to volunteer for that, Suh! Yes I would! I'd like to pick the man to come with me though, if'n you would allow it!"

Martin knew he and Dunker Tim had the same thought, though neither spoke it out loud; never kill a man yourself, when pirates are around to do it for you!

Instead Martin said, "I want you and Jackson to find a position behind these trees and wait for ten minutes. Then you two bring fire on the pirates. I'll take the rest of the men over to the right about a hundred yards, and lay up in that ditch we rode past. Once we hear you open up, and after you draw their fire, we'll open up."

Martin was, first and foremost a German Anabaptist, and even as he spoke, he was becoming more uneasy with his thoughts about what he and Dunker Tim were about to do. God was man's judge and Martin had no right to place Jackson in Dunker Tim's hands. Still he did need a distraction or all of his men would be dead, so all he did was look at his friend, and say. "Keep your damn head down. If you get into trouble, we won't even be able to see you from that ditch!"

Within a minute, Dunker Tim held the reins of Jackson's horse, and merely said, "Now come along with me Mr. Jackson, Suh. We got a mission for a brave man. We's gon' draw their fire!" He led the horse away down the trail, as Martin, Able Ward, Gator Jim, and Willie Koonce dismounted. Those four men lay about ten feet apart, in a shallow depression in the ground, and laid their weapons beside them. Beside those four men, twenty two rifles, muskets, and pistols were loaded, cocked, and ready for firing. Each of these men, by that point, recognized the wisdom of carrying multiple firearms. They waited only a couple of minutes, watching the terribly exposed pirates all the while.

Dunker Tim meanwhile, took Jackson back to the tree, and without saying anything further, he knocked him off his horse, and tossed several more ropes around him, including one around his neck. These ropes were tied to various trees and stumps, carefully making sure that Jackson couldn't move, and that his torso was mostly exposed to fire from the ship. With one rope around his neck held tight to a high tree branch, Jackson could not even duck behind the tree in front of him without hanging himself. With the pirates looking the other way and firing at the men on the *Henry*, none saw either Dunker Tim's movements, or the man all done up in ropes, tied out to their rear. When he was finished Dunker Tim unloaded his oldest musket and carefully tied it to Jackson's arm. Jackson had so much rope on him he looked like a man caught in a giant spider web.

Then Dunker Tim leaned in to Jackson, and said. "Don't make no noise now, Mr. Jackson!" With that Dunker Tim ripped the gag out of Jackson's mouth, and Jackson immediately began to curse loudly. However, with the ongoing shipboard rifle and cannon fire, those curses did not immediately draw attention, so Dunker Tim carefully hid behind a tree about fifteen feet from Jackson, took aim, and plugged one pirate on the *Revenge* squarely in the back. He didn't watch to see what happened however; he was running like hell to get away from Jackson.

With that shot only fifty feet behind them, the pirates could not help but notice, and just as they turned to the new threat, four Kentucky rifles opened up, and four pirates fell dead. Before the pirates even had a chance to consider that those shots had come from a slightly different direction than the first one, three more rifles fired from the ditch and several more pirates fell.

Stede himself was on the slanted quarterdeck of his ship, and he shouted the obvious though irrelevant question, "Where in hell did they come from?"

Just then Dunker Tim dropped into the ditch beside Martin, lifted his rifle and fired on the ship, and then the whole ditch seemed to explode!

Martin then shouted a question that was very similar to Stede's. "Where the hell did that come from?"

A pirate on the *Revenge* had loaded a swivel cannon up on deck and fired it at them. While Martin was correct that the *Revenge* could not bring her heavy cannon to bare on his men ashore, the swivel cannon was light enough to be instantly portable, and could turn in any direction. The second shot of that swivel cannon tore one of Martin's men ashore completely apart, but that pirate never realized that he had done Dunker Tim's dirty work for him. The third shot however, was again fired at Martin and the men shooting from the ditch, and Martin was terrified.

He had sinned mightily, and he was certain he was now feeling God's wrath for his sin in killing Jackson so blatantly. He shouted his guilt to Dunker Tim, who lay beside him. "We have overtaken God's punitive work. We have sinned against God! We are being punished, and there is nothing we can we do!"

As if to prove that assessment correct, another shot from the swivel cannon tore into the ditch, and wounded almost every man there. Martin caught a pellet in his shoulder but for some reason it did not penetrate deep. Gator Jim and Able were hit, leaving flesh wounds in their legs. Willie Koonce was wounded the worst, catching a ball in his arm that broke his bone, and then entered his chest. Still, he was tough, and didn't whimper one bit. He was sixteen years old that day, and had been fighting with the New Bern Militia since he was ten.

Dunker Tim saw the inevitable clearly. "Saints or sinners Suh', makes no damn difference! We facin' pirate cannon, and all of us gonna' die in this hea' ditch!"

Just then a blast from all four cannon of the *Henry* attracted the attention of the pirates, and they refocused in that direction. To a man, those pirates became instantly terrified. The *Henry* was righting itself in the changed current and would soon refloat, giving her a great advantage over the heavier, much larger *Revenge*. A quick glace down river showed that the *Sea Nymph* was already under sail and bearing down on the *Revenge* with fresh guns and fresh gun crews!

All of the men in the battle, from those beside Martin in the ditch across the water to Col. Rhett on board the *Henry*, heard Stede try to coax his men to greater strength and courage, but pirates tend to be a superstitious lot and they believed that their luck was clearly running out. Two enemy ships would soon be sailing under their own power, while the *Revenge* was still grounded, and the pirates were receiving fire from all sides. Within less than a minute, Stede found himself tied to his own mast, as his Jolly Roger came down and a white surrender flag was raised.

## A Hero's Death

Col. Rhett stood on the shore, and looked down at the corpse, or more accurately what was left of the corpse. "Surely this was the bravest man I have ever heard of, volunteering to draw cannon fire! I wish I had known the man!"

Martin and Gator Jim stood by silently, and neither could bring themselves to say anything. Able Ward however, was never one to keep his mouth shut in any situation, so he spoke right up. "He was a brave one indeed sir. Please to report that to your superiors in Charleston, if that'd be your choist. It would help us get recognition for this man's bravery, in the face of those pirate cannon! Awful cannon they was too!"

"I will indeed, my good sir." Col. Rhett said. "I will indeed. Jackson, did you say?"

Able replied, "Yes Sir. John Berry Jackson it was, owned a tavern only two days up the trail. A fine, hard workin' man what never turned a stranger away! Never was a braver man what fought with the New Bern Militia."

Martin thought Able was laying it on a bit thick, but what could he do? He'd not seen the many ropes that suspended Jackson's body for all the world to see! For all he knew, based on what he had actually witnessed, Jackson had died a glorious death drawing fire away from his comrades in battle. Dunker Tim had had the presence of mind to remove all of the ropes before Col. Rhett even got ashore. In fact, after the surrender flag was raised, the Colonel was much more concerned with the pirates than with this small band of New Bern Militia.

Col. Rhett spoke again. "Indeed I will report this man's bravery, as well as the assistance of the New Bern Militia in capturing this cutthroat band. South Carolina offers thanks to each of you gentlemen, and your names, and that of Sergeant Bender as your commander, will be mentioned in the dispatch I send to Charleston. So will Mr. Jackson here. Indeed his bravery will be mentioned prominently!"

As Col. Rhett headed back to his sloops, both of which amazingly could still sail, he left five men of the New Bern Militia alone, four of them wounded, to bury their comrade. He would have been shocked to hear the final word over the body of this man Jackson. Martin was still feeling guilty, and said nothing. Dunker Tim spit his tobacco chew on the remains of the torso, since after the cannon fire not much else was left. Gator Jim, who was usually quite quiet, ended up speaking the final epitaph over the body of John Berry Jackson. "They's near' as many gators here as Catfish Lake. They'll eat well tonight, I recon."

As Col. Rhett sailed away in his two sloops and his prize, the *Revenge*, the five men of the New Bern Militia mounted their horses for the ride back north. Jackson's body was left on the north bank of the Cape Fear, and was indeed drug off and eaten that night by the alligators of the Cape Fear, and rightly so! No sorrier man has ever lived or died anywhere in the Carolinas!

{Author's Note: Col. Rhett's subsequent report was actually printed in one of the Charleston papers, proving that no wise man ever trusts what he reads in a newspaper, no matter how reputable the paper may seem to be. It seems that several months later Martin Bender acquired a copy, which forced Martin to write a more accurate version of these events. Both that newspaper and Martin's written version of this story are available in the family records. Those dingy acidic sheets of paper were found, barely legible, in the final case of documents opened three centuries later, having been stored in the closet of Mildred Bender for over fifty years. These documents have become one of the foundations of the family legacy, for reasons which will soon become clear.}

Two immediate things resulted from that newspaper article however. First, a move quickly gained momentum in the North Carolina Colony to honor Jackson for his heroism against the pirates in some fashion. As a result, the town at the headwaters of the New River bares his name to this day, Jacksonville, North Carolina. That name and that town are famous worldwide, since two hundred years later in the early years of World War II, Jacksonville became the location for the largest single Marine base in the world, Camp Lejune. Both Jesus and I trained there prior to our days in South Vietnam, more years ago that I care to count.

Second, a low ranked Naval Commander, Lt. Maynard, who served on a British man-of-war in Hamptons Roads, Virginia, apparently read that paper. He noted the name of another low ranking commander, Sergeant Bender of the New Bern Militia. Lt. Maynard figured that this man Bender did indeed fight pirates, when the governor of the North Carolina Colony would merely take bribes from them. If he ever needed to, Lt. Maynard guessed that he'd found one North Carolinian that he could trust to help him catch pirates. That tidbit of data would come in handy in only a few months.

A second news article was located among the family records, apparently saved by Martin Bender. He wrote no notes related that that article. The news item dealt with an execution. On November 8, 1718, twenty eight pirates from Stede Bonnet's crew were hanged in Charleston, and by special order of the court as a warning to other pirates, their bodies were left aloft and swinging in the lazy sea breezes for five days. Charleston was indeed finding her revenge against the brethren of the seas! This singular event still holds the record as the largest mass execution in American history. A month later, on December 10 in that same year, Stede Bonnet himself was strung up in Charleston. All were eventually buried below the high water mark, so that sea creatures could digest their flesh and eat their bones.

Before the New Bern Militia left the Cape Fear region, Martin deposited Willie Koonce at a farmer's cabin only five miles inland from the scene of the battle to allow him to recover from his wounds. He paid the farmer to tend Koonce, and promised more funds from the New Bern treasury for Willie's upkeep. Koonce would stay at that cabin for two months, recovering completely, and then he eventually rejoined his mother again at their farm in Trent Mill.

As soon as that was taken care of, Gator Jim said, "I believe I'll go hunting." With no good bye and no further preamble, he headed off into the swamps near Catfish Lake. He never rode with the militia again, but the next time Martin saw him in Mallard's Tavern, he made sure that Gator Jim received his pay for his service. Those two hunted together for several more decades.

Thus, on that particular ride, only Martin, Dunker Tim, and Able Ward headed back north again toward Jackson's Tavern. Each had been thinking about what to do with Beatrice and her baby at Jackson's Tavern. They knew that Jackson had no real kin to speak off. When he wanted a woman, he merely took his pleasure from one of his several slaves. Based on that, no one was expecting any real trouble with Jackson's death, since nobody really cared if the man lived or died, and of course, that ultimately says something about who this horrid man truly was.

Able and Martin discussed various possibilities, clearly planning to tell Sheriff DuVal the story of Jackson's heroic demise.

Dunker Tim merely said, "Do what you need to do, Sergeant, Suh, but I believe Beatrice and her baby be coming wid' me!" Knowing that this man, Dunker Tim, had probably arranged to have John Berry Jackson blown into tiny pieces of human sausage by a pirate's cannon, neither Able nor Martin had any real desire to argue with his position on that matter!

"I guess the county 'll get ownership of the tavern and the other two nigger slaves," Able said. "There'll be a sheriff's court, I recon."

Martin had been contemplating that very thought for some time, and he still felt guilty about the manner of Jackson's death. He was sure Dunker Tim had done something to assure that death, but he had been wise enough not to ask and he'd already prayed for forgiveness several times. Then he realized that only three of them would be riding back into New Bern from his original five, and he thought he'd come up with a solution that would prohibit too many questions at a Sheriff's court to determine property ownership. He turned to his companions, and said, "Able, I think you look like Jackson a bit! In fact, you may be cousins!"

Able didn't think much more of Jackson that Dunker Tim did and he was about to get angry, until Dunker Tim grinned, and then joined Martin in his assessment. "Yes, Suh! I could 'a tol' ya myself! Able Ward is surly a cousin of ol' John Berry Jackson! Yes, suh!"

Able looked at Martin and said, "Uh? What the hell do you mean, cousins? I ain't kin o' that filthy cur, nor any other sorry son-of-a-bitch in these parts!"

Martin merely grinned and said, "Yes, you are! I'm sure of it! You two are definitely cousins, on your mama's side! That makes the tavern your problem, don't it?"

Able said, "What the hell?"

Dunker Tim grinned, and said, "Yes Suh! He is definite yo' cousin, and you gots to deal with the tavern and them other two slaves. In fac' you may owns 'um!"

Able, again repeated himself, "What the hell?"

With no relatives in the area, and few settlers near Jackson's Tavern to ask any questions, Jackson's death didn't attract much local attention. When these three arrived at Jackson's Tavern later that same day they told Beatrice to pack her few clothes. She and her baby would be moving up the road to New Bern. They also informed the other two slaves that they now belonged to Able Ward, as did the tavern itself. With a sworn statement of Sergeant Bender that Able Ward was, in fact, a first cousin of John Berry Jackson, the tavern and Jackson's two slaves became Able's property within a week of their return to New Bern. All of this was legally documented in a Sheriff's Court that served as the probate court of those days.

Able never even went back to New Bern on that return trip, but stayed at the tavern to begin his management that very day. He managed that tavern in the growing settlement of Jacksonville for three more decades until his death. He maintained the name, Jackson's Tavern, throughout that period in honor of the local hero, and often told of Jackson's bravery in facing Stede Bonnet's pirate cannon along the Cape Fear to draw fire away from his comrades!

That arrangement still left one big problem, Beatrice and her baby. Dealing with their status was a bit more delicate since Dunker Tim, a slave himself, clearly could not assume ownership of a mother slave and her baby. Martin had Able write out a bill of sale for one female tavern slave and her baby, but he left the buyer blank, thinking maybe he could talk Captain Brice, or maybe even Johannes into a slave once he arrived in New Bern.

Those three, Martin, Dunker Tim, and Beatrice rode north out of Jackson's Tavern, on towards New Bern. Beatrice, holding her baby, rode one of the mules from the tavern in front of the two men, allowing them to ride side by side to discuss the matter.

"Suh. I believe you should owns'um!" Dunker Tim expressed his opinion. "No slave woman can be free and get along, and leaving 'um here ain't right. No baby boy should know his ma is a tavern whore! It ain't right! You should owns 'um, fair and square!"

Martin could see some logic in that thought, but he did not own slaves and did not aspire to do so. Most of the original Germans living in New Bern itself had not acquired slaves at that point. Historians have often questioned that fact. Was it a result of their Anabaptist beliefs, or merely because they were hand-picked as tradesmen rather than farmers or plantation owners that they were slow to acquire slaves? At any rate, Martin had no intention of taking on slaves, though he did recall that Johannes had discussed it at one time in order to get some help in the cooper's shed.

Martin said, "I have no farm on which to work any slaves." He thought a bit longer on the matter, and then continued. "Katheryn and I have no real land in New Bern itself to build any slave cabins, and I don't think Beatrice would be of use in the cooper's shed or out in the wilderness felling old-growth oaks."

The two rode along for a mile or so, not speaking. Then Martin said, "I think we should discuss this with Captain Brice and seek his help."

Dunker Tim, reflected on that a moment, as he rode beside Martin. "We could tell the Captain, that you bought 'um from Jackson at the tavern before he went with us to the Cape Fear. That way maybe you could sell 'um to him. He ain't bad to none of his slaves, unless one gets a hankerin' to run!"

It was at that point that Beatrice spoke for the first time, and her words changed Martin's life. "You don' wana sell me and this baby to nobody else, Mr. Martin."

Dunker Tim quickly interrupted his sister. "Don't go spouting off your mouth, now Beatrice! Now don't do dat!"

Beatrice had stopped her mule and turned him in the trail to block the two behind her. They pulled up short as both men stared at Beatrice. She looked at Dunker Tim, and said. "He oughts to know! He's a right to know!"

Martin watched this exchange while getting a sinking feeling in his chest, just like when the governor had told him his ma was dead on the shores of New Bern those many years before. Sometimes a single statement can change a man's life, and some men like Martin, have an uncanny ability to tell just before that type of statement is uttered.

Beatrice then looked at Martin, and in a quiet voice, she said, "Dis baby of mine, he yor' baby, Mr. Martin. You don' wana sell your own chil' away, do ya?" After a moment, she pulled the head of her mule around, and added one final word. "His name Burdine." She then started on to the north toward New Bern. Without another word, Martin and Dunker Tim followed along down the trail.

## *Blackbeard Tries the Straight and Narrow*

Blackbeard, by the autumn of 1719, had lived the life of the brethren for eight long years and he grew tired of that life. He thought he might settle down, and he knew of the King of England's promise of pardon to all pirates who took an oath to commit no more crime. He had decided to take the king up on that kind offer.

At that point, in 1719 Blackbeard still had a wife in Bath, and if truth be known in several ports in the Caribbean as well. Given his wealth, and his choices of homes and wives, he could have gone most anywhere, and it says much about the "protection" he received in the Carolina Colony that he chose Bath. He wanted to take the oath and receive his pardon from Governor Eden of North Carolina Colony, so he headed his massive fleet toward those waters without telling anyone of his intentions.

However, he was somewhat troubled in one particular. Piracy had never offered a retirement plan, and severance packages were unheard of, so Teach was greatly concerned about his lifelong comfort. Clearly Blackbeard's Navy, four ships filled with pirates who expected their share of the loot, was an impediment to his pending retirement. Such a division of wealth would not leave much for Blackbeard himself. As they sailed to the north, he thought and thought and after much reflection, he came up with a way to steal most of the booty rightfully belonging to his shipmates, at least the riches belonging to a couple hundred or so. To put his plan into action, he first announced to his several crews that Blackbeard's Navy would sail to New Bern, and hold that town hostage just as it had Charleston the previous year! He then indicated that he would steer into the nearest inlet, Beaufort Inlet, careen his ships for safety sake, and then make for New Bern. His men all cheered that decision and happily followed this cagy pirate to their own doom.

However, when Blackbeard steered into the inlet itself, he sailed a bit too much to starboard, and ran the *Queen* hard aground on the dangerous shoals. Because he'd come in at high tide and carried too much speed into the inlet, there was little hope of refloating her on her own. His third Captain, Israel Hands, sought to get his sloop, the *Anne* close enough to use her sail, along with Blackbeard's to refloat the *Queen*. Unfortunately, within only fifteen minutes of that maneuver, Hands had run the *Anne* aground also. If any of the other pirates found it strange that two of the most accomplished sailors in the world had made such mistakes, they didn't mention it at the time.

Of course, the pirates cursed a great deal, and then set out longboats with oars to pull against the *Queen*. They even set out ground anchors to use with the ship's winches to "rope" the *Queen* from the bottom, all to no avail. They were all pretty sure that the smaller *Anne* would refloat at the high point of the next tide, but the mighty *Queen Anne's Revenge* seemed stuck for good in the muddy, sandy bottom of Beaufort Inlet.

Of course, all of this was merely theater staged for the benefit of two hundred and sixty vicious cutthroats. Blackbeard had let Israel Hands, the Claw, Black Jambo, and several others in on his plans to steal the loot from the rest of the men. He'd instructed Hands to run the *Anne* aground in an effort to help him. Over the previous two days, all three of them had talked to other pirates, those that had been with them the longest, about the plan. Blackbeard figured he'd keep the other two ships of his Navy with him, the *Adventure* and the *Trent,* and he needed only forty men or so to sail those!

When all had seen that the *Queen* was aground to stay, Blackbeard put the final stages of his plan into effect. He ordered many of the men to build a barricade, sort of an "earthworks fort" on the nearby shore, since they would have to wait for a combination of heavy rain and high tide to refloat the *Queen.* Meanwhile other pirates were ordered to load all the loot in her hold aboard the *Adventure* and the *Trent.* Perhaps some of those men noticed that the richest items in that treasure were loaded on board the *Adventure,* while lesser items were loaded on the *Trent,* but again, none mentioned it or raised any question. Through careful orders and timing, there came a point where most of the pirates were ashore working on the fort, or aboard the two stranded ships, leaving only the forty trusted men aboard either the *Adventure* or the *Trent.* Blackbeard didn't even have to give the order. He merely smiled at the Claw who commanded the *Trent,* and both the *Trent* and the *Adventure* hoisted sail and headed for the open sea.

The pirates on shore and on the grounded ships, some two-hundred and forty eight of them, had little option but to disappear into the hinterlands of the Carolinas. Curse though they might, they could do nothing against Blackbeard as he calmly sailed into the open ocean, and they certainly didn't want to stay near two grounded pirate vessels, least they be captured and hung! They headed inland en mass, and disappeared. Many eventually sailed again as legitimate seamen, while others took jobs all along the Carolina coast. Some eventually acquired farms anywhere from the Albemarle down to the Cape Fear, and a few rose to prominence in one Carolina community or another. They all chose to avoid Bath, since they had walked those streets many times with Blackbeard himself, but with that one exception, virtually every town, tavern, and settlement in the colony acquired one or two new residents from this mass migration of pirates. To repeat the common theme, "Scratch a Carolinian, find a pirate!"

{Author's Note: The *Queen Anne's Revenge* was never refloated from that grounding, and the remains of that mighty ship rest two miles south of Beaufort

Inlet today less than a mile off the coast of the Carolinas. After much searching, an archeological team located the wreck in 1996, and has been bringing up artifacts since that time. Many of these are viewable by the public in a museum in Beaufort, North Carolina. The wreck site itself is now protected by law. Over twenty seven cannon have been identified at that site, proving this was, indeed, a mighty pirate ship, and evidence has confirmed it was the *Queen Anne's Revenge.* It is one of only two wrecks of known pirate ships that have ever been found.}

Neither Hands nor Blackbeard wanted the *Trent* recognized in the waters around the Carolinas, so Blackbeard ordered Israel Hands to take a small crew and sail the *Trent* all the way to New Port in the New England colonies, and to toss most of his cannon into the ocean prior to arrival. Hands then sold that ship to a shady businessman who was looking for a good size ship to run untaxed cargo along the coastal routes in the northern colonies.

Blackbeard himself, along with most of his band boldly sailed the *Adventure* into Bath and requested the King's Pardon from Governor Eden. With a healthy payoff to the governor and his secretary, Tobias Knight, the pardon was quickly granted. The remaining goods were then sold and the funds divided among the men, with Blackbeard and the Claw claiming the shares for Israel Hands and the small crew that was soon expected to return from New Port. When they did, they too were paid off, and they also accepted the King's Pardon. For a while some of these men lived in Bath, but over the next few years most scattered into the hinterlands of the Carolinas or Virginia, again contributing pirate genes to the Carolina colony. Blackbeard, now using the name of Teach, kept the *Adventure* for "trading in the West Indies" and everyone, including the governor ignored the fact that that sloop was armed with eight guns.

## No Forgiveness

As Martin rode along in silence that day behind Beatrice and beside Dunker Tim, he struggled to come to grips with Beatrice's newly revealed secret. He had already said several silent prayers to God, asking again for forgiveness, as well as for guidance. He could not see what to do, and New Bern was getting closer with every hour. Then as he reflected on the whole matter, he suddenly realized something so he turned to Dunker Tim. He didn't even raise his voice, though his anger knew no bounds at that moment, as he sought to verify his suspicions. His voice cut into the afternoon ride; "You arranged that evening in the tavern with Beatrice!"

At first Dunker Tim didn't respond, so Martin repeated himself, his voice getting louder. "You arranged that evening in the tavern. That is why Beatrice spent the evening with me!"

Dunker Tim rode on in silence.

"Answer me, damn you!" Martin had sworn, one of the few times in his life.

Dunker Tim took a deep breath, looked directly at Martin and responded, as they rode along. "You my Sergeant and you my friend. Least I hopes you is. But I had to do somp'in." Dunker Tim took another breath and continued. "I paid for that night, 'cuse I needed to get my sister ou'n that whorehouse! He beat her terrible! You seed it, Sergeant Martin. You seed it! I was hoping you would buy her! What it is you want I could 'a done?"

Beatrice rode on in silence, close enough to hear, but wise enough to keep quiet.

"You could have told me," Martin said. "You could have told me about it!"

Dunker Tim rode on, but he began to shake his head side to side. "No Suh! Ain't no way I could 'a tol' you! What it is you could 'a done, had I tol' you?"

They rode on for a time in silence. Martin still seethed. He was livid with anger, and he felt that debased feeling, so unworthy, so low, of truly enjoying his rage at Dunker Tim for laying such a trap for him. Still, he was an honest man, and deep in his heart, he knew Dunker Tim was right. What could he have done to help, had he known?

Silence. A heavy painful silence, as all three considered their options.

It was clear to Martin that he now had an obligation, and angry though he was, he would not shrink from that responsibility. As so often happened in his life, he recalled a brief Bible passage on the duty of man; such was his solace in life's troubled times, and in those words, as always, he found some comfort.

*"It is good that thou should take hold of this, yea also from this withdraw not thine hand. For he that fearest God shall come forth of them all and do his duty."*

While some men walk away from challenges in life, that had never been in Martin's character. Neither his faith nor his makeup as a man would allow that. Martin was a man who, even as a boy, had helped toss his father's body over the side of a ship when called upon to do so. He had responded to every call of the New Bern Militia, and had followed every order ever given him by Captain Brice, Col. Moore, and even Barnwell. He was a man who sought God's will, and did, indeed go where God told him to go. He would meet this responsibility, as he did all of his responsibilities, head on.

On the other hand, he had no idea how to tell Katheryn about this problem. What does one say? "Sorry dear, there was one woman before you, a tavern whore, and she and her baby now live with us?"

They rode an hour or more in silence. Martin could not say a word, fearful of what he might say in his rage. After another hour, Martin had reached a decision that he thought he could live with. He didn't wish to discuss it or debate it, so he merely announced it to his companions. "Beatrice, you and the baby will belong to me. We'll build you a cabin on our land and you will work in the cooper's shed and with Katheryn as she sees fit. I will see to your freedom, and that of Burdine, on the day of my death."

"Thank you, suh!" Beatrice said, quietly understanding the depths of the man's anger, even if Dunker Tim did not.

Dunker Tim smiled as he looked at Martin, but he could see that Martin was still troubled by this situation, and he knew what that expression might portend. He spoke up, when he shouldn't have. "Sergeant Martin, Suh. I can see you troubled, and I recon you might be thinking about telling Ms. Katheryn about your boy Burdine here. I don't think that 'd be wise. She might end up hatin' Beatrice, and …"

Martin, still angry, interrupted and said something that he'd never said before in his life. "Shut the hell up, nigger."

The calmness in his voice, and the anger still etched in his face told Dunker Tim all he needed to know at that moment. Martin's statement was harsh, cruel, and as ugly as it could be, and he realized that immediately, even as he gave it voice. In the very next second, his remorse tore his heart out. He and Dunker Tim were comrades in arms, having fought beside each other more times than Martin could count. In less than a second, Martin's anger was drained, and he was mortally sorry, but by then of course, it was too late. The impact of those cruel words on Dunker Tim was even worse, and every bit of that pain showed clearly in that black man's face!

They rode the remaining miles into New Bern in silence.

### *Blackbeard's Boredom*

Philosophers have long pondered why some men never seem satisfied with life. Why can some men not be happy and fulfilled by the woman who loves them? Why does a man with a pretty, reasonably sweet wife and more money than any one should have, find reason to be dissatisfied with his life? Why does a man with a satisfying job, toss his future and his security to the winds and begin a new career in an entirely different field? What is it at the heart of maleness that causes many men to decide, usually at some point in their forties or fifties, to change everything in their lives? Answers to these questions range from psychological, to religious, to philosophical, to the mystic, and none are satisfactory. While it is hard to contemplate any such psychological or religious reasons applying to a man like Edward Teach, it is a fact that once he had everything he wanted, and everything he could reasonably want in life, Blackbeard simply got bored.

His new domestic life in Bath with his nice wife and the respect of the community, as a result of his friendship with Governor Eden, should have been quite satisfying. Still history records that this stage of his life was unbelievably short. For only eleven months did Blackbeard go to the parties of the governor and the planter class in and around Bath. He only visited the local whorehouse once or twice a month during that time, about average for the gentlemen farmers in those days. He even hosted parties at his mansion, with his young, sweet wife playing the grand hostess!

Still, within a year of his receiving the King's Pardon, he was taking his ship the *Adventure* out on the high seas again, and sailing with many of the other men who had taken the King's Pardon with him. Yes, indeed, the old gang was back together again! The Claw was among those receiving the call to sail again with Blackbeard, as did Israel Hands and Black Jambo. They made several voyages into the shipping lanes just off the Carolina coast and came back with several remarkable cargos. Some of Blackbeard's tales about how he acquired the cargo stretched credibility.

Once during this period, he took the *Adventure* to the open ocean for only fifteen days, and was then seen sailing back upriver to Bath with a large French frigate, *La Concorde*, loaded down with a rich cargo of sugar, cocoa, spices and iron implements from Europe. Teach saw to the anchorage and then calmly marched to Governor Eden's office to report his claim. His story bordered on ridiculous! He claimed that *La Concorde* had been abandoned, and the he had "found" it, with sails flying as the hull drifted unguided through the current. The governor, helpful as always where Teach was concerned convened a Vice-Admiralty Court, which was necessary to determine ownership of the French ship, and Tobias Knight, the governor's secretary presided. With both Governor Eden and Knight himself taking a portion of Teach's profits on every trip, everyone in the Carolinas could have predicted the verdict well in advance of the court judgment!

The "prize" was deemed legitimate, and Teach was allowed to sell the cargo, as well as the ship and keep any proceeds he received. The payoffs were quickly delivered to the governor and his secretary which left everyone happy. Even the merchants and farmers all through Bath Province got a goodly supply of excellent merchandise at wonderful fire sale prices!

However, Israel Hands voiced some concern about selling *La Concorde* locally similar to his concerns about the *Trent*, thinking that she might be recognized at some point after the sale. He need not have worried however. Strangely enough, *La Concorde* caught fire that very evening, spontaneous combustion of ships at anchor being a significant problem in those days, at least when Blackbeard was nearby. She burned to the waterline while at anchor in Bath Creek, and the hulk was towed up the creek and then sunk. This episode with *La Concorde* was to impact Martin Bender, and once again he would go chasing pirates.

# A Day of Reckoning

Unfortunately for Teach, *La Concorde* was in route to the Virginia Capes with some expensive cargo when Blackbeard seized her and the Royal Governor of Virginia, Governor Spotswood, was a partial owner of some of that cargo. Within a week Spotswood heard of the loss of this vessel to pirates off the Carolina coast and he became furious! He had lost a fortune with that capture, and to make matters worse, he knew that his counterpart, Governor Eden, had probably profited handsomely, in some way or another based on those stolen goods! He'd heard the many rumors of pirate protection in the Carolinas, and he was concerned that they might be true.

Moreover, it was about this time that rumors began to circulate that the infamous Blackbeard intended to make Ocracoke Inlet a haven for pirates. Apparently Blackbeard had enjoyed the Ocracoke Orgy so much, that he planned to merely take over the small village near that inlet and make it the next Port Royal! Spotswood cringed to think how that many pirates within ninety miles of the Virginia Capes would handicap shipping into his colony. At that point, no one knew if Blackbeard had truly reduced the size of Blackbeard's Navy and for all the governor knew he could still command three or four large pirate ships!

This was enough for Spotswood, and he began immediately to plan an expedition to rid the Carolinas of this nest of pirates once and for all. Not only had he personally lost considerable wealth with *La Concorde*, but the idea of a settlement dedicated to piracy only a hundred miles from his colony was unimaginable. If word spread of this possibility, the rumor alone would be enough to result in canceled shipments and lost revenue for the Virginia ports. After all, what captain would willingly sail into pirate infested waters, when Blackbeard commanded an entire navy?

At that moment, two British men-of-war, the *Pearl*, and the *Lyme*, were anchored in the James River, and each held forty guns; these were mostly massive six-inch cannons! Governor Spotswood knew that he had the firepower he needed on those ships, so he ordered them to sail to Bath immediately in an attempt to recover *La Concorde* and her cargo if possible. However, their orders were clear; their first priority was to capture or kill every pirate in those waters!

Unfortunately, it was then that the governor of the Virginia Colony got a terse lesson in geography and navigation and the result shocked him. With the strongest navy in the world, more powerful ships by far that every other nation on earth and with two of those powerful ships at his immediate disposal, Governor Spotswood learned that both he and the whole of the British Empire were virtually powerless against pirates in the Carolinas! They were preempted from action by the same shallow sounds and bays that had prevented the early settlement of his neighbor colony to the south. His large ships couldn't even begin to navigate into the Pamlico toward Bath without the certainty of running aground.

Not a man to be defeated easily, Spotswood stewed in his own rage for a whole day, but then he devised a plan that seemed like it might have a chance of success. He wanted to act in secrecy, so he accessed some of his own funds and rented two small sloops, the *Ranger,* and the *Friendly Seas.* If the might of the British Crown could not protect commerce along the Virginia shore, Governor Spotswood intended to use these small ships and do it himself. As to a crew, he informed the captains of the *Pearl* and the *Lyme* of his intentions with the strong admonition that they share his plan with no one. They quickly volunteered their own contingent of riflemen from their own ships for this venture against the pirates of the Carolinas.

At that point, every man in the British Navy had basic seamanship skills. While the riflemen's shipboard job in the early 1700s was generally ship security or firing a musket at one's enemies from the high rigging of the ship during battle, those riflemen could, when necessary, man the riggings and sail the vessel themselves. Once sixty riflemen were selected to sail the two smaller sloops it became merely a matter of who would lead these ships, ships that were essentially the "bait" in this expedition.

A junior officer from the *Pearl,* Lt. Robert Maynard, was chosen for that command for the most ordinary of reasons; he was known to have fairly good political connections and his rank was low enough that no one cared if he lived or died. However, his superiors in the Royal Navy thought they had seen some leadership potential in the young man, so Maynard it would be. He wasn't really supposed to fight the pirates. Rather, his mission was to sail into Bath and flush the pirates out of that shallow harbor, so that the *Lyme* and the *Pearl* could catch them in open seas. A junior commander could certainly manage that task, and the real fighting would be done by the heavy cannon on the two men-of-war on the open ocean! So went the general plan, and the idea of a massive heavy-gun battle between two men-of-war and Blackbeard's Navy put a sparkle in the eye of Spotswood, as well as the senior captains of the *Lyme* and the *Pearl.*

Lt. Maynard did make one hesitant suggestion after hearing the overall scheme of the operation. He realized that he would be sailing his small sloops into the waters of another colony, so he thought it prudent to request liaison from that colony. Spotswood immediately objected to anything that involved contacting Governor Eden for obvious reasons, but Maynard maintained that he could request a liaison in such a way that Governor Eden wouldn't be aware of it. When Maynard explained his plan, Governor Spotswood reluctantly approved.

For that reason, Maynard sailed his two sloops not to Bath directly but into the Pamlico and up the Neuse, finding his way to the Trent River docks just below Union Point. At the insistence of Governor Spotswood, Maynard wanted to keep his mission secret so he first contacted Sheriff Jack DuVal upon arriving in New Bern to inquire about borrowing someone from the militia. He was quickly directed to contact Captain Brice. That is how Captain Brice and Lt. Maynard managed to show up together one afternoon at the cooper's shed on South Front Street.

Martin had noticed two sloops stop by the Trent River docks only two hours earlier, and he also saw them sail on up the Trent less than thirty minutes later. Still, he didn't think much of it since commerce was growing with each passing week, and with the Tuscarora threat fading into memory, more colonists were coming to the growing town. Ships sailed upriver all the time now, and the farmers and large landholders in Trent Mill even ran a daily flatboat downriver to the New Bern docks. Martin knew that those farmers, working in unison, had purchased a fairly large ship to conduct their own trading with Virginia, but he'd heard that ship, the *Trent,* had been taken several months before by pirates.

Johannes was slightly under the weather on that day in November of 1719, and Martin had just completed giving the seven workmen their instructions for the day. Four would be returning to the Banks farm to fell trees, while three, including Beatrice, would be fashioning barrel staves in the cooper's shed. Since Martin had acquired her, Beatrice had indeed proven her worth in that task, not to mention many others in the cooper's shed. She also helped Katheryn in the garden behind the cabin, and often tended to Daniel and Burdine, both of whom were now fifteen months old. On days when the boys were asleep and chores were done in the cabin, Beatrice could work in the cooper's shed, and she had become quite good at shaving the finished wood into the proper shape for barrel staves or hogsheads, or even special furniture pieces that Johannes or Martin were building. Sometimes Dunker Tim, was allowed to earn some extra money, and he would come by and help fashion some of the wood for furniture. He and Beatrice were both learning much about the cooper's trade as well as making furniture from the many fine hardwoods of the Carolinas. However, there was still a cool reserve between Martin and Dunker Tim that neither of them was happy about.

"I say, Sergeant Bender!" Captain Brice hailed Martin, again from outside the cooper's shed. As always Martin came to the door of the shop, to see the Captain standing there with a British officer.

"Captain! Good to see you, sir!"

"Good to see you, too Sergeant," the Captain said. "This is Lt. Maynard, of the Royal Navy. He would like a word with you, if you please."

Martin looked over his visitor. Maynard was a young man, but he exuded confidence. That was one of the reasons his superiors were positively disposed towards him. Martin, on the other hand, was always cautious until a military man had shown his worth while being fired upon. Still, his first impression of Maynard was positive.

Maynard took over the conversation at that point. "Indeed, I would like a word, Sir!" He looked Martin over, and continued. "First, I'd like to shake the hand of a man who assisted in the capture of Stede Bonnet and his band of thieves! You and your contingent of the New Bern Militia did quite well at the Cape Fear." Maynard reached out to take Martin's hand and he then gave it a good shake.

Martin barely had time to get in his response of, "Thank you, sir," before Maynard continued. "I've read the reports from Captain Rhett, you see. Your decisions in that engagement were spot on. Spot on, I say! Very good work!"

Captain Brice then suggested, "Perhaps we could talk a bit in private, Martin. The Lt. has requested secrecy related to his request for this particular mission. Could we move to your cabin?"

"Of course, Sir." Martin replied. He thought it strange that the Captain wanted privacy, since it had never been requested before, but he hurried to honor the request. He turned to Beatrice, and said, "Bea, please tell Katheryn that we have guests coming and we'd like coffee." Bea hurried to the cabin, to let Katheryn know that company was coming. She immediately saw that Katheryn was gone, but the water pot was boiling in the fireplace nonetheless, so she began to fix the coffee.

As the men walked toward the cabin by the cooper's shed, Captain Brice continued. "Thank you, Martin. It seems that our Lt. Maynard here has a fancy to catch a few pirates, but we wish to keep a tight wrap on that information. Tight indeed!"

Lt. Maynard wasn't quite ready to discuss the mission yet. "I say, based on those reports from Captain Rhett, I was most impressed not only with your handling of the attack on the grounded pirate ship, but the decision to split off a few men and draw their fire in several directions. That is thinking while under fire, and I commend you for that. Spot on! Spot on, I say." Here Maynard took a brief break as they entered the cabin. "I would have liked to have met that man, Jackson too! A real hero to volunteer to draw cannon fire away from his comrades. Amazing that; drawing cannon fire! What bravery!"

Martin didn't want to tell him that he suspected Jackson had been given no real choice in the matter. In fact, by this point, Martin was fairly sure that Dunker Tim had tied Jackson out before those guns like a fly trapped in a spider web! Martin really didn't know what to say, so he merely said, "Yes, Sir."

As the three men entered the cabin and sat down at the small table, Beatrice herself served them coffee. Katheryn was nowhere to be seen, and Martin recalled that she had planned to take the two boys and go to the market where farmers sold their autumn vegetables over on East Front Street. Still, it made little difference. This was to be a council of war, and war had always been a purview of men. Beatrice placed a cup of steaming coffee before each of them and then quietly left them alone.

Lt. Maynard took a sip of the hot liquid, and then continued. "I need a small contingent of the New Bern Militia, really only a liaison, as it were. We have all the riflemen we need, trained men who are good fighters, and I have a pilot who knows the Carolina waters, the sands and shoals, but I want a liaison from your colony for this expedition."

Captain Brice merely said, "Indeed," and that was all the encouragement Maynard needed to continue.

"We are going to root out the vermin, the pirates at Ocracoke Inlet and Bath itself. Two men-o-war, the *Pearl* and the *Lyme,* with forty heavy cannon each are just offshore, and will rendezvous with our two sloops the *Ranger* and *Friendly Seas.* The sloops will then sail to Bath and identify the villains, and maybe fire a few shots to engage their interest. Then we sail to Ocracoke and out to the Atlantic with them in pursuit. Once the pirates are outside the bar, the men-of-war will encircle them. They will do the heavy fighting, and our only job is to lure the pirates into the open ocean. I'd like for you, Sergeant Bender and perhaps one or two of your most trusted men to ride with me in the *Friendly Seas.* We'll be most unfriendly to the brigands, I assure you!"

Here Maynard paused for the expected laughter. Martin smiled, as required, and Brice laughed outright. Still each was thinking the same thing, as they smiled together. Each of the three men at that table knew that the phrase "pirates at Ocracoke Inlet and Bath itself" meant Maynard was targeting one man, Blackbeard.

Then Captain Brice asked. "So you require only two or three men?"

Lt. Maynard replied. "We really require merely the liaison. Just Sergeant Bender here, and perhaps his manservant. We have sixty riflemen from His Majesty's Royal Navy onboard the two sloops. We need no more guns, merely cooperative liaison, since we sail in Carolina waters."

Captain Brice knew that Martin didn't have a manservant, but rather than admitting that to this upper class English Naval Officer, he merely said. "I'd prefer to send a slave of mine, Dunker Tim. He is a slave whom I trust completely, and he can act as Sergeant Bender's manservant. He has proven his worth in various battles before, and can provide me the information I shall need in any future reports of the action, which may be required of me."

Lt. Maynard didn't notice anything out of the ordinary with that request, so he merely grunted, and asked, "This will be acceptable then?"

Captain Brice looked at Martin and smiled, realizing that Martin had said absolutely nothing. "What say, Martin? Do you feel like a nice sail to the Ocracoke this evening?"

Martin merely smiled, and said, "At your orders, Captain."

"Jolly good!" Lt. Maynard responded and hopped up off his stool. "Jolly good, I say! Good to have proven men at one's side in battle! Sergeant, we leave from the Trent River docks in two hours when the tide turns. The *Friendly Seas* has only a partial hold so bring a deerskin blanket or two."

Again Martin said, "Yes sir. I will be there, sir."

Captain Brice said, "Dunker Tim is in town, and I'll have him at the docks, also. I guess that does it. I do wish you good hunting, gentlemen."

With that Captain Brice and Lt. Maynard left the cabin and headed back toward the river. Two hours later, the *Friendly Seas* and the *Ranger* sailed with the tide from the Trent River docks, with Martin, Dunker Tim, and Maynard aboard the *Friendly Seas*. Once again, Martin and his friend, Dunker Tim were chasing pirates.

### *Old Friends Talk Again*

During the thirty-six hour sail out to Ocracoke, Dunker Tim and Martin were quite civil to each other as they had been for the previous year, but they still avoided meaningful conversation during the early part of that voyage. They had bedded down beside each other on the deck of the *Friendly Seas,* along with the many soldiers on board. Still, it was the first time these two had spent any time together since that horrid day on the trail from the Cape Fear almost a year previously. Each knew that much needed to be said between them, but each was reluctant to begin such a serious discussion. Men through the ages have been reluctant to talk about serious emotional relationships, a fact that women most often find laughable. Still some twenty-four hours into that sail, these two had merely spoken a greeting to each other, and talked about what each had been doing lately. Dunker Tim had spent most of that time at Tintarkle Ridge cooking out turpentine for Captain Brice, while Martin had made barrels for that very product as well as others. That conversation, covered fairly quickly, led to silence.

Finally, Dunker Tim, thought it time to approach the dangerous subject. "I seed Beatrice only a week ago, when I's in New Bern for Cap'n Brice." He said. "She says she fine and Burdine is doin' fine and that he'd near as big as Daniel now. I wanta' thank ye a'gin, Suh, for making a home fo 'um." Dunker Tim paused, as he saw Martin's face turn to stone, but he had decided that some things needed to be said, and that he needed to apologize once again to his friend. He was grateful, a moment later, when he saw Martin get control of his anger.

Before Dunker Tim could continue, Martin spoke, and to Dunker Tim's ears, it sounded like the old Martin, his companion, and his friend. "Burdine is a fine strappin' boy, as is Daniel. I intend to begin preparation in Bible with both of them when they turn three. Right now, they scamper all over the cabin and eat anything they can get their hands on."

Dunker Tim's grin seemed even broader than his face. "Yes suh! I bet day do eat everything in the cabin. Yes Suh! I'm sure day do!"

Martin then wanted to continue more deeply into what needed to be said. Simply put, he wanted his friend back, and sailing into a fight with pirates only accentuated the matter. Martin was not the first, nor would he be the last man to discover that a pending battle and one's possible death put petty grievances, or even serious disagreements, in perspective. At those times, men generally wish to make things right with each other. Further, it seemed like the right time for him to make things straight with Dunker Tim, but he didn't think he could find the words. Still he had to try. "Dunker Tim, I…"

But Dunker Tim pre-empted him. "Suh, I's sorry 'bout settin' ya wid' my sister, and I knowd it wrong and all, but I had to do sompin'! Don' ya see? Wid you an her, well, I jes hoped that she'd end up to be livin' in New Bern and not some damn whorehouse, where she beat near to death every single week!"

Martin let him speak, realizing with great sorrow the incredible irony of Dunker Tim apologizing to him. Martin knew it had been his own words, and not the actions of Dunker Tim that had destroyed so much of their friendship, and he knew well that the most heart felt apology must come from him and not Dunker Tim. His rage and anger, not Dunker Tim's actions, had been the most painful thing, the most destructive thing, for both of them.

But Martin, like most men, was limited by his time. Unlike truly great men who occasionally rise above those limitations, unlike those rare men who can truly enlighten and enrich our world, Martin could not reach beyond the perspectives and beliefs of the society that had nurtured him. In truth, he was no saint; no great philosopher, or preeminent thinker. He was, in many ways, rather ordinary, and he certainly bore many of the most horrid prejudices of his day. He could no more apologize to a slave than he could fly!

Still, his pain was such that he had to do something and in that thought, for the first time in months, Martin felt his anger, his rage, dissipate. As he felt that wonderful release of rage, Dunker Tim droned on, without noticing. Martin then found that another of those wonderful Bible passages came to mind, a passage that has brought rest and peace to the human heart through the ages.

*"Though I speak with the tongues of men and of angels but have not love, I am become a noisy gong or a clanging cymbal. And though I have the gift of prophecy and understand all mysteries and all knowledge and have all faith so that I can move mountains, but have not love, I am nothing. And though I give all my goods to the poor, and though I give my body to be burned and have not love, it profits me nothing. Love rejoices not in the wrong but in the right. Love bares all things, believes all things, hopes all things, endures all things."*

Martin realized that he had missed most of what Dunker Tim had said. Moreover, he knew at that moment that he had missed his friend terribly. He loved Dunker Tim in some profound way, even as he loved Johannes. But such things could not be said between men in those days, and some might argue that the same profane limitation still exists today.

Dunker Tim had, by that point, paused in his conversation, waiting for some sign. Dunker Tim needed to know Martin's thoughts, and again Martin faced that most imponderable and frustrating limitation of men of all ages, men who do not and cannot seem to express themselves well, if at all!

What Martin could manage was a relatively simple declarative statement. "Tim. I am glad you will be fighting with me again. I could ask for no better man at my side."

He had never called this man Tim before, and somehow that was both more personal, and more intimate. That was enough. As strange as it may seem, between these two long-time comrades, veterans of many battles together, these men who had literally saved each other's life, that simple statement was enough.

## A Failure to Anticipate

The *Ranger* and the *Friendly Seas* sailed on toward their meeting with the larger men-of-war. They would make for the inlet at Ocracoke and sail over the bar into the Atlantic to meet the mighty ships, the *Lyme* and the *Pearl*. The plan was to let the captains of those massive vessels board the smaller sloops and thus have some opportunity to explore the shoals just off the inlet. There they could pick their location from which to jump the pirate vessels in the open ocean. Then the two smaller sloops would head to Bath to see if they could lure the pirates out.

While this overall plan seems somewhat naive today, it was not faulty in those circumstances. Every Royal Navy commander in the Atlantic knew that Blackbeard was fearless and was likely to accept the very type of challenge that would leave other pirates quaking in their boots. Also, many pirates were known to use the Ocracoke Inlet to careen their ships, so exploration of that inlet would be beneficial for these Royal Navy captains, even if Blackbeard was nowhere to be found. With that said, there was little likelihood of finding a pirate thus engaged at Ocracoke on any given day, so the rendezvous there made sense.

Still the best laid plans do go awry from time to time. As soon as the *Ranger* and the *Friendly Seas* came within sight of the inlet, it was apparent that an armed ship was anchored there. Maynard struck his colors (lowered his flags), and sailed on toward the ship to investigate. Some men were seen on the shore and so, at first, Maynard thought he'd merely jumped another band of pirates either just before or just after they careened their vessel. With dusk approaching, and the pirate ship at anchor, Maynard chose to anchor his smaller sloops to the windward side to partially box in the pirate vessel, and settle in for the night. He would demand surrender and, if necessary fight the pirates in the morning.

At that moment, Blackbeard was better informed than the British Royal Navy. While Maynard did not realized which pirate he was up against, Blackbeard knew full well what was happening. It has been established by historians that Blackbeard did know of an expedition to hunt him down in Bath and the Ocracoke Inlet. Governor Eden's secretary, Tobias Knight, had kindly sent a letter to Blackbeard telling him so, and that letter was actually found later on the *Queen Ann's Revenge*. As a result of that communication, all of Governor Spotswood's secrecy about this expedition was to no avail. While Maynard spent the entire night preparing for an attack on the pirate vessel, Blackbeard spent the entire night carousing in his cabin with the Claw and Israel Hands. Such was the makeup of this pirate leader. In the face of eminent attack by the Royal Navy, the most powerful navy in the world at that time, he partied most of the evening!

At dawn the next morning, Lt. Maynard put several smaller boats in the water to take soundings of the depth of the water between his sloops and the pirate ship. He planned to attack this pirate ship, knowing that if he could get close enough, his riflemen could knock those pirates off the deck of their own ship fairly easily, and he didn't really care which pirate it might be. Since the ship had just careened, he was relatively sure she mounted no cannon at all. However, as the boats were taking soundings, they were fired on with muskets and one of the swivel guns in the rigging of the pirate vessel, so the small boats scurried on back to the *Ranger*.

It was at that instant that Blackbeard identified himself. Climbing up into full view on his quarterdeck, he shouted to them. "You bastards! From whence come you?"

Before anyone could answer, the *Ranger's* bottom tore into the sand, as she ran fast aground. At least for now, she was out of the fight. Maynard, at that point had lost half of his power, and he was about to attack a fearless brigand. Historians have long debated his decision to continue the attack, and it may indeed have been fool-hearty. Still, at that exact moment he ordered his ensign aboard the *Friendly Seas* to run up the British flag. Then he answered Blackbeard's taunt, and shouted, "You may see by our colors that we are no pirates!"

Blackbeard took a sip of his morning rum, and shouted again. "Perhaps you should send a boat over, and we can discuss that matter!"

Maynard responded across a hundred yards of water. "I cannot spare my boat, but I shall come aboard as soon as I can with my sloop!"

Blackbeard shouted across the waves one final time. "Damnation seize my soul if I give you quarters or take any from you!" He ordered Black Jambo to run up his Jolly Roger, and the fight was on!

He shouted orders to his men to cut the anchor cable, hoist sail, and man the guns. Every man aboard the *Friendly Seas* heard that order, and knew in an instant that they were to face the cannon of Blackbeard! The *Adventure* held eight guns during this fight, and Blackbeard first fired his starboard battery of four six-inch cannon at the grounded *Ranger*. The effect was devastating, as one might expect. Eighteen men died as all four cannon hit the *Ranger* in her broadside; one of the dead was the captain.

Again, it might have been wise of Maynard not to challenge this brigand so blatantly. Least we forget, Maynard had no cannon at all! Both the *Ranger* and the *Friendly Seas* were essentially "rentals!" They were sloops that had no cabin to speak off, but only a partially covered hold, and neither had ever before been used for warfare. They were typically used to ship corn up and down the Chesapeake Bay, or loads of tobacco from a plantation dock to the larger tobacco market in Williamsburg. In fact the last documented shipment aboard the *Ranger* only two weeks prior to the battle had been a load of crabs that was shipped across the Chesapeake to Baltimore. The ship still stunk to high heaven from that cargo! Certainly neither ship had ever before had cannon mounted on them. Their intended role in this fight was merely to antagonize Blackbeard enough, and present him an "easy" target or two, not engage the deadliest pirate on the high seas in a running cannon fight.

To Blackbeard, this challenge from these puny, unarmed freight haulers was laughable. His *Adventure* had serious cannon, he would soon have the wind in his sails, and his gunners could rival the finest gunners in the Royal Navy. As the *Adventure* began to make headway, he ordered more rum brought to the quarterdeck, and then said. "That damned grounded dinghy presents no challenge. Let's make for the other one!"

The Claw, at the helm of the *Adventure*, grinned and shouted, "Aye, Captain!" He was, at that very moment, quite proud to be serving with Blackbeard.

Blackbeard then ordered his gunners, "Man the port battery, and quick about it! Make me a coffin of that damned sloop!" He pointed to the *Friendly Seas* as he said that, and then took more rum. He stood on the quarter deck, in full view of the riflemen on the *Friendly Seas,* but even a small rise in the ocean will throw off a rifleman's aim over a hundred yards of water.

The next forty seconds seemed like an eternity, as the *Adventure* slowly turned in the light wind. Every single man on the *Friendly Seas,* Martin included, had heard Blackbeard's remark, and every single one knew what was about to happen as soon as the *Adventure* tacked enough to bring the port battery—four six inch cannon—to bear on their ship. Each man on that deck expected to die. All they could do was load their rifles, rifles that seemed so small and insignificant at that moment, and fire at the various pirates on the *Adventure,* knowing that their aim would be compromised by the waves and wind. One lucky shot, probably aimed at Blackbeard himself, actually hit one of the pirates that was firing a swivel cannon from the quarterdeck. Thus, Black Jambo received his first wound of the day on the deck of the *Adventure,* but he remained at his gun.

Just before that horrid cannon blast, Blackbeard's laughter could be heard across the waves, and he shouted a final curse. "I'll see you in hell, but by God, you'll get there before me!" Then four heavy cannon fired as one!

The *Friendly Seas* seemed to shudder with the devastation of that explosion, and four large gaping holes were torn in planking on her port side. Several men lay wounded horribly at each hole. Seven other men died on the deck.

After he heard the explosion, Martin was somewhat surprised to find himself still thinking about what might happen. He reloaded automatically, as he quickly realized he would live a bit longer, at least until the pirates could reload their cannon. Then strangely enough a Bible verse came to mind. No, now wasn't the time for that. Then he realized it wasn't him. He was hearing that verse, a mumbling, was someone quoting the Bible? He thought for a moment he was going crazy. While he often reflected on the Bible—often recalled verses himself—he didn't do that in the midst of battle! What kind of fool did? Someone behind him was loudly quoting scripture.

"*Yea, though I walk through de valley of de shadow of death, Oh Jesus, I fear NO EVIL! For you're wid me and yor' rod and staff, comfort me, Oh Jesus, Oh damn! You will prepare a... Oh God, Oh Damn! You prepare a table before me in de presence of my enemies... Oh God! My blood runs over!*"

Martin was fairly sure that verse didn't go like that. He completed the reload of his rifle, stood to see above the gunwales, and took a quick shot at the pirate vessel. Then he glanced behind him. On the deck by a large hole in the planking lay Dunker Tim, loudly cursing and quoting any scripture that came to mind. He launched into another one of the Psalms at that moment.

"*I lift up my eyes to duh hills. Oh God! From where comes my help? Oh my good God! My help comes from the Lord, maker of heaven and de earth!*"

Martin looked him over. Dunker Tim was holding his left leg above the knee, just where the blood was soaking through his pant leg. The rest of his leg was gone.

Maynard was at the helm of the *Friendly Seas,* and he did the only thing he could do. He steered directly toward the *Adventure,* using a time honored move of desperation familiar to soldiers and sailors throughout history. When you have no other options, charge! You will either carry the day and be celebrated through all time, or you will die quickly, and thus, you won't really care what happens.

Maynard didn't see his action in that light, of course. He merely knew that another broadside would fill his hull with a large measure of the Pamlico Sound. He had to get close enough to the *Adventure* to board her, and then he and his men could fight on equal terms with Blackbeard.

Then in an instant, he had two quick thoughts and each was brilliant. First he ordered all of his riflemen to load and fire the next volley together. That probably wouldn't do much damage to the *Adventure,* but the smoke resulting from that many rifles would bury his deck in gun smoke for a few brief seconds. It was a way to hide! He shouted the orders, "Load your weapons but hold your fire!" No one fired for about twenty seconds, until all were reloaded. Then Maynard shouted, "Fire!" Twenty nine rifles, including Martin's, and a few muskets went off at once, and within only a second, every man on the deck of the *Friendly Seas* realized that he could not see more than four feet from his own face!

Maynard then put his next brilliant idea in place. He shouted to a man at his side to take the helm and hold the current course. He then moved along his line of riflemen hiding behind the gunwales. In a quiet voice he issued the simple orders. "Hide in the hold. Load all your weapons, and have your knives and swords at the ready. Come on deck at my command after they board us. Quiet now, but move!"

Giving the orders to small groups, sometimes five men, sometimes seven or eight, Maynard repeated the same orders four or five times on that deck in less than a minute. All his men readily complied, and just before the gun smoke cleared from the deck, the last of the riflemen joined his comrades below. Maynard joined the group at the front ladder into the hold.

By then Blackbeard had his starboard battery ready for firing again, but as he turned the *Adventure* to bring those guns to bare, the light breeze finally cleared the deck of the *Friendly Seas* of smoke. Blackbeard saw only a few men, so he steered the *Adventure* closer. Rather than firing, he thought at that point that he might steal this ship and sell it, and he chose not to damage it any more with another broadside. Thus, he ordered his men to toss homemade grenades, small boxes filled with powder and a lighted fuse, onto the deck of the *Friendly Seas,* to kill anyone left alive.

He then had to wait once more for the smoke to clear, but when it did he could see only three or four men on the deck, and most of them seemed to be wounded. He shouted his orders. "Let's jump on board and cut 'um to pieces!" He laughed, again and continued. "They may have some rum or some British coin we might put to use! What say, lads?"

The Claw was the only man that ever dared question Blackbeard on the high seas, and while others cheered, he did question him on that day. "Should we give 'er another taste o' cannon before we board her, sir?"

Blackbeard's answer was heard on both ships as they were within thirty feet of each other at that point. "No need. She's done for, and I've seen her end."

That was one of the only mistakes Blackbeard was ever known to make while at the helm of a pirate ship. That mistake would cost him his life.

Maynard listened to these comments, the laughter and several cheers of Blackbeard's men. The *Adventure* closed on the *Friendly Seas,* and all gunfire stopped. Martin, meanwhile, was busy tying a calico shirt tightly around Dunker Tim's leg and that seemed to stop most of the bleeding. He knew he was the only man left on the deck of the *Friendly Seas* that could fight.

For a moment all was quiet, then… "Sergeant, watch yo' ass when they come over! I won' be around to keep track o' you!" Dunker Tim whispered, as Martin struggled to tie up the leg.

"Don't be a fool, Tim. I'll see you after this is over. Meanwhile, just lay there and look dead!"

Dunker Tim continued. "Always figured it'd be a Tuscarora arrow in Cap'n Brice's barn, a rattlesnake along the Trent; maybe a 'gator at Catfish Lake. Not no damn pirate! Dem cannon is a bitch! Hard to face 'um alone out here."

Martin finished the knot. "I'm here and I ain't going anywhere. Now I told you to shut the hell up, friend." As he said it, both he and Dunker Tim realized the similarity to his earlier statement that had caused so much pain. They looked into each other's eyes for only a second, as they both recognized the difference, too.

With no further word, Martin ran toward a dead man only six feet away, and grabbed the rifle that lay beside the corpse. He had it loaded just as the first pirate jumped on the deck. He lay the rifle beside Dunker Tim, and noticed that Dunker Tim had passed out. But then, he faced the business end of a pirate's pistol, as the first pirate on board pointed his blunderbuss at Martin's face, so Martin slowly lay his knife aside too. Within ten seconds, fifteen pirates were on the deck of the *Friendly Seas,* including the Claw, Black Jambo, and Blackbeard himself.

Blackbeard looked at Martin, who was clearly the only man on the *Friendly Seas* not wounded, and said, "Ah! We have a live one! And he's patchin' up a slave!"

Martin answered simply, "He's my friend."

{Author's Note: That statement was carefully recorded within a week of the event by Martin Bender himself in his notes. That was the only time Blackbeard ever spoke to our great, great, great, great, great, great grandfather.}

At that exact second, Maynard sprang from the forward hatch, and another group of riflemen jumped from the stern. Within a second over twenty pistols, muskets, and rifles went off. The pirate holding the pistol in Martin's face, turned to the stern deck hatch and fired, and one man went down with a hole in his chest. Martin had the presence of mind to hit the deck beside Dunker Tim, thankful that that particular pistol shot had not killed him. He grabbed the rifle he'd loaded only a moment before, and shot the next pirate coming toward him. That man fell dead right on top of Dunker Tim.

By then almost every gun had been fired, and not a single man on that deck even thought of reloading. The deck itself was thirty eight feet long and just over nine feet wide and in that space nineteen pirates and twenty two riflemen from His Majesty's Navy were locked in deadly battle. They fought with cutlasses, swords, knives, fighting irons, rifle stocks, bayonets, fists, and anything else available. Blackbeard himself drew his pistols one at a time—he wore six across his chest that day, as always—and calmly fired at any man that charged him. No less than four men died from those shots alone, since it was hard to miss any target in those close quarters. Blackbeard was better armed than anyone else on that deck.

Martin had already fired his rifle, and Dunker Tim was either passed out or dead. Martin turned his rifle into a club and used it to fight off several advances of various pirates. He fought alone for a time on the starboard deck near the center, since most of the riflemen were still clustered around either the forward or the stern hatch. Within thirty seconds the battle degenerated into a free-for-all. A rifleman used a bayonet to parry a blow from a pirate cutlass, only to be stabbed from behind by another pirate! Blackbeard, now with cutlass in hand, cut a man's arm clean off at the elbow with one vicious blow, and Martin watched as that man fell to his knees while his arm spurted blood. Blackbeard's next hack was at the man's exposed neck, and his head was almost cut from his body but not quite. A flap of skin on the left of his neck held the head on, letting it lay to the left along the dead man's shoulder as he fell flat on the rough deck planking.

Another pirate rushed and Martin had to duck, and cover himself with his empty rifle. The mighty blow of that pirate's cutlass actually cut the rifle stock clean off, leaving Martin all but defenseless. This man was huge and just then Martin recognized that big, flat, black face, the massive dark beard, and the hole in the side of the man's head where his ear was supposed to be! Black Jambo looked at Martin and grinned—he may have recognized Martin from his days in New Bern. He didn't hesitate even for a moment; he lifted his mighty arm as he prepared to swing that cutlass at Martin's head. Martin could do nothing.

Then a rifle fired right beside him and Martin saw a large pool of blood soaking through the calico shirt Black Jambo wore, dead center, just over his heart. That pirate, as mean as any buccaneer in history, fell dead at Martin's feet.

Above the noise of battle, Martin heard Dunker Tim's shout, "Here's a loaded pistol, suh! Now wid' Black Jambo dead, please get yo' ass back down hea' least 'till I get loaded again!"

Martin ducked and began to load another rifle that lay nearby, but his attention was drawn to a fight taking place not quite six feet from him.

Maynard and Blackbeard by that time were face to face in the center of the deck, and both fired pistols at each other. Blackbeard's pistol misfired somehow, but Maynard's shot was true! Blackbeard's massive body shook as it took the musket ball dead center in his chest, but he seemed to absorb that blow somehow and he didn't stop! He seemed, at that moment, to be a demon from hell, immune to hot lead, and made for killing. He raised his cutlass higher and would have taken Maynard's head clean off, had Maynard not drawn his own sword in an instant to protect himself. With that mighty swing Blackbeard's cutlass slashed clean through Maynard's blade and drove Maynard to his knees on the deck. Then it seemed as if the battle froze at that moment, with Blackbeard slowly raising his cutlass for a final blow to take Maynard's life.

In an instant, Martin saw the opening, and in a tenth of a second he took two strides, while snatching his knife up from the deck, as he approached Blackbeard from the side. While that devil's attention was focused totally on Maynard kneeling on the deck before him, Martin buried his knife in the pirate's neck, then tore the blade out through Blackbeard's throat. Blackbeard looked sideways at Martin then, during the final seconds of his life. The devil was still fixated on killing, and Martin saw rage in his eyes, then fear, then nothing. Blackbeard fell to the deck dead as a stone. He died with five pistol wounds and twenty slashing cuts on his massive body, and his entire throat was torn out!

Maynard looked up at Martin and said simply, "Indeed! It is good to have you with us, Sergeant Bender." Then he passed out.

The battle ended at that moment. When the remaining pirates saw Blackbeard fall, and took a look at the odds on that small deck, they lay down their cutlasses. Nine pirates, including Blackbeard, Black Jambo, and the Claw lay dead. Six more were captured and all of them were wounded, but four who could swim, jumped over the side at that moment and swam to shore. They were never captured, adding even more pirate blood to the Carolina gene pool!

Martin knew what had to be done, and in the next few seconds of silence, he grabbed the closest rifleman to him, and said, "Tend to Maynard." He then turned to another and said, "Come with me."

That man, an eighteen year old rifleman named Jim Lovorn, was bloody from his neck down, but he laid his rifle aside, and jumped to Martin's order. Together they picked up Dunker Tim's body, and moved him to the center of the deck, as other men did the same with other wounded. Within five minutes a small fire was built, and a barrel of gun powder sat dangerously close to it. Dunker Tim passed out several times briefly, and then returned to consciousness. Once when he came to, Martin handed him a bottle of rum that one of the sailors had retrieved from the *Adventure*.

"Drink this," Martin said. "Drink as much as you can." Martin then spread some of the gun powder in the blood at the stump of Dunker Tim's leg. With no further preamble, Martin grabbed a burning stick from the fire, and pressed the smoldering end into the gun powder. Flames shot skyward, and the odor of burning flesh and gun smoke was horrible. Martin later stated that Dunker Tim's scream could have been heard in Bath over fifty miles away.

Maynard decapitated Blackbeard and hung his head from his bowsprit on the *Ranger*. He ordered his second to take command of the *Friendly Seas* and deliver Sergeant Bender and his slave back to New Bern, but he didn't let Martin depart without another heartfelt thanks! He and Martin stood over Dunker Tim's prostrate body on the deck of the *Friendly Seas* as they said their goodbyes.

"I say, Sergeant. I'm fortunate you were here to help, and I do believe I owe you my life. Thank you for that, and for your service here!" He offered his hand, and Martin took it.

"At your orders, Sir. And may I say you fought quite well. I'm proud to serve with you!" Martin replied.

"Quite right! Sir. Quite right! I do believe we may have done some good here! Maybe we put an end, at least to this nest of pirates. What?" Maynard then looked down at Dunker Tim on the deck. "Your slave will not live through the trip, I'm afraid. Not with that wound. A pity that."

Martin didn't wish to correct him on the ownership of Dunker Tim, so he said again. "He is a fighter, Sir. He may yet live. He is my friend."

"I see," said Maynard, though he didn't see at all. He then turned back to Martin. "I am honored to have fought with you. Good sailing to you, Sir, and thank you again!"

## A Final Trip Home

Maynard departed and the *Friendly Seas* sailed to New Bern, where they landed thirty six hours after the battle. Dunker Tim's leg smelled horrible during the entire trip, so he remained in the breeze on the upper deck, and Martin stayed beside his friend for the entire voyage. It reminded him of tending his father aboard another small ship, so very many years before.

Dunker Tim suffered sweats and chills for the entire transit, and was delirious much of the time. Martin kept a deerskin blanket over him. Tim sometimes spoke nonsense, calling Martin by various names. Once or twice he called Martin "Mama." At other times, he would seem to be competent, though he did carry a high fever.

In the middle of that first night, as a low moon silhouetted the *Friendly Seas* casting a long shadow across the Pamlico, Dunker Tim was coherent for a few minutes, while lying on the open deck. He looked at Martin and said. "Beat 'um all to hell, did we Sergeant Martin?"

Martin smiled at his friend, "Yea, we did, Tim. We beat o'l Blackbeard all to hell! Beat him good and proper!"

"You kilt him, didn't you Sergeant? You kilt Blackbeard?"

"Sure did, Tim! Deader'n all hell! I killed him deader 'n you killed John Berry Jackson's sorry ass!"

That brought a smile to Dunker Tim's face, just as Martin hoped it would. Tim said, "May they both rot in hell!" They both chuckled a bit, at that.

A pause, then Tim said, "I'm mighty hot, Sergeant. Could I have a lil' water?"

Martin hurried up to get a ladle of water from a bucket on deck, and helped Dunker Tim take a sip. Thus, the white man now waited on the slave. If anyone on that ship thought that to be a bit strange, they kept it to themselves.

Dunker Tim said, "Thank ya! That's pow'full good!"

Martin looked at the horrid black flesh of Dunker Tim's leg. The coagulated blood and the burned flesh smelled like rotten eggs. Dunker Tim said, "Don' look good, do it?"

Martin said, "It ain't truly rotten yet. Don't look good, though."

Dunker Tim seemed to resign himself then to the inevitable. "Never thought it'd be dis' way! Maybe a damn savage, or somepin' in de woods, but never dis' way."

Martin looked at his friend, in silence.

Dunker Tim was becoming more reflective, as he turned to look at the low moon over the water. "Al'ays thought somehow I'd die a free man. Didn't know how, mind you. I mean, Cap'n Brice a good massa, an' all. Still, I al'ays thought…."

Martin didn't know what to say. He then found himself talking without thinking. "You're free now, ain't ya? Right now out here on this wide open ocean? You're free right now, as free as any of us. Ain't it beautiful? Ain't we all free right now? This as free as any man can be!"

Dunker Tim looked at his friend. "It's beautiful, sure 'nuf, but it ain't de same, Sergeant." Tim then paused and for a moment his breath seemed ragged. Then, "You and me, Sergeant. We fight 'side each other more 'n either of us knowd, and we is friends, as much as men can be, but it still ain't de same."

Dunker Tim was quiet for a bit, and Martin thought he'd drifted off again, but then he spoke. "Naw, suh! I'm gonna die out hea' on dis' hea' ship, right enough, and it is mighty pretty hea' but it ain't de same. If'n I did live, I don' know what Cap'n Brice gone do wid a one-leg nigger. I can't take out his sloop no more, can't ride, or fight no mor' or cook his turpentine pots. What good is a one-leg slave?"

Martin thought for a moment, then strangely, he began to grin at his friend. "You right about that! You sure ain't worth much now, to nobody."

Dunker Tim didn't understand the smile on Martin's face, at first, or understand his gentle giggle afterward. Then Martin continued. "Yeah, I bet anybody that comes along could buy you real cheap right now."

Dunker Tim was losing consciousness again and didn't understand as he looked at his friend. Why would his Sergeant say such a thing right then? He was losing strength, about to slip back into sleep.

Martin was still grinning, and didn't know at the time if Dunker Tim heard his next statement or not. "I'll own you by this time tomorrow Tim, and the very next minute, may God witness my vow, you'll be a free man!"

Dunker Tim was gone by then. He'd passed out once again, but Martin carefully made sure he was still breathing. The breath was quite shallow, but it was there.

Martin closed his own eyes for a moment when the tears came, but only for a moment. He then cried openly and unashamed. After a minute or two, there on the deck of the *Friendly Seas*, in the beautiful moonlight on Pamlico Sound, he continued speaking to his sleeping friend.

"You may be crazy with fever then, you may not know it at all, Tim. But if you can just live all the way to the Trent River docks, you'll be a free man when you die!"

# Epilogue
## The Bender Legacy
### *A New Hope for A New World*

This then, is the story of the Bender family legacy, the story of Jesus' and my family, the story of our common blood. Those papers and records so carefully preserved by this family for so many generations, most recently by Mildred Carmichael Bender, tell all of this and more. There is a richness here of unimaginable value for our family and really for all progeny of those rugged German and Swiss settlers of New Bern so long ago. This is the story of New Bern, of the Carolinas, and in some larger sense, this is the story of America. This is a story and a legacy for us all.

This intoxicating narrative brought tears to our eyes many times, as Jesus and I explored these documents, and discovered this story together. It was and is powerful. It proclaims many individual truths, the value of faith, strength in the face of adversity, nobility in the common man. Still, Jesus and I came to believe that the most fundamental message herein is a message of hope. These settlers, with every action they took, showed an undying, unyielding hope for a better life and a better world, even in the face of constant lifelong struggles.

Of course, any historic culture clash is a bloody, horrid affair, and the settlement of New Bern and all the Carolinas was steeped in that horror, witnessing many tensions between many different cultures. As there is no innocence among men, there are no innocents in history—there is only hope.

Who could have known that Cary would decide to fight Hyde and turn the colony into a festering, bleeding wound? Who would guess that the Tuscarora would get angry simply because whites stole a few of their women and children for slaves? Why should slaves like Beatrice, Black Jambo, or even Dunker Tim long so very much for their freedom? Why should pirates pick this particular patch of nowhere to ply their deadly trade?

In retrospect, most things do make sense, at least in their own time. Slaves long for freedom in all cultures, and all peoples, like the Tuscarora in this instance, will fight for their way of life when invaded by others. The pirates of the Carolinas merely did what pirates do everywhere, steal everyone blind. Still, amid all of this, somehow, life went on for the Simmons family, for Charlotte May Koonce and her son Willie, for Franz Tuber, the miller, and for Archie Carmichael sleeping there on his stool at Mallard's Tavern, for the Banks family, or for the Foscues, for Martin and Katheryn Bender, for Captain Brice, and even for Beatrice and her son Burdine. The question is not how this colony managed to succeed in the face of starvation, drought, yellow fever, pirates, armed rebellion, and the Tuscarora Massacre. The question is how each single man, woman, and child survived against all odds and almost every hardship known to man? The only possible answer is hope.

These German and Swiss immigrants, the Simmons, Koonces, Ipocks, Tubers, and all the rest struggled with every ounce of their being, and met every hardship as they hoped for a world in which they could practice their religion, work, and live their lives free from the persecution they suffered in Europe. The hope they found in their undying belief in a merciful, loving God was their reason, their strength, and their sustenance. For these our ancestors, God was the basis of all hope. These Anabaptists sensed that Divine presence with every breath they took. Individually, and as a people, they went where God commanded, and we today, could benefit from that lesson and that example. These peoples were enriched by their faith, as we are enriched by their struggles even today; for their faith allowed them to create for us, this beautiful city.

The indentured servants and orphan apprentices on these shores, men like Martin Bender, the distant ancestor of Jesus and I, all hoped for a better life here than they had previously, and they fought for that hope every day of their lives. The English and the Scots who came to this city, the Brice family, the Mallards, Foscues, and Carmichaels, wanted a life of freedom, the right to own land, and to farm that land free from the surf system still so prevalent in Europe.

Even the slaves, Beatrice, Dunker Tim, and Black Jambo, whose ancestors were not willing immigrants to these shores, had their own deeply personal hopes and dreams. They hoped for a better day in this new colony, even while under the lash of slavery. These most persecuted of peoples recognized the dream of freedom in a new world as a worthy dream, even though they knew that they were building that dream for others. They saw the value of that goal, and in many cases they fought for that dream as they did that day so long ago in Brice's barn, while they were yet denied their rightful portion of it. Black slaves fought for that dream in the American Revolution, the Civil War, and black sharecroppers fought for it in World War I, even before they could realistically participate. Why? The answer, again, is hope. Hope for that dream was their engine of freedom in this new world, and therein lies yet another lesson from which we, today, could well benefit.

That hope for freedom and a better life, is, and should evermore be, one of the highest aspirations of man. That is the message of this story, as these, our ancestors shout to us from their very graves. After all, in the darkest, earliest days of this city, hope was all these people had.

As Jesus and I came to grips with this story, we saw the power here, and we both experienced a profound humbleness. We talked these things through for hundreds if not thousands of hours, as we read the extensive notes by Martin Bender or his son John. We searched libraries, tax records, land deeds, wills, and anything else that might help us unravel this history. How many times did we reconstruct this story, as we found new information in tax records or hidden within those old documents? God only knows. As we talked it all over, again and again, our most frequent reaction was "Wow! How could these people survive these things?" Again, the answer is hope.

There are questions here that will never be answered. What was Charlotte May Koonce feeling when she fired that musket in Brice's barn? How could Katheryn have been so certain about her marriage to a young man who seemed destined to rush into every battle? Could King Hancock have chosen a different path, a path that would have let his people survive a bit longer in the Carolinas? Was Barnwell as sorry as some suggest, and did Col. Moore really walk on water? What remorse did Dunker Tim experience, when he tricked his friend into his sister's bed? How could Martin have felt, knowing full well that Dunker Tim had no other options?

We can never know these answers, but we can sense, we can feel, and perhaps experience in some degree the marvelous determination of these ancestors of ours. Jesus and I came away from this story knowing that our personal trials are trivial when compared to these early peoples of New Bern. Our struggles, while sometimes serious and on rare occasions life threatening, are really relatively minor. If history teaches anything, if it does anything at all for us, it should at least leave us humble, and in the case of Jesus and I, this historical story had exactly that effect!

Moreover, their success in founding this city and this state challenge us today. If these ancestors of ours could survive when hope was all they had, can we not do the same? If they could get beyond the color of a man's skin and see his strength and his character, can we not do as well? Are we more limited today somehow, than they? What does that say of us?

Tax records from the Craven precinct document that Martin and Katheryn Bender moved out of the city of New Bern within three months of the death of Blackbeard. They cleared land on Martin's original land allotment, the Bender Plantation, on Mill Creek trail just outside of Trent Mill, the small town now named Pollocksville. They are buried there today. As it turns out Martin Bender had fought his last major battle when he faced Blackbeard at Ocracoke Inlet. All of his wars, he fought before he turned twenty three years old. From then on, he merely lived his life, while building both his plantation and his family. He and Katheryn had other children, built a plantation home, and farmed for several decades. In short Martin lived a rich full life, with Katheryn by his side every step of the way. Martin's children Daniel, John, Solome, and Mary grew up on that farm on Mill Creek, not knowing in their childhood that their father's favorite slave, Burdine, was their half-brother.

In time they knew. In time they were told, but that came later.

Martin's three sons, Daniel Bender, his younger brother John, and Burdine Bender each founded a family as free men in the Carolinas, the first two white and the last, black. Daniel and Burdine moved to Tennessee, apparently together in their later years, and several of their children either moved with them or had already settled there. Those families remained intertwined for three or four generations as far as Jesus and I could tell, honoring these family relationships and this legacy. At some point after the Civil War, the white Benders of central Tennessee either moved on or died out completely. One can only wonder how long the legacy, as described below, was shared, father to son, in that family.

Among the children of John Bender, the legacy was passed down through six generations, until my grandfather, John H. Bender Sr. shared it with Mildred Carmichael Bender. She guarded that legacy for her entire life, long after he died, but I do not know if she shared it with my father or not. He never mentioned it to me in any way.

Martin Bender's handwritten will was among the papers filed with the Craven Precinct. It was dated 1750. It granted hundreds of acres of farmland to the four children above, and named four slaves, which were likewise left to various children. However, in that will, an older female slave named Beatrice was granted her freedom, as was her grown son Burdine. They were each given a hundred acres of land. Both then took the last name of Bender.

However, that will also makes several strange references to "other directions and papers, which I hereby leave to my sons Daniel and John." Jesus and I searched diligently, but found nothing in the old records. As far as we could tell, no other instructions or papers were ever filed with the court in New Bern by Martin Bender.

Until we managed to open the final box I found in my Grandmother's closet, we had no idea what those other instructions might be. Then as Jesus and I explored the last of the boxes, we found it, the Bender legacy, written in Martin Bender's own hand. Thus, our common ancestor spoke to us from his very grave.

We read it together.

Jesus wept. I did too.

It came in two parts. First, there were over two hundred pages of notes on experiences Martin had in his life, revealing his views of Col. Barnwell, Captain Brice, and Col. Moore, as well as the true story of things like John Berry Jackson's death, and Blackbeard's one statement to Martin. Much of the story above comes from that source, as well as notes written later in John Bender's diary.

The other part was the oath, the legacy itself. It is powerful and poignant, even today. I believe it fitting that this legacy be left not only to the Bender family, but to all descendents of those early settlers, and moreover, to all others who live in, and who love this wonderful city of New Bern today. In some broad sense, this is who we are.

## *The Legacy*

*As a codicil to my last will and testament, I write these instructions, as a legacy to my sons Daniel and John, as to the maintenance and help they shall provide to my other children. As Daniel and John are both of age at the date of my writing, I leave this legacy as binding on both of them, or either of them that shall survive the other. Because of my illness, my sons and I have discussed this legacy together, within the last week, but I put it down herein for clarity, written by my own hand.*

*It is my wish that they leave this legacy and commitment, each in their own line, for their sons through the generations. I state and require them to commit, by their own oath, before God, as follows.*

*1. My sons, their sons, and all my progeny shall know that Burdine Bender, a Negro son of the slave Beatrice, is my son. By my last will and testament he and his mother Beatrice are, and shall remain forevermore, free. I have provided additional written notes, by my own had, on this matter and the many other things in my life that my sons should know of my reasons for this.*

*2. Knowing that others do not look kindly on free Negros, I require that my sons Daniel and John, prior to accepting their inheritance from me, do swear before each other, before their mother, and before Almighty God a promise to keep Burdine Bender and his progeny close to their farm or place of business, and to assist Burdine as he wishes and as he sees fit, and to assist all of his children through the generations, in learning trades that they may survive and thrive. These are your brothers and sisters before God, as shown in these notes and this legacy, and it is my hope and prayer that ye all assist each other whenever needed.*

*3. In my lifetime, I have made certain that Burdine learned his Bible, his letters, and his numbers, as I have all my children. I require that you each, Daniel and John, shall assist Burdine and see that his children and all those generations of his children learn to read the Bible and other writings, and learn their numbers.*

*In this new world, family lineage counts little. In this colony, if knowledge is the real power, then education is the real freedom. Mrs. Margaret Simmons taught me that when she took me in, and I most strongly admonish you to never forget that lesson. Read everything you can; learn everything you can, and work hard to assist Burdine, that his children may do the same.*

4. I have sought forgiveness before Almighty God for my sin, and I have received such bountiful forgiveness as a benevolent and loving God may provide. I attest hereby that I die in peace with God, as is the blessing of his grace, his forgiveness, and his will. But herein I also testify, before God, that in spite of my sin, much joy and happiness has been afforded me by my son Burdine, as also from my sons and daughters by Katheryn Simmons Bender. I have loved Burdine as a son, as you know, and I urge you to love him as a brother, as you have thus far in life. He is a worthy man, and friend, and a brother you can count on, even as you count on each other. You are very fortunate to have such a man as he by your side, as I had such a man by mine, as these papers and this legacy hereby attest. Honor him, as you honor each other.

5. As this oath requires actions not condoned and not legal in this world, but right and true in God's eyes, as also in my beliefs, this oath shall be kept secret from all others through all the generations. However, I do most earnestly urge you, my sons, and the sons in those future generations, to share this legacy with your wives, as have I. Your wives are your strength and the backbone of this colony and I urge you to trust them and seek their guidance as to how to carry out this legacy, and in all other important matters as long as you shall live.

I do instruct and admonish you to read the story of the women in Brice's barn. They are strong women, and such women will be a blessing to you through all your generations. These are the women of the Carolinas; these are your mothers, your sisters, and your wives. If I have sired wise men through all the generations herein bound by this legacy, then by your acceptance of this legacy and as sworn before Almighty God, each of you shall marry a woman stronger than you are.

6. Finally, I also troth my sons to tend and to keep their Uncle, known to them as Uncle Dunker Tim, the one-legged Free Negro who has lived with us these many years, for as long as he may live. He has built much fine furniture, as you know, and you will keep him supplied with timbers that he may continue that work in his cabin at Mill Creek as long as he desires. By earnings from those pieces, and your help for this man, he will be provided for comfortably in his cabin, and well fed, and doctors provided when needed. He has saved my life more than once, as I have his. Many notes attached hereto attest to our battles together. He has been at my side throughout my life in tough times, and I have no doubt he is standing at my side, even as I lay in my coffin, and helping my family as you read these words in the days of my death.

I began my life in New Bern alone, as you know, but I did not live alone. God in his benevolent grace granted me a wonderful wife, Katheryn Simmons Bender, five fine children, and a great and true friend, Dunker Tim. I hereby testify at my death before Almighty God, that no two men could be more closely brothers than Dunker Tim and I, in this life or the next.

*As I believe God has willed, I have identified a slight rise of one half acre, in the field behind my home, the Bender Plantation on Mill Creek, where I and my wife, Katheryn, shall be together buried. It is my wishes that this Free Negro, my friend Dunker Tim, likewise be buried in that half acre plot near to me, should he wish it. He often sat at my table to sup, he fought with me, and we bled together many times. I will be proud indeed to share my final patch of ground with both my wife and my friend.*

{Authors Note: No graves are marked in the Bender Plantation Cemetery on Mill Creek for Martin, Katheryn, or Dunker Tim, but neither Jesus nor I doubt in the slightest, that they, our common ancestors, rest in that hallowed ground today. It has long been known in the family that the oldest graves in that cemetery are unmarked. The oldest gravestone there today is for John Knox Bender, who is Martin Bender's great grandson.}

*This legacy and commitment, as well as all my notes on these events in my life, I leave to my sons. If you honor me as is proper, as your children will be made and taught to honor you, I confirm you to this legacy and make it binding unto you for all your years. I urge you to make this legacy binding on your sons in those future generations.*

*This responsibility has been and can be, a great joy in life and not a burden, as I have endeavored to show you in all my days. That is always a choice that a man can make, and I pray I have taught you to make that choice wisely.*

*Martin Bender, May, 18, 1750*

*Sworn before Katheryn Simmons Bender, my loving wife, who may hereby attest to the truth of this legacy, and take the oath of my sons, Daniel and John, to abide as described herein.*

## *Author's Final Note and Postscript:*

Shortly after we finished this research, my cousin and my friend, Jesus, died.

Dr. Julian Christopher Bender passed away of a heart attack on October 2, 2008, just as we were beginning to write this story of our ancestors and our family. At his memorial service, the church in Nashville overflowed with his former patients and his many friends. He would have been very pleased, but not in the least surprised, to see so many white faces and black faces there together. He was interred in Leesville, Tennessee in the churchyard of Rutland Church.

Thus, Jesus left me alone to finish this story, a story both his and mine. It was the only time in my life when I needed Jesus, and he was not there.

He rests now with his family. Many Benders, white and black, have been buried at Rutland Church over the centuries. The family records indicated that both Daniel Bender and Burdine Bender are buried there, but as the early markers were made of wood, each of these sons of Martin Bender, like their father before them, rests forever in an unmarked grave.

While most of the research for this was done together, and some sections were written by our joint hand, I had to complete most of the actual writing alone and publish this work after his death. He knew everything that is contained in this story and this legacy before he died. He indicated to me many times that this legacy pleased him greatly. We are both very proud of our ancestor Martin Bender, and this large family. Because of our many discussions, I believe I have done this work, as Jesus would have wanted it done.

It is my hope that this book, this story of our family and this legacy, honors not only Martin and Katheryn Bender, but all those rugged Germans and Swiss who created our wonderful city. I hope and believe that it also honors Jesus, as well. He was my cousin, my brother in arms, my companion in struggle, and my friend.

## Geographic Locations of New Bern and The Tuscarora War

*Albemarle* – or "The Albemarle" describes settlements along the Albemarle Sound, in the North Carolina Colony just south of Virginia. That was the first area of the colony settled by whites, who mostly came from Virginia.

*Bath* – first town in the North Carolina Colony, charted in 1705.

*Brice's Creek* – a tributary of the Trent river three miles below New Bern, and the location of a plantation owned by William Brice.

*Brice's Garrison* – The name used for Brice's Plantation three miles up the Trent river from New Bern, once it was fortified during the Tuscarora massacre of white settlers in September of 1711.

*Cartouca* – the name of the Tuscarora settlement at the union of the Neuse River and the Trent River, where New Bern would be located.

*Catechna* – King Hancock's town, and head town of the Southern Tuscarora. It was located thirty-five miles to the west of New Bern.

*Contentea Creek* – tributary on the North Bank of the Neuse River on which King Hancock's town was located.

*Fort Barnwell* – A fort constructed by Col. John Barnwell of the South Carolina Militia in February of 1712, on the on the South Bank of the Neuse River thirty miles northwest of New Bern. Earthworks of this fort survive today, as the only physical remnant of the Tuscarora War.

*Hancock's Fort* – a fort with a palisade wall and blockhouses, constructed by King Hancock across the creek from Catechna in December of 1711.

*Island Creek Trail* – the only trail to the south of New Bern in 1710. To take this trail, one crossed the Trent River at New Bern by ferry, and then came down the South Bank of the Trent to the settlement of Trent Mill.

*Mill Creek* – a tributary of the Trent River labeled on De Graffenreid's early map of the New Bern settlement. He ordered that a grist mill, a saw mill, a church, and a blockhouse fort be constructed, and while the grist mill and blockhouse were built, the saw mill and church were not built until much later.

*Narhantes* – A fortified Tuscarora Town with nine blockhouses, and several small palisade areas located fifteen miles up the Neuse River from New Bern. Built in December of 1711.

*Neoheroka* – The largest fort ever constructed by the Tuscarora, or any native American tribe in the Carolinas. It was attacked by Col. Moore in 1713. His victory at Neoheroka broke the back of Tuscarora power in the Carolinas.

*Neuse River* – named the News River by John Lawson, name was changed to Neuse by misspelling. A navigable waterway well past New Bern, and into the heart of the North Carolina Colony.

*North Trail* – the name of the trail from New Bern to the North, leading to Bath and the Albemarle, then into Virginia. Much of this trail is known as Highway 17 today.

*Ocracoke Inlet* – Inlet that was a favorite hangout of Blackbeard where the Ocracoke Orgy took place.

*Topsail Inlet* – Inlet in which Blackbeard sank his own ship. It is now called Beaufort Inlet, and is near Beaufort and Morehead City, North Carolina.

*Trent Mill* – the original name for a settlement twelve miles south of New Bern on the Trent River. It was pictured on De Graffenreid's map as including a church and blockhouse fort. Later this was called Trent Bridge, and still later that name would change again to Pollocksville, in honor of Col. Thomas Pollock.

*Trent River* – named after a river in England, it was first settled by French religious refugees from the Virginia Colony in 1694, since it was navigable for much of its length. That French settlement ceased to exist by 1705, and the next settlement along this river was Trent Mill.

*Union Point* – the location where two very stubborn rivers, the Neuse and the Trent, merge. This is located in downtown New Bern.

## Disclaimer

While various historic characters are presented herein, many traits and characteristics ascribed to them are fictional, and should not be considered accurate. This is a work of fiction and my primary motivation was to make this amazing history come alive in the minds of the reader. I have changed history, in some relatively minor ways, to accomplish that. Some notes on the actual history behind this novel may be found at the publisher's website (**www.curraheebooks.com**). Also, while some names for characters in this novel may appear similar to various acquaintances over the years, these characters in this novel are not intended to portray any real person, living or dead, with the obvious exception of historic characters that lived between 1700 and 1750.